Dark City Lights

NEW YORK STORIES

Dark City Lights

NEW YORK STORIES

EDITED BY
Lawrence Block

THREE ROOMS PRESS

New York, NY

Dark City Lights: New York Stories
A HAVE A NYC EDITION

EDITED BY
Lawrence Block

ISBN 978-1-941110-21-8 (trade paperback)
ISBN 978-1-941110-22-5 (ebook)
ISSN 2333-1291 (print)

COVER AND BOOK DESIGN:
KG Design International
www.katgeorges.com

DISTRIBUTED BY:
PGW/Perseus
www.pgw.com

Three Rooms Press
New York, NY
www.threeroomspress.com
info@threeroomspress.com

TABLE OF CONTENTS

IT'S TIME TO LOWER THE LIGHTS . . .
A FOREWORD BY LAWRENCE BLOCK

THE WORLD, ACCORDING TO DANNY Boy Bell, is in urgent need of two things: a dimmer switch and a volume control.

Now Danny Boy's an albino, which might help explain his perspective. (He's also a recurring character in a series of novels I've written about a fellow named Matthew Scudder.) Still, one needn't be genetically predisposed toward photosensitivity to share his sentiments. The world, I'd submit, is often louder and brighter than a person might wish it.

And, if Paris is the City of Light, New York is certainly the city of bright lights, burning away twenty-four hours a day. No wonder it's the city that never sleeps. How could it, without ear plugs and a sleep mask?

And yet it's also the capital of Noir.

Thus *Dark City Lights*.

WHAT DO SHORT STORIES NEED with an introduction? The twenty-three that constitute *Dark City Lights* can certainly stand on their own without any words from me to prop them up. But a volume of this sort seems to require some compendium of prefatory remarks, if only so that the reader will have something to skip. (And please feel free to do just that if you're so inclined. The book's first story is Ed Park's "Amsterdam in the 90s," and it's terrific. Why don't you slip out and read it now, without further delay? My feelings won't be hurt, honest.)

Still here? Well, okay. I promise I won't keep you long. I'll just take a few minutes to tell you a thing or two about what's in store for you.

First of all, the one common denominator here is that all of these stories are set in New York City, which is home to many but not all of the writers.

Aside from their New York setting, the stories vary widely. Many of them are crime stories, but quite a few are not. Most of them have a contemporary setting, but several are set in the past, and Robert Silverberg recounts a fictional event that occurred in 2003, when visitors from outer space landed in Central Park. (You don't remember the incident? Really?)

Bob's story was set well in the future when he wrote it. It's one of two reprints in *Dark City Lights*; the other is my own "Keller the Dogkiller," one of that thoughtful assassin's few New York adventures. All the other stories appear here for the first time.

Most—but not all—are dark. Noir, you might say, or at least noirish. Many are the work of writers who've been doing this for decades, but a few constitute their authors' first published short fiction. (And that's unusual in an invitational anthology, because who would be daft enough to solicit a contribution from someone who's never done this before? Well, *I* would, as it turns out, and it paid off bigtime, as you'll see.)

Besides wheedling stories out of people with plenty of other ways to spend their time, my chief contribution has been to put the contents in order. One could waste hours, even whole days, trying to figure out what story might best follow what other story, but I decided to be guided by the example of a literary hero of mine, John O'Hara. He published many collections of his short fiction, and in later years simply put them in alphabetical order by title. (I took that tack in my own most recent collection, and so far no one has complained.)

There's one exception. I've placed my own effort last, as evidence of the modesty and humility in which I take so much pride.

AMSTERDAM IN THE 90s
BY ED PARK

I. MINDFULNESS

SOMEONE ON WNYC IS TALKING about mindfulness, how it's not about quote unquote checking out at all.

I am sort of interested and sort of not. Mostly I am thinking about my medication.

I only need to take two pills a day, one in the morning, to stop the dizziness, and one in the evening, to counteract the possible side effects of the first pill, which include nausea, discolored discharge, and—I don't understand this part—dizziness.

Something's off, I realize.

But around the time I'm supposed to take each pill, whether it's the main pill or the counteracting pill, I will forget whether I've taken it or not. I'll visualize myself opening the pill container, but that might just be a memory of all the dozens, hundreds of times now that I've pushed down and turned the lids off containers and tapped out a pill and knocked it back with a glass of water.

I listen to the radio when I'm in the kitchen. Maybe that's the problem. I'm easily distracted.

Duane Reade loves me. I wonder what the fetching pharmacist thinks.

The mindfulness guy is still talking. He's talking about anger, how it's causing divorce, it's causing assault, it's causing war.

So today: have I taken my pill, my morning pill? This is the question. I remember I did, or do I? My wife told me to get one of those day-of-the-week pill sorters, but I said those were for old people.

Then it occurs to me that I *am* old. I'm staring forty in the face. How did that happen?

It seems like only yesterday I was staring thirty in the face.

I can remember staring twenty in the face, though I know that *was* a long time ago.

Nearly twenty years ago, as a matter of fact. Twenty doesn't seem like a huge number, except when it does.

It's hard to believe, but I remember being *nine* and staring *ten* in the face. There was no terror then, only excitement at achieving the zero I could tote around for a full year.

So here's an example of forgetfulness. I just forgot that I actually *do* have a day-of-the-week pill sorter. I got one about a month ago, while walking by some sort of community health camper van on Amsterdam between Ninety-ninth and 100th, near that strange cluster where the police station and the Department of Health and the Bloomingdale branch of the public library are. I'd never seen the van before, though who knows: Perhaps it's always on that particular stretch of road, at that particular hour—around 2 p.m., not my usual time for being out and about in the neighborhood.

An extremely pretty woman in a blue smock was handing out the pill sorters. As I walked toward her, I couldn't tell what she had in her basket. I saw her offer one of these myste-rious slim objects to an old lady, an old man, another old lady. She did not offer any to a pack of teenagers, nor to a young woman strolling a tot.

She offered one to me and before I even saw what it was, I extended my palm to accept. Anything for a few seconds' communion with her.

For a second I thought she'd given me some kind of toy. Then I thought it was a device to mold very small popsicles.

I told her it was just what I needed. She smiled. I thought about how sometimes you get handed promotional food sam-ples, bottles of a new energy drink, and how you just consume them without thinking: *What if this person is trying to poison me? What if it's all a weirdly orchestrated mass-murder scheme?*

The pill-sorter seemed okay, though. Plastics aren't ideal for hot liquids, I read, because of leaching. BPAs get into your system. I don't know what BPA stands for, but in general you don't want anything to get into your system that isn't already there. Especially anything that just goes by its initials.

This pill-holder won't hold liquids, hot or cold. Only pills. Dry, room-temperature pills.

Worrying doesn't add any value, says the mindfulness guy. The host jokes that she certainly hopes her mother is listen-ing to the program. Her mother, she says, is a *chronic worrier.*

I didn't spend any more time at the health van, which maybe was the point of the freebie, but the pill-sorter has the web address on it so I will probably look it up online sometime.

So I said to myself back then.

The upshot of the pill-sorter episode is that I started using it but then had trouble remembering whether I'd put a pill in the appropriate daily compartments in the first place, and also whether, assuming that I had stocked the sections correctly, I'd taken the pill from its box and swallowed it.

That's not supposed to happen, I know. But somehow my pill-sorter predicament was just as confusing as my regular pill-taking amnesia.

It's ten minutes to noon right now. Soon it will be too late to take the morning pill. Though, of course, I might have already taken it. In which case, all is right with the world.

What I need is a third kind of pill, one to counteract the forgetfulness. It's not a general forgetfulness. It's not amnesia. It's just a very precise bit of fogginess that surrounds whether or not I've taken my pill.

The host is talking to another guest. She says, *It is a real treat to have you here today.*

II. RUNNING THE RED

I know what I saw that day, but I understand why no one will believe me. Not that I've told a soul. I'm not *that* dumb.

I was in a bad way at work—nothing dramatic, but I was coming in later and later, making more mistakes. It was getting so that if I didn't course-correct, my boss, Dr. Awkwa, would notice. But still. I could have my mornings, couldn't I? A little slice of time to myself. After I dropped off Emma at school, I'd grab a coffee and a muffin or a breakfast sandwich at the bodega, ham and egg on a bagel, and talk to the guys working the counter or Miranda who worked the till. We didn't discuss important matters of the day, just boom our greetings. They'd call me boss and I'd call them boss. Who's the boss, I'd wonder. I sat with the paper for a long time. Sometimes do the crossword. The puzzles get harder from Monday to Friday, but

I always had a smoother time with the later ones. Mondays were *too* simple; I would second-guess every other answer, read hidden depths into the clues. By Friday, though, I was in my zone; I could polish off the puzzle in twelve minutes, even ten, and reward myself with a second pastry.

One morning, puzzle and pastry disposed of, I was walking the eight blocks home when a long black car peeled around the corner, from Ninety-eighth to Amsterdam, nearly decking an old man who was using his rolled-up umbrella as a cane. Something got into me. What if the car had hit the man, or hit me? What if I'd been with Emma? Earlier that year, indeed on the very same corner, a sixteen-year-old joyrider had jumped into an unattended Acura in the East Village, whizzed across town and up the West Side, until finally coming to rest by smashing into a Japanese restaurant at ten past eight—just seven minutes later than the time when Emma and I typically walk by. A little girl and her grandfather were there in our place. He suffered a broken leg and two broken arms; his granddaughter, pinned between the stolen car and the grating, was dead by the time the EMTs arrived. The item in the *Times* struck a portentous and somber tone: "The teenager had no destination in mind, just an urge to press down on a pedal and see the blocks go by. But the city had misery on its agenda."

I wasn't remembering this on that morning when the long black car ran a red in order to snag a parking spot on Amsterdam. The pedestrian who had almost been hit shook his head, eyes wide open in fear and fury.

"I can't believe that guy!" I said.

"It's no good—no good at all," he replied, as we passed each other in the middle of the crosswalk. I saw the long black car backing into its precious parking space, the driver making adjustments as the back wheel neared the curb.

I got back on the sidewalk, stomped back in the direction I had come from. I was going to peer into the driver's seat. If the guy was big—well, I wouldn't say anything. No sense in being stupid. The last physical fight I'd subjected myself to was in the seventh grade (it was a draw). I am not what you would call a formidable specimen—I barely clear five foot five and my arms are jokes—yet I wanted so much to make the driver . . . what? Apologize? To whom—me? The old man, now already heading east and out of sight? The ghosts of the grandfather and his precious charge, run down on this same awful stretch of pavement?

Why not.

Apologize.

Break down.

Beg forgiveness on the sidewalk.

As I approached the car, I saw that the driver was a man of roughly my height, older by at least five years if not a decade, face plump but by no means fat. His arms could be strong but somehow I didn't think so. He had a Mets cap on, a little mustache thin and dark.

Strange glasses with round frames. I could see a wide, almost cartoon version of myself, miniaturized. He must have been too cheap to spring for the anti-reflective lenses that the eyeglass shops always push on you. Maybe it just meant he could stand his ground. I thought and I thought, during those two seconds as I moved past him, me on the sidewalk, him in the car, gripping the wheel. Finally I decided the glasses meant he was weak. Someone I could confront. Torment a bit. Why not? Make him at the very least never attempt such a maneuver again.

"Hey," I barked, my voice louder than I had anticipated, like the quality of the air was amplifying it. "You *ran* that *red*."

He paused his parking job and turned around to face me through the window. He pushed a button and it lowered halfway. "Yes," he said. "I know."

"You just *ran* it."

"Thank you."

His calmness was infuriating. I could read his mind: *Don't engage with this nut in the raincoat.*

What was I going to do—punch him through the crack in the window, which even now he was closing noiselessly? Pretend to call the cops? The longer I stood there, the more foolish I felt.

I wheeled around, blood thrumming in my head. I walked a bit. Then I whipped out my phone, turned back.

Flicked open the camera app.

Pointed and shot.

An image of the front of the car swam up in my screen. I closed the camera, buried it in an inside pocket, and walked quickly away. "Hey," I heard him behind me. "Hey, *motherfucker.*"

I knew he wouldn't come after me—he wasn't done parking. I picked up the pace on 98th, though, and hustled toward the subway station once I got to Broadway.

All day at work I congratulated myself on my quick thinking. He had thought he'd gotten rid of me, made me look like an idiot. But now I had him. His face. His car. All day, who knows, all week, he'd be living with the fear that his misdeed would be reported to the police. Maybe he'd begin to imagine that I'd been photographing or recording him all along—that I'd captured the moment when he turned that corner so violently, nearly clipping the old man with the umbrella. Right there, right on the same corner where the girl had been killed by a thoughtless joyrider. The cops couldn't ignore that, he'd think, especially now that the mayor had come out with a program to eliminate pedestrian fatalities.

I was fantasizing about what the driver might be fantasizing. I loved thinking about him squirming.

When I got home that evening, after another shapeless and pointless day at the office, I told my daughter what I had done. "Are the police going to get him, Daddy?" Emma asked, looking up from her book. She had, in the last few months, been formulating her ideas of crime and punishment. When the little girl had been killed on Ninety-eighth, the fate of the teenage driver troubled and fascinated her for weeks. Shouldn't *he* be run over, in fairness to the girl's family? Who would do the running over? The grandfather should, once his casts came off and he could get behind the wheel. But then the teenager's family would be sad. And would demand justice.

"Did the man see you take a picture of the car?"

"Yes."

"Then you should *do* something."

"I don't know," I said. "I just want him thinking about what he did. Something to remember. That's just as important, in the end."

Emma went back to her book, about a pigeon who wants to drive a bus. It occurred to me that I hadn't looked at the photo of the car since taking it. I wondered how clearly the license plate would read. The morning light diamonded the hood. A New York plate, one of the white ones.

A New York plate that said YOU DIE.

Clear as day.

YOU and then a space in the center and then DIE.

My back broke out in chills. I swiped up on the screen and stared at the driver's face. He had lined cheeks, wrinkles everywhere. The mustache was thicker, the glasses were tinted. There was no Mets cap, just dark hair snarled into a hive.

"Daddy?" Emma said.

It was hard to see anything. What I thought were dark glasses were the eyes themselves, but what I thought were the eyes themselves were depthless spots, so black they couldn't be reproduced in a photo. In my terror I found myself zooming in. The lines on his face weren't wrinkles but various symbols and figures, like emblems from some lost alphabet. The tattoos marched across his face and his white grin was filled with sharp teeth.

"Can I see, Daddy?" said Emma, walking over.

"No—it's—the picture didn't come out," I said, reflexively wondering if the front door was locked, if the windows were shut. And in my haste to close the photo I hit delete.

Something to remember.

THE BIG SNIP
BY THOMAS PLUCK

WHEN THE NEW GIRL GOT in the van, all Sharon saw was a sunbaked skinny-ass white girl with chicken legs, and she wasn't sure how long she'd last. Probably couldn't lift more than fifty pounds, at least without complaining. She wore long sleeves and kept her nails trimmed to the quick, her dishwater hair tied back, tucked down the back of her shirt. Smelled like she'd just sneaked a cigarette.

Sharon gave her a week.

But she had lasted three, long enough for Sharon to call her by name.

"Good morning, Christina," she said, and climbed into the passenger side. She placed two boxes of syringes and vials of Telazol on the floor between her feet. "First stop's on Dyckman."

Christina had a driver's license, and wasn't afraid to bully her way through traffic with the Neuter Scooter. They usually sent her fresh-faced girls from Queens or Long Island, who couldn't parallel park worth a damn. All pink and scrubbed and so full of love for animals that they'd eagerly serve three months spaying feral cats and snipping pit bull balls on the street before they were allowed to intern at the veterinary hospital.

True, in the operating rooms you had a sense of urgency, like on a medical TV show. Except instead of second-string Broadway actors playing the patients, you got pampered pets who probably ate better than you did.

The Neuter Scooter was the front lines, where you earned your bones at People Who Love Animals. Every morning, they drove the modified Econoline van to pet owners who'd signed up for an appointment to alter their dog or cat at the PWLA (pronounced Poola) subsidized rate. You had to work quick and follow procedure, handle dogs that the owners often barely knew, plenty of "outdoor" pets and friendly strays, and cats who'd nuzzle your hand and then flay your arm a moment later.

Sharon had just lost Lynndie, a plump powder-white Minnesota girl she'd trained into an op table warrior, to the hospital staff. Even though she'd known all along that her protégé wanted to work inside—she was on her way to a vet degree—it stung of betrayal. They'd been a good team, had some laughs. It always hurt when the techs left. The unspoken words lingered like the stink of smoke on the new kid: if you worked in the van, it meant you were the B team.

When Fort Tryon Park loomed, Sharon pointed for Christina to cut right.

"I got it," she said.

Sharon didn't care for her driving. She hung in the far lane too long before a turn, and was a little too liberal with her use of the horn. But she couldn't complain; she was a lifelong New Yorker, and had avoided getting her license first because there was no need, then out of stubbornness, and finally out of a strange sense of pride. She'd been born on Convent Avenue, a block downtown from City College, in what was now called Hamilton Heights. The street crested a ridge on land once owned by Alexander Hamilton, whose house, now a museum, had been moved three times that Sharon knew about. Nearby St. Nicholas Park had a fine dog run, and she'd inherited her parents' building, living in one half and leasing the other to three white girls who'd been chased out of Williamsburg by hipster-inflated rents. Girls that reminded her of Christina.

Their first patient was a gray bully mix named Tuco, a rambunctious boy whose ears and tail were intact. Christina double-parked and left the engine running. The Scooter had twin tanks to fuel the equipment.

"Tuke's not dog aggressive, but he humps just about any-thing in sight," his owner said. The sun lit up her natural puff of burnt-orange hair. "He's gonna break his lead and get himself killed one day, I know it."

"He'll settle down when we're done," Sharon told her. She ran the woman's credit card on a little gadget attached to an iPhone while Christina squatted down to play with the dog.

"Who's a good boy?"

He mounted her knee like it was the southbound end of a northbound Shih Tzu.

"Not you," Christina laughed. "Not you."

They carried him in the back and closed the doors. The van had an extended roof so they didn't have to hunch over. Tuco stood on the steel operating table, wagging his tail, breathing in the smells of hundreds of other dogs and cats who'd been there before him.

"Gimme your paw," Sharon said. When Tuco obliged, she stuck him with a syringe of Telazol. He yipped and looked up like he'd done something wrong. Sharon rubbed his foreleg, easing the drug up the artery. "That's all, sweetie. That's all."

The wooziness hit his eyes, and Christina rolled him onto his back and strapped him to the table. Sharon checked his pulse, then gave Christina a nod.

"You're gonna end up doing it anyway," Christina said.

"If you don't practice, that's what we call a self-fulfilling prophecy."

Christina turned her head, but Sharon caught the eye roll. No one liked intubating when they first started. It was simple empathy, jamming a tube down a living creature's throat. They'd gag when they heard the slick and crunchy noises and felt the flesh resist. She held the dog's head as Christina unfurled the hoses hooked to the gas, and watched her angle of entry. "There it is. Ease it on in. You got it."

Christina bit her lip. Sharon gave her another try, then saw the confidence leave her hands. She took over. "Prep him," she said. "It's alright."

The tube went right in for Sharon; she'd done enough of them. It was like anything else: you needed the confidence to not be overly gentle, but not so cocky you didn't listen to your hands and wound up hurting them. She got the isoflurane flowing, and watched him breathe until she was satisfied.

Christina sighed and pulled a surgical drape over the dog. She took out a Bic razor and shaved a square of fur just above the testicles. "If I knew I'd be shaving balls when I made it to New York, I would've stayed home."

Sharon shook her head, then inflated the cuff on the endo-tracheal tube to hold it in place, so Tuco wouldn't vomit and aspirate during the procedure. "Least it's just dogs," she said. "Do they do men at those Brazilian places?"

Christina wet a gauze pad atop a blue gallon jug of chlorhexidine and scrubbed the square of pink-gray skin she'd shaved on Tuco's belly. "No," she said. "Far as I know, guys have to do that themselves."

"I don't know how you let someone down there," Sharon said. She could sign up for social security next year, but the flow of young vet techs kept her in the know. They talked about everything, including shaving their business.

"I don't," Christina said. "Couldn't afford to have someone else do it, even if I wanted them to." She squinted at the now-shiny patch of skin, and lifted up Tuco's genitals. "Fully descended. Ought to be a breeze."

When only one dropped, they called it a cryptorchid. The day Sharon told Christina that, she'd snorted like a wild hog. "You know a guy came up with that. Like they're a friggin' bouquet, or something. Hello, honey! Wanna put your tulips on my orchids?"

Sharon ran a gloved finger over the prepped area, then quickly made an inch-long cut. She held one orchid with thumb and two fingers, like a tiny bowling ball, and squeezed it up its roomy sac until it popped out the incision she'd made. Then she closed the forceps around the vesicle so it wouldn't disappear back inside like a fleeing bait worm.

"Come on, do the snip," she told Christina.

Christina took the scalpel and leaned in.

"Just slice and go." On her granddad's farm the animals didn't even get anesthesia. Just cut and cauterize.

The razor severed the vesicle like overcooked spaghetti. "Now ligate." Christina tied it off and tucked it back inside.

Sharon tossed the freed testicle into the gut bucket. "Now number two. Come on, we got a long list."

The farm was one reason Sharon had headed for vet school. Seeing horses suffer from impaction colic, billy goats castrated with nothing but a clasp knife and a pair of pliers, and how the farmhands dealt with an explosion in the barn cat population. No, sweating in the back of an old van giving feral cats the Big Snip wasn't menial. For her it was a kind of penance.

She watched Christina perform the second removal, then closed the incision with a single stitch and a thin line of surgical glue. Christina cut the iso gas and removed the tube, and after he came to, they brought the sleepy pup, sans testicles, back to his owner.

"Plenty of water, keep him inside. He can go for a walk tomorrow, but no running for a couple of days. If he opens it up somehow, bring him in and we'll stitch him up."

THEY FOLLOWED THEIR CLIPBOARD NEARLY all the way up to Inwood. They snipped two toms, spayed a momma cat who'd littered twelve adoptees two weeks prior, then a yappy Chihuahua, and a fat black Lab mix.

"Cryptorchid!" Christina called. She treated them like four leaf clovers.

On the ride back toward the clinic, a big bald man in a cardigan waved them down from the crosswalk.

"Pull over," Sharon said. It was Timothy, an actor who walked dogs down in Morningside Heights on his off time. He had two Afghans on leashes.

"Hey girl." Timothy was built like a football player, with a smile almost too big for his face. "How's the nut cutting biz?"

"You know," Sharon said. "Our job's never done. How about you? Who you got there?"

Timothy lifted one leash, then the other. "This is Tazi, and this is Karzai. They're dolls, but so prissy." Tazi put her paws on the side of the van and stuck her long nose in the window to lick Sharon's hand. "Oh, that thing you did? Worked like a charm. They never even noticed."

Sharon nodded, "Told you they wouldn't."

"Oh, and I have an audition for *Jersey Boys!*"

A cab honked behind them. "We'll see you later. You can give me those tickets you owe me."

Christina pulled back into traffic, and cut crosstown. She squeezed the van into a spot in front of a Jimbo's Hamburger Palace, and they washed up in back before breaking for a late lunch.

Jimbo's cooked their patties on the griddle, and finished them under a steel cup made for ice cream sundaes. It steamed them, and kept them tender. There were few things Sharon was nostalgic about, but her father taking her to the first Jimbo's to open in Harlem was one of them, and their burger was the only one she'd eat.

They sat on Duct-taped red vinyl stools and waited for their burgers. Christina with a Diet Coke, Sharon with black coffee.

"How's Alex doing?" Sharon said.

"Alexie's good. Getting ready for pre-K already. I can't believe it."

"And Hester?"

"Kyle doesn't like her, but Lexie just adores her. He even flushes her poops down the toilet." She thumbed through her phone, and showed a photo of little tow-headed Alexie hugging a plump tortoiseshell. Cute little thing. The cat hung limp with a tolerant mother's grin.

They ate their burgers, the kaiser rolls soaked with grease and onions. A man ordering to go swept Sharon with his eyes. His hair and beard trimmed close, shot through with gray. She frowned at her burger and cut it in half with a wood-handled steak knife.

"What was your friend talking about?"

"Oh, just another snip."

Christina ducked and lowered her voice. "Remember what you said about guys shaving their junk? Kyle asked me to shave his, because he heard it would make him look bigger."

"Honey, no."

"One little nick, and that was the end of that," Christina said, with a snort. "I didn't have all this practice then."

Sharon shook her head. She'd heard on NPR that the popularity of shaved genitals had put the existence of crab lice in jeopardy. No big loss, that.

"The snip job for Timothy was on the sly," she said. "This couple he knew, theater patrons. You'd know their name. Big dog they brought home from Italy, where they were married." He was a Neapolitan mastiff named Otto, the size of a large black panther or a small bear, and the owners kept him intact. The woman wanted him neutered, but the husband wouldn't allow it. He was a good dog, but they couldn't control him, and he got dog aggressive. Timothy got his hand cut up, trying break him off another dog.

"They paid him and the other dog's owner off, to keep Otto off the vicious list. I met Timothy walking him in St. Nicholas, where the big dog run is. I had Caesar with me, and he put that Otto in his place with one look, no balls or not."

Caesar was her boy, a big white whale of a boxer mix with one brown eye and one ice blue.

"He told me about the disagreement between Otto's owners, and I suggested a solution."

"What did you do?"

"Neuticles," Sharon said. "You know. Those prosthetics." Some owners preferred their dogs to look intact. They'd crop the ears and the tail, but wanted two balls swinging around back there. "So we didn't shave him, I did the incisions, kept it real clean. Squeezed those fake nuts in there, like I was putting pits back inside a plum."

"No way?"

"Yup. Glued him up and you couldn't tell the difference, not even up close. And he settled down soon enough. He's still a spoiled, hyperactive dog, just like his owners. Hell, Timothy brings him to the dog park by car service. That dog gets a cab faster than he does."

The gray-bearded man stopped by Sharon's shoulder. "I could put a smile on that face."

Sharon set her burger down. "You know what'd make me smile? Not getting told to smile all the time."

His grin twisted into a sneer. "Well you don't got to be a bitch."

"Go on, now." Sharon wagged her steak knife, the teeth gristly with red. "I worked all day in back of a hot van snipping off dog balls, I can cut one more pair."

Christina covered her mouth not to laugh. She looked over her shoulder as the man slammed the door.

"Can't even eat my lunch," Sharon said, and wiped the shreds of meat off her knife with a napkin.

TUESDAY WAS TNR DAY AT the shelter uptown. Trap Neuter Release. They drove up to assist with the cats the shelter had caught. Feral things with matted coats and crusted eyes. Interns gave them shots and shaved the snarls from their fur. One tom yowled in protest, his voice roughened like a seasoned smoker's. It took three interns to hold him down and inject the sedative.

Sharon put Christina on prep and intubation.

"I don't know," she said. "You always end up doing it."

"This assembly line's just what you need to get over that hump."

The shelter was an old building with a lean to it, and no air conditioning except a few overworked window units. Sharon peeled off her lab coat and worked in a tank top. Christina wore her long sleeves and wiped her brow between the motions.

"Why don't you take that off?"

"Don't want to get scratched."

Sharon shrugged. The cats were sedated already. She was a firm believer that once an adult, a person had already decided whether or not they were going to be happy or miserable. She'd found happiness early in life, then lost it to her own pigheadedness; in the years that followed, happiness seemed difficult to find and harder to hold onto, and she slowly embraced the adage that if you wanted devotion, a dog was a sure bet, while people of either sex could only be counted on until they saw the next best thing.

So she didn't care whether Christina was comfortable, but she did mind if she learned to intubate. Sharon kept on her back until she worked through her hesitation. It took a few tries and some guidance, but five cats later she was doing it. Maybe not like a machine, but with enough confidence to keep things running. She had one slip with the cuff, and a pink and gray female regurgitated. The vomit smelled like fermented fish heads.

Christina gagged. "It smells like garbage bags in Chinatown!"

To her credit, she fixed the cuff before running for the sink.

A goateed intern brought her a pair of clean scrubs to change into.

"Nice ink," he said, eyeing her lean forearms.

Sharon looked over while she glued up a scrawny female's belly. Christina's arms were covered in tattoos. The artwork showed talent, and her pale skin made for a good canvas.

Swirls and autumn leaves and symbols. Over the inside of one elbow, a sailor's heart tattoo with her boy Alexie's name and birthdate in engraver script. Sharon didn't understand why anyone would want one tattoo, much less that many, but it wasn't the art that bothered her.

She put it aside and got back to work. There were always more ferals than they could snip in one shift, and today was no exception.

THE SHELTER PROVIDED LUNCH IN the form of cheap greasy pizza from the dollar a slice joint around the corner. They washed up and ate outside, where it was cooler, leaned against the brick.

Christina held out her arm and ran a finger over a track mark. The silver pocks showed through the ink. "These are from a long time ago," she said. "I'm a sponsor now."

"That's good," Sharon said. She tossed the spongy crust of her pizza toward a trio of pigeons. "See you inside."

AFTER WORK, SHARON WALKED AND fed Caesar, then took a blue train downtown to the Cubby. She drank Stoli and Seven; the fizz lingered on the tip of her tongue. A napkin around her drink absorbed the sweat, and the glass didn't touch the bar until she'd finished it.

She had lost her eldest brother to heroin when she was a little girl. She asked her mother: why would anyone give themselves a needle? Her mother had no answer, and in the fifty-two years since, Sharon hadn't found one. We all dealt with pain in different ways, even animals.

It always amused her, that adage about veterinarians being the best doctors, because the patient couldn't tell them what hurt. If you couldn't tell, maybe you had no business being a doctor. At least animals were honest about pain, and growled or snapped. People, they liked to bury it, in all sorts of ways.

The clinic had been broken into several times over the years, for syringes and sedatives. But more often, half-used vials of ketamine went missing. Her previous tech, Lynndie, had put herself through vet school by tending bar; she told Sharon that ketamine was called Special K, and it was used both recreationally and as a date rape drug. There were bars where if you wanted to remember the rest of your night, you finished your drink without it ever leaving your hands.

But it wasn't Christina's track marks that had bothered her. Like the tattoos, it was something you got used to seeing. There'd been something else just as familiar, around the wrists and forearms.

A woman half her age with close-cropped hair and a beauty mark beneath her left eye bought Sharon's next drink. They talked about the music and the weather and dogs, and Sharon forgot what it was she'd noticed until the next morning, when the young woman pulled a shirt over her tattooed shoulders, petted Caesar on the head, and let herself out of the apartment.

Bruises beneath the inkwork, on the inside of the wrists. Right where you'd hold someone's hands when you had them up against the wall, nose to nose. Thumbprint smudges between the radius and ulna, some yellowed and faded, others red-rimmed, fresh, and purple.

She thought Christina was smarter. But over the years, she'd learned that if a horse wanted water, it found the corral on its own, and leading them to it often engendered more resentment than gratitude.

She'd been kicked enough to know.

THEY WERE BUSY ENOUGH THAT Sharon stopped noticing when new bruises joined the old, and she was thankful she'd minded her own business. For all she knew, the marks could be from anything. Maybe Christina took judo, or liked being held down as a kink.

Christina's sense of humor didn't waver. Fridays, when the other techs on the shift went around the corner for a drink, she always bowed out, saying she had to pick up her son from his grandparents. And as her skills improved, she showed no inclination to abandon van duty for a cushier gig in the clinic.

The show of loyalty softened Sharon's view of her.

The last snip on the clipboard was a bull mastiff female on Riverside Drive by the tennis courts. The owner was a little man who had half his hair pulled back in a little ponytail knot, leaving silver locks framing his face. Plaid shirt with the sleeves rolled, revealing nice, strong arms. The kind of man who looked like a sculptor or Buddhist priest, but usually turned out to be a financial planner or a hand model.

"Jonquil's in heat," he said, rubbing her immense forehead. "Will that be a problem?" Jonquil was one hundred-and-ninety pounds of black-and-tan jowl and slobber, sitting spread-legged on the sidewalk, her pudenda swollen and red.

"There's a greater chance of bleeding," Sharon said. "I usually recommend waiting until she's out of her cycle."

"This guy at the park's got a Doberman he can't handle, he's all over her."

Christina raked her nails over the dog's back, and Jonquil butted her head into her, begging for more.

"You should bring her to the clinic."

"I can't really get away, is the problem. I've got clients all day, during your hours. And weekends, you're booked for months. I called."

He squatted and kissed Jonquil on her wet coal nose. "I just don't think Jonny girl wants puppies."

It took them both to lift Jonquil onto the table after the Telazol kicked in. Christina intubated her like a pro, and Sharon strapped her down and crossed her paws.

"Jesus," Christina said, as she shaved the belly. "She's red as a baboon's ass."

"Get her prepped," Sharon said. Usually she appreciated the sense of humor, but the lack of urgency set her off.

She made the cut with care, but blood welled immediately. Christina soaked it up with gauze and Sharon quickly inserted the spay hook, to fish out the first horn of the uterus. She extracted the grape-bunch of ovarian follicles, clamped it at both ends, and cut them at the bud.

Blood formed like red beads of sweat, then pooled. The dog's belly heaved beneath the surgical sheet. Christina inhaled sharply.

"More iso," Sharon said. "Quarter turn."

Christina adjusted the flow of gas and Jonquil's breathing settled. Sharon sponged the blood and ligated the uterus with three quick loops of surgical thread. She kneaded the flesh, leaning in close to see, but no blood appeared.

Sharon followed the pink worm of the uterus to the second horn, and squeezed it out. "You can see why we don't go for hot dogs much," she said.

Christina let out a breath of relief, and shook her head with a little eye-roll. Her fingers clawed for a cigarette.

Sharon repeated the cut, this time ready for the blood. She moved slow and smooth with practiced motions, cinched tight little stitches, and checked for bleeding several times before tucking everything back inside Jonquil's belly.

"Ease up on the iso," she said, as she finished tying up the knots to close the abdomen. "Let's get things cleaned up. Detube her."

"I'm too jittery," Christina said, her face flushed.

"She'll be alright. She's just got a big old heart."

Sharon flinched as Christina stepped in to give her a hug. Her hair smelled of strawberries and stale smoke.

Sharon patted her shoulder. "Your first scare?"

"Yeah." She rubbed her nose then looked away, cleaning up the operating table.

"I'll bandage her up," Sharon said. "Go have a puff."

"Thanks."

As Sharon bent to get the adhesive tape, she saw Christina squeeze toward the front of the van. Her hand went into the pocket of her scrubs, and came out empty.

OUTSIDE, SHE GAVE JONQUIL'S OWNER the papers for postoperative care.

"Doesn't she have to wear a cone?"

"No, just keep an eye on it. If it gets dark red, like her cookie, bring her in. And keep her out of the park for a few days, let her rest. She'll still be in heat a day or two, it'll take a while to get the hormones out of her system."

He handed them both a folded twenty, before walking sleepy Jonquil slowly up the stoop.

In the van, Sharon waited for the doors to close, then turned off the ignition.

"What—"

"What's in your pocket? That's the only question," Sharon said, clutching the keys in her palm.

"My cigarettes, what are you talking about?"

"Don't insult me now. Don't." The pleasant mask melted from her face, into the look she'd inherited from her mother.

Christina reached in her pocket and removed a pair of Neuticles. The expensive ones, soft as a breast implant. The largest size, like the ones Sharon had put in Otto the mastiff.

"What, you selling them?" Sharon said. "They cost a few hundred, wholesale. Am I gonna have to inventory the whole truck?"

Christina's lower lip trembled, and she mashed her palms into her eye sockets. She kicked the floorboards and rocked with silent sobs.

SHARON DROVE THEM TO A shady spot in Riverside park. Christina gripped the cracked beige dashboard the whole way. After they parked, she hiked her scrubs. Leopard spot bruises between her ribs.

"He likes to jam his thumb in there," Christina said. "Don't say it. I'd leave if I could. But he'll get custody. His parents, they say it every time they can. 'Oh we just *love* having little Alex over. Wouldn't you like to live here all the time, instead of your tiny apartment?' His name's *Alexie,* bitch!"

Sharon felt cold around the edges, like she'd barged into a house where the heat had been turned off. "If you need a lawyer, I know a few."

"It won't matter." Christina held out her arm, ran a finger over the track marks. "Kyle says they'll use my record against me. I'm clean five years, I'm not even on fucking methadone."

"Then why are you stealing, if you don't want a lawyer?"

Christina lit a cigarette, and rolled down the window. The cherry ember bobbed as she laughed out an exhale.

"Well, that's where I ask a big favor."

Besides the Neuticles, Christina had palmed a syringe and a fresh vial of Telazol. Needle, a scalpel blade, surgical glue, and thread.

Sharon told her she was out of her mind.

"Well then Alexie goes to Kyle's parents, or protective services. My parents ain't worth a damn, so don't even ask. I can't take this anymore."

"Does he hit . . ."

"No, he just takes it out on me and the cat, for now. The last straw was when Alexie started talking. He uses the same condescending voice on him, when he gets mad. Next thing, he'll stand there smoking in the door of his bedroom while he sleeps." She looked out the window. "Looking at him like he's less than shit."

There was more. On the drive back, she learned where the bruises came from. When she said no.

She listened without comment, until Christina told her the plan. Then she laughed.

"You need the gas to keep him under," Sharon said. "He would've woken up with you down there, screaming and bleeding, then you'll really lose your boy. Pretty sure there'd be jail time."

No, this was a van job. And she would need a partner. A smart one.

Sharon took the spare set of keys to the Neuter Scooter home Friday night. Kyle's favorite bar was one of those new speakeasy types out in Bushwick, where the only thing bigger than the ice cubes was the check. It smelled of old wood and music blared from cheap speakers, muffling any attempt at conversation.

Sharon wore a short dress that she sometimes took to Cubby's, or a hunting ground uptown when the mood struck her. She kept the makeup light, like a neighborhood holdout enjoying herself, someone who refused to let the trust fund kids take over.

It wasn't a difficult role to play. Gentrification had begun its creep into Hamilton Heights. She enjoyed the restaurants, but not the accompanying shift in neighborhood tone forced by increases in rent. You could always take a train to try a new place, but home was home.

Here the barflies were uniformly young, and mostly white. A couple had a stroller with their conked-out child, but most were singles out hunting. The kind of bar Lynndie had warned her about.

Sharon played with her phone until a spot opened at the bar near Kyle and his group, and ordered a Vodka Seven. They didn't have 7 Up, so she nursed a Moscow Mule instead.

Kyle wore a checked shirt and a knit bow tie, a long but neat beard, and those stretched horn rims that everyone seemed to wear. He was tall but not built, and dominated conversation among his friends with sweeping gestures reminiscent of a stage magician.

A young man cozied to the spot beside her and tried his game. Perhaps he felt it was his duty to talk to her, alone as they were in the crowd. He bought her a drink, and she bought him one, to let him know where they stood, and while he pouted, she used his body as a shield to spritz an entire vial of ketamine into Kyle's Rock & Rye.

She hugged her would-be friend goodbye and told him he was sweet, then cleared her bill with the bartender, as Kyle's friends slowly drifted off in pairs. He gripped the mahogany for purchase. She turned, brushing him with her hip.

"Oh hello there," Kyle said, with a gleam of eye teeth. "How'd I miss you?"

"I could be your grandmother," she said. His great-grandmother, maybe. She been the first to break the streak of motherhood by sixteen on her mother's side.

"No way," Kyle said. "Well, know what they say. Black don't crack."

She feigned a smile and sipped her drink. She saw why Christina had once liked him. He put on a good show. But there was a layer of demanding beneath the ready smile, a hunger for attention, that Alexie's sudden appearance must have offended. Her own father had it, but he'd been pleased to have a captive audience in his children. He may have pouted when they complained of hearing a story for the thousandth time, but he'd never become petulant. It was their mother who'd driven them away, one by one.

She let Kyle talk, as the K and alcohol loosened his rivets. When she suggested he might like to go home, he assumed she meant hers and leaned in to whisper. As she pushed him away, she thumbed the empty vial of ketamine into his jeans pocket.

She checked her phone. Christina would have Alexie in bed by now. She let Kyle snake an arm around her waist, and guided him out the front door onto the dimly lit, crooked sidewalks.

Down the block, Christina would be waiting in the van.

But Kyle would never make it there. The dose of ketamine was surely fatal, and that was the only way. Sharon had tried to explain, that dogs were one thing, and people were another.

And besides, it wasn't the balls that were the problem.

It was the brain.

BOWERY STATION, 3:15 A.M.
BY WARREN MOORE

I saw a food vendor at his cart near the corner of Bowery and Delancey. He didn't look too busy—which made sense for a Thursday night, with almost an hour before the bars closed. The Ballroom on Christie had disgorged its concert-goers a couple of hours earlier, but thank God there was a little more time to drink like civilized people, and there had to be some of those somewhere—it was the Bowery, but even so. The vendor would be busy enough later, but right now it was alone enough and cold enough that the heat from his grill made him seem to shimmy under the amber streetlight glow. Straight ahead were the green-and-white subway globes and the stairs down. Just behind me was the streetcar shelter.

The JZ entrance on the southeast corner—my corner—was bright, white fluorescent lamps set above tile walls with concrete stairs down. I walked down the stairs, carded my way through the turnstile and made my way down to the platform.

A Queens-bound J train receded along the west side of the platform as I came down the stairs. The newsstand was long gone—a mosaic still said there should be one, but it had been gone since before I ever set foot there. But a copy of the day's *Daily News* sat abandoned on one of the benches. I picked it up and, like a good citizen, dropped it into the trash. I breathed in deeply. It was the usual underground clammy, but it wasn't warm enough yet to start smelling like a urinal. That would wait until July.

I read somewhere that Bowery Station is one of the least-used stops in the system. I guess that made sense—for a long time, most folks didn't want to go there, and the folks who were there may not have had much reason to get out. That's starting to change, I guess; the rising tide of urban home-steaders and folks who can't afford Williamsburg or Park Slope is starting to lap against this beachhead, too. But since it isn't used too much, the station is pretty low on the mainte-nance list. You can't even spot a CCTV camera to stand under on the platform.

I saw the girl standing on the Brooklyn-bound side of the platform. You might not have noticed anything, but I saw the fists clenched at her sides and I saw her lips moving, and I knew what she was gearing up to do.

The subways average about one jumper a month—one person who decides that if they can't make it here, they won't make it anywhere, and decides to call it a day under the wheels of a few tons of subway train. Most of the time it doesn't make the papers—the editors don't see much point in encouraging copycats—so you don't hear about it except for really flashy cases, like the guy last year who pulled his three-year-old off the platform with him. But even without much publicity, we get about one a month, and this girl—she couldn't have been more than twenty-five—had decided it was her month.

I heard the Brooklyn train before I saw the light—it sounds like a giant exhaust fan a good ten seconds before it shows up. I ran across the platform as she bent her knees to tumble onto the tracks, grabbed the collar of her fake leather trench coat and jerked her back as the cars roared by. I had let go by the time the car doors opened, but no one got off the train, and after a moment, the warning tones sounded, the doors closed, and the train rumbled away.

She looked at me. She was blonde, with that leftover seventies middle-parted Marcia Brady hair that so many of them seem to like these days. Not much makeup, or it was applied well enough that I couldn't tell. A little on the pretty side of average, I guess. She just glared at me for a moment and said, "What the fuck did you do that for? I'm never gonna have the guts to do that again."

"Then maybe you shouldn't have tried," I said. "I mean, it seems kind of drastic."

"Of course it's drastic," she said. "That's the point. If it wasn't drastic, I wouldn't be doing it. Not that I will now."

"Glad to hear it. Suicide's wrong, you know."

"What's it to you?"

"Well, not much to me, I guess. But I kind of figure that you didn't pick when you got here, so I'm not sure if you should pick when you leave. That's God's decision, and it's not like there's much chance to get right with God when you're doing it, huh? When it's your time, He'll make sure it happens, I think."

"You believe in God?"

"Yeah, there are even a few of us who live in town."

She shook her head. "Well, I haven't had much proof lately."

"I don't know," I said. "I mean, I just stopped you from becoming subway mulch. That would seem to indicate something."

"Yeah. It indicates that you're a Jesus freak who can't mind your own fucking business." She was probably right, but she smiled when she said it, and her hands had relaxed out of their fists. We both knew she wouldn't jump now.

I asked her why she had wanted to do it. It was about like I had figured. The job hadn't come through, which meant the rent wasn't gonna make, which meant that she'd have to hitch back to Antelope Springs or Sioux Falls or some other city named after animals or Indians. Another big city success story, except that I hadn't let her write that last chapter. But I knew, even if she didn't, that she hadn't wanted to die with that last decision on her soul.

Another train rolled in, headed for Queens. A couple of guys got off and made their way up the stairs, and to the streets above, I guess. The girl and I just stood there and the train rumbled away.

"So I guess this is where we're supposed to fall in love and I get my happily ever after, right?" she said. Her voice seemed to trail off, but it was just the beginning of the roar of the oncoming train.

I smiled, but shook my head.

"So what happens next?" she asked.

I saw the headlight. "This," I said, as I hooked my left foot around her right ankle and shoved her off the platform.

The train hit her with the sound of a meat-filled Hefty Bag smacking the pavement, and the effect was much the same, I guess. Not that I stayed to watch. I was already running up the stairs, my feet light, the screaming of the brakes still in my ears. I had helped her leave without sin, and I knew I had done God's work. Why else would He have put me there?

I felt cash in my pocket as I went up the steps opposite the ones I had gone down a few minutes earlier. I could get dumplings. Life was good. Amen.

CHLOE
BY JERROLD MUNDIS

I HEAVED INTO BEING, CAME out of the stone, the bricks, and
other elements, and took form. Because I was lonely. More,
wanting. The two are confusing sometimes. Less as I age, but
still, sometimes. It was both then: an emptiness, a whimper, a
longing, coiled round and merging into a focused tremble in
my loins, a swelling of my breasts. I wanted. I needed.

People drink themselves stuporous over that, or cry into
their pillows, or take and hurt. Sometimes they love, and find
and offer solace.

Nothing was different from when last I was, when I had
walked through the dark pipes and channels for months mus-
ing with small companions and reading the debris: the lost,
the discarded—in a way, the entrails—of the city above to
learn what, if anything, had changed. It is not often anything
truly does. Mostly it is just the trivia, the distractions of the
moment, the colors in which the verities are currently painted.

To me the air here is neither fetid nor dank, the gloom
is not gloom, nor the little rivulets, swirling eddies, and
coursing streams of corruption corrupt. They are as sweet

to me as a spring-fed meadow is to you, and the scurry of little clawed feet and dragging hairless tails as welcome as the flit and song of birds among the grasses and trees to you. I have seen those things of yours, and while they mean nothing to me and are even a little unpleasant, I can understand through my own my own causes of charm and delight what they are to you.

I am happier and more content than you. Happy just in being, when I am.

You were never that. You were more so once, in the days before the fierce mono-gods rose—*I and no other!*—and more content, too, when we were all abo ut you, and you saw us. Few of you do that now, and mostly we do not come where we are not loved, or at least seen.

Not that I was ever loved or supplicated much, but I *was* known. And appreciated. Which was enough for the small needs I had of you. We all have need of you, the greater and lesser among us. We are not complete without you. Deprived of you, we languish. Sometimes we have simply taken you. In the past when we did so, it was often crude or violent or both. Leda was not welcoming, Europa did not consent, nor did Ganymede desire.

Rubens knew. Yeats knew.

I want, too, sometimes. But I do not raven.

I wanted that night, and was lonely, and so I came out of the stone, the archways, beds and joints, where somehow I am when I am not, and heaved into being.

I made my way through the darkness which is not darkness to me, through the tunnels, to a place where I knew there would not likely be anyone above. I waited, casting about for any of you, and then when I sensed nothing, lifted the manhole cover in the small private street in Kips Bay a little past the Riverpark Restaurant, toward the river, and came up into the city, into Manhattan and the night.

THE SKY WAS EMPTY BUT for a half moon and a single planet, Venus. It is always astonishing to me to see nothing in the night sky now but the moon and a planet or two, and sometimes a point of light that is a satellite and perhaps dimly another one or two in an otherwise empty vaulting field of dark blue. The sky at night was once black as pitch, black as a cave with a sealed entrance: deep, infinite, voluptuous, shot through with stars—so many!—like shattered crystals or scattered diamonds. It summoned awe. It engendered peace, gave solace. It was wondrous.

But it is gone from the cities of the earth now, at least to you who live in them, and you are poorer for it and made more mad.

There were cities before, of course, even great ones, and I have lived in many of them, but it is only recently that they have eaten the nighttime sky. Not that I ever saw that sky much myself. I didn't, only on the infrequent nights I rose and came up onto the streets of whatever city beneath which I was living, but it did please me to see it then, even if I did not miss it otherwise.

I have seen how its loss has ravaged you, taken some of your very heart from you.

Some of your cities devoured it earlier than others, with their thickened air and lights. London was one, the place where I last emerged before that night in New York and where I took as my lover a poet and dramatist, and a good a lover he was, for the night. I took him because he was often about on the streets nights as well as days and because he was one of the few in his time who had ever shown interest in me and my works. (I grant he showed interest in many other things as well. His fascination was broad. As was his waggishness, which was also of appeal.) I had read most of his works, which had found their way from the streets as pamphlets, broadsheets, and dailies, along with other debris, and lost or partly ruined and discarded editions into my channels and byways, on their way, eventually, more deteriorated and transformed, and only partly recognizable as what they once were, and sometimes not at all, out to the Thames with the other effluents and discharges. I knew him, even if he had only dimly sensed me, and I felt a certain draw to him. So I emerged in a place and at a time as to encounter him. Which I did.

Only once before had I done that, sought out a man in particular rather than at random, and him for encounters over several months (something I have never done since), until he died one day in the sands of the arena. I missed him when that happened, while it could not be said that I mourned him. I didn't know then what it was, to mourn, except through what I had read or heard. One needs to love before one can mourn. I imagine it was as close as I had ever come or thought I could to either loving or mourning, until the night in New York. At least as I understand those things now. I was young then, when I was with Albus.

I was older that night in London (and other nights in other cities, too). On some, I took a lover. Others, I simply walked along the streets among you, out of loneliness. And I was older still—but unchanged to the eye and even mostly in how I experienced myself on that night, which is now just a little gone, at least as I reckon things—when I lifted and set aside the manhole cover and emerged into the semidarkness of the starless night over Manhattan. I paused. I looked about, cast outward, and when I sensed and found nothing, picked up the iron cover and lowered it back into its seat, careful not to make a sound.

While there was no sky, at least as I have known it, and most of your ancestors, too, only the half moon and below it and off to the side Venus—at least the planet (might that be a joke or an approximate of one?)—against the empty gray-blue field, there were still lights, a myriad of them from the cars on the FDR Drive and the buildings across the river in Queens and even from some of the windows of the buildings along the street on which I was, and the street lamps, and blooming up into the thickened air from First Avenue and the rest of the city behind me.

I went to the rail at the end of the street to look out over the river and the expanse of empty sky beyond, where it was not carved into narrow strips as it was by the tall buildings that rose above the canyon streets of Manhattan. Only a handful of weak scattered little points of light blinked in and out of view in the dead sky as companions to the moon and planet. Still, it was vast, a universe to me, who lives in and melds with such small tunnels and byways. Its immensity quickened me.

And my earlier trembling became a pulsing.

His name was Dovid.

I sensed him before he actually approached, while he was still preparing to make himself known to me.

He was back a little down the street, considering me. He was young, hormonal. He wanted, too. Powerfully. His *life* was powerful. I shuddered with the beat of his heart, the surge of oxygen-rich blood through his arteries, the vitality of him. There was heat in him, his loins. *Strength*. But he was not dangerous. No man is to me, actually. Still, I avoid those who are dangerous to others: they are not pleasant to consort with.

(But what about my first lover, you might ask. Was he not dangerous? No. He killed as a professional; died as one.)

"Hi," he said.

I turned my head. He had taken up a position on the rail near enough to speak easily but enough apart from me as to be reassuring. Young, driven by the wants of his youth, but wise, too.

"Hi," I said, and smiled.

He was tall, with dark curly hair. He had strong, attractive features, the lean build of a basketball player. I know about such things as basketball, and most else that is important to the time and city in which I happen to live. I always have, in the same way I did the works of my London poet and dramatist.

"Nice moon," he said. "It's peaceful down here, with the water and the open sky."

I nodded.

"I usually stop by for a little after work."

"You work near here?" I asked. "And nights?"

He motioned with his head back down the street. "At the Riverpark, the restaurant. You?"

"I'm just out for a walk," I said.

I loosened my posture, opened it.

He noticed.

"I'm Dovid," he said.

His voice was deep and friendly and had a guilelessness that, while almost certainly not genuine at the moment, was still convincing.

He reminded me of Josephus, that priestly, aristocratic, defeated Jewish warrior-turned-historian whom I met once on the streets of Rome while walking about with my lover, Albus, he whom I missed but did not mourn after he died. (I do not think I can rightly call any of the others, with whom I spent no more than a night—and there were not many of those, either—a lover.) I would not have been surprised if Dovid descended from that line, from Josephus. It is a smaller world than one might suppose, and always has been.

"Chloe," I said.

"Nice to meet you, Chloe."

"Are you a chef there, at the Riverpark?" I asked.

"Nothing so exalted," he said "A waiter."

"And an . . ."

He laughed. "Actor."

"Of course," I said.

"You?

"I am a helper," I said. "I serve."

"Well, that's evasive," he said.

"Yes. It is."

"And a little intriguing. Intentionally?"

He had moved just a little closer.

"Perhaps," I said. "Maybe even a bit more than perhaps."

We talked for a while, then walked a while more, and then we went back to his apartment in Yorkville. It was a freshly painted one-bedroom with inexpensive but pleasant drapes, and carpets, books, and a nice reading chair. There were a handful of framed playbills with Dovid's name in them, a couple of framed photos of him on stage and two more with friends, one taken on a small sailboat. He had worked in his craft a lot for someone so young.

Twenty-six, he had said when I'd asked.

He hadn't asked me. If he had, I would have said twenty-seven, and it would have been believable—though I would have been that age, by his reckoning, far, far back in the distant past, if I had ever been an age at all. I don't remember. I just remember *being*, where a moment before I had not.

I have been as I am now always. It is simply how I am, though I think those of you who see me when I am abroad each do so a little differently, according to your own predilections.

"You have beautiful eyes," he told me.

I do. Green, with flecks of gold that pick up the color of my hair. I am fair and lovely despite who I am and what you might think at first. I serve, and lovingly. "Goddess of the Tide," my London lover for the night wrote of me, "Whose sable Streams beneath the City glide." And still they do, as they did then, in every city, though I live only in the great ones (except for an occasional holiday in a country hamlet) and only one at a time. But John, which was my London lover's name, dissembled after that line, and wrote:

"A mortal Scavenger she saw, she lov'd;
The muddy Spots that dry'd upon his Face"

It was he, John, and not some scavenger I saw and lov'd (though lov'd was not the proper word), and not mud upon his clean-shaven face but a bit of powder.

"Swift the Goddess rose," he wrote,
"And through the Streets pursu'd the distant Noise,
Her Bosom panting with expected Joys.
With the Night-wandring Harlot's Airs she past,
Brush'd near his side, and wanton Glances cast;"

Yes, I did that.

"In the black Form of Cinder-Wench she came,
When Love, the Hour, the Place had banish'd Shame;
To the dark Alley, Arm in Arm they move:
O may no Link-Boy interrupt their Love!"

No, it was not as a cinder-wench but rather as my comely self I came, even if in the guise perhaps and manner perhaps of a gentleman's daughter; and not to a dark alley, but rather back to his quarters we went. By night's end, he knew me, as I was, as I am—the only one of my lovers (if they were that) ever truly to do so, even if he dissembled some when he later wrote of it. I do not know how he knew, or why, but he did, classicist, poet, dramatist, and man of many curiosities that he was, and maybe that was all there was to it, that he was those.

"Thank you," I said to Dovid.

He had to imagine that many before him must have said that to me, or at least known that it is a tired thing to say to any woman whose eyes are not forcefully unpleasant, and yet he did not hesitate to say it to me himself, was unafraid of sounding trite. Because it was true and how indeed he found them.

We made love in his small bed, and again, and then yet again.

He had greater appetite than Albus, less guile and calculation than John.

He fell asleep holding me, with his breath gentle upon my shoulder. I lingered in it, and in his arms.

Thank you, Dovid, I wrote to him on a notepad on an end table in his living room when finally I rose and made ready to leave. At the door, I stopped and returned to it, and wrote, *O, thank you!*

I felt what I think you must feel when you are ready to cry.

I WAS PREGNANT. I HAD been so before. From Albus with a daughter, John with a son. To both of whom I gave birth.

I prepared a nursery in the drains, from which I had not emerged again since my night with Dovid. (I rarely do, often for decades, sometimes even centuries. I am not usually lonely; nor do my loins tremble much.) Though my babies have been like you and not like me, still they can live without harm here in the few days I keep them, which I know I should before I bring them up to you, which I also know I should and which I do not mind, never having felt before anything more than faint connection with them, and only fleeting interest once they were no longer within me; as I might with anything new and novel that entered my realm, stayed briefly, then left, as it should, along with everything else. They can live here without harm during their brief tenancy because of the suckling of my breasts, which protects them.

I did remember Dovid's hands, though. And his breath upon my shoulder. And how he had held me, as if he would have done so forever, as if he had thought it was all he had ever wanted.

I would have gone back to him again, I believe. No, I am *certain*.

And somehow we would have . . .

But no, that is just fancy. (Even though I am not given much to fancy.)

We wouldn't have. We couldn't have.

But while I think that, it cannot be proved. Partway through my pregnancy, it was made impossible.

I WAS *NOT* BEFORE I was. And then I *was,* where I had not been before.

I *was* the moment Lucius Tarquinius Priscus touched me, or rather the marble form he perceived to be me. That is the moment I came into being, brought forth, so far as I can determine, by Priscus's very act of perception.

I was not; and then I was.

They had found me, or what they perceived to be me—they knew as well as I that it was a statue they saw—but whence and how it had come to be in that broad ditch, that stream, that open drain that cut along the floor of the valley between the seven hills and which would become the center of the city as it grew, they did not know any more than I. They wondered at it, especially Tarquinius Priscus, who was the king, there still being kings then, long before the Republic that supplanted them and the Empire that followed, who had been summoned to look, to witness, and who in some wonder touched me, as he perceived me, named me, and I was.

I served the city as it grew, and it propitiated and appreciated me and built for me a great arched tiled home beneath itself, running the length of the valley so I could continue to drain down the marshy parts that once were there and keep it dry and habitable, and also to carry away their wastes as the greater houses multiplied over the years and connected to me, and the public facilities, too. As the city grew, an ever carefully planned and multiplying number of subsidiary ducts were connected to flow into me. I also carried away the waters from great storms for them, feeding it all out into the Tiber, just as much later I would do for London into the Thames, Hamburg into the Elbe, and for other places into other rivers and lakes.

I served them in that, my first city, and they reverenced me and even erected for me a small shrine in the center of their dry valley which they now called a forum, along its main thoroughfare which they called the Via Sacra, in front of a building they called the Basilica Aemilia. It was a modest shrine, but sincere. They understood the importance of what I did for them and wished to honor me, and I regarded them well for that and pledged to serve them tirelessly. They built my little shrine over the central drain of my home, the *Cloaca Maxima*. It was a round, raised platform with a low railing and two statues of me (though some have claimed one was of a greater being like me, and not me, but it was not) and in the center a covered opening that gave ingress into my great tunnel, as if into me.

That was long ago, as you count time. Long before any fancy I might have had about Dovid and me.

MIDWAY THROUGH MY PREGNANCY FROM Dovid, a great, terrible storm struck the long island to the east and north of Manhattan, and even Queens and Brooklyn and some of the eastern edge of Manhattan itself. The East River, which is not truly a river but a tidal strait open to the ocean on both ends, surged up from the south against Governor's Island and Roosevelt Island and Randall's Island in the strait which separates Manhattan from Queens, and surged again, and then yet again, frenzied and wild.

Raging, the crazed waters flowed backwards into my systems, pounded into them, carried debris and things from the sea swirling into them, and among those things a pod of little sea nymphs who became trapped beneath a grate that secured a passage between the tunnel in which I stood witnessing the rape of my home and the tunnel below, and they were hurled up against the grate by the thrusting backflow, the salty water erupting up past them into the larger tunnel where I was, streaming their golden hair up over their heads in wavering filaments through the small square openings in the grate. They raised their faces and pushed their slender fingers up through the grate toward me in panicked supplication and shrilled in terror with their high-pitched voices. And I could not help these lovely fragile creatures who in common days rode the crests of waves in the bright sunlight under a blue sky in delight, known long ago for who and what they were, but no longer now, not by you who cannot see the stars in the sky but rather who see these creatures only as glinting little puffs of spray as the wind whips against the curling tops of those waves. All I could do was stretch out my hands toward them in pity and hold their eyes with my own so they could see that they were not alone, for though I am greatly strong I cannot wrench heavy iron from its embedment deep in concrete. And I watched the little pod of these frightened creatures drown, which is all I could do, and then watched them sink back down lifeless into the roiling waters and be carried away.

The storm killed Dovid, too.

He had gone out to a marina on City Island in the Long Island Sound to help his friend Michael Shannon re-moor the small sailboat Shannon kept there. A boom broke free in the driving wind, swung wildly, struck Dovid, knocked him overboard, and he drowned.

It was that simple, and that sudden.

Beneath the city streets, I felt a wrench within my belly when it happened. I cried out and lowered myself to sit on a ledge from which the rats, who normally find me congenial and I them, had gone scurrying away at my cry. I held my rounded belly, surprised. I do not much feel pain, if this had actually been pain. I was uncertain. If it had *not* been pain, it had at least been unfamiliar: a sudden twisting, a turn, a breaking of some kind.

And in truth I did not know if it was I who had experienced it or my forming child, whom I would later learn was a boy; if I had not instead felt a rippling outward from him, of what *he* felt at that moment. I do know that as I sat with my hands cradling my belly, my forming child was thrashing about within me and that it took time for him to become quiet again. But I do not know which of us had actually felt this loss, sensed Dovid in his death, and in our agitation had disturbed the other. I think perhaps it was the child, connected to his father through the agency of the small part of him that was me. As later, through that same agency he would—dimly—know me.

I loved my child. That had never happened to me before. With my first two, I felt some regard—or at least that I *ought* to—and I saw that they were not destroyed, that they could exist without suffering the more violent pains of their times and live out their natural lives that way.

The girl, whom I had by Albus, I was able to place into the house of one of the lesser noble families, a house more kind than most at that time, as a household slave. The boy, from John, I got situated as an infant with a servant couple who had lost a child of their own, and later apprenticed to a cobbler so he could have a decent trade.

Had Dovid lived, I would have brought Ben—for that is what I named my son, and he *was* my son, not just a child I had borne—to him, and I believe Dovid would have loved him, would have wanted him. And I would have found ways to help, make it not only possible but even easy for him to raise our son, even though I would not, I think I have to admit, have been able to be with them.

I know Dovid would have loved Benjamin. Though we had had but a single night together, he had loved me. His touch had become too gentle, his eyes too open to me, his body figured to mine too easily as we slept, and his arms around me too cherishing and protective, his breath too soft on my shoulder, for him not to—even with the swell of his hormones, which is what had first impelled him to me at the side of the river. After that swell, beneath it, Dovid was a man capable of love. He would not have been able to resist loving his child. I think that was part of why I loved Ben myself, however much I can love, which is at least some, I have learned. Because his father had loved me.

And I think Dovid would have liked the name Benjamin. I don't know why. I just do. Which is mostly why I chose it.

The sea god might have killed Dovid. Out of anger, or jealously, or both. He was once a suitor to me, some say. Others that he was my father, who carelessly tossed me aside. I don't think either is true. If so, it was somehow before I *was,* and I cannot see how that could be. Still others say he might simply hold me in contempt, I being so much less than he, a corrupt little mimicry in a corrupt domain, or because in his eyes I foul his own. Again, I do not know. Perhaps it was just that he goes into rages sometimes, needing no reason, and it was only by sad coincidence that Dovid was killed along with the little nymphs and other creatures of the sea that day, and even some of the air and land, too, and the borders between sea and land so badly ravaged.

Whichever, Dovid was dead; and months later Ben was in my arms and suckling at my breast.

I HAD LAIN WITH DOVID in the summer. It was late in a night the following spring when I rose up into the streets again, with Ben in my arms. He was but seven days old, swaddled in a light wool blanket, with a little cap on his head, and sleeping contentedly, having suckled his fill. When there was no one to see, I emerged onto Seventeenth Street, walked east a little, crossed to the other side of Sixth Avenue and turned south. Within a few steps I was at the closed glass doors of the New York Foundling Hospital. I lifted Benjamin, kissed him on his forehead, then quickly bent and set him gently to the pavement. I stood and rapped on the glass. Within, the guard looked up. I pointed down to Benjamin, and then I left, moving rapidly, and turned east onto Sixteenth Street before the guard could open the doors.

A taxi was pulled to the side there, the driver talking on a cell phone, gesticulating as he spoke. I could not return to my home with a witness. I walked past the taxi to Fifth Avenue, where cars were moving down toward Washington Square, as they always are—the city never wholly sleeps—went to Fifteenth Street, and saw there would soon be a lull in the scant traffic there. I turned onto it, waited, and when the lull did come stepped off the sidewalk into the street, lifted the manhole cover there, slipped down, replaced the cover behind myself, and was home again . . . and alone.

More alone than ever.

I did not want form anymore, in which there is more feeling, so I merged back into the brick and concrete, melded into the stuff of the tunnels and passageways, and became without form—still being in a way, but in a way where not much was poignant.

Time passed.

I sensed the boy now and then. He was content, he was happy, he was lonely. He was frightened, he was angry, he was amused. He felt terribly, terribly alone: friendless, unloved. I stirred in the tunnels, in the brick, the concrete, the cast-iron. His loneliness touched me, even in my attenuation. I nearly took form, but in the end did not. There was nothing, really, I could do for him.

I could do only what I had always done. I drained the city, and kept it from sickening itself.

But one night, suddenly, without intent, I heaved again into being. Just *did*.

I was afraid, something I had never been before. Terrified, I think—if I understand what people mean by that word.

(If it is, I can only pity them. I cannot imagine how they can bear to live with something like that in their life.)

I took form below a manhole on East Fourth Street, off Avenue D, rose up, threw aside the iron cover, which clanged atop the pavement when it fell, and surged onto the sidewalk and up the stairs of one of a pair of abandoned buildings there. I plunged through the splintery gap in the broken plywood that ineffectually sealed a glassless window to the side of the landing, which was half a level up from the street.

"Please, please! Don't!" cried Benjamin.

"I'm going to cut your dick off, you little shit."

I saw them in what was the near darkness to them but was not to me, two boys, young men really, greasy, dirty, both with knives advancing on Benjamin, who was equally unkempt but younger, much younger, and smaller, and who had already been cut on his arm, from which blood was dripping down onto the dirty floor, his shirt wet with it around the wound.

I said nothing. I just moved.

I ripped the head from one of his attackers and seized the other as blood sprayed from the neck of the corpse that was still standing beside him. I lifted him above my head and hurled him against the scarred, stained, hard plaster wall a dozen feet away in what had once been the sitting room of this old, tired building. Many of his bones broke when he struck it. He dropped heavily to the floor.

"Please!" Benjamin wailed.

He was pressed against the far wall in front of me, away from the street, half crouched, his head down, trying to protect it with his arms.

The decapitated corpse collapsed.

There was blood on the ceiling from it, and on the near wall, and blood now began to pool slowly out of the torn neck, no longer pulsing with the heart no longer beating, just trickling some now.

"I don't *have* any more money," Ben cried.

"Ben," I said.

"Please!"

"Ben. Benjamin. It's alright. You're safe now. No one is going to hurt you."

He raised his head a little, peered fearfully over his forearm, trying to see in the gloom.

"It's alright, Ben."

He could not make me out clearly, but he could see that I was not them.

"Ben," I said, letting him hear my voice, my woman's voice.

I took a step toward him, held my hands out to him.

"I . . . my name is Tom," he said. "Tom."

"It's Ben," I said. "That's what it first was. But you can be Tom if you wish. Either way, you're safe now." I extended my hands further. "Come, let's leave this place."

He pushed himself erect, took a tentative step toward me, then another, looking about for the two young men who had hurt him, who had intended to kill him. In the blackness, he didn't see the body at the foot of the wall against which I had thrown the one. I moved a little away from the other, crumpled at my feet, which I did not think Ben would recognize as a body in the gloom and amid the boxes and other debris on the floor. He was looking for standing figures, dangerous figures.

"Come."

I reached for his hand, touched his fingertips. He flinched, but did not draw his hand back. I took it and began to lead him toward the broken plywood and the street. I could feel the years through his hand, could feel his heart, could *know* him. I ached for him. Too many foster homes, too many indifferent or bad people, and finally the awful one, who had hurt him and caused him to run away, to be living on the streets as he was. I have never wept. If I could, I think I would have then.

Ben was turning his head, trying to see into the darkness around us.

"Where are they?" he asked. "What happened to them?"

"They're gone," I said.

I helped him out through the broken plywood onto the landing at the top of the steps.

"Stay here a moment," I said, touching his shoulder. "I need to go back and get something I dropped."

He tensed.

I touched his cheek. "No, no. Don't worry. There's nothing to be afraid of. I'll be back in just a moment. Truly. A moment."

I was quick. I went through their pockets and took the money that was there, which wasn't much but was enough for what I needed. The one at the foot of the wall moaned once, a little moan. I broke his neck.

Outside, I took Ben's hand again and led him down to the sidewalk. He was, I think, somewhat in shock. But I could see him struggling against that, working to take control of himself. I walked him to beneath one of the sodium street lamps, which cast a light that had an orange tint but was brighter than one might have thought. He needed to see me. To feel comforted, to feel safe, and he needed to see me examine his wound in the light, which I could have done in what was the dark to him, but which would not have been a good thing to do.

"It will need cleaning and stitches," I said.

"Who are you?" he asked.

He was trying to toughen himself, to stand straighter.

"Just a friend," I said. "Someone who cares about people. At least sometimes. I heard you cry out. I went to see what was wrong," I said.

"There were two of them," he said. "They were going to kill me. They could have killed you."

"No. They couldn't—they . . . wouldn't have. I think they were cowards."

"Thank you," he said.

I took the moment to look at him more completely. He was gangly, but I could see that he would grow up to be tall and lean like his father. His dark hair was the same, curly and thick, even if in need of a washing now. And his eyes.

That was a mistake, looking into his eyes.

They were not Dovid's eyes.

They were my mine: green with flecks of gold that picked up the color of my hair.

In the light of the street lamp, even with its orange tint, he saw that, too: his eyes in mine. He saw *me*, even if he did not understand what he was seeing. He made a sound that seemed torn from his heart and threw himself into my arms and clasped me.

I held him, and rocked him, and kissed his head.

"There," I murmured. "There. It's alright now. It will be alright. No one will hurt you again. There," I said, holding him.

I took him in a cab to the Downtown Hospital on William Street at the foot of the Brooklyn Bridge, to the emergency room. There were only two other patients waiting at this late hour. The bleeding from Ben's wound had slowed, and we were given a compress to keep pressed to it. It was not long before the nurse called us over to take our information.

"Name?" she asked.

Ben looked at me. Into my eyes. "Ben," he said.

"Last name?"

He waited, looking at me.

"Davidson," I said, after only a moment. "Benjamin Davidson."

"Davidson," Ben said.

That had not been Dovid's last name. But it was a true name for Ben.

"And you are?" the nurse asked me.

Ben was waiting, intently.

"His sister," I said. I could not have been his mother, did not look old enough.

"Your name?"

"Chloe."

"Davidson?"

"No. Purificare. Chloe Purificare," I said, using one of the old words.

The nurse wrote it down. "Your date of birth, Benjamin?"

I did not answer for him. When he saw that I was not going to, he gave her a date. It was not the true date, but close enough, probably assigned to him by the Foundling Home.

"Address?"

He gave her one in the West Village that was not his, that had never been his. He gave it to her easily, naturally. I could see some of the charm of his father in him, as his father had begun to speak to me by the East River that night fifteen years ago.

"How did this happen?" the nurse asked, lifting the compress and looking at the wound.

"I was trying to fix a broken window pane. I slipped. I got cut."

The nurse wrote that down. She may have believed it. It was clear that she had noted his clothes, which looked like the clothes of a boy who was living on the streets, and his grime. My robe, which some see as a kind of gown when they see me, or as a simple dress, was not blemished. It never is, by anything, as I myself am not. I have been called a purifier.

"Parents?" she asked.

I said, "They're dead."

"You're his legal guardian?"

"Yes."

"Insurance card, please."

"I don't have it with me. I'm sorry. We left the house in a hurry. I'll go back and get it. How long before the doctor sees him?"

"Within the next few minutes."

"I'll leave now," I said. "It won't take me long. Here, Ben," I said, pressing the money I had taken from the two corpses into his hand. "Keep this till I get back."

I saw that he knew I would not return. I saw the longing in his eyes, my eyes, the tears welling in them.

"Just give us a moment, please," I said to the nurse, taking Ben's hand and raising him up from his chair. "He can finish the remaining questions you have without me."

"Sign here, first," the nurse said, pushing a form across the table of her small station along with a pen. "We need you to authorize treatment. Also to acknowledge that you are responsible for any costs not covered by your insurance."

I signed the form and drew Ben off to the side.

"They'll treat you," I said. "They have to. You won't get in trouble. Not much, anyway. Just tell them someone robbed you in the subway. They cut you. I found you bleeding in the subway car and brought you here."

"Why won't you come back?" he asked.

"I can't, Ben. I can't."

"Then I want to go with you," he said.

I took his face in my hands. I kissed his forehead.

"I can't, can I?" he said.

We looked into each other's face

"I'm sorry," I said.

And I saw the need he had.

"You can say it," I told him. "It's alright. Go ahead."

Tears spilled out of his eyes.

"I love you," he said, hugging me.

"I love you," I said. I held him close. Then I said, "Your father would have loved you, too."

The nurse called out. "We do have more questions, about medical history," she said.

"Yes. He'll be right with you," I said.

Quietly, I said to Ben, "For the rest, afterward, just tell them the truth—who you are, why you ran away. Ask them to put you back into the care of the Foundling Hospital. The hospital will probably be willing to take you in temporarily, before you can be placed in a new home. Whatever the case, get up to the Forty-second Street library three days from now. Outside, at the base of the southernmost of the two lions, the downtown side. Be there at noon. Someone will meet you there, to help. If you can't get there three days from now, then go on the fourth. If you can't get away on the fourth, then go on the fifth. As soon you can get there, there will be someone looking for you."

"Please!" the nurse said. "He can't be seen until the form is completed."

"Goodbye, Ben," I said.

"I love you," he repeated, wiping away the tears from his cheeks.

"I love you," I said. "I always will."

And I left.

I WAS AT HIS GRADUATION from St. Ann's School in Brooklyn Heights four years later, though I stood in a hall looking into the chapel through a partly closed door. The chapel was too small for him not to have seen me otherwise. I saw him look for me from the podium as he made ready to deliver the valedictory address. He smiled at his adoptive parents, who were in the chapel, at his classmates and at the other parents, but still his eyes moved about in search of me. He had kept the name Benjamin, I saw on the program. Benjamin Davidson, though as a middle name he had assumed the surname of the couple who had taken him in and treated him as their own.

I had seen to his safety and future.

I had done that through Dovid's friend Michael Shannon, who had been with Dovid on the day he died. I had called Michael Shannon's offices as soon as they were open the morning after I had left Benjamin at the Downtown Hospital and made—insisted on—an appointment the following morning.

"It involves administering a sum of between two and three million dollars," I told him over the telephone. "With a commensurate fee. And because you once had a friend named Dovid, to whom you were close."

Michael Shannon had done well. He was not one of the overwhelmingly powerful men in the city, but he was not unknown to those who were.

He seemed bemused by me when we met. But only *seemed* so. It was a tactic to disarm me. His questions, when he asked them at intervals, as if something had only just then occurred then to him, were subtle and probing. I allowed him none of them.

I had brought a leather satchel with me. In it were cash, gold coins, jewelry (much of it antique), and other small valuables: a fine miniature English enamel portrait someone had brought from England that fell into me in the early nineteenth century, a rare Qianlong jade someone else had brought home from China and that had found its way into my domain in the 1930s, and more.

"It is all worth easily more than two million net," I said to Michael Shannon. "Probably closer to three. And not difficult to sell."

"And you know that how?" he asked, smiling.

"I simply do," I said.

"Do you have papers of provenance for the more costly items?"

"No. But I have possession of them. And my right—your right—to that will not be challenged."

Things valuable as well as foul regularly find their way into my domain, lost, discarded, stolen, and then abandoned in fear, cast off by accident or in anger. In every city I have ever lived over the years, I have taken up some of this and set it aside. It was useful to have sometimes, as now.

We agreed on his fee. I was generous in it.

"You will administer the money for the boy's security and well-being," I said. "In seeing him placed in a good home, for his education, for any other needs and reasonable wants he has. Until he reaches the age of thirty, at which time you will disburse to him in full whatever amount remains."

"And you wish no papers on this, nothing binding me to fiduciary duty. No papers of any kind."

"No. None."

"And I won't see you again. Ever."

"That is correct."

"Nor any agent or representative of you."

"Nor any agent or representative."

He had been leaning back in his chair. Now he rocked forward, put his forearms on his desk, clasped his hands, and looked into my eyes. "Tell me, Ms. Purificare, then what would stop me from simply taking this money for myself?"

"I would know," I said. "And I would hurt you."

After some moments, looking at me, he said, "I believe you would."

"It is good to believe the truth."

"I wouldn't, you know. I wouldn't do such a thing." He sat back.

"I know. That is part of why I am here."

Michael Shannon had led the funeral service for Dovid, at the marina out on the small wharf where Michael's sailboat had been tied that day. He had wept for his lost friend.

I was there. In the water, watching, listening. I had come out of my home for it. I saw the man then for who he was. And I had read of him over the years, noting his name because he had been Dovid's friend.

Michael Shannon was studying me now that our business was done.

He asked, "How did you know Dovid?"

"I just did."

He nodded, not having really expected much more from me.

"You're what, twenty-seven, twenty-eight?" he asked.

"Twenty-seven," I said.

"You would have been young when Dovid died, twelve or thirteen."

"I was younger then," I said.

I stood, ready to leave. I offered my hand.

Michael Shannon got up from his chair. He paused, searching my face: my hair, my brow, my eyes, my skin, my mouth.

"Do you have an older sister?" he asked.

"No."

He came around his desk. He took my hand, shook it politely.

"Dovid told me about a girl once," he said. "He spent only a single night with her. She was gone in the morning when he woke. Dovid liked women, but he wasn't a one-night-stand kind of guy. She really got to him. He spent months looking for her. In fact, he still was, right up to the day of the storm. I think she might have looked something like you."

I finished our handshake. "Thank you, Mr. Shannon. I appreciate your services."

"You're welcome."

He was reluctant to let me go.

"And the boy, he's never to know anything of you, anything at all. You're sure of this."

"Only that there has been a benefactor, someone who cares about his well-being."

He nodded. "Well, then thank you, Ms.—may I call you Chloe, this once? It's nice to meet someone who was Dovid's friend."

"Yes, you may. And yes, it is nice for me, too, to meet someone who was Dovid's friend."

"Well. Thank you, Chloe."

"Thank *you,* Michael."

I kissed him on the cheek.

Then I left. I always do. I always must. It is the nature of things.

I WAS THERE WHEN BEN graduated from Columbia, too, this time seated in the much larger audience, my hair darkened for the day and pulled back, face rouged, wearing a mannish suit. I wanted to be nearer him. And again he looked for me, eyes roaming the audience as he mounted the stairs in the moving line of graduates, stepped onto the platform and walked toward the dean to receive his diploma. They passed over me, went beyond and further back to the seats behind me—then stopped and snapped back to the row in which I sat. I coughed, covering my mouth with my hand, and lifted my program, bent my head to it. Ben was forced forward by the continuing call of graduates. He crossed the stage, still running his eyes over the row in which I sat, then descended and had to take his seat again with the other graduates.

I left before the assembly was dismissed. He had not actually seen me, but I knew the part of me that was him had sensed me. I probably should not have gone, but was glad I had. I could only hope my presence had been better for him than not.

I had seen Michael Shannon there, too, tanned, fit, temples graying, in an elegantly tailored suit. He sat with his wife, his equal physically and in dress, alongside Ben's adoptive parents, and looked affectionately at Ben as he accepted his diploma and shook the dean's hand. He did not see me. He had no reason to expect to, but would not have recognized me if he had.

Ben had graduated summa cum laude, bearing out what he had accomplished at St. Ann's and presaging well for his future.

I was glad for him. What lingered for me, though, was the *language* of that honor, the dead language no one spoke anymore. It was still sometimes read in schools, used in medicine and law, and graven into cornerstones and monuments. But not spoken.

I missed it. I do not miss things much, or places I have left. Things rise, things fall. As do days: here a little while, then not. As for places, I have always simply gone where it was best for me to go. Sometimes where I was most needed, others where I was most wanted, or appreciated, and still others just because I wished to.

I began to think in those months after Ben's graduation that a leaving might lie ahead.

It did.

But I saw Ben once more before then.

I went to his wedding.

He married a young woman who had studied with him at Columbia. They waited till she had finished law school, passed the bar, and had her first hire. Her name was Flora, which I liked, having had a friend in Rome from whom it had come down, a being like me and who, also like me, had wandered to many places over the years, as most of us did. Ben was with the mayor's office by then. There was talk of a political future for him.

I had read of them together and seen photographs of them: with the mayor, the borough president, the senior senator from the state, Flora to the side and just slightly behind Ben; with joined hands at a reception at the Metropolitan Museum; she speaking at a symposium, he in the front row of the audience. She was graceful and intelligent. Ben looked at her in a way that spoke to me of how I thought Dovid had come to feel about me as I lay on my side nestled back into him, he cupped to me, his arm around me, his breath soft and warm on the skin of my shoulder. And that I felt for him in those few short hours before I rose to leave.

I sensed that now in Benjamin, deep below the streets of the city, the love he had for her and the love he knew back from her.

I was made peaceful by it, calm, content—and knew I could leave.

They were married in St. Bartholomew's Church on Park Avenue, an important church in the city, a lovely edifice,

Byzantine in design, beautifully domed. The mayor was there, and other people of note.

As was I.

I sat on the groom's side midway back from the altar, two people in from the aisle. It was pretty ceremony. I have always liked ceremonies, of any kind. Dovid would have liked it, too, I think, though it was not of his faith. As it was not of mine.

Ben and Flora were joyful it as they came walking back down the aisle at its completion, the organ playing, swinging their clasped hands, smiling and nodding to people, stopping spontaneously once to embrace and kiss one another, followed by the bridesmaids and groomsmen, happy and smiling, too, and waving to people they knew.

And Benjamin saw me.

Me.

His face froze—for an instant, less even. Then it softened, became softer than I have ever seen a face become before. He smiled ever so gently, and looked lovingly into my eyes, which were the mirror of his own. It was as if, for a moment, we were suspended outside of time, outside of anything else at all, that there was only he and I. My own face softened, and I opened my heart, fully, and I looked lovingly into his eyes. And then he was gone, passed on with his bride, into his life.

I left New York that night.

I went home. I could now, it was right now. And when I arrived there, after all those years, all those other cities, I was indeed home, and it was good and I was made glad.

In the spring, I spent an afternoon with Flora—*my* Flora, the first Flora—who had also come home. We spent it in a meadow outside the city on a late spring day. We walked, laughed, rested, and caught one another up on two other dear friends, Pomona, whom Flora had last seen in an orange grove outside Valencia, in Spain, and Ceres, with whom I had visited at the edge of a broad field of wheat near Topeka, in Kansas, back in the United States. We picked wildflowers and wove them into wreaths which we wore in our hair, and listened to the laughter of nymphs in the woods nearby and the rutting cries of a pair of satyrs who pursued them. There was no one else about—which is why they were.

It could have been a day from long, long ago.

We gossiped, Flora and I, about the doings of the greater ones of which we had heard since last we met, though there is much less of that now since your kind have turned away from them as well as from we lesser ones. We stayed the afternoon and most of the night, too, lying on our backs in the meadow, the wreaths of flowers still in our hair, feeling the lovely, temperate, timeless breeze blow softly across us and listening to the sounds of the satyrs exhausting themselves with the handful of nymphs who had allowed themselves to be caught, and looking up in dreamy pleasure at the night sky, which, we being far enough from the city and any town or village of significant size, was filled with glittering stars, many of which were arranged in the shapes and forms of, and named for, some of the more notable among us.

I have never, as I said, really missed any place I have left, or time, or thing that is gone, but it was good to be there that night with Flora, lying on our backs, holding her hand, the breeze gentle, with the fragrance of our wreaths, listening to the rioting of the nymphs and satyrs, the stars abiding and abundant above us, like crystals or diamonds, and wondrous to see.

I saw Ben once more.

He came to me. Ostensibly, to my city. He arrived with others who did what he did in other cities to meet and speak of their work with one another, of what was effective and what was not, to talk of remedies and the future, what might be and how it might. Ostensibly. I knew he was here the moment he set foot on the soil (rather, the paved-over soil) of my city. I felt him, and knew why he had come. I had known of the impending conference, of course; in a way, it was in my honor—focused on my being and purpose, to the extent its organizers and participants understood me. They didn't, not actually anyway. They saw *me* as a metaphor, knew me only in my secular guise. Still, they had chosen my city, the place of my coming into being, in honor of that.

Benjamin was now Director of New York City's Bureau of Water and Sewer Operations, the most extensive of its kind in the world. That it was such was partly why I had the stayed the time I had in New York, which was longer than I usually did in a city (though London and Paris both held me for goodly lengths, too).

The significant work of the conference was finished by the end of the third day, and the event was formally ended at a breakfast convocation the next morning. Some of the conferees left immediately after to return home. Others remained for what many considered the highlight of their trip, an afternoon tour of me that had been arranged for them. They were taken by bus to an entry point of the *Cloaca Maxima*—the Great Drain—the central, most ancient, and most important part of my domain, and led down into me by an historian from Sapienza University, the largest in Europe and the oldest in the city (though not nearly as old as I).

I watched them from within the stones and concrete, the terra cotta and brick. They marveled at me, not in flattery but rather in genuine admiration and appreciation, and such as I had not been given in a very long time. They were, after all, men and women who cared for me, who maintained and wished my well-being, my flourishing, through all my domains in all of their cities.

I was pleased, touched even, and renewed in my desire to serve.

Still, it was Benjamin on whom I dwelt. While the rest esteemed me, they did not *see* me. He did. He looked deeply at the parts and pieces of me during the tour, and into them, and *saw* me. I watched his body loosen at the moment he actually perceived me, saw the softening in his face again, the comfort and love within him.

Benjamin went up and out of the drain and into the Forum again with the rest of them when the tour ended, from which their guide led them to the Tiber, near the bridge Ponte Rocco, the Basilica Julia. A stone stairway descends here down to a suspended walk overlooking a tall, arched opening that is the place of my outfall into the Tiber and that has been for longer than the stones that arch over it now, for longer than men have actually recorded.

From this vantage, Benjamin and the others looked upon me and the easy, not very powerful flow out from me down into the river. These days, I no longer carry waste and debris out and away from the city through the *Cloaca Maxima*. That is done through other, newer parts of my domain, and handled in another manner. But still I continue to serve the city through it, draining off rain and storm water in the bed of its main course, which remains wide enough for a narrow boat to navigate between the stone blocks of its sides, which blocks themselves have narrow walks upon which a man can walk erect beneath the vault of its ceiling.

I waited.

When the tour members had seen enough of this, my final place, they began their way back up the stairs to the Basilica Julia and the street. One called goodbye to me, jokingly, by my old name, my first name, my original name, in that dead language.

"Vale, Cloacina!"

Some of the others laughed, and one joined him in bidding me farewell:

"Yes. Goodbye, Cloacina!"

From within the stone, I watched Benjamin remain.

"Coming, Ben?" the historian called, looking back over his shoulder.

"I want to stay a while," Ben answered. "I'll make my own way back."

The guide nodded.

Ben waited.

I did, too—till the French couple also on the walkway finally left, arms about each other's waist, and then a little longer till the Italian teenager who had been leaning on the rail with his forearms and looking moodily out to the Tiber, finished his cigarette, flicked the butt out into the river, turned, stuffed his hands into his pockets, and left.

When the teenager was gone and there were no others, and as the sun began to sink into the horizon sending streaks of orange through the western sky, I heaved into being, into form, and came to Benjamin on the walkway.

If my heart could be broken, I think it might have broken then, with what welled up in me as I looked at Benjamin and with what I felt filling him. Broken with joy, with grief.

He took a step toward me, hesitant, as his father had first been that night at the side of another river, only with a different kind of longing, a different need, and deep, deep as any I have ever seen.

I opened my arms to him.

He came to me, wrapped me in his own arms as I took him in mine, held me tightly, his face buried into my shoulder. I held him, and rocked him, and said, "Sshhh, sshhh now," as his breath caught in his throat. "It's alright," I said. "It's alright. I'm here."

He sobbed into my shoulder. Just once. But from within his heart.

"Hush," I said, stroking his hair, his father's hair, and rocked him.

After a short while, he straightened in my grasp, put his hands on my hips and stepped back. He was older now, his face a little fuller, small lines at the corners of his eyes. I was not. At least not as he saw me, I looked no older than I had to him the night I had taken him out of the abandoned house on East Fourth Street in Manhattan.

He saw me as I am, which is how I was then. How I have always been.

He nodded slowly.

"Thank you," he said. "Thank you for coming to me."

"I couldn't *not*, Benjamin."

"I knew you'd be here. I knew somehow that this is where you had gone. Home."

"Yes, home."

"I don't know how I knew."

"We just know some things about one another. *Feel* them."

"Yes, that's it," he said. "I wanted to show you something."

"Alright."

He took his wallet from his back pocket and opened it.

"There," he said, holding it up for me, so I could see a closeup photo of a young boy, a young boy with dark black hair and a familiar smile.

I smiled back at him, the young boy. Again, I couldn't *not*.

"He's very good looking. He seems to be a wonderful boy," I said. "He has his father's eyes."

"Yes," Benjamin said, turning to the photograph to look at it himself. "And your eyes, too."

"Yes," I said, looking into his own, which were green with flecks of gold—my eyes looking back at me.

"What is his name?" I asked.

"Davide," he said.

"Ah. That is a good name. Why did you name him that?"

"I don't know," he said. "It just seemed right. A good name."

"I think it is a very good name."

"Do you think my father would have liked it?"

"Yes. Very much. And he would have loved Davide. And he would have loved you. He wasn't able to. He died. But I know he would have loved you, and then Davide."

"Would he?"

"Yes."

"Thank you."

"I will need to go now," I said gently. "It is how things are."

"I know," he said. "I don't know how I know, but I know."

We looked into one another's eyes, into the green of them, with the flecks of gold.

It was all, truly, that could be done. And it was enough. It had to be enough.

I stepped back from him.

"Once more," he said, opening his arms. "Please."

I held him again. He sighed, loosening, and seemed almost

to melt into me, this man, this grown man, this capable man, this father of Davide who for instant was an infant himself again, and then the boy to whom I had never been able to give all that he needed and that he deserved, and whom I could only hold now, and let whatever comfort and succor he could draw from me flow forth to him.

He let go, stood looking down at me, tall, like his father.

He held my shoulders. He bent and kissed me on the cheek.

"I love you," he said.

"I love you," I said.

He sighed. There was contentment in the sound, peace. He accepted. And would carry with him what he needed from me.

"How does this work?" he asked. "Should I leave first, leave you here?"

"Yes," I said. "That would be best."

He stepped away. "Goodbye . . ." He struggled over the word, over what he wanted to call me.

"I love you," I said.

He nodded, understanding. He turned and walked away. And did not look back.

I waited till he was out of sight.

Then I went back into my domain.

It was comforting there, quiet, soothing. I sat. I put my face in my hands. I have never wept. I would have then, I believe, were I able. For grief, joy. For all the blessing, and all the hurt.

In gratitude.

In gratitude for Dovid. In gratitude for Benjamin. In gratitude for Davide, whom I would go to see some day, though I would not let him see me.

I wished I had been able to do this, what I had just done now, for my daughter here in Rome long ago.

And for my son in London.

I knew I would never to be able to do it again. That somehow it would burst my heart.

I would need to be careful in the future never to bear another child.

But I was glad I had had Benjamin.

I knew that he was glad, too, even in the face of all he had suffered. I knew that he had several times been up north of his city and seen the myriad stars glittering over the Hudson River, and that he would take Davide to see them, too, and that he would continue to know peace through the sight of them and the wonder of them, and that he might well hear things moving about in the night beneath them that others did not. And that Davide, too, would come to know something of me through them even if he could not form what it was that he knew into thought, only felt it at times, understood it in his heart.

Whatever was to become of me, and all else, including the stars, in time I was glad that long ago I had first come into being—and that this day my son had come to embrace me.

THE DEAD CLIENT
BY PARNELL HALL

NEW YORK'S CHANGED. WHEN I started working for Rosenberg and Stone, shortly after the dawn of time, the City was a fearsome place, at least for me. Attorneys had just been allowed to advertise, and a young, hotshot lawyer named Richard Rosenberg took full advantage, bombarding the airwaves with clever TV ads strategically placed on syndicated sitcom reruns on the local independent channels. The ads, all similar, were variations on a theme: an impoverished-looking man, usually black, with his leg in a cast, side-spied sheepishly up at his long-suffering wife, who stood stoically with her arms outspread in the living room of what was obviously a project apartment, and declared, somewhat petulantly, "What we gonna do now, George? How we gonna pay the rent?"

The answer, of course, was to call Rosenberg and Stone. The lure was it wouldn't cost you anything and you could make a pile of money. "Free consultation! No fee unless recovery! We will come to your home!"

Richard wouldn't, of course; he'd send me, and I'd come walking in in a suit and tie, flop down a briefcase on the table, and say, "Hi, I'm Stanley Hastings from the lawyer's office," and if they thought I was an attorney, hey, that wasn't my fault.

I would take down the facts of the case, all similar, usually the client tripped on a crack in the sidewalk, fell down, and broke a leg. I would fill out the fact sheet and get them to sign a number of forms, one to get their hospital records, one to get the police report, if any, and one, of course, retaining Richard Rosenberg as their attorney to act on their behalf.

That form was always last, and by the time they got to it most people were so used to signing forms they signed it without reading it. Which wasn't bad, they weren't getting taken, the form was a standard retainer; still it always gave me pause.

My job, though boring, was a piece of cake. It was also dangerous as hell. Because the people who called the lawyer they saw on TV tended to be, to put it politely, less than affluent. I plied my trade in slums and crack houses and projects with elevators that didn't function and stairwells that reeked of urine. I worked alone and unarmed and fully expected to be mugged and/or killed. The only reason I wasn't was because everyone thought I was a cop, otherwise why would I be there?

But that was way back when. Then Giuliani cracked down on crime and Bloomberg cracked down on soda and the City changed.

Cosmetically.

Disney cleaned up Times Square and Columbus Avenue got a bike lane, and the nice neighborhoods got nicer and the not-so-nice neighborhoods didn't. And do you think that created some resentment? Good guess. The junkies and muggers and crack whores and gangs are just more concentrated in the neighborhoods I frequent. And I'm older but no wiser and still look like a cop. But some things are different.

One thing that disappeared, and I wasn't sorry to see them go, was the squeegee guys. If you don't know what they are, you're not from New York. They're the guys that hang out on street corners and wash your windshield against your will. Squeegees are windshield-washing implements, an amenity you used to find in buckets of water next to the gas pumps in service stations. Few squeegee guys had squeegees, and fewer still had water. Most had a rag, usually dirtier than the windshield they were attempting to wash. They would appear out of nowhere, plaster themselves to the hood of your car, and smear your windshield with all kinds of unmentionable filth. They were gone, and no one missed them.

Which was why Nelson Jones was a surprise.

I was driving back from an assignment in Queens, signing up a woman who had gotten her hand slammed in her apartment door. It was her boyfriend who slammed it, which made the liability questionable, but Richard would probably sue the City of New York for building a project with a defective door that injured its occupants.

I was tooling past LaGuardia Airport when I got beeped. I have a cellphone, but I don't want to answer it when I'm driving. They page me and I call in.

I got off the Grand Central Parkway just before the Triboro Bridge and called the office.

"Rosenberg and Stone," Wendy/Janet said. Richard has two switchboard girls with identical voices, so I can never tell them apart.

"It's Stanley. You beeped me."

"Stanley. Glad you called."

She always says that, at least one of them always says that, as if I just happened to ring.

"What's up?"

"I got a case for you."

"I figured as much."

"Got a pen?"

"Always."

"The client is Nelson Jones. He broke his leg."

"What's his address?"

"Well, that's the problem."

"You don't have an address?"

"*He* doesn't have an address. Don't worry, he'll meet you on the corner."

"You're kidding."

"No, that's what he said."

"Great. I suppose you'll call him on his phone and let him know I'm coming."

"*He* doesn't have a phone."

Irony goes right over Wendy/Janet's head. As does practically anything else. Besides a voice, Wendy and Janet share the brains of a labradoodle. I don't know who got the larger half, but then I wouldn't know if I was talking to her anyway.

"So how will I know he's there?"

"You'll go and see."

"Any particular street corner?"

"Huh?"

"What corner will he be on?"

"125th and Broadway."

"Which corner?"

"He didn't say."

"Doesn't sound promising."

"You better find him. Richard really wants the case."

I came off the Triboro Bridge at 125th and Second Avenue, which sounds convenient, but Second Avenue and Broadway are about as far apart as you can get and crosstown traffic is the worst. The lights aren't staggered *or* in unison, like up and downtown streets, so you usually hit every one. I've had taxi drivers curse when I gave a crosstown address.

There's no good place to stop on the northeast corner of 125th and Broadway, so I pulled up on the northwest corner instead. There's no good place to stop there either, but you're less likely to piss off a bus driver. I hopped out and looked around.

Across the street a black man with a cloth was washing the windshield of a car that had pulled out of the McDonald's parking lot and been caught by the light. He hobbled around the front to wash the driver's side and with a sinking feeling I realized he was my client.

He had a cast on his leg.

He was the grungiest man I've ever seen. His clothes were not rags, but enough of them were missing to render it questionable. The pants were slit from the ankle to the crotch. Which might have been to accommodate the cast, but only one leg was broken and both legs were slit. The right leg was a different color from the left, as if the man had lain in paint, though which was the painted leg was not entirely clear.

He wore a sleeveless white T-shirt. It hadn't always been that way. The sleeves had been ripped off in jagged tears. It was a wonder there was enough fabric left to keep it on his shoulders. He had probably torn them off to use as windshield cleaning cloths, though the one he was currently clutching looked like it had been stolen from a garage, where it had served to wipe the oil off dipsticks.

Things did not look good for our client's sale. The driver had not rolled down his window, and when Mr. Jones knocked on it he gave him the finger.

The light changed and the car roared off while our client was still leaning on it. Had he fallen, I'd have gotten the license number.

"Nelson Jones?" I called.

He spun around, a one-legged man, ready to take on the world. "Yeah?" he snarled.

"I'm from Rosenberg and Stone. You called the office."

That rang a bell. Our client lurched out into the street right in the path of a car. The driver leaned on the horn and fishtailed around him. Nelson Jones took no notice. He motored across the street without benefit of a crutch in a serpentine style all his own, swinging his cast in a semicircle and hopping his good leg forward. He made remarkable progress, which was good, as every car in uptown Manhattan was bearing down on him. He clung to the side of my car and demanded, "You the lawyer?"

"I'm Mr. Hastings from Rosenberg and Stone."

He scowled, spit. "She-et! You Rosenberg?"

"No."

"I call Rosenberg. Where he at? Wanna talk to the man on TV."

Richard had let a slick advertising executive talk him into appearing in a couple of his own TV commercials. I'd warned him it would be trouble.

"Mr. Rosenberg handles the case in court. He doesn't go out in the street."

"You tell him he gots to."

"He won't."

"You tell him."

"I'll tell him. He won't. You'll never see him again. You wanna see him you do one of two things. You talk to me, or you go to his office."

"Where the office?"

"Downtown."

"She-et!"

"Wanna talk to me?"

"No."

I got back in my car.

He frog-kicked his way around it, plastered himself to the windshield, banged on the glass.

I took that as a sign he'd changed his mind. I got out of the car, opened my briefcase, and took out a signup kit with a fact sheet on top. The usual procedure was to fill in the name, address, phone number, age, sex, marital status. I figured I'd skip the usual procedure. "Why don't you tell me what happened."

"Muthafucka knock me down."

I did not write that on the form. "With his car?"

He glared at me. "What are you, comedian? Wit' his car." He waved his hand in the general direction of his face. "You think a car did this?"

I saw immediately what he meant, kicked myself for not seeing before. His face was covered with cuts and bruises, only I couldn't tell because it was black, dirty, unshaven, hard to look at, and if you did you were immediately transfixed by those hostile, gleaming eyes of a demon from hell.

"Who beat you up?"

"Muthafucka."

I almost said, "What motherfucker?" but I was afraid he'd think I was mocking him. "Who was it? Who did this?"

"Muthafucka got outta his car."

Which told the story. Some driver hadn't taken kindly to our client cleaning his windshield and had cleaned his clock.

I figured that was about as much as I was going to get. I figured right. Our client couldn't describe the man who hit him or the car he drove. He thought it was a white man but he couldn't tell if the car was a Mini Cooper or an SUV. Apparently our client's earnings, if any, went immediately for drink, and his assailant had caught him on a particularly good day. I got virtually no information.

Richard wouldn't be pleased.

"GOOD JOB, STANLEY."

"Good job? I got nothing."

"You got a signature." Richard settled back in his desk chair and smiled. "That's all I need. The guy's a goldmine. Victim's victim. Gotta love him."

"Who you gonna sue?"

"The City of New York."

"How are they liable?"

"I don't know, but they are. It's just a question of how many ways. Be fun adding them up."

"What about the guy who hit him?"

"What about him?"

"You don't care about him?"

"No, do you?"

"He's to blame."

"Stanley, I don't indulge revenge fantasies. I make my clients money. That's what they need."

"Don't you want to sue him?"

"For what? You think our client was beaten up by a neurosurgeon or a bank executive? Ten to one the guy who decked him was a muscle-bound wage slave pissed off at getting stuck in yet another snarl of rush hour traffic after a dreary day of slogging through his dead-end nine-to-five job. The type of poor schmuck who's mortgaged to the hilt, has no savings, and can't afford liability insurance. I'm really gonna bother suing him? It wouldn't be worth the cost of finding him, assuming you could even do it."

"I see your point."

"In other words, you totally disagree. Luckily, this is not a democracy. I am a majority of one, my vote is the only one that counts. I will have to learn to live with your disapproval. Just don't go looking for this guy and expect me to pay you for doing it. Is that clear?"

"Hell, yeah. I never wanted to take the case in the first place."

"I understand. I'll try not to bore you with how much money it makes."

As FAR AS I WAS concerned, that was the end of the case. That's the way it works in the negligence business. You sign the clients, turn in the fact sheets, and never hear of them again. A large percentage Richard rejects. Of the ones he takes, most are routinely settled out of court, just a matter of the insurance companies crunching the numbers. The ones that are contested eventually come to trial, but that's a year or two down the road. I'm occasionally employed to serve a summons on an elusive defendant, but generally that's handled routinely, too. And even the ones that go to court I'm rarely asked to testify. So I never expected to hear of Nelson Jones again.

It was three weeks and probably about fifty signups later and I was out in Newark, New Jersey, signing up a family who'd been injured in a tenement fire—probably one they started themselves, the mother and her boyfriend and her oldest son all smoked like chimneys—when my beeper went off. I called the office expecting yet another assignment, and got a message to call MacAullif.

Sergeant MacAullif is my cop friend in homicide. Sometimes I help him out and sometimes he helps me out, and sometimes he tries to push me through the wall. It rankles him not to have my cellphone number, but I don't want him calling me when I'm driving either. I'm sure if he wanted it bad enough he could get it; I've heard the police have connections.

I hadn't seen MacAullif in a while, because I hadn't gotten in trouble and business had been slow. Not my work for Richard, that was steady as a Chinese water torture drip, but the occasional walk-in who showed up at my office wanting help. They were always trouble, but they paid better than Richard and rent in Manhattan isn't cheap. I'd often gone to MacAullif for help with a client, and after a tirade of abusive vulgarities he was usually willing to oblige.

It was a little different when he came to me. It was not often that he wanted my help. It usually meant I'd gotten involved in something so bad he wished I were never born. So if MacAullif wanted me, it couldn't be good.

It wasn't.

"Got a John Doe down at the morgue I'd like you to take a look at."

"Who is he?"

"If I knew, would I call him John Doe? A scraggly black bum with a cast on his leg."

"Oh?"

"You know him?"

"We're in the same Pilates class."

"Don't be an asshole. Someone beat the shit out of this guy. I gotta know if it was on his own account or if I got a bunch of gangbangers getting off on killing homeless. That shit I don't need."

"Why you asking me?"

"Guy had a business card in his pocket, Rosenberg and Stone. I called the office, the girls asked Richard, he said to ask you."

"They give you a name?"

"Are you serious? A lawyer divulge a client's name when he's not even sure it's a client? These guys don't lay themselves open to lawsuits. So, you wanna take a run down to the morgue, see if it's the guy?"

"I'm not a lawyer."

"So?"

"Sounds like it is."

It was. He didn't look pretty. Not that he did before, but someone had used his head for batting practice. One eye was bulging out of its socket, the jaw was askew, teeth in the lopsided, gaping mouth were broken off.

"Well?" MacAullif said. He looked disappointed I hadn't blown lunch.

"That's the guy. His name is Nelson Jones."

"He's your client?"

"Not anymore."

I WAS WRONG ON THAT count.

"Don't be silly," Richard said. "The client may be dead, but the cause of action survives. I can file suit on behalf of the estate."

"You want me to track down the heirs?"

"No need. The girls are on it."

"The girls?"

"Wendy and Janet."

"*They're* doing investigative work?"

"On the computer. They're checking vital statistics, birth, death, marriage, family trees. They're doing a computer search."

"They can do that?"

"Why not? They're on the computer all day long. With their Twitters and tweets and Facebook and whatever the latest wrinkle is. They know enough to do it."

"Yeah, but tracing somebody."

"Hey, it's not rocket science. A lot of it consists of doing a Google search and hitting 'I'm Feeling Lucky.'"

"They find anyone?"

"No. Doesn't mean they won't. Doesn't mean they will."

"If they don't?"

"Doesn't matter. I win my suit, take my third. The rest will go into trust."

"Yeah, but . . ."

"But what?"

"Someone killed him."

"Yes, they did. That's why we're in this situation."

"You think it was the same guy who beat him up?"

"That would be incredibly unlucky, wouldn't it? Pick the same car again."

"Unless he did it intentionally. To show the guy he couldn't be intimidated."

"Oh, my God," Richard said. "The pride of the squeegee guy. 'My faddah was a squeegee guy and his faddah before him, and I will stand in front of the gates of hell and let this guy beat on me until he realizes what he has done.'"

"Richard—"

"Stanley, it doesn't matter if the same guy beat him up, or if a different guy beat him up, or if half a dozen guys took turns beating him up. The fact is he's dead. In terms of liability that's a big one. Kind of beats a fat lip all to hell. Though you wouldn't believe the settlement I got that Birnbaum kid."

"Richard—"

"Stanley, your involvement in the case is over. You fill out your timesheet, and you get paid, and that's the end of it. And you don't do anything more on the Nelson Jones case unless I specifically ask you to. And I'm not going to specifically ask you to, so you don't. Is that clear?"

"Absolutely."

MacAullif grimaced when I came in. "It's like a bad dream."

"Relax, MacAullif. I just want to know if there's any progress in the Nelson Jones case."

"Of course you do. And you know the answer. There's no progress in the Nelson Jones case, nor is there likely to be. A fed-up driver beat the shit out of a squeegee guy. It's a wonder it doesn't happen more often."

"The squeegee guys are gone."

"Someone forgot to tell this one."

"What makes you think that's why he got beat up?"

MacAullif grimaced. "He had a rag stuffed in his mouth."

"You didn't mention that."

"It was irrelevant."

"You showed me the body."

"I showed you the body. I didn't show you the evidence."

"Evidence of what? You taking this case to trial?"

"Not without a defendant."

"What progress have you made on that front?"

"I told you. None."

"Why, because he wasn't rich?"

"No, because he wasn't seen."

"Did anyone look?"

"I'm sure they did."

"You don't know?"

"It's not my only case. I had no idea you'd come waltzing in here today, and I didn't bone up on it."

"Well, could you check?"

"Thought you'd never ask."

MacAullif pulled the file. "Body was found seven o'clock in the morning. According to the coroner he was killed around midnight. Search for witnesses turned up zero."

"Where was he found?"

"Empty lot on East 124th Street between Second and Third Avenue."

"Closer to Second?"

"Yeah, why?"

"Then you know exactly where he was killed. 124th Street feeds into the Triboro Bridge right on that corner. As you cross Second Avenue it's a little jog to the left and up the ramp. The northwest corner of 124th is where the cars all get caught by the Second Avenue light. That's where Nelson Jones was washing windows and that's where someone jumped out and beat him up."

"Yeah, well no one saw it."

"It's a street corner, MacAullif. At a high-volume bridge entrance where cars are apt to run the light. There's surveillance cameras on those corners."

"Oh, for chrissakes."

"You check the surveillance tapes?"

As MacAullif lunged to his feet and lurched around his desk I realized two things. No one had checked the tape, and I'd better get the hell out of his office.

Richard looked like every student's worst dread, the strict disciplinarian headmaster who has just summoned you into his office. In this case I couldn't imagine why. I hadn't done anything wrong.

"Yes," I said.

"Sergeant MacAullif called."

Oh.

"Yes?" I said.

"Wanted me to give you a message. I don't know why he couldn't give you the message himself."

"I wasn't here."

"You're never here. The girls beep you and you call. This time he asked for me."

"What did he want?"

"He wanted to avoid taking to you. Because he didn't think you'd like what he said. He's probably right, because I didn't like what he said."

"I can explain."

"Spare me. Since I told you to leave the Nelson Jones case alone, you've hardly worked on anything else. You were working for free, by the way, but you knew that. I got the girls going over your time sheets, and any day in the last week your hours come to eight I'm gonna wanna know what cases you're padding to hide the time you spent on Nelson Jones."

"You really think I'd do that?"

"No, I think MacAullif just thinks you were working on the case because he's a stressed-out old homicide cop and he's having senior moments."

"Richard—"

"Did you or did you not go to MacAullif and ask him about the Nelson Jones case?"

"We may have had a conversation."

"Yes, you may. And, yes, you did. And did you ever stop to think what effect that might have on *my* case? Which is the only one I'm concerned with. I'm filing suit against the City of New York. You wanna prove someone other than the City of New York is guilty, fine, you do that. It doesn't mean I can't sue. It just makes it that much messier. Then I gotta spend money on trial prep, when there is no guarantee I'll come out of this with anything. Trust me, I will, but I shouldn't have to depend on me to bail myself out."

"Richard, what happened?"

"You know what happened. You went to MacAullif made a big stink about some surveillance camera being aimed at the corner where Nelson Jones died."

"Wouldn't you like to have that evidence?"

"I could give a flying fuck about that evidence. It's not important in the least. And I don't have it because the police don't have it, because no one has it, because it doesn't exist. Which means if I get to court, the defense attorney will be able to make a big deal out of the fact that we don't have it. It doesn't matter in the least, but some asshole attorney will be able to strut around like he scored a telling point, and if the jury falls for it it will take a big bite out of the settlement."

"There's no videotape evidence?"

"No, there's not. Thank you for pointing it out. If you hadn't, no one could possibly give a shit. Now that you did it's going to be a pain in the ass, thank you very much."

"I don't understand."

"What's to understand?"

"Wasn't there a camera at that intersection?"

"It wasn't working."

"It wasn't working?"

"No, it wasn't. Which shouldn't be a big shock. The cameras are old, they break down. Like the stop lights, and the street lights, and everything else."

"How long had it been out?"

Richard took a breath. "I don't know how long it had been out, I didn't ask how long it had been out, I don't *care* how long it had been out. Don't concoct some conspiracy theory based on a broken surveillance camera. The damn thing wasn't working. I'm sorry you don't get to sit and watch twenty-four hours of pointless surveillance video, but you don't. Because you live in the real world, not some storybook world where such things happen. Like it or not, the Nelson Jones case is a dead end. Leave it and go back to work."

I sighed. "Okay."

MacAullif's face was livid. "Motherfucker!"

"That's what our client said. With more inflection."

"You come in here and ask me if I'm involved in a massive police cover-up?"

"That's not what I said."

"Bullshit. I tell you the camera's broken, and you wanna know if it's really broken or if the commissioner's nephew beat the shit out of the guy and the tape is just conveniently missing."

"Or just some cop on the block who got pushed too far. People aren't going to rally around him?"

"They're not gonna cover up a homicide. Jesus Christ, you got a lot of gall. Come in here with an accusation like that."

"I wasn't accusing anyone."

"You're asking if it happened! I'm telling you it didn't, and you're asking anyway!"

"Was the camera out for weeks, or just for the day of the murder?"

"Now you're pissing me off."

"Because I'm touching a nerve?"

"Because you're here at all."

"I'd have thought that was beneath you, leaving a message with Richard."

"Beneath *me*? You talk about beneath *me*? I was trying to spare you the mistake of accusing the police department of corruption. I should have known you'd do it anyway."

"You're willing to swear for each and every officer?"

"I swear I'll kick your ass if you won't let go of this. It's a no-win situation. You wanna go after the police department, be my guest. Just don't count on me. My official position is the guy's full of shit."

"You'll turn your head if I get beat up?"

"I won't even blink if you get killed. You know why? You'll deserve it. You'll have brought it on yourself."

MacAullif picked up a file and began reading it as if I weren't even there.

THERE HAD TO BE A way. I knew it. In every detective story ever written, when the situation is hopeless, the hero finds a way. He picks, he pokes, he prods, and some insignificant detail, some tiny kernel of information inexplicably rings a bell. All you had to do was look. That was the key. To have the grit, the determination, the tenacity not to give up. To refuse to be defeated.

And I knew I was going to fail. Utterly, completely, devastatingly. And it killed me that it was a homeless black beggar. An anti-social, unlikable son-of-a-bitch. A squeegee guy, the scourge of the City, in whose disappearance I had rejoiced. Did that make it easier to let it go?

No, it made it harder. I had to deal with the nagging doubt would I have done it if it had been some sympathetic, white, family man who just happened to be in the wrong place at the right time? I wouldn't have. I just would have had less guilt.

MacAullif hadn't told me how many homicides went unsolved, but I knew it was a lot. That it would be another was not an earth-shattering event. I could live with that, couldn't I?

My beeper went off. I called the office and Wendy/Janet gave me a slip-and-fall in the produce section of a Stop & Shop.

I took down the information, headed out to Queens.

Of course I had to go over the Triboro Bridge. I drove up Third Avenue, turned onto 124th Street. The light at Second Avenue was red. I ran it, dodged a taxi that gave me the horn, and went up the ramp. I went over the bridge, turned around, came back, and did it again. This time the light was green. I pulled off to the side, stopped, waited for it to change. I ran it, turned around, came back, did it again. The third time I went out to Queens and signed up the client.

MacAullif stopped by my office. He didn't look happy. I figured he'd been watching a lot of surveillance video.

"You here to beat me up?"

"I might throw you out the window."

"When will you know for sure?"

"Asshole."

He pushed by me, flopped down in a folding chair. It shuddered but did not break. MacAullif had put on a few pounds, and he didn't start slim.

I hadn't seen MacAullif since I'd subpoenaed him into court to fight my traffic ticket. He hadn't killed me then, but I think he was still stunned. He couldn't quite believe I'd done it.

The judge couldn't believe I'd done it either. People occasionally showed up in court to fight traffic tickets, but few showed up with a lawyer, and fewer still subpoenaed a police officer to testify in their defense. I'd not only subpoenaed MacAullif into court, but Richard was ready to get him declared a hostile witness if he had to.

It turned out he didn't have to. In response to my defense that there couldn't be any photographic evidence of me running a red light at 124th Street and Second Avenue because the surveillance camera was broken, the judge had demanded the videotape, which was forthcoming, and the video technician testified readily enough that while one camera at that intersection was indeed broken, the other two weren't, and the evidence of my guilt was clear.

I got off with a hefty fine. It was a miracle I got to keep my license, but Richard was eloquent, and the judge was interested, actually had been since reading the complaint. Evidently, three separate violations for running the same red light at the same intersection within a ten-minute span was a unique event in the annals of crime, and judicial cognizance was taken.

"What's up, MacAullif?"

"We arrested Bert Hogg."

"Who's Bert Hogg?"

"A fry cook for Burger King. Also a walking billboard for tattoo parlors. Every muscle-bound inch of the moron is covered with colored ink."

"You arrested him for that?"

"We arrested him for the murder of Nelson Jones."

"Oh?"

"A slam dunk, even without the video. The dumb shit still had the bat in his trunk. With the victim's blood on it."

"Nice."

MacAullif heaved himself out of the chair. "For your information, Bert Hogg is not the nephew of the Commissioner, or a policeman, or anything of the kind. No one gives a flying fuck about him. There was no cover-up. Just poor communication between traffic and homicide." He jerked the door open, muttered, "Asshole," and slammed out.

So, that was that. It was, as far as I was concerned, a perfectly satisfactory ending. The Nelson Jones murder was solved, Richard could go ahead and sue, and the integrity of the police department had been upheld.

There was no conspiracy. Just incompetence.

Yeah, the City's different.

But some things never change.

THE GARMENTO AND THE MOVIE STAR
BY JONATHAN SANTLOFER

IT WAS THE SUMMER OF '62. I was twelve and working for my father, a tough boy from Queens, who'd earned a business degree from CCNY at night while apprenticing in the garment industry by day before opening his own company specializing in cocktail dresses that often graced the covers of fashion magazines like *Mademoiselle* and *Harper's Bazaar*. My father was the owner not designer, the nuts and bolts guy, the production man who made sure everything ran smoothly.

The shop, as it was called, was on Seventh Avenue—then the heart of Manhattan's garment industry—a quarter-floor in a prestigious *schmatta* building, famous designers of the era, Oleg Cassini (who was dressing Jackie Kennedy) and Norman Norell (née Norman Levinson) each with their own shop one floor above or below.

A year earlier my parents had moved us out of the city to a split-level on Long Island, their idea of the American dream, which meant it was now an hour-and-a-half commute via the 7:06 from Hicksville to Penn Station every morning.

The train rides were tense. My father rarely spoke. He'd sit across from me reading the *Post* (a respectable newspaper back then), or *Women's Wear Daily*, the trade paper for his industry, while I daydreamed or stared at passengers trying to imagine their lives.

Our first item of business was always the same, a shoeshine in Penn Station, a ritual I didn't understand or enjoy, perched on a throne-like chair while an elderly black man buffed and shined my Thom McAns to a high gloss.

From there we'd make our way north among the throng of commuters and workers, a crowded and noisy trek, fire engine sirens, taxis blaring horns, buses spewing exhaust into hot summer air already heavy with ambition, resignation, and smog.

Back then the garment center was a small strip of Manhattan real estate on Seventh Avenue between Thirty-fourth and Forty-second Streets teeming with guys pushing racks of colorful gowns along gray concrete streets crowded with hot dog and pretzel vendors, newspaper and magazine kiosks.

We were always the first to arrive, so my father had time to arrange and rearrange his little empire, test the alarm, inspect the showroom, turn on the three air conditioners—showroom, designer's workroom, his office (the rest of the place was sweltering)—before he would settle behind his desk to review the same orders and bills he'd looked at the night before. The routine never varied.

My job was errands, picking up packets of sequins or beads for the seamstresses, delivering bills or swatches of fabric, but mainly fetching coffee and tea for everyone, the specifics forever etched on my brain: Andrea, the receptionist, light with one packet of saccharine; Izzy, the designer, Sanka with three sugars; Arthur, my father's partner, a slick handsome man who handled sales, tea with saccharine; his wife, Vera, an anorexic gorgon, sent me out for three or four black coffees a day; the two in-house models, Terri and Suzi, who alternated days though occasionally overlapped, both black coffee with saccharine and both starving themselves to maintain their model-size figures. Pretty and fun, they treated me like a pet and I'd do anything they asked, my favorite request, "Can you zip me up?" a coy tease they enjoyed.

Suzi, button-nosed, blonde and nineteen was cute in a Christie Brinkley way with small breasts and surprisingly large nipples (yes, I saw them; lots of times). Terri, a dark Italian beauty, was twenty-five or -six, divorced with a two-year-old son and hazel eyes that went black when a buyer would accidentally-on-purpose feel her up as he examined a dress, something the models endured on a daily, sometimes hourly basis, over-groomed old men in pinstripes and pinky rings turning up hems of dresses for a better look at the stitching while they slid a hand against the girl's thigh.

I'd watch Terri's or Suzi's face turn to stone while they stood there quietly, later calling the guys pigs and leches and horny bastards, and when it happened with a woman, as it did with the tough blonde Neiman Marcus buyer from Texas, that "bull dyke" or "butch" bitch, new words for me. My father always said modeling was no job for a nice girl, but was very protective of his girls and always a gentleman, which made him beloved by the models, if no one else.

How to describe him? A Pit Bull in *garmento* garb: expensive Italian suit, Brylcreemed black hair, gold ID bracelet on his wrist, star sapphire ring on his pinky. A short, stocky, dandified tyrant, who could change the air in the room in a matter of seconds, who killed with a look and ruled by fear. Behind his back his employees called him "Little Napoleon," which my father knew. He liked that he was feared by his employees—all but Vera, the partner's wife, who was even scarier than my father and who my mother later blamed for my father's massive heart attack at age forty-two (that summer he was thirty-eight, hard for me to imagine).

It took the staff some time to relax around me, the boss's son, to see that I was just as scared of my father as they were. Like them, I avoided him as much as possible, maybe more (they didn't have to live with him) running errands and keeping out of his way.

The dressmaking business was different back then, no shows in tents or galleries or Lincoln Center for fashion week. Instead, the buyers came directly to the showroom five times a year—fall, winter, spring, summer, and "cruise wear"—a few at a time or individually, and the models would change clothes, over and over, to show the new line. For each of these seasons my father hired more models, which meant I got to see lots of beautiful girls in their underwear, though my father tried to keep me away from them in the same way he tried to keep me away from the designer, Izzy the Fag, my father's full name for him, a hilariously funny guy with bleached blonde hair and wild print shirts opened to the navel exposing gold chains and chest hair, and who I will always picture with a cigarette hanging out of one side of his mouth, a bunch of pins in the other, creating a dress (usually on a form, sometimes on Terri or Suzi) a fascinating process of layering, pinning, cutting, twisting, belting, and gathering. Watching him, I understood the beauty and intensity of the creative process for the first time, the man totally lost in his work, grimacing and cursing.

My father tolerated Izzy because he was talented (years later he became famous), though his flamboyant gayness was in direct contrast to my father's Napoleonic machismo.

Despite the garmento costume, my father was a man's man with no time for small talk or gossip, which Izzy relished and I enjoyed ("Oleg says Jackie Kennedy is a total ice queen, no wonder Jack fucks around").

I got to see my father at a distance that summer, though I understood him no better. His parents had lost most of their relatives to the Nazis, and his mother, at eighteen, had gone back to Europe and rescued her own mother and one sister from pre-war Poland. She was a cold, tough woman who, according to my mother, never showed her children any kind of affection, which I could imagine as she showed none toward me.

My father, her second son, was born in Poland and brought to this country at age two. He had an older brother, Max (called Mac), and a younger one, Murray, both of whom my father took care of for as long as he lived.

That summer Mac was working in the shop as a pattern-maker. My father had paid for his training, his union dues, and his salary, which he monitored, as Mac spent most of his money on the horses. A lifelong gambler, Mac was often beaten up and left for dead, bookies and loan sharks threatening to kill him and his family—a wife and two sons, who would once or twice a year hide out with us on Long Island.

Mac was a tall, skinny guy who wore wife-beater tees and had longish dirty nails and thin greasy hair. He was the complete opposite of my neat-as-a-pin father, who had total disdain for him but protected him until he no longer could.

But Mac had a sweet side (something I rarely saw in my father) encouraging me to go to college and make something of myself, though he countered that advice by bragging about his association with the Gambino crime family. Even as a kid I could see that he was just trying to be somebody, which he never was. When he got older and life had beaten him down (he was a two-time Gamblers Anonymous dropout whose wife finally left him and kids stopped talking to him) he became the saddest man I ever knew.

My father was dead by the time Mac was found shot to death in a Manhattan transient hotel, a crime the police never bothered to pursue.

But that summer, Mac, who was probably forty or forty-one, still a young man (though he'd already had his teeth kicked out and wore dentures), was making all of the shop's dress patterns and displayed a deft hand for drawing huge free-hand arcs and dotted lines on heavy, buff-colored paper, an artistic feat that impressed me.

THE SHOP HAD SEVERAL FAMOUS customers who would come in to buy wholesale. Among them, Polly Bergen, a beautiful actress with a smoky voice and dark blue eyes who was in the original *Cape Fear,* and Bess Myerson, a former Miss America (the only Jewish Miss America, idolized by my mother and every other Jewish woman, all of whom failed to note that Bess was the country's post-war way of saying Jews were okay— sort of). A tall girl, Bess would swoop in like a condor, blowing air kisses and openly flirting with my father. Izzy called her "that horsey tramp" and years later when she was arrested for shoplifting and involved with a gangster and city shenanigans in what the newspapers referred to as "the Bess Mess," I was sure he must have been thrilled.

Izzy, always a star-fucker (a term he may have invented; at least it was the first time I'd ever heard it), was friendly with the designer Norman Norell, who was "remaking Marilyn Monroe and giving her some class," and he convinced Norell that Monroe needed to have at least one of *his* dresses. And so it was sometime in late July, about three weeks after I'd started working, that Izzy broke the news Marilyn Monroe would be coming into the shop with "intent to buy."

My father tried to act nonchalant, but the day before her visit he insisted we both get haircuts. (He also got a manicure and wanted me to get one, but I refused.) That morning he changed his suit three or four times while my mother reminded him that she wanted a full report—what Marilyn was wearing, how she acted, what she said. While he attended to my tie I could smell that he'd put on his expensive floral-smelling cologne rather than his usual Mennen Skin Bracer, and his hands were clumsy as he tied and retied my Windsor knot.

Everyone showed up early that day. Andrea, the receptionist, had her hair teased into a high lacquered beehive; the salespeople were all at their desks rather than out courting buyers. Both Terri and Suzi came in, though it was only Terri's day to work, and they too had had their hair done and were wearing skirts rather than slacks, and Suzi was upset because she'd smudged the nail polish she'd put on while riding the subway. Even Mac was wearing a real shirt, light blue, though ruined by semi-circle sweat stains.

Izzy sent me out twice, once to buy cigarettes, then aspirin. He was chain smoking and popping pills (not just aspirin, but small blue pills), straightening and re-straightening his work-room, moving stacks of designs from one spot to another, pinning up magazine covers that featured his dresses, opening his shirt buttons, then closing them and spraying his blonde hair into place. He'd bought two bottles of Dom Perignon because "that's all she drinks, you know, the best and most expensive champagne, the spoiled little bitch," though according to Norman Norell by way of Izzy, "she's a doll, an absolute doll but a little crazy," and had been recently fired from a movie because "she never showed up, I mean *never*," and was addicted to pills, "uppers *and* downers, and everyone knows she's having an affair with JFK and maybe his brother Bobby, too," which I didn't believe because Kennedy was my hero and I said so. "Darling," said Izzy, "it's common knowledge. Where the fuck have you been?"

"In junior high," I said.

"That's no excuse," Izzy said, exhaling a long plume of gray smoke for emphasis.

Marilyn's appointment was set for one.

At two, there was still no sign of her.

By three, people were getting annoyed, and hungry, as no one had gone out for lunch, but Izzy kept reassuring them, "Don't worry, she's notoriously late, she'll be here," though I could see the strain in his manic smile.

By four, everyone but Izzy was losing faith.

At five, the seamstresses left, muttering in Spanish.

By six, the sales team left.

By six-thirty, Andrea and Uncle Mac gave up.

At six-forty-five, Izzy huffed into the showroom. "Maybe she's OD'd and I fucking hope so!" his final words before slamming the shop door.

My father told him to watch his language, too late, then packed his briefcase and turned out the lights. He set the alarm and when he opened the door to test it as he always did, she was standing there, a kind of ghostly apparition.

"Ohhh," she cooed softly. "Am I too late?"

"Of course not!" my father boomed, turning off the alarm and flipping on lights.

I don't know what I had expected. The big celluloid star I'd seen on the movie screen, I guess, but she was a normal-sized woman. When we stood side by side I was aware that we were about the same height, 5'6". She was thin and somewhat fragile-looking, wearing big sunglasses and a scarf over her hair. Her pale, luminous face had a sprinkling of freckles across her nose and there was soft but noticeable down on her cheeks. She was wearing tight, lime-green pants with a zipper up the back and a striped, sleeveless blouse, nothing special, but I took note so I could give my mother and sister a report in case my father forgot, and I could see he was nervous, talking too much, guiding Marilyn around the showroom by the elbow, pointing out magazine covers and industry awards while I hung back.

Was she pretty?

I'm trying to remember what I really thought, and I'd say yes. But not especially so. Not dramatically so. I'd seen "The Seven Year Itch" and the girl standing in front of me (that's what she seemed like, a *girl*) was nothing like her, though she emitted a kind of light and it wasn't just the pale skin and mostly hidden white hair.

When my father finally stopped leading her around, she focused on me, took off her shades, and beamed a glittery, jittery smile, then asked me a string of questions: My age, likes and dislikes, what I wanted to be when I grew up?

Before I could answer my father indicated a few of my sketches, which he'd framed and hung on a narrow strip of wall near the fire door. "He wants to be an *artist*," he said, underscoring the word with sarcasm, but Marilyn said, "How wonderful!" and took her time looking at them, commenting and asking more questions: "The girl in this one looks sad. Are there people living in this house? Do you always use charcoal? Why not some color, color is so happy . . ." After a few minutes she said, very seriously, "I think . . . they . . . are . . . very . . . good," slowly enunciating each word as if rehearsing for a play.

I didn't know what to say—I was embarrassed, and proud—but it was one of those defining moments, something in my mind that I could not yet grasp, an inchoate longing to be appreciated, noticed by people, people who mattered—and to be famous one day.

Marilyn said she had a cold and kept dabbing at her nose with a tissue and my father said, "I know what will make you feel better," then disappeared and reappeared with Izzy's champagne and Marilyn made a Lorelei Lee sort of "Ooooh" as he opened a bottle and poured her a glass and she kicked off her shoes and tucked her bare feet under her and settled onto the couch. She downed a glass or two and then, for the next few hours, with my father's assistance, tried on dresses.

"Try this one, dah-ling," he'd say in his Jewish-garmento way, not Izzy-darling way, handing her a dress.

Marilyn would go behind the changing screen, unzip her pants and slip off her blouse—and she was naked, no underwear, no nothing. She didn't parade around, but the mirrors broadcast her refection in multiple CinemaScope views and I caught glimpses of her breasts (smaller than I'd imagined), and flashes of blond pubic hair, and it was startling, like trying to hold onto lightning, exciting and dangerous.

Marilyn would emerge hugging a dress to her body so that she was covered but half exposed, study herself in the floor-to-ceiling mirrors that lined two of the showroom walls, lost and dreamy for several minutes, fluffing her white-blonde hair, trying on a variety of expressions and staring hard as if she were looking for someone or something, then duck behind the screen and come back with another dress, this one slipped over her head, zipper open, and she'd turn to my father and ask in her small soft voice, "Lou, do you mind?"

Lou?

He'd zip her up and she'd trill a laugh and he'd throw me a look, once even a wink (a first) and later made a point of saying, "Your mother need not know about the zip."

The whole time I sat on one of the showroom's two couches and watched, hands tucked under my thighs. Each time Marilyn emerged from behind the screen it was a little vignette though pretty much the same. She would stare in the mirror turning this way and that, fluff her hair, smile, frown, lick her lips, occasionally cup her naked breasts under the dress, then turn around to assess her rear end. Her expressions changed often but in slow motion: happy to sad to mad to determined or lost. A couple of times she turned to me and asked my opinion about a dress and I always said she looked beautiful.

"Really?" she'd say, as if no one had ever said that to her before and I'd bob my head up and down like a puppy and say, "*Really*," and she'd throw me a smile like a bunch of wild flowers tossed into the air.

A couple of times she called my father over and cupped a hand to his ear and whispered like a child would, and when I think about it now that's exactly how she seemed: childlike.

At one point she sagged onto the couch beside me in a half-unzipped dress and sipped champagne and asked me more questions—if I liked school, if I had siblings, what I liked to read (I could not come up with a single title, not even one of my Hardy Boys books or Classic Comics), so I turned it around and asked her, "What's your favorite movie you ever made?" and she thought a while before saying, "*Bus Stop*, because . . . Cherie was a . . . *real* girl, you know, sad but . . . trying to be happy," her pale face inches from mine, and I said, "Oh, you were great in that," though I hadn't seen it and again she said "*Really?*" as if my opinion mattered, and I said,

"Yes!" and she smiled and asked me if I got along with my sister and I said "sort of," and I asked her if she had any kids and she blinked and pulled back as if slapped and her eyes welled up with tears and in a quivering whisper said, "I . . . have not been . . . lucky," and my father cut in and said, "Kids? Who need kids? Brats, all of 'em!" and swatted me on the head a little too hard and forced a laugh, then quickly fetched a new dress. Marilyn dashed behind the screen looking as though she might shatter to pieces but emerged in less than a minute in a white satin dress with a tight bodice of white lace and the same lace trim along the bottom, all smiles and absolutely radiant, the movie star, Marilyn Monroe.

After the usual posing she asked, "How about some color, Lou? Or a pattern?"

"No patterns," my father said shaking his head, "We make only white, black, or red cocktail dresses. It's about elegance, darling. This isn't Hollywood."

"Well," she said, "Hollywood is *anything* but elegant," and sounded tough for the first time, though she followed it up with a high-pitched laugh.

"With your coloring you should only be in black or white," my father said, and he was right, I could see it, her white hair, skin, the dress, her reflection in the showroom mirrors shimmering like a ghost, there and not there, like something imagined or remembered.

He brought her a black dress next with thin straps and a snug torso, the bottom edged with black ostrich feathers, and the contrast was startling, her face and arms and legs like an alabaster statue against all that black.

Marilyn seemed to know it, too. She stood perfectly still, her finger slowly tracing the edge of the black neckline over and over and over.

She bought that dress and three others, gave my father a check and asked that he send them to her home in California, which she said was her first and explained how she was decorating it Mexican-style and asked my father if he'd ever been to Mexico and he said no but he'd been to Cuba and she talked more about the house, obviously proud, though her voice sounded nervous, edgy.

"Nothing like a new home to cheer you up," my father said as if he'd bought dozens of homes in his lifetime, and she said, "Thank you, Lou," with so much emotion it was almost embarrassing, then hugged him.

She wrote her address on a piece of paper after making my father promise never to divulge it to anyone and he crossed his heart, a meaningless gesture for a Jew. He told her he would have the dresses altered to her "specifics" and she said that she'd recently lost a lot of weight and asked how he knew her size and he said, "Darling, I've been in the *schmatta* business since I was sixteen, I know exactly what needs to be done," and she trilled another laugh and kissed his cheek and said, "Oh, I shouldn't have done that—my cold," and he swatted her sentence away and it was the only time I ever saw him blush.

Marilyn changed back into her green pants and sleeveless blouse, then stopped to look at my sketches again.

"They're really . . . *good*," she said. "You must promise me that you will keep making them." I nodded and meant it and she said, "And you'll let me see them, won't you?" and I said, "Sure!" and she kissed my cheek, got her sunglasses in place and hugged my father once more. At the door she turned back and said, "Don't forget, I want to see those new sketches," and I nodded and smiled and bobbed my head up and down and she gave a little girl wave and I waved back and then she was gone, taking all of the light with her.

My father pinned some notes to the dresses she'd chosen, put them aside, then locked up, and we walked to Penn Station in our usual silence. The city streets were less crowded now, the air sticky hot, the top of the Empire State Building dissolving into a fuzzy pewter sky.

On the train, we sat opposite one another, my father behind the *Post*, me replaying everything Marilyn had said and daydreaming about the new drawings I would make and show Marilyn and how one day I was going to be a famous artist.

Halfway home, my father lowered his paper and said, "Nice girl," and I said, "Really nice." A moment later I asked, "What did she whisper to you, Dad?" and he said, "I can't remember," and that was all we said until we got home where my mother and sister were waiting, fidgety with questions.

"Was she beautiful?" my sister asked.

"Kind of," I said. Then corrected myself, "Sometimes."

"What does that mean?" my sister asked.

"She changed a lot," I said.

"You mean her clothes?" she asked.

"Yes," my father said.

"That's not what I meant," I said, seeing Marilyn's face in my mind morph from happy to sad, from plain to beautiful.

"She tried on lots of dresses," my father said, "and is buying four."

"How exciting," my mother said. "Did you think she was pretty?"

"Sure," my father said, "but not nearly as pretty you."

My mother waved a hand at him, but smiled.

"Was she nice?" my sister asked.

"Yes," my father said. "A sweet girl. Without airs."

Then he told them how Marilyn had admired my artwork

and had kissed my cheek (neglecting to tell them she'd kissed and hugged him several times or that he'd zipped her up more than once) and after that my mother and sister teased me by referring to Marilyn as my "girlfriend." But not for long.

It was only two or three weeks later that my mother awakened me with the words, "I've got bad news. Your girlfriend died."

"*What?*" I said, still groggy.

"Marilyn," she said, and I could see she regretted the flip remark and was struggling to figure out what to say next. "It's—all over the news. She was so young. Only thirty-six."

"Really?" I said, images of the freckled, fuzzy-cheeked blonde hugging dresses to her naked body playing in my half-asleep mind. "I thought she was a lot younger."

"Thirty-six *is* young," my mother said, and I realize now that at the time my mother was thirty-seven. "It's so sad," she said.

"What happened?" I asked.

"Sleeping pills," my mother said. "She overdosed." She sighed and I pictured Marilyn staring into the showroom mirrors looking for something or someone, and her eyes filling with tears.

It was a weekend and my father was off playing golf and I wondered if he had heard the news and was thinking of the nice girl who didn't put on airs, who had called him Lou and kissed his cheek. He never said a word, but that Monday I saw him looking at the dresses Marilyn had bought. The alterations had been finished but they were never shipped and he never cashed her check.

HANNIBAL'S ELEPHANTS
BY ROBERT SILVERBERG

THE DAY THE ALIENS LANDED in New York was, of course, the 5th of May, 2003. That's one of those historical dates nobody can ever forget, like July 4, 1776 and October 12, 1492 and—maybe more to the point—December 7, 1941. At the time of the invasion I was working for MGM-CBS as a beam calibrator in the tightware division and married to Elaine and living over on East Thirty-sixth Street in one of the first of the fold-up condos, one room by day and three by night, a terrific deal at $3,750 a month. Our partner in the time/space-sharing contract was a show-biz programmer named Bobby Christie who worked midnight to dawn, very convenient for all concerned. Every morning before Elaine and I left for our offices I'd push the button and the walls would shift and five hundred square feet of our apartment would swing around and become Bobby's for the next twelve hours. Elaine hated that. "I can't stand having all the goddamn furniture on tracks!" she would say. "That isn't how I was brought up to live." We veered perilously close to divorce every morning at wall-shift time. But, then, it wasn't really what you'd call a stable relationship in most other respects, and I guess having an unstable condo, too, was more instability than she could handle.

I spent the morning of the day the aliens came setting up a ricochet data transfer between Akron, Ohio and Colombo, Sri Lanka, involving, as I remember, *Gone With the Wind*, *Cleopatra*, and the Johnny Carson retrospective. Then I walked up to the park to meet Maranta for our Monday picnic. Maranta and I had been lovers for about six months then. She was Elaine's roommate at Bennington and had married my best friend Tim, so you might say we had been fated all along to become lovers; there are never any surprises in these things. At that time we lunched together very romantically in the park, weather permitting, every Monday and Friday, and every Wednesday we had ninety minutes' breathless use of my cousin Nicholas's hot-pillow cubicle over on the far West Side at Thirty-ninth and Koch Plaza. I had been married three-and-a-half years and this was my first affair. For me, what was going on between Maranta and me just then was the most important event taking place anywhere in the known universe.

It was one of those glorious gold-and-blue dance-and-sing days that New York will give you in May, when that little window opens between the season of cold-and-nasty and the season of hot-and-sticky. I was legging up Seventh Avenue toward the park with a song in my heart and a cold bottle of Chardonnay in my hand, thinking pleasant thoughts of Maranta's small, round breasts. And gradually I became aware of some ruckus taking place up ahead.

I could hear sirens. Horns were honking, too: not the ordinary routine everyday exasperated when-do-things-start-to-move honks, but the special rhythmic New York City oh-for-Christ's-sake-what-*now* kind of honk that arouses terror in your heart. People with berserk expressions on their faces were running wildly down Seventh as though King Kong had just emerged from the monkey house at the Central Park Zoo and was personally coming after them. And other people were running just as hard in the opposite direction, *toward* the park, as though they absolutely had to see what was happening. You know: New Yorkers.

Maranta would be waiting for me near the pond, as usual. That seemed to be right where the disturbance was. I had a flash of myself clambering up the side of the Empire State Building—or at the very least Temple Emanu-el—to pry her free of the big ape's clutches. The great beast pausing, delicately setting her down on some precarious ledge, glaring at me, furiously pounding his chest—*Kong! Kong! Kong!*

I stepped into the path of one of the southbound runners and said, "Hey, what the hell's going on?" He was a suit-and-tie man, popeyed and puffy-faced. He slowed but he didn't stop. I thought he would run me down. "It's an invasion!" he yelled. "Space creatures! In the park!" Another passing business type loping breathlessly by with a briefcase in each hand was shouting, "The police are there! They're sealing everything off!"

"No shit," I murmured.

But all I could think was Maranta, picnic, sunshine, Chardonnay, disappointment. What a goddamned nuisance, is what I thought. Why the fuck couldn't they come on a Tuesday, is what I thought.

WHEN I GOT TO THE top of Seventh Avenue the police had a sealfield across the park entrance and buzz-blinkers were set up along Central Park South from the Plaza to Columbus Circle, with horrendous consequences for traffic. "But I have to find my girlfriend," I blurted. "She was waiting for me in the park." The cop stared at me. His cold gray eyes said, *I am a decent Catholic and I am not going to facilitate your extramarital activities, you decadent overpaid bastard.* What he said out loud was, "No way can you cross that sealfield, and anyhow you absolutely don't want to go in the park right now, mister. Believe me." And he also said, "You don't have to worry about your girlfriend. The park's been cleared of all human beings." That's what he said, *cleared of all human beings.* For a while I wandered around in some sort of daze. Finally I went back to my office and found a message from Maranta, who had left the park the moment the trouble began. Good quick Maranta. She hadn't had any idea of what was occurring, though she had found out by the time she reached her office. She had simply sensed trouble and scrammed. We agreed to meet for drinks at the Ras Tafari at half past five. The Ras was one of our regular places, Twelfth and Fifty-third.

THERE WERE SEVENTEEN WITNESSES TO the onset of the invasion. There were more than seventeen people on the meadow when the aliens arrived, of course, but most of them didn't seem to have been paying attention. It had started, so said the seventeen, with a strange pale-blue shimmering about thirty feet off the ground. The shimmering rapidly became a churning, like water going down a drain. Then a light breeze began to blow and very quickly turned into a brisk gale. It lifted people's hats and whirled them in a startling corkscrew spiral around the churning shimmering blue place. At the same time you had a sense of rising tension, a something's-got-to-give feeling. All this lasted perhaps forty-five seconds.

Then came a pop and a whoosh and a ping and a thunk— everybody agreed on the sequence of the sound effects—and the instantly famous not-quite-egg-shaped spaceship of the invaders was there, hovering, as it would do for the next twenty-three days, about half an inch above the spring-green grass of Central Park. An absolutely unforgettable sight: the sleek silvery skin of it, the disturbing angle of the slope from its wide top to its narrow bottom, the odd and troublesome hieroglyphics on its flanks that tended to slide out of your field of vision if you stared at them for more than a moment.

A hatch opened and a dozen of the invaders stepped out. *Floated* out, rather. Like their ship, they never came in contact with the ground.

They looked strange. They looked exceedingly strange. Where we have feet they had a single oval pedestal, maybe five inches thick and a yard in diameter, that drifted an inch or so above ground level. From this fleshy base their wraith-like bodies sprouted like tethered balloons. They had no arms, no legs, not even discernible heads: just a broad dome-shaped summit, dwindling away to a rope-like termination that was attached to the pedestal. Their lavender skins were glossy, with a metallic sheen. Dark eye-like spots sometimes formed on them but didn't last long. We saw no mouths. As they moved about they seemed to exercise great care never to touch one another.

The first thing they did was to seize half a dozen squirrels, three stray dogs, a softball, and a baby carriage, unoccupied. We will never know what the second thing was that they did, because no one stayed around to watch. The park emptied with impressive rapidity, the police moved swiftly in with their sealfield, and for the next three hours the aliens had the meadow to themselves. Later in the day the networks sent up spy-eyes that recorded the scene for the evening news until the aliens figured out what they were and shot them down. Briefly we saw ghostly gleaming aliens wandering around within a radius of perhaps five hundred yards of their ship, collecting newspapers, soft-drink dispensers, discarded items of clothing, and something that was generally agreed to be a set of dentures. Whatever they picked up they wrapped in a sort of pillow made of a glowing fabric with the same shining texture as their own bodies, which immediately began floating off with its contents toward the hatch of the ship.

PEOPLE WERE LINED UP SIX deep at the bar when I arrived at the Ras, and everyone was drinking like mad and staring at the screen. They were showing the clips of the aliens over and over. Maranta was already there. Her eyes were glowing. She pressed herself up against me like a wild woman. "My God," she said, "isn't it wonderful! The men from Mars are here! Or wherever they're from. Let's hoist a few to the men from Mars."

We hoisted more than a few. Somehow I got home at a respectable seven o'clock anyway. The apartment was still in its one-room configuration, though our contract with Bobby Christie specified wall-shift at half past six. Elaine refused to have anything to do with activating the shift. She was afraid, I think, of timing the sequence wrong and being crushed by the walls, or something.

"You heard?" Elaine said. "The aliens?"

"I wasn't far from the park at lunchtime," I told her. "That was when it happened, at lunchtime, while I was up by the park."

Her eyes went wide. "Then you actually saw them land?"

"I wish. By the time I got to the park entrance the cops had everything sealed off."

I pressed the button and the walls began to move. Our living room and kitchen returned from Bobby Christie's domain. In the moment of shift I caught sight of Bobby on the far side, getting dressed to go out. He waved and grinned. "Space monsters in the park," he said. "My my my. It's a real jungle out there, don't you know?" And then the walls closed away on him.

Elaine switched on the news and once again I watched the aliens drifting around the mall picking up people's jackets and candy-bar wrappers.

"Hey," I said, "the mayor ought to put them on the city payroll."

"What were you doing up by the park at lunchtime?" Elaine asked, after a bit.

The next day was when the second ship landed and the *real* space monsters appeared. To me the first aliens didn't qualify as monsters at all. Monsters ought to be monstrous, bottom line. Those first aliens were no bigger than you or me.

The second batch, they were something else, though. The behemoths. The space elephants. Of course they weren't anything like elephants, except that they were big. Big? *Immense.* It put me in mind of Hannibal's invasion of Rome, seeing those gargantuan things disembarking from the new spaceship. It seemed like the Second Punic War all over again, Hannibal and the elephants.

You remember how that was. When Hannibal set out from Carthage to conquer Rome, he took with him a phalanx of elephants, thirty-seven huge gray attack-trained monsters. Elephants were useful in battle in those days—a kind of early-model tank—but they were handy also for terrifying the civilian populace: bizarre colossal smelly critters trampling invincibly through the suburbs, flapping their vast ears and trumpeting awesome cries of doom and burying your rose bushes under mountainous turds. And now we had the same deal. With one difference, though: the Roman archers picked off Hannibal's elephants long before they got within honking distance of the walls of Rome. But these aliens had materialized without warning right in the middle of Central Park, in that big grassy meadow between the Seventy-second Street transverse and Central Park South, which is another deal altogether. I wonder how well things would have gone for the Romans if they had awakened one morning to find Hannibal and his army camping out in the Forum, and his thirty-seven hairy shambling flap-eared elephants snuffling and snorting and farting about on the marble steps of the Temple of Jupiter.

The new spaceship arrived the way the first one had, pop whoosh ping thunk, and the behemoths came tumbling out of it like rabbits out of a hat. We saw it on the evening news: the networks had a new bunch of spy-eyes up, half a mile or so overhead. The ship made a kind of belching sound and this *thing* suddenly was standing on the mall gawking and gaping. Then another belch, another *thing*. And on and on until there were two or three dozen of them. Nobody has ever been able to figure out how that little ship could have held as many as one of them. It was no bigger than a schoolbus standing on end.

The monsters looked like double-humped blue medium-size mountains with legs. The legs were their most elephantine feature—thick and rough-skinned, like tree-trunks—but they worked on some sort of telescoping principle and could be collapsed swiftly back up into the bodies of their owners. Eight was the normal number of legs, but you never saw eight at once on any of them: as they moved about they always kept at least one pair withdrawn, though from time to time they'd let that pair descend and pull up another one, in what seemed like a completely random way. Now and then they might withdraw two pairs at once, which would cause them to sink down to ground level at one end like a camel kneeling.

They were enormous. *Enormous*. Getting exact measurements of one presented certain technical problems, as I think you can appreciate. The most reliable estimate was that they were twenty-five- to thirty-feet high and forty- to fifty-feet long. That is not only substantially larger than any elephant past or present, it is rather larger than most of the two-family houses still to be found in the outer boroughs of the city. Furthermore a two-family house of the kind found in Queens or Brooklyn, though it may offend your esthetic sense, will not move around at all, it will not emit bad smells and frightening sounds, it will never sit down on a bison and swallow it, nor, for that matter, will it swallow you. African elephants, they tell me, run ten- or eleven-feet high at the shoulder, and the biggest extinct mammoths were three or four feet taller than that. There once was a mammal called the baluchitherium that stood about sixteen-feet high. That was the largest land mammal that ever lived. The space creatures were nearly twice as high. We are talking large here. We are talking dinosaur-plus dimensions.

Central Park is several miles long but quite modest in width. It runs just from Fifth Avenue to Eighth. Its designers did not expect that anyone would allow two or three dozen animals bigger than two-family houses to wander around freely in an urban park three city blocks wide. No doubt the small size of their pasture was very awkward for them. Certainly it was for us.

"I THINK THEY HAVE TO be an exploration party," Maranta said. "Don't you?" We had shifted the scene of our Monday and Friday lunches from Central Park to Rockefeller Center, but otherwise we were trying to behave as though nothing unusual was going on. "They can't have come as invaders. One little spaceship-load of aliens couldn't possibly conquer an entire planet."

Maranta is unfailingly jaunty and optimistic. She is a small, energetic woman with close-cropped red hair and green eyes, one of those boyish-looking women who never seem to age. I love her for her optimism. I wish I could catch it from her, like measles.

I said, "There are *two* spaceship-loads of aliens, Maranta."

She made a face. "Oh. The jumbos. They're just dumb shaggy monsters. I don't see them as much of a menace, really."

"Probably not. But the little ones—they have to be a superior species. We know that because they're the ones who came to us. We didn't go to them."

She laughed. "It all sounds so absurd. That Central Park should be full of *creatures*—"

"But what if they do want to conquer Earth?" I asked.

"Oh," Maranta said. "I don't think that would necessarily be so awful."

THE SMALLER ALIENS SPENT THE first few days installing a good deal of mysterious equipment on the mall in the vicinity of their ship: odd intricate shimmering constructions that looked as though they belonged in the sculpture garden of the Museum of Modern Art. They made no attempt to enter into communication with us. They showed no interest in us at all. The only time they took notice of us was when we sent spy-eyes overhead. They would tolerate them for an hour or two and then would shoot them down, casually, like swatting flies, with spurts of pink light. The networks—and then the government surveillance agencies, when they moved in—put the eyes higher and higher each day, but the aliens never failed to find them.

After a week or so we were forced to rely for our information on government spy satellites monitoring the park from space, and on whatever observers equipped with binoculars could glimpse from the taller apartment houses and hotels bordering the park. Neither of these arrangements was entirely satisfactory.

The behemoths, during those days, were content to roam aimlessly through the park southward from Seventy-second Street, knocking over trees, squatting down to eat them. Each one gobbled two or three trees a day, leaves, branches, trunk, and all. There weren't all that many trees to begin with down there, so it seemed likely that before long they'd have to start ranging farther afield.

The usual civic groups spoke up about the trees. They wanted the mayor to do something to protect the park. The monsters, they said, would have to be made to go elsewhere—to Canada, perhaps, where there were plenty of expendable trees. The mayor said that he was studying the problem but that it was too early to know what the best plan of action would be.

His chief goal, in the beginning, was simply to keep a lid on the situation. We still didn't even know, after all, whether we were being invaded or just visited. To play it safe the police were ordered to set up and maintain round-the-clock seal-fields completely encircling the park in the impacted zone south of Seventy-second Street. The power costs of this were staggering and Con Edison found it necessary to impose a ten-percent voltage cutback in the rest of the city, which caused a lot of grumbling, especially now that it was getting to be air conditioner weather.

The police didn't like any of this: out there day and night standing guard in front of an intangible electronic barrier with ungodly monsters just a sneeze away. Now and then one of the blue goliaths would wander near the sealfield and peer over the edge. A sealfield maybe a dozen feet high doesn't give you much of a sense of security when there's an animal two or three times that height looming over its top.

So the cops asked for time and a half. Combat pay, essentially. There wasn't room in the city budget for that, especially since no one knew how long the aliens were going to continue to occupy the park. There was talk of a strike. The mayor appealed to Washington, which had studiously been staying remote from the whole event as if the arrival of an extraterrestrial task force in the middle of Manhattan was purely a municipal problem.

The president rummaged around in the Constitution and decided to activate the National Guard. That surprised a lot of basically sedentary men who enjoy dressing up occasionally in uniforms. The Guard hadn't been called out since the Bulgarian business in '94 and its current members weren't very sharp on procedures, so some hasty on-the-job training became necessary. As it happened, Maranta's husband Tim was an officer in the 107th Infantry, which was the regiment that was handed the chief responsibility for protecting New York City against the creatures from space. So his life suddenly was changed a great deal, and so was Maranta's; and so was mine.

LIKE EVERYBODY ELSE, I FOUND myself going over to the park again and again to try and get a glimpse of the aliens. But the barricades kept you fifty feet away from the park perimeter on all sides, and the taller buildings flanking the park had put themselves on a residents-only admission basis, with armed guards enforcing it, so they wouldn't be overwhelmed by hordes of curiosity-seekers.

I did see Tim, though. He was in charge of an improvised-looking command post at Fifth and Fifty-ninth, near the horse-and-buggy stand. Youngish stockbrokery-looking men kept running up to him with reports to sign, and he signed each one with terrific dash and vigor, without reading any of them. In his crisp tan uniform and shiny boots, he must have seen himself as some doomed and gallant officer in an ancient movie, Gary Cooper, Cary Grant, John Wayne, bracing himself for the climactic cavalry charge or the onslaught of the maddened Sepoys. The poor bastard.

"Hey, old man," he said, grinning at me in a doomed and gallant way. "Came to see the circus, did you?"

We weren't really best friends anymore. I don't know what we were to each other. We rarely lunched anymore. (How could we? I was busy three days a week with Maranta.) We didn't meet at the gym. It wasn't to Tim I turned to advice on personal problems or second opinions on investments. There was some sort of bond but I think it was mostly nostalgia. But officially I guess I did still think of him as my best friend, in a kind of automatic unquestioning way.

I said, "Are you free to go over to the Plaza for a drink?"

"I wish. I don't get relieved until 2100 hours."

"Nine o'clock, is that it?"

"Nine, yes. You fucking civilian."

It was only half past one. The poor bastard.

"What'll happen to you if you leave your post?"

"I could get shot for desertion," he said.

"Seriously?"

"Seriously. Especially if the monsters pick that moment to bust out of the park. This is war, old buddy."

"Is it, do you think? Maranta doesn't think so." I wondered if I should be talking about what Maranta thought. "She says they're just out exploring the galaxy."

Tim shrugged. "She always likes to see the sunny side. That's an alien military force over there inside the park. One of these days they're going to blow a bugle and come out with blazing rayguns. You'd better believe it."

"Through the sealfield?"

"They could walk right over it," Tim said. "Or float, for all I know. There's going to be a war. The first intergalactic war in human history." Again the dazzling Cary Grant grin. Her Majesty's Bengal lancers, ready for action. "Something to tell my grandchildren," said Tim. "Do you know what the game plan is? First we attempt to make contact. That's going on right now, but they don't seem to be paying attention to us. If we ever establish communication, we invite them to sign a peace treaty. Then we offer them some chunk of Nevada or Kansas as a diplomatic enclave and get them the hell out of New York. But I don't think any of that's going to happen. I think they're busy scoping things out in there, and as soon as they finish that they're going to launch some kind of attack, using weapons we don't even begin to understand."

"And if they do?"

"We nuke them," Tim said. "Tactical devices, just the right size for Central Park Mall."

"No," I said, staring. "That isn't so. You're kidding me."

He looked pleased, a *gotcha* look. "Matter of fact, I am. The truth is that nobody has the goddamndest idea of what to do about any of this. But don't think the nuke strategy hasn't been suggested. And some even crazier things."

"Don't tell me about them," I said. "Look, Tim, is there any way I can get a peek over those barricades?"

"Not a chance. Not even you. I'm not even supposed to be *talking* with civilians."

"Since when am I civilian?"

"Since the invasion began," Tim said.

He was dead serious. Maybe this was all just a goofy movie to me, but it wasn't to him.

More junior officers came to him with more papers to sign. He excused himself and took care of them. Then he was on the field telephone for five minutes or so. His expression grew progressively more bleak. Finally he looked up at me and said, "You see? It's starting."

"What is?"

"They've crossed Seventy-second Street for the first time. There must have been a gap in the sealfield. Or maybe they jumped it, as I was saying just now. Three of the big ones are up by Seventy-fourth, noodling around the eastern end of the lake. The Metropolitan Museum people are scared shitless and have asked for gun emplacements on the roof, and they're thinking of evacuating the most important works of art." The field phone lit up again. "Excuse me," he said. Always the soul of courtesy, Tim. After a time he said, "Oh, Jesus. It sounds pretty bad. I've got to go up there right now. Do you mind?" His jaw was set, his gaze was frosty with determination. This is it, Major. There's ten thousand Comanches coming through the pass with blood in their eyes, but we're ready for them, right? Right. He went striding away up Fifth Avenue.

When I got back to the office there was a message from Maranta, suggesting that I stop off at her place for drinks that evening on my way home. Tim would be busy playing soldier, she said, until nine. Until 2100 hours, I silently corrected.

ANOTHER FEW DAYS AND WE got used to it all. We began to accept the presence of aliens in the park as a normal part of New York life, like snow in February or laser duels in the subway.

But they remained at the center of everybody's consciousness. In a subtle pervasive way they were working great changes in our souls as they moved about mysteriously behind the sealfield barriers in the park. The strangeness of their being here made us buoyant. Their arrival had broken, in some way, the depressing rhythm that life in our brave new century had seemed to be settling into. I know that for some time I had been thinking, as I suppose people have thought since Cro-Magnon days, that lately the flavor of modern life had been changing for the worse, that it was becoming sour and nasty, that the era I happened to live in was a dim, shabby, dismal sort of time, small-souled, mean-minded. You know the feeling. Somehow the aliens had caused that feeling to lift. By invading us in this weird hands-off way, they had given us something to be interestingly mystified by: a sort of redemption, a sort of rebirth. Yes, truly.

Some of us changed quite a lot. Consider Tim, the latter-day Bengal lancer, the staunchly disciplined officer. He lasted about a week in that particular mindset. Then one night he called me and said, "Hey, fellow, how would you like to go into the park and play with the critters?"

"What are you talking about?"

"I know a way to get in. I've got the code for the Sixty-fourth Street sealfield. I can turn it off and we can slip through. It's risky, but how can you resist?"

So much for Gary Cooper. So much for John Wayne.

"Have you gone nuts?" I said. "The other day you wouldn't even let me go up to the barricades."

"That was the other day."

"You wouldn't walk across the street with me for a drink. You said you'd get shot for desertion."

"That was the other day."

"You called me a civilian."

"You still are a civilian. But you're my old buddy, and I want to go in there and look those aliens in the eye, and I'm not quite up to doing it all by myself. You want to go with me, or don't you?"

"Like the time we stole the beer keg from Sigma Frap. Like the time we put the scorpions in the girls' shower room."

"You got it, old pal."

"Tim, we aren't college kids any more. There's a fucking intergalactic war going on. That was your very phrase. Central Park is under surveillance by NASA spy-eyes that can see a cat's whiskers from fifty miles up. You are part of the military force that is supposed to be protecting us against these alien invaders. And now you propose to violate your trust and go sneaking into the midst of the invading force, as a mere prank?"

"I guess I do," he said.

"This is an extremely cockeyed idea, isn't it?" I said.

"Absolutely. Are you with me?"

"Sure," I said. "You know I am."

I TOLD ELAINE THAT TIM and I were going to meet for a late dinner to discuss a business deal and I didn't expect to be home until two or three in the morning. No problem there. Tim was waiting at our old table at Perugino's with a bottle of Amarone already working. The wine was so good that we ordered another midway through the veal pizzaiola, and then a third. I won't say we drank ourselves blind, but we certainly got seriously myopic. And about midnight we walked over to the park.

Everything was quiet. I saw sleepy-looking Guardsmen patrolling here and there along Fifth. We went right up to the command post at Fifty-ninth and Tim saluted very crisply, which I don't think was quite kosher, he being not then in uniform. He introduced me to someone as Dr. Pritchett, Bureau of External Affairs. That sounded really cool and glib, Bureau of External Affairs.

Then off we went up Fifth, Tim and I, and he gave me a guided tour. "You see, Dr. Pritchett, the first line of the isolation zone is the barricade that runs down the middle of the avenue." Virile, forceful voice, loud enough to be heard for half a block. "That keeps the gawkers away. Behind that, Doctor, we maintain a further level of security through a series of augmented-beam sealfield emplacements, the new General Dynamics 1100 series model, and let me show you right here how we've integrated that with advanced personnel-interface intercept scan by means of a triple line of Hewlett-Packard optical doppler-couplers—"

And so on, a steady stream of booming confident-sounding gibberish as we headed north. He pulled out a flashlight and led me hither and thither to show me amplifiers and sensors and whatnot, and it was Dr. Pritchett this and Dr. Pritchett that and I realized that we were now somehow on the inner side of the barricade. His glibness, his poise, were awesome. *Notice this, Dr. Pritchett*, and *Let me call your attention to this, Dr. Pritchett*, and suddenly there was a tiny digital keyboard in his hand, like a little calculator, and he was tapping out numbers. "Okay," he said, "the field's down between here and the Sixty-fifth Street entrance to the park, but I've put a kill on the beam-interruption signal. So far as anyone can tell there's still an unbroken field. Let's go in."

And we entered the park just north of the zoo.

For five generations the first thing New York kids have been taught, ahead of tying shoelaces and flushing after you go, is that you don't set foot in Central Park at night. Now here we were, defying the most primordial of no-nos. But what was to fear? What they taught us to worry about in the park was muggers. Not creatures from the Ninth Glorch Galaxy.

The park was eerily quiet. Maybe a snore or two from the direction of the zoo, otherwise not a sound. We walked west and north into the silence, into the darkness. After a while a strange smell reached my nostrils. It was dank and musky and harsh and sour, but those are only approximations: it wasn't like anything I had ever smelled before. One whiff of it and I saw purple skies and a great green sun blazing in the heavens. A second whiff and all the stars were in the wrong places. A third whiff and I was staring into a gnarled twisted landscape where the trees were like giant spears and the mountains were like crooked teeth.

Tim nudged me.

"Yeah," I said. "I smell it too."

"To your left," he said. "Look to your left."

I looked to my left and saw three huge yellow eyes looking back at me from twenty feet overhead, like searchlights mounted in a tree. They weren't mounted in a tree, though. They were mounted in something shaggy and massive, somewhat larger than your basic two-family Queens residential dwelling, that was standing maybe fifty feet away, completely blocking both lanes of the park's East Drive from shoulder to shoulder.

It was then that I realized that three bottles of wine hadn't been nearly enough.

"What's the matter?" Tim said. "This is what we came for, isn't it, old pal?"

"What do we do now? Climb on its back and go for a ride?"

"You know that no human being in all of history has ever been as close to that thing as we are now?"

"Yes," I said. "I do know that, Tim."

It began making a sound. It was the kind of sound that a piece of chalk twelve feet thick would make if it was dragged across a blackboard the wrong way. When I heard that sound I felt as if I were being dragged across whole galaxies by my hair. A weird vertigo attacked me. Then the creature folded up all its legs and came down to ground level; and then it unfolded the two front pairs of legs, and then the other two; and then it started to amble slowly and ominously toward us.

I saw another one, looking even bigger, just beyond it. And perhaps a third one a little farther back. They were heading our way, too.

"Shit," I said. "This was a very dumb idea, wasn't it?"

"Come on. We're never going to forget this night."

"I'd like to live to remember it."

"Let's get up real close. They don't move very fast."

"No," I said. "Let's just get out of the park right now, okay?"

"We just got here."

"Fine," I said. "We did it. Now let's go."

"Hey, look," Tim said. "Over there to the west."

I followed his pointing arm and saw two gleaming wraiths hovering just above the ground, maybe three hundred yards away. The other aliens, the little floating ones. Drifting toward us, graceful as balloons. I imagined myself being wrapped in a shining pillow and being floated off into their ship.

"Oh, shit," I said. "Come *on*, Tim."

Staggering, stumbling, I ran for the park gate, not even thinking about how I was going to get through the sealfield without Tim's gizmo. But then there was Tim, right behind me. We reached the sealfield together and he tapped out the numbers on the little keyboard and the field opened for us, and out we went, and the field closed behind us. And we collapsed just outside the park, panting, gasping, laughing like lunatics, slapping the sidewalk hysterically. "Dr. Pritchett," he chortled. "Bureau of External Affairs. Goddamn, what a smell that critter had! Goddamn!"

I LAUGHED ALL THE WAY home. I was still laughing when I got into bed. Elaine squinted at me. She wasn't amused. "That Tim," I said. "That wild man Tim." She could tell I'd been drinking some and she nodded somberly—boys will be boys, etc.—and went back to sleep.

The next morning I learned what had happened in the park after we had cleared out.

It seemed a few of the big aliens had gone looking for us. They had followed our spoor all the way to the park gate, and when they lost it they somehow turned to the right and went blundering into the zoo. The Central Park Zoo is a small cramped place and as they rambled around in it they managed to knock down most of the fences. In no time whatever there were tigers, elephants, chimps, rhinos, and hyenas all over the park.

The animals, of course, were befuddled and bemused at finding themselves free. They took off in a hundred different directions, looking for places to hide.

The lions and coyotes simply curled up under bushes and went to sleep. The monkeys and some of the apes went into the trees. The aquatic things headed for the lake. One of the rhinos ambled out into the mall and pushed over a fragile-looking alien machine with his nose. The machine shattered and the rhino went up in a flash of yellow light and a puff of green smoke. As for the elephants, they stood poignantly in a huddled circle, glaring in utter amazement and dismay at the gigantic aliens. How humiliating it must have been for them to feel *tiny*.

Then there was the bison event. There was this little herd, a dozen or so mangy-looking guys with ragged, threadbare fur. They started moving single file toward Columbus Circle, probably figuring that if they just kept their heads down and didn't attract attention they could keep going all the way back to Wyoming. For some reason one of the behemoths decided to see what bison tastes like. It came hulking over and sat down on the last one in the line, which vanished underneath it like a mouse beneath a hippopotamus. Chomp, gulp, gone. In the next few minutes five more behemoths came over and disappeared five more of the bison. The survivors made it safely to the edge of the park and huddled up against the sealfield, mooing forlornly. One of the little tragedies of interstellar war.

I found Tim on duty at the Fifty-ninth Street command post. He looked at me as though I were an emissary of Satan. "I can't talk to you while I'm on duty," he said.

"You heard about the zoo?" I asked.

"Of course I heard." He was speaking through clenched teeth. His eyes had the scarlet look of zero sleep. "What a filthy irresponsible thing we did!"

"Look, we had no way of knowing—"

"Inexcusable. An incredible lapse. The aliens feel threatened now that humans have trespassed on their territory, and the whole situation has changed in there. We upset them and now they're getting out of control. I'm thinking of reporting myself for court-martial."

"Don't be silly, Tim. We trespassed for three minutes. The aliens didn't give a crap about it. They might have blundered into the zoo even if we hadn't—"

"Go away," he muttered. "I can't talk to you while I'm on duty."

Jesus! As if I was the one who had lured *him* into doing it.

Well, he was back in his movie part again, the distinguished military figure who now had unaccountably committed an unpardonable lapse and was going to have to live in the cold glare of his own disapproval for the rest of his life. The poor bastard. I tried to tell him not to take things so much to heart, but he turned away from me, so I shrugged and went back to my office.

That afternoon some tender-hearted citizens demanded that the sealfields be switched off until the zoo animals could escape from the park. The sealfields, of course, kept them trapped in there with the aliens.

Another tough one for the mayor. He'd lose points tremendously if the evening news kept showing our beloved polar bears and raccoons and kangaroos and whatnot getting gobbled like gumdrops by the aliens. But switching off the sealfields would send a horde of leopards and gorillas and wolverines scampering out into the streets of Manhattan, to say nothing of the aliens who might follow them. The mayor appointed a study group, naturally.

The small aliens stayed close to their spaceship and remained uncommunicative. They went on tinkering with their machines, which emitted odd plinking noises and curious colored lights. But the huge ones roamed freely about the park, and now they were doing considerable damage in their amiable mindless way. They smashed up the backstops of the baseball fields, tossed the Bethesda Fountain into the lake, rearranged Tavern-on-the-Green's seating plan, and trashed the place in various other ways, but nobody seemed to object except the usual Friends of the Park civic types. I think we were all so bemused by the presence of genuine galactic beings that we didn't mind. We were flattered that they had chosen New York as the site of first contact. (But where *else*?)

No one could explain how the behemoths had penetrated the Seventy-second Street sealfield line, but a new barrier was set up at Seventy-ninth, and that seemed to keep them contained. Poor Tim spent twelve hours a day patrolling the perimeter of the occupied zone. Inevitably I began spending more time with Maranta than just lunchtimes. Elaine noticed. But I didn't notice her noticing.

ONE SUNDAY AT DAWN A behemoth turned up by the Metropolitan, peering in the window of the Egyptian courtyard. The authorities thought at first that there must be a gap in the Seventy-ninth Street sealfield, as there had at Seventy-second. Then came a report of another alien out near Riverside Drive and a third one at Lincoln Center and it became clear that the sealfields just didn't hold them back at all. They had simply never bothered to go beyond them before.

Making contact with a sealfield is said to be extremely unpleasant for any organism with a nervous system more complex than a squid's. Every neuron screams in anguish. You jump back, involuntarily, a reflex impossible to overcome. On the morning we came to call Crazy Sunday the behemoths began walking through the fields as if they weren't there. The main thing about aliens is that they are alien. They feel no responsibility for fulfilling any of your expectations.

That weekend it was Bobby Christie's turn to have the full apartment. On those Sundays when Elaine and I had the one-room configuration we liked to get up very early and spend the day out, since it was a little depressing to stay home with three rooms of furniture jammed all around us. As we were walking up Park Avenue South toward Forty-second, Elaine said suddenly, "Do you hear anything strange?"

"Strange?"

"Like a riot."

"It's nine o'clock Sunday morning. Nobody goes out rioting at nine o'clock Sunday morning."

"Just listen," she said.

There is no mistaking the characteristic sounds of a large excited crowd of human beings, for those of us who spent our formative years living in the late twentieth century. Our ears were tuned at an early age to the music of riots, mobs, demonstrations, and their kin. We know what it means, when individual exclamations of anger, indignation, or anxiety blend to create a symphonic hubbub in which all extremes of pitch and timbre are submerged into a single surging roar, as deep as the booming of the surf. That was what I heard now. There was no mistaking it.

"It isn't a riot," I said. "It's a mob. There's a subtle difference."

"What?"

"Come on," I said, breaking into a jog. "I'll bet you that the aliens have come out of the park."

A mob, yes. In a moment we saw thousands upon thousands of people, filling Forty-second Street from curb to curb and more coming from all directions. What they were looking at—pointing, gaping, screaming—was a shaggy blue creature the size of a small mountain that was moving about uncertainly on the automobile viaduct that runs around the side of Grand Central Terminal. It looked unhappy. It was obviously trying to get down from the viaduct, which was sagging noticeably under its weight. People were jammed right up against it and a dozen or so were clinging to its sides and back like rock climbers. There were people underneath it, too, milling around between its colossal legs. "Oh, look," Elaine said, shuddering, digging her fingers into my biceps. "Isn't it eating some of them? Like they did the bison?" Once she had pointed it out I saw, yes, the behemoth now and then was dipping quickly and rising again, a familiar one-two, the old squat-and-gobble. "What an awful thing!" Elaine murmured. "Why don't they get out of its way?"

"I don't think they can," I said. "I think they're being pushed forward by the people behind them."

"Right into the jaws of that hideous monster. Or whatever it has, if they aren't jaws."

"I don't think it means to hurt anyone," I said. How did I know that? "I think it's just eating them because they're dithering around down there in its mouth area. A kind of automatic response. It looks awfully dumb, Elaine."

"Why are you defending it?"

"Hey, look, Elaine—"

"It's eating people. You sound almost sorry for it!"

"Well, why not? It's far from home and surrounded by ten thousand screaming morons. You think it wants to be out there?"

"It's a disgusting obnoxious animal." She was getting furious. Her eyes were bright and wild, her jaw was thrust forward. "I hope the army gets here fast," she said fiercely. "I hope they blow it to smithereens!"

Her ferocity frightened me. I saw an Elaine I scarcely knew at all. When I tried one more time to make excuses for that miserable hounded beast on the viaduct she glared at me with unmistakable loathing. Then she turned away and went rushing forward, shaking her fist, shouting curses and threats at the alien.

Suddenly I realized how it would have been if Hannibal actually had been able to keep his elephants alive long enough to enter Rome with them. The respectable Roman matrons, screaming and raging from the housetops with the fury of banshees. And the baffled elephants sooner or later rounded up and thrust into the Coliseum to be tormented by little men with spears, while the crowd howled its delight. Well, I can howl too. "Come on, Behemoth!" I yelled into the roar of the mob. "You can do it, Goliath!" A traitor to the human race is what I was, I guess.

Eventually a detachment of Guardsmen came shouldering through the streets. They had mortars and rifles, and for all I know they had tactical nukes, too. But, of course, there was no way they could attack the animal in the midst of such a mob. Instead they used electronic blooglehorns to disperse the crowd by the power of sheer ugly noise, and whipped up a bunch of buzz-blinkers and a little sealfield to cut Forty-second Street in half. The last I saw of the monster it was slouching off in the direction of the old United Nations Buildings with the Guardsmen warily creeping along behind it. The crowd scattered, and I was left standing in front of Grand Central with a trembling, sobbing Elaine.

THAT WAS HOW IT WAS all over the city on Crazy Sunday, and on Monday and Tuesday, too. The behemoths were outside the park, roaming at large from Harlem to Wall Street. Wherever they went they drew tremendous crazy crowds that swarmed all over them without any regard for the danger. Some famous news photos came out of those days: the three grinning black boys at Seventh and 125th hanging from the three purple rod-like things, the acrobats forming a human pyramid atop the Times Square beast, the little old Italian man standing in front of his house in Greenwich Village trying to hold a space monster at bay with his garden hose.

There was never any accurate casualty count. Maybe five thousand people died, mainly trampled underfoot by the aliens or crushed in the crowd. Somewhere between three hundred and fifty and four hundred human beings were gobbled by the aliens. Apparently that stoop-and-swallow thing is something they do when they're nervous. If there's anything edible within reach, they'll gulp it in. This soothes them. We made them very nervous; they did a lot of gulping.

Among the casualties was Tim, the second day of the violence. He went down valiantly in the defense of the Guggenheim Museum, which came under attack by five of the biggies. Its spiral shape held some ineffable appeal for them. We couldn't tell whether they wanted to worship it or mate with it or just knock it to pieces, but they kept on charging and charging, rushing up to it and slamming against it. Tim was trying to hold them off with nothing more than teargas and blooglehorns when he was swallowed. Never flinched, just stood there and let it happen. The president had ordered the guardsmen not to use lethal weapons. Maranta was bitter about that. "If only they had let them use grenades," she said. I tried to imagine what it was like, gulped down and digested, nifty tan uniform and all. A credit to his regiment. It was his atonement, I guess. He was back there in the Gary Cooper movie again, gladly paying the price for dereliction of duty.

Tuesday afternoon the rampage came to an unexpected end. The behemoths suddenly started keeling over, and within a few hours they were all dead. Some said it was the heat—it was up in the nineties all day Monday and Tuesday—and some said it was the excitement. A Rockefeller University biologist thought it was both those factors plus severe indigestion: the aliens had eaten an average of ten humans apiece, which might have overloaded their systems.

There was no chance for autopsies. Some enzyme in the huge bodies set to work immediately on death, dissolving flesh and bone and skin and all into a sticky yellow mess. By nightfall nothing was left of them but some stains on the pavement, uptown and down. A sad business, I thought. Not even a skeleton for the museum, memento of this momentous time. The poor monsters. Was I the only one who felt sorry for them? Quite possibly I was. I make no apologies for that. I feel what I feel.

All this time the other aliens, the little shimmery spooky ones, had stayed holed up in Central Park, preoccupied with their incomprehensible research. They didn't even seem to notice that their behemoths had strayed.

But now they became agitated. For two or three days they bustled about like worried penguins, dismantling their instruments and packing them aboard their ship; and then they took apart the other ship, the one that had carried the behemoths, and loaded that aboard. Perhaps they felt demoralized. As the Carthaginians who had invaded Rome did, after their elephants died.

On a sizzling June afternoon the alien ship took off. Not for its home world, not right away. It swooped into the sky and came down on Fire Island: at Cherry Grove, to be precise. The aliens took possession of the beach, set up their instruments around their ship, and even ventured into the water, skimming and bobbing just above the surface of the waves like demented surfers. After five or six days they moved on to one of the Hamptons and did the same thing, and then to Martha's Vineyard. Maybe they just wanted a vacation, after three weeks in New York. And then they went away altogether.

"You've been having an affair with Maranta, haven't you?" Elaine asked me, the day the aliens left.

"I won't deny it."

"That night you came in so late, with wine on your breath. You were with her, weren't you?"

"No," I said. "I was with Tim. He and I sneaked into the park and looked at the aliens."

"Sure you did," Elaine said. She filed for divorce and a year later I married Maranta. Very likely that would have happened sooner or later even if the Earth hadn't been invaded by beings from space and Tim hadn't been devoured. But no question that the invasion speeded things up a bit for us all.

And now, of course, the invaders are back. Four years to the day from the first landing and there they were, pop whoosh ping thunk, Central Park again. Three ships this time, one of spooks, one of behemoths, and the third one carrying the prisoners of war.

Who could ever forget that scene, when the hatch opened and some three hundred and fifty to four hundred human beings came out, marching like zombies? Along with the bison herd, half a dozen squirrels, and three dogs. They hadn't been eaten and digested at all, just *collected* inside the behemoths and instantaneously transmitted somehow to the home world, where they were studied. Now they were being returned. "That's Tim, isn't it?" Maranta said, pointing to the screen. I nodded. Unmistakably Tim, yes. With the stunned look of a man who has beheld marvels beyond comprehension.

It's a month now and the government is still holding all the returnees for debriefing. No one is allowed to see them. The word is that a special law will be passed dealing with the problem of spouses of returnees who have entered into new marriages. Maranta says she'll stay with me no matter what; and I'm pretty sure that Tim will do the stiff-upper-lip thing, no hard feelings, if they ever get word to him in the debriefing camp about Maranta and me. As for the aliens, they're sitting tight in Central Park, occupying the whole place from Ninety-sixth to 110th and not telling us a thing. Now and then the behemoths wander down to the reservoir for a lively bit of wallowing, but they haven't gone beyond the park this time.

I think a lot about Hannibal, and about Carthage versus Rome, and how the Second Punic War might have come out if Hannibal had had a chance to go back home and get a new batch of elephants. Most likely Rome would have won the war anyway, I guess. But we aren't Romans, and they aren't Carthaginians, and those aren't elephants splashing around in the Central Park reservoir. "This is such an interesting time to be alive," Maranta likes to say. "I'm certain they don't mean us any harm, aren't you?"

"I love you for your optimism," I tell her then. And then we turn on the tube and watch the evening news.

JIMMY TAKES A TRIP
BY ELAINE KAGAN

"So, she picked him up, right?" Stan said. He looked around the restaurant. It was already crowded at six thirty.

"What?" Al said.

"I said *she* picked *him* up," Stan said, pushing a crust of bread through a pool of olive oil on his plate.

"No."

Stan lifted his eyes to Al. "No?"

"I said no," Al said.

"No."

"No—she—didn't—pick—him—up." Al said the words slowly and separately as if he were speaking to someone Chinese. He had a distinctive voice—strong and resonant. Once upon a time he had auditioned for the Met. *The Metropolitan Opera*—his mother used to say it as if it were in all caps. He'd made it to the second-to-final round singing the role of the father in Verdi's *La Traviata*. The baritone part. Not too many people knew that.

"Well . . ." Stan said, straightening his shoulders, "*Maury said* . . . you know . . . that she picked him up."

Al swirled the scotch around the melting cubes in his glass and gave Stan a long look. "Maury's got a hell of a lot of nerve saying that's what happened. He wasn't even there."

Stan frowned. "He wasn't?"

"No, he wasn't."

"Well." Stan said. "I thought it was the six of you."

Al settled himself; moved his broad back against the slick red leather booth. He cracked the knuckles of his left hand and then his right. He readjusted the quarter-inch of white French cuff at the end of his gray suit jacket sleeve on each wrist and folded his big hands neatly in front of him. The muscles in his upper arms strained against the gabardine. The diamonds in his cuff links flashed. His fingers were large and stubby, the skin of the third finger of his left hand deeply indented by a thick gold wedding band. He was a formidable man with ice-white hair, chopped into what once would have been called a flattop. "Maury wasn't even in the city," Al said.

Stan shook his head. "Well, I'll be . . ."

"You believed him?" Al said, "That he was there? That fat jerk."

Stan shrugged.

"He was on the island. He had a family to-do."

"Uh huh," Stan said.

"Cancelled at the last minute. Some family thing that Suze had to do," Al said. His eyes narrowed. Pale blue eyes. "Which you'd think he would have known about in the first place and we wouldn't have made the date in the first place and we wouldn't have even gone there."

"Right."

"The whole thing was Suze's idea anyway. She read about it in some magazine."

"No kidding," Stan said.

"No kidding," Al said. "Would I go into the city if I didn't have to?" he said in his booming baritone, and polished off the scotch. "Would I go to a fucking hotel? Where I could look across at Jersey?" He shook his head. "I'm already in Jersey. Do I need to look at it?"

"I guess not," Stan said.

"Suze got Lil and Cheryl all excited with the idea. I couldn't talk Lil out of it. And Jimmy said, oh, c'mon, we'll take 'em, what's the big deal?"

"Uh huh," Stan said.

The waiter put thick white plates down in front of them, the china making a thunk sound against the tablecloth. New York strippers sizzling, baked potatoes the size of rats, and creamed spinach, individual bowls of creamed spinach to the left of each plate. Sorrentino's had excellent creamed spinach. The secret ingredient was nutmeg. Everyone knew that.

"Ketchup," Al said to the waiter, lifting his knife and slicing through his potato. It let off a cloud of steam like a volcano.

"Ketchup?"

'That's what I said."

"Yes, sir."

"He always does that, Maury, acts like he knows everything, tells everybody else's goddamn story like he was the one standin' there . . ." Al kept his eyes on the back of the waiter as he went to get the ketchup.

"Well, Maury didn't say he was *standing there*. He just said she picked him up," Stan said. He trimmed an edge of fat off the hunk of meat and carefully moved it to the side of his plate.

"Well, she didn't," Al said.

"Okay."

"It was me and Lil and Cheryl and Jimmy. That's all who went. The four of us. And I was the only one with him at the bar."

The waiter returned and set down a small silver bowl of ketchup. Al looked at the bowl; he looked at the waiter.

"Sir?" the waiter said.

"You poured this from the Heinz bottle?"

"Yes, sir."

"Well, okay then," Al said. The waiter turned and took off. "I don't know this guy," Al said, gesturing towards the parting waiter. "Must of just got out of the Army."

Stan gave a little chuckle.

Al lifted the silver bowl and spooned ketchup all over his steak. He looked at Stan. "Anyway, it was just the four of us," he said. "No sign of Maury."

"Who was on the island," Stan said.

"Yeah." Al made a face that was half smirk, half smile. The dimple in his left cheek was ironic—it gave the impression that he was sweet as a cupcake.

Stan picked up his knife and fork. "So . . ."

"So?" Al said.

Stan smiled. "So, go on."

"So, it was Saturday, you know that . . ." Al said, dropping two inches of butter onto his potato.

"Yeah, I know that. Saturday . . ."

"Nobody in their right mind would come into the city on a Saturday. You could lose your mind in the tunnel."

"Right," Stan said.

"You could shoot yourself in the head in the tunnel."

"You bet," Stan said.

Al took a deep breath, as if to steady himself. He looked at Stan.

"Hell of a thing," Stan said.

"Yeah," Al said. He wiped his mouth on his napkin.

Stan pushed his fork through the creamed spinach. "How long you two know each other?" he asked.

"Me and Jimmy?" Al spread the napkin carefully on his lap, took another swig of the melted ice. "Since Immaculate Conception," Al said.

"*THE* Immaculate Conception?" Stan said, eyes wide.

"What are you? Crazy?"

"I beg your pardon," Stan said, frowning.

"That was the name of our high school."

"In Short Hills?"

"No, Verona. I lived in Verona, Jimmy was in Newark."

"No shit."

"Where were you then?" Al asked.

"Boston," Stan said.

"Really. You a Red Sox fan?"

"Not anymore."

Al smiled. "We were fourteen."

"Wow," Stan said, "I don't think I know anybody from when I was fourteen."

"Yeah," Al nodded. "He was standing next to me when I passed out at mass."

"You what?" Stan said, pulling another piece of bread out of the basket and using it to scoop up the rest of his spinach.

"Oh, I hadn't eaten and I passed out at mass." Al smacked his meaty hands together making a big slap sound. "Splat," he said, grinning. The couple at the table closest to their booth turned their heads to look at him. He laughed. "Face down across the marble. Like LaMotta with Danny Nardico."

"Wow," Stan said.

"That's when they found out I was hypoglycemic." Al gave Stan a look.

"That's the blood sugar . . . you know, if I don't eat . . . blood sugar goes down . . ." he slapped his hand on the table, "kaboom."

"No kidding," Stan said. He set down the empty bowl. "Does it bother you?"

"No. I carry nuts in the car. You know, nuts, a Mars bar, things like that. Lil makes sure."

"Uh huh," Stan said.

"So . . . anyway . . . then . . . when I went down . . . I broke my jaw." Al said. "Big time. Wired for months." He laughed. "And Jimmy was standing next to me. He could sing a hell of a bass. Even then, when we were kids. Like in *Gloria en excelsis Deo*, you know? At the end."

"Who?"

"The Christmas carol, you know, in Latin. About the angels." He leaned forward and sang, "*En excelsis daaayyyyy ohhhhh*," he held the last note. He didn't belt it out or anything but it was definitely clear and strong and heard across most of Sorrentino's Steak House. People turned in their chairs. Stan's mouth gaped open about a half inch.

"Anyway," Al said, "Jimmy was next to me, and for some reason we never figured out, he went with me in the ambulance. It was probably Sister Mary Innunciatta's idea. She was great with ideas." He ate some of the inside of the potato, avoiding the skin. He cut another piece of steak. He polished off the scotch and raised his glass in the air. He didn't move the glass or anything; just held it high in the air in front of him like a running back does with the football after a touchdown.

Stan gazed at Al, transfixed.

"Did you want another drink, sir?" the waiter asked. He'd appeared out of nowhere like a Wile E. Coyote cartoon.

"Yeah," Al said. "A double."

"Two doubles," Stan said.

"Yes, sir."

Al kept his eyes on the back of the waiter. "He's a regular lieutenant."

"Maybe just a sergeant," Stan said.

They both smiled.

"Well, so . . ." Stan said. He ran his hand across his face. "So, you and Jimmy all these years, huh?"

"Yep," Al said, nodding. "A wild and crazy guy."

"Who said that? *A wild and crazy guy*—Robin Williams?"

"No. Steve Martin."

"Oh, yeah, Steve Martin, that's right," Stan said. "I saw him once. He did that arrow thing through his head. Did you ever see that?"

"Not that I remember," Al said. "He's no Robin Williams, Steve Martin, that's for damn sure."

"No, well . . . who is?" Stan cut a piece of steak.

They both ate for a few minutes.

"It's downtown, huh, the Saxony Hotel? I never went there. I've seen it lots of times but I never went in."

"West Village. Did you ever try to find a garage in the West Village?"

"You didn't give it to the hotel guy?"

"Well, finally," Al said, "finally I gave it to the hotel guy because Cheryl was having a fit. Like we were gonna be late or something. We're gonna be late, we're gonna be late, she kept harping at Jimmy. Like we were gonna miss the skyline. The skyline is forever, right? Or always. Always is what I said. No matter when you look out you see the goddamn skyline. Night or day."

"Maybe she meant the sunset. Were you trying to get there in time for the sunset?"

"The sunset in October? We would have had to leave Short Hills at what? Three? Three thirty?" He shook his head, took a breath. "Look, Cheryl's okay . . . I mean, we made our peace a long time ago . . . about a lot of things . . . whenever Jimmy went awry. Astray. Whatever. On many occasions . . . Lil used to say to me, take it easy, take it easy, but Cheryl always went against my grain . . . little things . . . I don't know."

"You all know each other a long time."

"Since he met her. I was *with him* when he met her. She was walking out of the Up-to-Date Luncheonette. That was a place we used to go—a kind of candy store, you know, where you bought a newspaper, had a soda. Those places don't exist anymore."

"Right."

"It's a damn shame," Al said, taking a slow breath. "Anyway, I'm godfather to their kids, you know, I stood up for him when they got married. And she's a good girl, Cheryl, a really good girl, but there are things . . . little things about her that always annoyed me . . ."

"The perfume," Stan said, interrupting.

Al stopped, the last forkful of steak midway to his mouth. "That's right. The perfume. The goddamn perfume. There you go."

"Cotton Candy," Stan said, "terrible."

"Could make you gag. Especially in an enclosed area. Like my car." Al ate the last piece of steak, placed his knife and fork in a perfect diagonal across the top of the plate, and gently pushed the plate maybe an inch forward.

Stan lifted his chin. "You don't like spinach?"

"I'm not so big on vegetables."

Stan laughed. "That's all I'm supposed to eat."

"You weren't supposed to have the steak, right?"

"No way."

"You lost a lot of weight. A hell of a lot of weight."

"They made me."

"The docs, huh?"

"Yeah, but mostly Deb. She turned into Stalin."

Al laughed. It was a big fat laugh. A baritone laugh. And, it was infectious. He probably hadn't laughed that hard for a long time and if you heard it you had to laugh too. Stan laughed until his eyes welled up. He wiped his face with his napkin. "I'm cryin' here," he said.

"Listen, I'm sorry I didn't visit you at the hospital," Al said.

Stan gave a little wave with the napkin. "It's fine. Really. Fine."

The waiter set down the double scotches.

"You're probably not supposed to have this either," Al said, raising his glass. "Does scotch have cholesterol?"

Stan laughed again. "Who the fuck cares?"

The busboy stood in front of the table. He nodded at Al's plate. "Finished, Mr. Ruban?"

"Oh, yeah," Al said. "You done, Stan?"

"Sure."

The busboy stuck his hand back and forth between them, lifting plates, clattering silverware onto a tray. He slid the crumbs off the tablecloth with what looked like a letter opener.

"Good steak, huh?" Al said to Stan.

"Terrific."

The busboy smiled like he owned the place. He was a squat man, about fifty, dark, Puerto Rican.

"How you doin', José?" Al said to the busboy.

"Fine, Mr. Ruban. We are okay."

"Your family?"

"Mucho bueno, sir."

"Mucho bueno," Al said, "well, that's good to know." He gave the busboy a nod. The bus boy nodded back and took off for the kitchen with his tray.

"So, did you eat at the Saxony?" Stan said, taking a swig of scotch.

"We were going to. We'd already had drinks at our house. Lil made appetizers. Cheese, salami, stuff like that."

"Sure."

"So we'd already had a little something when we got there. And a couple." He shook his head. "Lil was drinking gin and tonics. With cherries. Can you imagine? Somebody drinking gin and tonics when it isn't summer?"

"Deb likes martinis."

"Well, that I can understand," Al said. "Oh, and Lil made this thing with sardines . . . you wouldn't know it was sardines if I didn't tell you . . . all mashed up . . . really good."

"Sardines, huh?"

"Yeah. And, that's another thing about Cheryl. You can't ever eat there, at their house."

"Why not?"

"I don't know. She's got a thing about cleanliness. You can't touch anything. She's got the can of Pledge out before you even make prints. And the pillows on the couch are all puffed up and you can see it upsets her when you sit. You know, when you dent them. I don't wipe my hands on the towels if I have to go to the can there."

"No kidding."

"No kidding."

"So, the four of you never eat there?"

"Not for years. We eat at my house. We don't even go there. The kitchen is probably boarded up and painted black."

They were quiet for maybe a minute. "So, you were gonna eat at the Saxony," Stan said, "after the cheese and crackers."

"Yeah."

"It's fancy, huh?"

Al gave Stan a look. "Twenty-two bucks for a gin and tonic."

"You're kidding."

"That's what I said."

"Wow. Was it crowded?"

"Oh, yeah. Packed. Big time. The lobby, the elevator . . . that's after the mob scene at the valet."

"People clamoring to pay twenty-two bucks for a gin and tonic?"

"Young people. They're all over the city. They're all in black. The city is packed with young people wearing black. Hipsters, they call them. On the street, in front of the hotel. Not a suit in sight."

"They probably don't own suits."

"Right," Al said. "And after you get out of the elevator you gotta wait in a line. You get off at the Rooftop floor and there's a line. "

"Even with a reservation?"

"Oh, yeah. And a list. You gotta be on the list, or they send you away."

"Where do they send you? Back to New Jersey?" Stan said, chuckling.

Al laughed. "Right. Good one." He nodded. "Back to Jersey."

"So, you were on the list?"

"Sure," Al said, "Ciccolini fixed it. You know him?"

"I know who he is, I never met him."

"Oh, yeah, we know each other from the beginning. Me and Jimmy and Chick. He lived down the street from Jimmy. We did some things, the three of us."

"He's a big attorney, right?"

"Makes nine hundred fifty bucks an hour."

"You're kidding," Stan said.

"No." Al polished off his double.

"He can pay twenty-two bucks for a gin and tonic."

"You bet." Al moved his empty glass around the tablecloth. "If they only knew."

"Who?"

"His clients. If they only knew some of the stuff we did. In the day."

"You were a team?"

"We were a team, alright. Jimmy was the team leader." Al shook his head. "My ma used to call him *the instigator*. I mean, like it was his name. Like it was a title. *You hungry, Instigator?* she'd say. *I made gravy, Instigator, you want some?* She was really upset when he went away. Well, everybody was. A little bit of fraud, Jimmy called it. Like a little bit pregnant, you know? He was only gone ten months."

"Wow," Stan said.

"That's 'cause Chick was his lawyer. That's why he was only gone ten months."

"Where'd they send him? Allentown?"

"Yeah."

"Better than Dix."

"Oh yeah, Dix can be a heartache."

"A white-collar crime is not treated like a white-collar crime anymore," Al said.

Stan nodded. "Don't I know it."

"Dessert, sir?" the waiter said.

"You got the bread pudding?" Al said.

"Yes, sir. That's our specialty."

"I know that. I've been eating here maybe fifteen years."

The waiter blinked.

"Two bread puddings," Al said.

"I probably shouldn't," Stan said.

"It's got a brandy sauce," Al said, "very tasty."

"Okay."

"After all," Al said. He looked up at the waiter. "And two Rémys."

"Yes, sir." The waiter took off.

"He's probably a hipster when he isn't a waiter," Al said.

"When he's out of uniform," Stan said.

They both laughed.

"So did you have to wait a long time?" Stan said.

"Not for the table," Al said. "We got a table pretty quick. It was the size of a fucking coaster but you could see everything." He shook his head. "Amazing place. Amazing . . . there you are, outside . . . with a 360 right in front of you." He held one meaty arm high in front of them and moved his fat hand to the left and to the right. "New York, New Jersey, all of it lit up, like a movie." He brought his hand down and folded it into his other hand. "It was warm, you know, for October. That's why it was still open; they close it when it gets cold." He looked across the room and then back at Stan. "Gorgeous view."

"Well, you can't beat the city when you're up above the noise and the smell and the squalor. Nothin' like it," Stan said.

"I don't go into the city unless I have to," Al said.

"Oh."

The waiter set a glass dish of bread pudding topped with whipped cream in front of each of them. "I'll be back, sir, with your Rémys."

Al didn't look up. The waiter took off. "This guy should get a job at the Saxony. They need waiters over there."

"Yeah?"

"Yeah. You couldn't get a drink, you couldn't even flag a waiter down, and you couldn't tell who was a waiter and who wasn't."

"They're wearing black?" Stan said.

"You got it," Al said. He lifted his spoon and attacked the bread pudding. "So, Jimmy and I went to the bar. We left Lil and Cheryl to hold onto this teensy table and we went to the bar. They got a bar on either side of the band."

"They got a band?"

"Oh yeah, playin' all kinds of stuff. Seven guys. Very slick. Lucent Fields."

"What?"

"That's the name of the band."

"Lucent?"

"Yeah."

"Never heard of it."

"Of course not."

Stan took a small bite of the whipped cream on top of his pudding.

"You make your way around the dance floor to get to the bar, or through the dance floor to get to the bar and then you gotta wedge yourself in between whoever else is standing there trying to get a drink. You gotta position yourself so the bartender sees you. And he's on a quest to see *nobody*. They probably got a bartender school where they go to learn that," Al said.

The waiter placed a cut-glass snifter of Rémy Martin before each of them. Neither looked up.

Al picked up his snifter and swirled the amber liquid around the inside of the glass. "That's when the girl showed up." He gave Stan a look. "I'd already banged my hand on the bar a couple of times to get the bartender's attention. Nothing. He was a skinny guy, looked like the guy who used to drive for Greenspan."

"With the pop-out eyes?"

"Yeah. He's a real pig."

"I knew his brother. He was okay."

"Yeah? He musta took after the mother." Al lifted the glass of cognac. "So, I said to Jimmy, *Maybe we should split up and I'll go to the other bar and you stay here.* And Jimmy says, *Maybe we should jump over the bar and give this guy a shot* . . . and we're laughin' . . ." Al shook his head. "And, there she is."

"The girl?"

"Yeah, the girl," Al said, his big voice rising. "Who the hell did you think I meant?"

"Sorry," Stan said.

"She steps right in between us, like she knows us . . . like she's with us." He took a big swig of the cognac. He lips pulled into a narrow line. "Like a float in the Easter Parade," Al said.

Stan put his spoon down, lifted his glass.

"And Jimmy and I give each other the eye."

"I'll bet."

"Good looking girl. Dark hair. Cut all short. Like she did it herself. She's wearing a dress. Not black." He gives Stan a look. "Burgundy." He takes another drink of the cognac. "Plain. Very nice. Classy."

"Uh huh."

"So, she slides in, she doesn't say anything, just stands there, staring straight ahead. I smack my hand on the bar another time, not that that skinny fuck of a bartender pays any attention. *I hate this guy,* I say to Jimmy. Jimmy grins. The girl does nothin'." Al frowned. Three deep lines across his forehead from end to end. "That's when it started," he said, "you can tell Maury that."

"Okay."

"Jimmy started it. He talked to her; she didn't say anything. You tell Maury that for me."

"What did he say?"

"'You got an evening gown back,' he said to her."

"No kidding."

"No kidding. He's lookin' right at her. They're practically touching. And he says it quiet, but I hear him and I know she hears him."

"Just like that," Stan repeated.

"Just like that," Al said. "You know Jimmy, with that low voice—he can sound like the guy in the middle of the night who plays jazz on WNEW. That's how he says it to her. Like it's a secret."

"Wow," Stan said.

"In a million years I could never say a thing like that to Lil. I might say, hey, that's a nice dress you got on, or your hair looks good, but an *evening gown back* is out of my range. Not Jimmy's—he probably threw his ma a line when he slid out of the womb."

"Ha," Stan said.

"He was always that way with girls. From the beginning." Al gave a sharp laugh. "He used to take girls to my Uncle Lawrence's furniture store and try out the bedroom sets." He shook his head. "We were fourteen."

"Your uncle let him?"

"No. What are you—crazy? He broke in."

"I'll be . . ."

"Yeah. Jimmy and the ladies. From the beginning. No big surprise."

"I guess not."

Al polished off the Rémy. "And then because she didn't react I thought maybe he didn't say it—maybe it's the music and the ice cubes hitting the glasses or everybody crowding around because she doesn't move, and he doesn't move, and I think, hell, maybe he didn't say it, maybe I'm hearing shit, maybe I better slow down on the Dewar's, and right as I'm about to say to him *Did you say something,* she pushes her hair out of her eyes. It wasn't in her eyes, but you know that gesture?"

"Sure," Stan said.

"And she looks at him." Al puts down his glass. "So I can't see her face because she's looking at him, but I can see his face and he says to her, 'You want to dance?' And he slips his arm around her waist and he dances her away from the bar."

"He dances her away from the bar."

"Yep," Al said. "Like they've been dancing together forever."

"Just like that?" Stan said.

"Just like that. Into the crowd."

"And where was Cheryl?"

"At the table with Lil. Where we left them."

"Wow."

Al rubbed his hand across his face. "He gave me a little lift of the chin as he went by me. Just a little lift of the chin," Al said. He looked hard at Stan. "That was it."

"I'll be . . ." Stan said.

"Did you want the check, sir?" the waiter said.

Al lifted his eyes to the waiter. "Did I give you that impression?"

"Oh, no, sir . . ."

"Did I gesture that I wanted the check?"

"No, sir. Not at all."

Al's eyes had narrowed, his back was straight, and the fingers of his left hand had curled slightly into a fist.

"It's okay," Stan said.

"It's not okay," Al said.

"It's okay," Stan said. "Take it easy."

"It's not okay," Al said again.

Stan looked up at the waiter. "Bring us two coffees," Stan said.

"Yes, sir," the waiter said and took off like a rocket.

The two men sat in silence. Finally Stan spoke. "Did you see it happen?"

"Yeah."

"Oh, man."

"I was trying to figure out how I was going to get four drinks to the table since the fucking bartender was not interested in giving me a tray—he gave me a look like he thought I was going to steal it—so I had two drinks in my hands and I thought I'd take those two and then I'd come back for the other two and they danced out of the crowd for a minute. Jimmy didn't see me, he had his back to me but then he spun her out, and he was facing me going backwards. *Dancing* backwards," Al said louder. "Let me emphasize. *Dancing* backwards." Al said in his baritone.

Stan nodded.

"He was smiling."

"Jesus," Stan said.

Al's lips pulled up against his teeth.

They were both quiet for maybe a minute.

"Chick is handling the lawsuit," Al said.

"Against the Saxony?"

"Oh, yeah."

"Well, that's good," Stan said.

"Negligence," Al said. "I guess that's what they call it. The barrier, the wall, whatever the fuck it was, behind the plants, you know, where it gave way."

"Right," Stan said.

"Did you see the fucking *Post*?" Al said.

"No. I missed that."

Al lifted his big hands and held them about a foot apart in front of him, cupped as if he were enclosing a caption. "*Jersey man dances off rooftop*. That's what they said. *Jersey—man—dances—off—rooftop*," he said it again—each word slowly and separately and distinctly, as if he were talking to someone Chinese. "As if Jimmy couldn't dance. As if Jimmy was some jerk who couldn't dance, who didn't know his way around because he was from Jersey. That was the headline. Do you fucking believe that?"

"Terrible."

"They should sue the fucking *Post*," Al said.

"They should." Stan shook his head again. "Jesus."

They sat quietly. Al picked up his glass of Rémy, realized it was empty and set it down again.

Stan leaned forward. "Well, he was a man who lived on the edge."

Al straightened his big shoulders against the red leather booth, looked at Stan hard, "Is that supposed to be funny?"

"Of course not," Stan said.

The waiter set a cup of coffee down in front of each man. He looked like he was going to run out of the restaurant. "Did you want cream, sir?" the waiter said.

KNOCK-OUT WHIST
BY DAVID LEVIEN

THE PHONE RANG AND JERRY Riser crossed his office and answered it.

"Your friends are coming up." It was Rodman, the green-jacketed, bow-tied doorman from downstairs.

"My friends," Riser said. He didn't have any.

"Two of 'em," Rodman said. Rodman also knew he had no friends. He was doing Riser a solid. They hung up in time for him to hear the old fashioned elevator's brass accordion-type gate open and heavy footfalls land on the steps.

Riser was out the glass door that let onto the roof and was climbing a fire ladder down to the neighboring building's parapet when he chanced a glance back. There were two of them and they were big, with dark suits and darker looks on their faces. They stalked around his office, trying to open locked file cabinets and log into his computer. One tapped the other with a ham hock hand and pointed at the fleeing Riser as he made it over the ledge to the roof of the next building and disappeared from their view. He took once last look back and saw that the bookends weren't pursuing, but leaving his office, going back down to the street, no doubt, to try and intercept him there instead.

North, south, or east, Riser had three choices in which to run, based on the neighboring buildings' roof doors he knew he could access. His pursuers could only cover two directions. The math was simple—for a guy who knew math. Riser chose north. He entered that building's fire door and hurried down the stairs.

TWO HOURS EARLIER JERRY RISER had been on top of the world, almost literally. He'd been standing in Ken Lewinter's office on the fifty-seventh floor of the MetLife building, taking in the view of the city while waiting to get paid.

"I don't know how the hell you do it . . ." Lewinter said of the job Riser had done for him. But Riser knew he was just saying it and didn't actually want to know. Sixty-five, with steel-gray hair and wiry eyebrows that evoked a horned owl's, Lewinter had run his investment fund with a penurious and iron fist for the last three decades and had plenty of enemies— he had multitudes—and as such, was a good source of employment for private investigators, security men, and various other operatives of Riser's ilk. This time around it had been Sheldon "Shelly" Kipniss. Kipniss was a rival Wall Streeter who was just starting a run for mayor on a platform of regulation and reform. If he won, he was going to raise taxes, specifically on the city's top earners. Riser was no fan of big gov or higher taxes, but in his mind they couldn't tax what he didn't have; it was nothing personal. Ken Lewinter and his cronies hated Kipniss, however, and everything he stood for. They wanted Kipniss out, so Riser had put him out.

"We're done here, Riser. If I need you, you'll hear from me," Lewinter said, and that was that. Jerry Riser was dismissed. If one was looking for an atta-boy, this Park Avenue office, with windows so large and clean they looked like television show trans-lights, was the wrong place. Riser wasn't there for that. It was his third time around with the titan, so he knew better. A barrel-bodied woman nearing retirement age appeared at his elbow holding an envelope. The check's memo line read: RESEARCH SERVICES. Riser took in the view for another moment—the city was a hive from this height, the people and the yellow cabs moving about in the street below like pre-programmed insects—then saluted Lewinter, who no longer recognized his presence, before turning and walking out across carpet so thick it swallowed all sound.

Once outside Riser walked over to Fifth Avenue and uptown, a row of palatial apartment buildings looming to his right and Central Park spreading out to his left. He had a cup of French press in his hand. There was an autumn crispness to the air and the leaves were just starting to go amber. He had just done a piece of work and had gotten paid for it, and for a moment Riser felt rich. He was the king of the city.

Then the M3 flatulated a black cloud of bio-diesel in his face by the gates to the zoo and corrected his impression. He wasn't a king, or even an heir to a minor dukedom. He was barely hanging on.

Riser kept walking. At times like these, he tended to get philosophical and try to parse the un-parsables like: who belonged to the City, and to whom did it belong? And how did a guy live in New York City nowadays? Not the Bronx, not Long Island City, not Staten Island, but the actual City herself, Manhattan island, the one they bought for a bag of beads, the one Frank sang about, the Apple. And not some corporate lawyer or doctor or Wall Street raider, but a regular guy. How does that guy pay the rent now that there is no Hell's Kitchen anymore, but just another row of glass luxury condo towers for investment bankers called "Clinton"? And if he lucked into a place he could afford, how the hell did he keep an office, too?

It was something Jerry Riser had asked himself many, many times before he'd finally come up with his answer. As a private investigator on what he couldn't deny was the low end of the scale, he charged a hundred bucks an hour. The equation was simple: he had to work a lot of hours in order to make rent on apartments that ran in the thousands, even for the shitboxes, and he didn't work that many hours. He couldn't really raise his rates and as far as *more* hours went, he was happy to book the ones he did.

The problem was: Riser wasn't one of those superstar ex-Feds who charged lawyers' numbers and hung out with the Commissioner, who wasn't just a friend but a personal rainmaker. No, Riser was what could only be called "a disgraced former cop." In fact, he had been called that in little known organs such as *The New York Times*. The *Post* had called him worse. He wasn't that disgraced cop who got drunk and left his gun on the sink in a men's room at a bar and only remembered it later when he woke up and it was gone. No, he wasn't that asshole. But he was like him.

He'd lost his gun in a slightly different way, on a slightly different drunk, and it had taken him three brutal days to get it back before it ended up gone for good or someone got shot with it. He hadn't had a drink stronger than coffee since then, but he also hadn't told his bosses while it was going down and then word had leaked out. And that was something a cop just didn't do. Then some grainy black-and-white security footage of him in a strip club acting in a manner unbecoming had emerged. So just after he'd recovered it, the NYPD had taken that gun away at the same time they'd taken his badge and had thanked him for coming and told him not to let the door hit him . . .

But that was then and this was now, and even though a cop who'd been stripped of his badge became invisible, that condition wasn't without its upsides. It went back to his question about the city and to whom it belonged. If certain people were asked, like those who lived between Sixtieth and Seventy-ninth, from Park to Fifth, they might say: Just us. When they saw someone like Riser, they saw a servant, or most likely they didn't see him at all. That's why it had been so easy to pick up a loose foot tail on Shelly Kipniss when he left his limestone mansion on Fifth and walked to the bank on Madison. Kipniss hadn't noticed Riser loitering around the table where deposit slips were filled out as Kipniss made a large cash withdrawal from the preferred client window. Riser wanted to be out on the street by the time Kipniss left the bank in order to resume his tail, but had gotten tangled up with some customers at the exit and actually ended up holding the door for his subject. Again, Kipniss hadn't really seen him. He thought it was his due that doors be held open for him as he went about town.

Riser followed Kipniss back to Fifth Avenue and a dozen blocks further south, to the Sherry-Netherland hotel, which Kipniss entered. He went to the desk, checked in and got a key, before disappearing into an elevator. Riser couldn't go up after him without attracting attention, so he dawdled around in the lobby and watched the floor counter as the elevator ticked its way up and stopped at eleven. Riser had an idea about what was coming. Rich men only checked into plush hotels just blocks from their homes for a few reasons, and it didn't look like Shelly Kipniss planned on jumping.

A few minutes later she crossed the lobby. Maybe twenty-two years old, she was five foot ten, one hundred-and-fifteen pounds with a whippet's body and a mane of mahogany hair. She wore a tan raincoat even though it wasn't raining and dark Jackie Os. She'd seen *Breakfast at Tiffany's* a few too many times, it seemed, but likely hadn't read it. She crossed to the elevator while the desk staff studiously looked the other way. It didn't take a clairvoyant to know the car would be stopping at eleven, and it did. There was no need to wait, it was going to be about two hours, because her kind had a minimum, so Riser went out and found himself a little café and bought a French press and a prosciutto panini that cost him a quarter of an hour's wages.

He was waiting on the corner ninety-five minutes later when the young lady emerged from the hotel, with slightly bed-ruffled hair, and undoubtedly four thousand dollars the richer for her trouble. She belted her trench coat and disappeared into the back of a black Uber car. Five minutes later Kipniss emerged looking steam cleaned and pressed with an expression of Dalai Lama calm on his face. Riser trailed the man to his office, and the hard part was done.

There were only two agencies in the city that provided the level of talent that Riser had seen, and he knew them both and their price. He'd been authorized plenty of slush to spread around in order to get the girl's name. The story hit the *Post* six days later, their photographer having camped out and gotten shots of both parties leaving the Netherland after a repeat performance. "Married Mayor Wannabe Sacked," read the headline, and the *News*'s "Shelly Caught With His Pants Down." The girl's name was Natalie. She was shocked and horrified to be revealed as an escort; she'd had plans to be a Knicks City Dancer. She liked Shelly, she admitted, but not the hard spankings he was partial to dishing out and receiving, nor the fact that he smelled like old feet. She had recently gotten engaged and had a new lingerie line to announce. Kipniss's run for mayor was dead in the starting gate.

RISER'S FRENCH PRESS WAS DONE and deposited in a garbage can by the time he was through the mid-sixties and had cut right, toward his answer to the riddle that was New York City: the Windsor Whist. The Windsor Whist was a fancy card club housed in a stately brownstone and populated by a moneyed set of what used to be called blue haired ladies. The old manse had a bar and a dining room that he couldn't frequent, not being a social member; it had that old cage elevator that ran from the lobby to the fifth floor, and there was a little spiral staircase that led up to his digs on the sixth. The place had high ceilings, and marble floors and fire places in most every room and was maintained by a half-dozen attendants all in bright green jackets cut down at the waist, with gold buttons and silk lapels, that had them looking like refugees from a Hollywood back lot in the 1950s. And then there was Rodman at the front, who was kind enough to give him a ring when trouble was coming up and always laughed when Riser congratulated him for winning the Master's.

Riser entered the club and gave Rodman a nod while moving through some of the duplicate players whose bridge games had just broken up. Fifteen years younger than the average member, male, and less than perfectly dressed, Riser stood out and caught some quizzical looks. Not everyone knew there were offices on six above the card rooms. Management had certain restrictions on his space, like no more than three meetings a week attended by no more than three outside people. It limited who would take the space but didn't present a problem for Riser who only wished he had that much business walking in. He had a suspicion that they liked a man in the security field on the premises, so they put up with him. He headed to the elevator when Rodman told him: "Elevator is being serviced. The guy is upstairs." The thing was a hundred years old, it was always being serviced. Riser gave Rodman a shrug and took to the stairs. Five flights and then the spiral staircase; fortunately he still had the legs for it. As he ascended, he passed the main card room on two, which had a few tables going.

"That's a dog's life for you, Janet," one of the doyennes announced to her partners, and Riser knew they were playing Knock-Out Whist, which was perhaps the most popular game spread at the club. He took a look inside and saw the old ladies, vicious as bull terriers, playing for pennies but acting like it was their entire estate. It was a pretty simple plain trick card game, Knock-Out Whist was. The Brits called it Trumps. The players are dealt seven cards and the uppermost undealt card is turned over and that indicates the trump suit. The highest trump wins each trick, and the players keep on with six cards in their hand, and then fewer and fewer. A player who takes no tricks at all in a hand is eliminated, is dealt no more cards, and takes no further part in the game, which was a pretty painful condition for the old gals. Getting put out seemed to hurt them even more than losing their money. The exception is the first player during the game that takes no tricks on a hand; she's not knocked out immediately but is awarded a "dog's life," or a second chance—which was what Riser supposed everyone was looking for—and gets to keep playing. It goes on from there. The rest of the rules, if they matter, can be found in Hoyle's. The winner of the trick on the final hand wins the game. Or if all but one of the players is knocked out before this, the surviving player is the winner. Surviving, that was the thing.

Riser climbed the spiral staircase and reached the landing to his office and was glad he'd quit smoking. Then he heard a man's voice speaking Dominican-accented Spanglish too loudly. He entered his office, and discovered it was occupied by the elevator repairman. There was a little locked trapdoor behind his desk that housed the elevator mechanicals, so Riser saw plenty of the repairmen over the last few years, though he'd never met this one before. They were usually expert technicians who kept the intrusion to a minimum, did their jobs and moved on. But not this time. No, this time the burly, sweaty guy barking into his cell phone wasn't really working at all. Instead he was sitting in Riser's desk chair and picking his fingernails with a letter opener while conducting his call through headphones. The gent had the name JOSE embroidered on the pocket of his grease-stained work shirt and didn't acknowledge Riser's presence whatsoever.

Live in New York long enough and you'll see all kinds, Riser thought, then crossed to the man, delicately relieved him of the letter opener and let it clunk to his desk. "Jose" looked up, seeming to notice Riser for the first time.

"Well?" Riser said.

Put out, the man got up out of the chair and went back to the trapdoor, sticking his head into the shaftway, but continuing his call.

"*Ai, mama guevo.* What do you mean 'who's that?' Some fucking guy, that's who," he said, taking out a vise grip pliers. "You just worry about you. I'm going out tonight and I'll see you late. I said: I'll see you fucking late, *cuero.*" The man clicked off the call.

"*Hijo de la gran puta,*" he said to himself, and then louder, for Riser's benefit, "fucking bitches, you know?"

"Jose" was some piece of work. Riser just shook his head, crossed his arms, and watched in silence for ten minutes while the man checked and adjusted the sheave, motor, counterweight, and cables, hoping the repairman felt the glare on his back. "Why you gots to eye bang me? I'll be done in a sec," he said.

Finally, the man pulled his head out of the shaft and closed the door, leaving a grease smudge on the paint. He noticed but left it, instead wiping his hands on his shirt and putting his tools away in a satchel.

"Yo, bro," the man said, as if he had nowhere else to be, "you live here or what?"

"No," Riser said. Technically, according to the terms of his lease, Riser could not and did not use his office as a dwelling.

"Okay, bro, whatever you say . . ."

"You have a point?"

"I saw that pillow and blanket on the couch and shit."

"Maybe I like to take naps."

"Isn't that sweet," he said, and then muttered "*pajero . . .*"

Riser was familiar enough with Dominican slang to know that he'd just been branded an onanist.

"You all set?" he asked, the invitation to leave clear in his tone.

"Thing's a piece of shit," the repairman said, "but yeah, it's all set."

He trundled down the stairs leaving Riser alone. Despite the boorish manner, the repairman had sized up the situation correctly. Riser lived there alright and had for the past two-and-a-half years. The office space had once been the porter's quarters, when there were such things as live-in porters. It had a tiny stall shower in the bathroom and a kitchenette with a full-sized refrigerator and a microwave. Riser would exit the club around closing time and make his way back later, when it was empty. He slept on the couch, and would be out in the morning before the staff arrived, so they could see him show up each morning. He took most of his meals out and his shirts went back and forth to the cleaner's in his briefcase. He'd even had a lady or two up for a visit when fortune smiled upon him. The system was a bit labored, but he had one rent and he'd been able to make it so far and he got to be right in the middle of it all. That's when Rodman had called to warn him about the pair coming up for him and he'd lit out.

RISER MADE THE STREET, CHECKING his impulse to run because it would cause him to stand out too much, and went north on Madison two blocks toward the Gucci store, where he intended to cut left and disappear into the park. It was a solid plan and he felt good about it, right up until he felt a hand, heavy and strong, on the back of his neck. The hand spun him around and drove him into the window of a high-priced optical shop.

"Who do you work for?" the big man asked. The garlic on his breath suggested he'd eaten Italian for lunch.

"Who do you?" Riser asked, though he knew the answer. This was Kipniss trying to find out which of his foes had gotten him. Riser wondered for a moment whether a deskman at the Netherland had described him or if it was the madam at the agency who'd sold him out and collected a second payday. But the hand on his throat chased away his musings.

"I'm doing the asking," the man said. "Who do you work for?"

"We all serve God and the IRS, don't we?" Riser said, but the man wasn't going in for bright repartee. Then the other half of the team loped around the corner, spotted them, and slowed to a menacing walk. Up close, the men were twin towers of beef, each well over six feet tall and north of two hundred pounds.

"Look, we can pay you off or hurt you, but you're going to tell us," the man holding him said. "What are you holding out for anyway, what would the guy really do for you?"

He made a good point. Lewinter wouldn't stamp him out if he passed by and Riser were smoldering. He could also use the cash. On the other hand it was a question of honor, the old vintage. There were still a few bottles of it left around, and once it was uncorked, it was sticky stuff.

"There are just some things a gal doesn't talk about," Riser said, wondering for how much longer he'd have teeth. The man let Riser's arm brush against the gun at his waist.

"You want to tell me now, or should I do it right here in the street?" the man offered. That was when Riser saw one of those uniformed Upper East Side guards who walk around with walkie-talkies in order to make the shoppers feel safe. Riser took his chance and slumped for a moment, as if his will had been broken, before ripping his arm free and cutting over to the guard.

"Excuse me, sir, can you tell me where the Hermes store is?" The guard pointed and started to explain. "Maybe you can show me, I'm not too strong with directions." The guard shrugged and started walking with Riser, who was steering him by the elbow.

The pair of hired men bumped past them and gave Riser a hard look. "You're a dead man the next time we meet, Riser," the one who hadn't previously spoken said. Riser believed him.

The guard's eyes bulged.

"Just some old fraternity buddies," Riser said with a smile that probably looked as weak as it felt, and he walked south with the guard for a few blocks before they reached the store and Riser peeled off.

BACK IN HIS OFFICE AN hour later, Riser sat and sipped his coffee, which had gone cold, and felt alone. He needed a drink, and a rent-controlled apartment, a week at the beach, and a good retirement plan and protection. What he had was an office with a couch and some wits. He hoped they'd be enough. He had an idea and a call to make. He made it and was still sitting there an hour and a half later, as afternoon came and went, when his phone rang like bad news.

It was Rodman from downstairs. "Those friends of yours are coming up again."

"Are you sure?"

"They're in the elevator now."

"You're positive?"

"Saw them get in myself."

"Alone?"

"Just the two of them."

Riser hung up, stood, and worked quickly. He wasn't running this time.

There is a legendary story from the late seventies, perhaps apocryphal, when the rock band the Eagles was at the height of its fame. At an after-show party, Joe Walsh pushed a grand piano out a hotel's penthouse window on a lark, because he "wanted to know what it sounded like when it landed." The band's manager cleaned up the ensuing mess so efficiently that it was barely reported. The crash downstairs at the Whist was stupendous as well. It shook the building louder than when the rich guy in the townhouse next door did demolition to put a swimming pool in his basement. There may not have been any strings or keys inside the elevator, but the noise was musical to Riser just the same.

RISER WENT DOWN THE STAIRS, slipping his tension tool and lock pick and grease-stained handkerchief back into his pocket. He'd watched very closely when old "Jose" had done his work earlier. Riser shook his head at the mess in the lobby and went out and got himself a French press. He took his walk on Fifth, along the park, and sipped his coffee as the sun dropped behind the trees.

As he walked, Riser pulled out his cell phone and dialed Shelly Kipniss's office.

"Tell him it's Jerry Riser," he said to the executive assistant, and lo and behold, Kipniss took the call.

"Yes?"

"Surprise," Riser said.

"What do you want?" Kipniss asked, his voice flat and tight.

"When this gets looked into and the reports are written up, they're going to find that the maintenance on that elevator hadn't been done correctly. The governor cable was disconnected and the motor failed, which left the brake off."

"I see."

"Yeah, modern elevators have lots more redundancies, but this one was an oldie. It was a tragedy waiting to happen," Riser said. The tech was surely going to lose his license. It was a real shame.

"And now?" Kipniss asked, livid.

"You're not going to learn what you were hoping to, not from me. Now, I know a man like you isn't accustomed to not getting what he wants, but this time you'd better get used to it. When the cops track me down and ask what your men were doing in my building I can tell them one of two things, depending on whether you leave me alone: one is the truth, about everything, right up until the *accident . . .*"

"Or?" Kipniss asked. That was pretty much it. After Riser told him, the line went dead. He and Kipniss were done with one another.

WHEN THE COPS FINALLY CAUGHT up with him later that night to ask why the pair of dead men in the elevator had been coming to see him, Riser had his answer:

"Job interview."

He had phoned Kipniss's firm and applied for a job in security that very afternoon, right after the men had come and threatened to kill him on the street, and if the call hadn't been logged, that was okay, because he'd gotten the names of the receptionist and the HR person to whom he'd spoken.

Riser didn't imagine Lewinter would be coming to him with more work anytime soon. He got things done, but he was going to be too hot for the near future. Maybe word about what had happened would leak in the right way, though, and another whale with a problem would give him a call. He sipped his coffee and walked. Deep down Riser believed the city belonged to everyone, if they could survive it. Surviving, that was the thing. He may have been just hanging on, but at least he was doing it in the best place in the world.

THE LADY UPSTAIRS
BY JILL D. BLOCK

IF I'D LEARNED NOTHING ELSE in my twenty-seven years on this planet, I'd learned that when someone gives you something totally unexpected and undeserved, you don't ask questions. Just smile, say thank you, and take it quick, before they change their mind. So when the flight attendant leaned over and whispered discreetly that there was a seat for me in first class, I just smiled, said thank you, and followed her to the front of the plane.

I smiled at the old guy next to me as I sat down and told my new best friend yes, I would love a glass of champagne, thank you. Then I settled back to watch the safety demonstration. Oh yeah, the finer things. I could get used to this.

An hour or so into the flight, Old Guy Next to Me introduced himself as George Rothstein, and asked me if I was coming or going. I must have looked at him like a total moron, so he asked again, patiently, if California was home, or New York? Oh, right. I get it. I told him that I was on my way home from my cousin's kid's bar mitzvah. He was also on his way home. He had been in Los Angeles on business, real estate. He asked me what line of work I was in. I couldn't come up with a glamorous lie, so I told the truth. Social work, autism study, art therapy. The truth was, I spent most of my days trying to connect with kids who wouldn't look at me or speak to me. It was like babysitting for kids who hated me.

He seemed really interested in me, which was maybe a little creepy, but flattering. I assumed that unlike me he'd actually paid for his first-class ticket. And he was wearing a nice suit, and I was pretty sure his big gold watch was real. So I decided to go with the flow. Who knew, maybe he could be my sugar daddy.

He asked about my family, where I grew up, where I had gone to school. When he asked me where I lived, I told him about my apartment in Chelsea. It was a tiny studio, a fifth floor walk-up. The shower leaked and half of the outlets didn't work. I left out the part about the scary black stuff growing in the corner of the bathroom. I told him it was an illegal sublet and I had to be invisible, so I couldn't get anything fixed. Any day now, I was going to have to give up and find a new place.

He asked if I wouldn't be happier in a larger place with a doorman. Well yeah, sure. He explained that he owned a building on Sixty-second Street, between Madison and Park. He said he only rented to his friends, something about keeping the apartments full so he could convert the building once it became empty. Which actually didn't make any sense to me, but I figured he must know what he was doing. He asked me how much I was paying in rent and said that I could have a one-bedroom apartment in his building for what I was paying for my shithole.

Don't ask questions. Just smile, say thank you, and take it quick, before they change their mind. I said yes.

So I called the number on the business card he'd given me, and a week later I met the lady from the management company. Three weeks after that I moved in.

It was a great apartment, a grown-up apartment—a real one bedroom with a big living room, a separate dining room, and a kitchen you could cook in, if you were so inclined. And I had a real lease, with my name on it. But they also had me sign a letter that said that the landlord could relocate me to another apartment within the building at will, and could terminate the lease on ninety days' notice, "For any reason or for no reason at all." Sure, whatever.

I felt like I was too young and too broke to belong. It was a neighborhood for rich people. Ladies who lunched, who got their hair done and wore stockings, even on the weekend. Housekeepers in uniforms walking fussy dogs. Jamaican nannies pushing white babies in fancy strollers. Black cars with drivers idling on the street, waiting to pick up kids to take them to school in the morning. Then there was me, in jeans and a hoodie, stomping down Sixty-second Street in my Doc Martens.

And the building! It was weird enough that there was a guy opening the door for me and asking if I needed a taxi. But an elevator man? That was just ridiculous. I was used to being invisible, and here I was, all of a sudden, living my life with an audience. These guys saw me coming and going. They were going to know every time I ordered in, if I didn't leave my apartment all weekend, when I stumbled home late at night, or worse, early in the morning.

I felt self-conscious each time I went in or out. Did they wonder where I was going? Did they compare notes about me, talk among themselves? Did they notice how often I picked up a pizza on my way home, and did they know that I some-times ate the whole thing in one night?

One thing about that building, you couldn't be anony-mous. Everyone pretty much knew everyone else. There were the rent-controlled tenants, who were old and had lived there forever, and then there were the people who had moved in within the past few years and had some kind of connection to Mr. Rothstein. His banker lived next door to me, with her husband and kids. One of the guys in 3A had decorated the Rothsteins' house in Connecticut. And I heard that his grand-son's math tutor lived on the sixth floor. I guess we'd all signed the secret letter, so that when the oldtimers someday moved on, we would all get kicked out and Mr. Rothstein would have his vacant building.

It was about a month after I moved in when I first noticed Margaret. It was cold out and raining. My shoes were soaked and my umbrella was dripping all over the floor as I walked through the lobby. She was sitting on a folding chair in the back, by the elevator. I thought maybe she was homeless, that the building guys were being kind, letting her stay warm and dry on a terrible night. Which was nice, but weird. Hey, who was I to judge? She smiled at me, so I smiled back.

Once I'd noticed her that first time, I saw her all the time. Not every day, but at least once or twice a week. She some-times rode up and down in the elevator, or else she sat in that little chair in the back of the lobby, or she hung out up front by the doorman. It turned out that she lived in the building, that she was the only tenant on the top floor. She'd been liv-ing there for something like fifty years.

She was old. Seventies maybe? Eighties? She was tall and thin, stooped over and looked very frail. You could see her veins through her skin. Everything about her was gray—her skin, her eyes, her lips, her long straggly hair. It was like all of the color had been sucked out of her. She wore a shapeless faded cotton dress, or maybe it was a nightgown. From the looks of things she had nothing on underneath it. She wore a beat-up pair of bedroom slippers. She had a big, baggy sweater that she wrapped herself in when it was cold outside.

I knew that she was harmless, but something about her made me feel like I needed to keep my distance. Like if I got too close I might end up like her someday. I started taking the stairs when I went out, to avoid her in case she was in the elevator, sitting on that little bench, riding up and down. Coming down the street on my way home, I would dread that she would be in the lobby when I came in. She seemed so lonely. Just seeing her felt like a burden.

But I have to admit, I was also curious about her. I tried to guess what her story was. I imagined her in the faded and dusty penthouse apartment, where once upon a time she and her husband had thrown swanky dinner parties with butlers and a uniformed staff. Or maybe she had been the mistress of some rich and powerful man. Was she a secret millionaire? Or was she eating ramen noodles for dinner? I figured she must have some kids and grandkids someplace, and I wondered if they ever came to visit. It seemed weird and sad that she didn't at least have some kind of nurse or aide to keep her company. I wondered if she had a cat.

For months I managed to avoid ever saying a word to her, to just give her a smile and keep moving. But eventually she wore me down. If she was in the lobby when I got home, it started to feel like she'd been waiting for me. She would comment on the weather, or ask me about my day, sometimes following me into the elevator. This was a challenge—if I didn't time it right, and finish my sentence just as we got to my floor, she would get off the elevator with me so we could finish our conversation. I would stand with her in the hallway, talking outside my door.

What was the etiquette here? Was I supposed to ask her in, offer her some leftover Chinese? See if maybe she wanted to watch *Jeopardy* with me? It took me a while before I figured out that I could just end the conversation when I wanted to. That I could deal with her like I dealt with my kids at work—I would just tell her, *Okay, I am going to go now,* and go inside while she stood there and stared at me. It felt pretty terrible, but how exactly had she become my problem? Where was everyone else? I was still new here, practically still a kid. Why did I wind up with the lady from upstairs?

One day she was in the lobby when I got home. I'd had a crappy day, and just wanted to go upstairs, change my clothes, and chill out for a little while. I was barely in the door when she handed me a letter and asked me to read it. Yeah, okay fine. It was from Rothstein Real Estate. Addressed to Ms. Margaret Sherman. So that was her name. They were offering to relocate her, at the landlord's expense, to a one-bedroom apartment on the seventh floor so they could start renovating the tenth floor. We stood in the hall outside my apartment and she told me that she didn't want to move, that she couldn't possibly move.

Seriously? I really didn't have time for this.

She was upset. She seemed frightened, desperate. So I let her come inside and I made her a cup of tea. I felt like I should offer her something to eat, but all I had was an open bag of pretzels sitting on the counter, and that just didn't feel right. Plus, if I fed her I was afraid she might never leave. I reread the letter and saw again how freaked out she was.

So I got into social worker mode. It was just an offer, I told her. You have a lease, right? They were just asking—you don't have to agree. They said that they would pay for the move—you won't have to do anything. I tried to stop myself, but I heard myself telling her I could help her find someone who could come and take the stuff she didn't need, the furniture or whatever that wouldn't fit into a smaller apartment. I don't know if she was even listening to me. She just kept saying how terrible it was, how unfair, how they were taking advantage of her. I wondered if it would help for me to call my airplane buddy, George.

I left her in my apartment and went down to the lobby. I got the doorman to give me the key, and then I went back and got her. We went upstairs together to look at the new apartment. It was fine, freshly painted, a lot like mine. She just kept shaking her head. It wasn't possible. They couldn't do this to her. They couldn't push her out of her home. It was all she had. So I asked her to show me her place.

Whoa. Let's just say, it was not what I was expecting. The tenth floor was not the penthouse. It was an SRO floor: single room occupancy. Eight tiny rooms with an old kitchen that looked like it hadn't been used in years, and a bathroom at the end of the hall. Seven of the rooms were empty, with their doors removed. She unlocked her door, two locks, and I followed her in. Her room was tidy, but absolutely crammed full of stuff. She had a twin bed, a table and a lamp, a wooden chair, and a chest of drawers. And lots and lots of boxes and shopping bags. I don't know what was in the boxes, but the shopping bags looked like they were mostly filled with other shopping bags. No pictures. No television. No books. It was no wonder she hung out in the lobby. It was the most depressing thing I had ever seen.

I had to get out of there. She had to get out of there. So first I tried tough love. This is not a good way for you to live. The other apartment is better. You'll be more comfortable there. She said I didn't understand. Well, yeah, that was certainly true. I realized that this was going to be a process, and it was going to require some patience. I told her that she didn't have to decide anything yet, that she should just think about it for a day or two. When I stood up to leave, she grabbed my hand and didn't let go. It made me wonder when was the last time she'd been touched. I took the stairs back to my apartment where I turned on the television and tried not to think about Margaret upstairs in her little room.

When I got home from work four days later, the doorman told me that Ms. Sherman had passed. That's what he said—that she'd passed. He said that when building guys realized that none of them had seen her for a few days someone went up to check on her. The door was chained on the inside, so they called the cops, who busted down the door. She was dead in her bed. The ambulance guy told him that it appeared that she had taken a bunch of Benadryl, tied a plastic bag over her head, and gone to sleep.

She fucking killed herself.

I should have been nicer to her. I should have offered to call Mr. Rothstein. I could have sat with her, talked to her. I should have let her tell me about herself. I should have given her a hug. I shouldn't have left her sitting there.

A week later the doorman said he that had something for me, and handed me a shopping bag from Galeries Lafayette in Paris. He said that they'd been clearing out Margaret's room and they found it with my name on it. It was heavy. I took it upstairs and put it down on the table. I poured myself a glass of wine and looked at the bag for a long time before I opened it. I wondered when she'd been to Paris.

There was an envelope inside the bag, sitting on top of the tissue paper, with my name written on it. The note inside was on a piece of expensive-feeling stationery with her name engraved on the top. In perfect old lady penmanship it said "Thank you for being a friend." Jesus, Margaret, really? Now I am going to have the Golden Girls theme song stuck in my head for a week. And then I remembered that she was dead.

The tissue paper was so old, it cracked when I touched it. Wrapped inside it was an Hermes Kelly Bag. Red. Alligator or crocodile or something. It was old, and you could tell it had been used, but also that it had been cared for. It was real. It was so beautiful it glowed. And it was mine.

I looked up, toward the tenth floor or heaven. I smiled, and said thank you.

MIDNIGHT IN THE PARK WITH HARRY
BY JANE DENTINGER

ONLY CRIMINALS AND MADMEN WALK into Central Park after midnight . . . or, occasionally, an actor. Harry Dillon was the latter. And he didn't mean to do it, but he had no choice. Harry had been "between engagements" for a *very* long time. So when he was cast in Shakespeare in the Park's production of *A Midsummer Night's Dream*, manna fell upon his actor's heaven.

He was cast as Flute, one of the mechanicals who perform the *Pyramus and Thisbe* play-within-a-play for the king's wedding banquet. Flute plays Thisbe, so Harry got to do Shakespearian drag, which is a rare, fun thing for an actor. Better yet, Flute is pretty much an idiot. Harry liked playing idiots. He felt comfortable in their skin somehow. But best of all, he got to do Stan Laurel. That's who he based his Flute on.

As a kid, Harry loved Laurel and Hardy the way his more athletic friends loved Mantle and Maris. Sure, the baseball stars could hit, catch, and run like demons. But could they do a slow-burn take like Hardy? Could they do Laurel's scrunched up I'm-about-weep-but don't-want-to face? Nah. As

Oliver Hardy once said, "We're always on the same page . . . and it's totally blank."

So that's how Harry played Flute, as the blankest page ever unwritten upon. And it was working. It helped that he had Laurel's thin, wiry physique, and mobile, hang-dog face. And he was getting more laughs every night. He was even getting fans.

This was a first for him; finding people outside the Delacorte Theater dressing rooms after the show—some of them girls!—who wanted to shake his hand, pat him on the back, and say ridiculously nice things like, "Dude, you are, like, Steve Martin stupid-funny!"

It was very gratifying. It would've given most actors a big head. But not Harry. He just wasn't built that way. He was that rare anomaly in the theater . . . a modest nerd. But he was grateful. So every night, he stuck around after the show and thanked every single person who came by to pay his or her respects. Because, hell, who knew when, if ever, he'd get another gig this good.

And that's why Harry was often the last person to leave the Delacorte. Other, more important actors would arrange to meet friends later at bars, restaurants, or someone's swanky apartment. Harry had no head for drink, couldn't afford fancy restaurants, and lived in a small studio apartment in Alphabet City with an ancient, mangy cat named Murgatroyd—a cat he'd inherited from his ex-girlfriend, Jeri, who had moved out after telling him, "Harry, I don't mind that you're not famous. I don't even mind that you're not rich. But, damn! You're an actor—you're supposed to be *hot*!"

That was almost three years ago and Harry had felt tepid ever since. Part of the problem was his eyesight—which was lousy. In his daily life, he wore the kind of glasses that Michael

Caine wore as Harry Palmer in *The Ipcress Files*. Caine's Harry had worn those glasses with an effortless élan. Harry Dillon wore them as what they really were—coke bottles. But that wouldn't do for his acting career, so he'd spent much time and money he could ill afford to get state-of-the-art contact lenses, really *amazing* contact lenses . . . and one of them had just popped out in the dressing room.

So after his fellow actors had left, after the audience had left, after even the stage crew had left, Harry was still on his hands and knees, like Helen Keller in *The Miracle Worker*, feeling the floor for his lost lens. Helen would have had better luck than Harry. The lens was nowhere to be felt or found. Worse still, Harry had forgotten to bring his glasses along that night.

He was going to have to walk out of the Park with one good eye only. And alone.

Or so he thought.

"MANNY, GEEZ, I GOTTA TAKE a leak, man!"

"So what? Damn, Jo, it's Central Park, asshole. The world's your toilet."

"Well, yeah, I know . . . but I don't wanna, you know, show my stuff."

"Show your stuff? Are you fuckin' crazy? It's black as your ass in here. And there's bushes every damn where."

"Oh, sure, I know that. But ya know, ya hear stuff . . . like what if there's a faggot hiding in one a those bushes, man?"

Thirteen-year-old Manny Ruiz plopped down on a nearby bench and gave a heavy sigh. Clearly his incipient life of crime was not going as smoothly as he'd planned.

"Jo-Jeff, how damn out of it are you? Don't you know those queers can marry each other now? Why the hell would they want your skinny black ass?"

Joseph Hardy Jefferson, two years Manny's senior, but his junior in most ways, slumped down beside his friend and said, "Yeah, I know that—but ya hear things, know what I mean?"

"Oh, fuggedaboutit. You down for this action or not, man?"

"Yeah, no—I mean yeah, I'm down for it, Manny."

"Good! So keep your eyes open for an easy mark—then we roll him, right?"

"Yeah . . . right."

BUT JO-JEFF WASN'T SO SURE. It had sounded like a good plan when they were up on the roof of their building, feeding Manny's pigeons and smoking some of his brother's weed. They could hear the ugly fight going on below in Manny's apartment as his parents went toe to toe about all the same old shit.

Jo-Jeff was kind of amazed that Manny's parents hadn't managed to kill each other . . . yet. While Manny, for his part, was mildly surprised that Jo's mother, a single woman on welfare with two kids, hadn't opted for throwing herself off that same roof. God knows she'd threatened to enough times.

This was how they had grown up together—in families with too little money and way too much angst and rage. They were both sick of it. And Manny had figured the way out—money.

So they had taken the subway from the Bronx down to West Eighty-sixth Street at a late hour. Manny knew about the free Shakespeare plays in the Park. In fact, he'd even gone to one once with a teacher who had actually cared about her pupils . . . before the system broke her back. The play had been *Hamlet* and Manny had dug it, even when that crazy Ophelia bitch drowned herself.

But he'd been more interested in the audience. Because he could smell the money in the house. Afterward he watched the audience stream en masse out of the Park. Most of them heading westward, past the Diana Ross Playground, to hop on the C train or the M10 bus or grab cabs to places nicer, lovelier than he'd ever seen. But he'd also seen the stragglers, the ones who left later and by themselves.

That's what he was looking for now. A late-leaver with money. An easy mark.

Manny was slight and small for his age. But Jo-Jeff was tall and bulky. Normally Jo-Jeff wouldn't hurt a fly. But Manny thought he could change that. He knew how to get Jo-Jeff mad.

That's what he was counting on when he saw, from a distance, Harry Dillon leaving the Delacorte.

"Jo! That's him—that's our pigeon." Manny said, nodding toward Harry, who was now heading east.

"Uh, I dunno, Manny. He's kinda tall."

"So what? There's two a us and one a him. And he's headed toward the underpass. We can nail him there. C'mon!"

Harry Dillon liked the Greywacke Arch that ran beneath the road that went by the Metropolitan Museum of Art. It was a short tunnel, but it had great acoustics. That's why street singers always hung out there during the day.

He went up to the mouth of the tunnel, stuck his head in, and let loose with a few lines from *Othello*: "He who steals my purse, steals trash." Which, in Harry's case, was pretty much the truth.

Jo-Jeff grabbed Manny's arm. "Shit! He saw us coming. And he's tellin' us to back off."

Manny shook off Jo's grip and hissed, "He ain't seen nothing, man. He's just one a them crazy-ass actors. Move!"

But before he could get Jo-Jeff moving, Harry swung away from the tunnel and headed up the slope to the road above.

"Nope. He seen us." Jo-Jeff shook his head. "Thas why he's goin' for the road. He'll be outta the park in no time."

But Harry didn't head due east to walk out past the Met. Instead he turned south. And Manny grinned. "Aw, the dumb fuck, he's takin' a goddamn *stroll*. We got him."

However, there was a vague method to Harry's apparent madness. He wanted to walk by the Loeb Boathouse Restaurant. His old girlfriend waitressed there. He knew the restaurant was closed by now, but he also knew the wait staff often hung out after hours to kick back a few. Maybe Jeri would still be around. Maybe he'd get to see her. Maybe Jeri would even be glad to see him. Maybe.

And lo and behold, there *was* a dim light on in the bar area. Harry made a stealthy approach and peered through the glass door. Then he saw her.

Jeri was seated on one of the tall bar stools surrounded by four other people, all chatting and laughing like old war buddies, in the way that a wait staff does after surviving another night of diners who expect the New York restaurant "experience" to waft them to the heights of Valhalla.

She looks tired, Harry thought. And she did. Her auburn hair was matted with sweat and there were dark shadows under her blue eyes. But those eyes still danced with laughter as she tilted her impossibly cute, freckled nose up toward a guy with smooth, olive skin and jet-black hair—long hair that he wore in a ponytail.

"Aw, *no*, not a ponytail guy." Harry moaned. As someone who religiously checked for follicle loss every morning, he hated ponytail guys. They were just flaunting it. And Harry suddenly wanted to rip that particular ponytail out by its roots. The guy had one arm casually thrown around Jeri's shoulder. Harry knew that move and there was nothing truly casual about it.

Through the glass door, he could hear Mr. Perfect Olive-Skin say, "Oh, you *must* come, Jeri! Mah fren has zees great house in the Hamptons."

"Fuck the Hamptons! I hate the Hamptons," Harry seethed. "*She* hates the Hamptons. What's wrong with the goddamn Berkshires?"

But he couldn't hear Jeri's reply as she picked up a paper cocktail napkin to wipe sweat from her brow. That was one of the things he'd always loved about her. Jeri didn't do standard girlie stuff. She didn't powder her nose; she just wiped sweat off. God, it was so sexy. And that little waitress outfit with the black vest and string tie . . . oh, it was killing him!

He wanted to knock on the glass, get her attention, but Harry found himself frozen. What if she frowned, instead of smiled, when she saw him? He couldn't bear the thought. It would kill him.

So he backed away from the glass door and stumbled blindly toward the Boat Lake—but he bumped into one of the outdoor tables, which made a loud clanking noise. He could see the heads inside the restaurant jerk round. Then he ran.

And Manny and Jo-Jeff, who had been lurking in the shadows, ran after him.

It was just at this same moment that the statues in the Poets Walk began to move. Of course, they normally moved at this same hour, but it was never seen.

THE POETS WALK—OR THE LITERARY Walk, if you prefer—is the only intentional straight line inside Central Park's walls. Just south of the Naumburg Bandshell, it is framed by a glorious row of American elm trees that create a cathedral effect over the walk, which is punctuated with statues of Robert Burns, Walter Scott, and Fitz-Greene Halleck, William Shakespeare, and, oddly, at the southern end, Christopher Columbus.

The statues had been there for many, many decades—but Halleck's was the first to get antsy. You could hardly blame him. He had been the most renowned writer of his day—i.e. from 1790 to 1867. Not to mention the only American author on the Walk. Damnation, President Rutherford B. Hayes and his entire cabinet had come to unveil his statue to the acclaim of thousands in 1877! But after that—bupkis! Worse still, his statue didn't even rate one of those piddling green boards on plinths that stood before his literary fellows, describing their life and works in white knock-out print. No, the elitist Central Park Conservancy hadn't seen fit to give him even *that*.

So he spent his endless days watching passers-by pass him by with nary a glance. Or if they did deign to look his way, they'd squint to read his name on the pedestal and then mutter, "Fitz-Greene *who*?" Then shake their heads and move on. Or they'd mistake him for someone else. But the unkindest cuts came from tourists who misidentified him. One horse's ass from San Francisco had confidently told his family that he was James Fenimore Cooper. Egads—Cooper!

Now days no one remembered a word from his poem "Fanny" or, for that matter, anything else from his *Alnwick Castle* collection. Halleck blamed that drunken bastard Edgar Allan Poe, who'd said of "Fanny": "To uncultivated ears it is endurable, but to the practiced versifier it is little less than torture."

Oh, yes, Poe had died ignominiously—and deservedly, Halleck thought—in a gutter. But still people quoted "The Raven" and "Annabel Lee" and all his other sodden rot. And all those endless film adaptations! It was hard to bear. Harder still for Halleck was the company he kept: There was smug Robbie Burns, who every damn day heard some passerby quote, "The best laid schemes o' mice an' men/Gang aft agley." Who would ever imagine you could get such mileage out of a mouse! And Walter Scott and his damned *Ivanhoe* and *Rob Roy* . . . and, again, the movie deals that followed.

And then there was Shakespeare . . . the insufferable Bard of Avon. This was and had always been the hardest pill for Fitz-Greene to swallow—because Will, frankly, did not give a damn. Why should he? He had statues and busts of himself scattered all over the globe. Halleck had only his one statue in the Poets Walk.

That's why he had decided, some one hundred years ago, to rise from his granite pedestal and strut about at night. He had suffered from lumbago in his lifetime and being cast in stone hadn't helped matters. A little exercise was in order. And whom did it hurt, really? The Poets Walk was never much frequented at night. During the Depression, the desperate folks living in shanties in the Park were too hungry and miserable (or drunk) to pay heed. In the sixties, the hippies were too stoned to believe their psychedelic eyes. And of late, crack cocaine had made the matter moot. So, gradually, the other statues had begun to join Halleck for a midnight stroll—except Shakespeare, the damnable snob!

Of course, the two Scotsman, Robbie and Walter had hit it off right away, gleefully swapping haggis recipes. Their description of the haggis ingredients had so horrified Columbus that he had finally been forced to come off his stone throne to upbraid these literary nincompoops with, "You do na know nuthin' bout food! I'm gonna tell ya how to make a real nice Bolognese."

But still Shakespeare didn't move . . . until tonight.

While the other four were cavorting—well, cavorting isn't an apt description, not when you're made out of granite, let's say shuffling up and down the Poets Walk—Will, from his pedestal, sensed rather than saw Harry Dillon running up the steps from Bethesda Fountain.

Methinks an actor approaches, he thought. While there was nothing overtly theatrical about Dillon, the Bard could sense a fellow thespian from afar. And then he sensed something dire—the two youths sidling out of the shadows of the under- pass just as Harry was passing by the Bandshell. *And methinks he is pursued by villains!*

For his part, Harry had no idea he was being followed. He just wanted to put as much distance as possible between him- self and the image of Jeri with Ponytail Guy.

For their part, Manny and Jo-Jeff were having a harder time than expected keeping up with the long-legged actor as they fumbled in the pockets of their baggy pants for their box cutters. Manny had tried to score a zip gun ear- lier with no luck. And Jo-Jeff had tried to borrow his big brother's switchblade—that hadn't gone so well either. And he had the bruised ribs to show for it. So box cutters it would have to be.

MEANWHILE, HALLECK, BURNS, SCOTT, AND Chris Columbus were oblivious to the approaching trio. So Shakespeare whis- tled. (Well, again, you can't *really* whistle with stone lips. He made more of a slow, grating sound with his mouth. Still, it got their attention.)

"Huh?" Halleck stopped and looked up at Shakespeare. "My stars! Is that really you, William, deigning to address *us*?"

Columbus attempted to shake his head. "No, it canna be! He tinks we are too stupid-o to talk with."

But Robbie Burns wasn't so sure. "Nae, you're wrong, laddies. I ken our William finally has something to say to us!"

While Walter Scott, having been a baronet and so every bit Shakespeare's equal, if not his better, just snorted and said, "I doubt it will be of much interest."

Then Shakespeare slowly raised one arm and pointed toward the hastening Harry. "See what draws near, my friends. A lone man who knows not that Hell is on his heels!"

Now *this* Scott got. After all, he had also been a judge and sheriff-depute of Selkirkshire in his day. So he knew a thing or two about criminal behavior. But he also knew a thing or two about playwrights and, frankly, the one in front of him now had a tendency to overdramatize, Walter felt. *Let us not forget* Titus Andronicus, he thought.

Still he thought it best to take a gander, so he shifted his bulk around to face north and spied Harry Dillon on the run.

Yet Harry still didn't realize that there was real danger to run from. He was still lost in thoughts of his lost love. Robbie Burns was the first to pick up his vibe.

"Och, the poor man has no idea that he's doomed! His heart, t'is breakin', I ken. Do you not see?"

Halleck, who'd long ago ceded the poetic high ground to his cohorts, observed dryly, "I'd say it's more than his heart that'll be broken. Look at those ruffians coming up behind him! In a nonce, they'll jump his ass." (Fitz-Greene had also, despite himself, picked up street slang.)

IT WAS AT THIS MOMENT that Jo-Jeff grabbed Manny's elbow and said, "Slow down!"

Manny jerked his arm away and hissed, "You nuts? We almost got him!"

But Jo-Jeff had freakishly good night vision. He could see the unawares Harry, but he could also perceive something that was just *not right* ahead of him. "Uh, Manny, those statues—they're not where they s'posed to be."

"Huh?"

"They not, like, in place."

"Wha' the fuck! 'Course they are. They're fuckin' statues. They gotta be *in place*, man."

"I dunno, dude."

Of course, Jo-Jeff was right. But, in case you're wondering, it's no easy task for statues to just hop back up on pedestals. It takes some doing. Right now, the statues on the ground were, uh, playing Statues. They froze as they were, scattered around the revered William, and waited for matters to unfold.

For Harry Dillon, matters weren't so much unfolding as imploding. At least that's how his chest felt; he wasn't used to running long distances—or short ones, either. He wasn't one of those actors who spent time between auditions at the gym or jogging. So his flight from the Boathouse had left him winded, bent over, and gasping for breath.

When he finally managed to stand erect, he was vaguely aware that something was *off* on the Poets Walk. But he couldn't say what. His night vision wasn't the best and now, with only one contact lens in place, it was the worst. Still he sensed things were somehow amiss.

Well, sure they are, dummy. You're alone in Central Park, running away from Jeri. You're a damn fool . . .

"Sirrah, you are Fortune's fool if you tarry here a moment longer."

"What?" Harry clamped a hand over his contact lens-less eye and squinted.

There appeared to be a gray man with a high-domed forehead standing in front of him. From somewhere to his left, he heard another gravelly voice groan, "Oh, spare me. He's paraphrasing his own stuff. How trite!"

Harry spun round toward the other voice but he couldn't see Fitz-Greene, who was in the shadows. What he did see was a short figure hurtling toward him with an outstretched arm. At the end of that arm was a fist that held something ominous.

"I'm gonna *cut* you, sucka!" Manny cried. By now, he was just one hundred-and-thirteen pounds of pent-up frustration, out for blood and money. But even to his own ears, his voice sounded shrill rather than terrifying.

Jo-Jeff started to run after him, but he was stopped short by a deep voice with a funny accent intoning, "Ah, Man's inhumanity. Makes countless thousands mourn."

"Really, Robbie? You, too?" Halleck sighed as he started to lumber forward.

Harry Dillon was vaguely aware of figures shifting in the dark but he couldn't take his eyes off that arm and that fist and what it held. And he found he couldn't budge.

Son of a bitch, he thought. *That guy wants to kill me. I should do something.*

But before he could move, a cold, heavy hand clamped down on his shoulder and a voice said, "Move not. But speak the speech, I pray you, as I pronounce it to you . . . "

The rest of the words Harry heard, not with his ears, but oddly reverberating in his head. By now, he was pretty sure he was either A) Going to die or B) Losing his mind. So what did he have to lose by following directions? He shot his arm out, pointing toward the accelerating Manny and shouted, "Is that a dagger I see before me?"

Manny shouted back, "Bet your ass, mother fuc—"

Then Manny went down like a sack of bricks.

Drawing back one granite foot—the one Manny had just tripped over—Walter Scott smiled down at the unconscious would-be mugger and said, "How darest thou, then, to beard us lions in our den?"

"Oh, Scott, come *on!*" Halleck was hopping mad now, though actual hopping was out of the question. Upstaged again, he fumed at the others, "I am the *only* American amongst you and yet you leave me out. Come on, Christopher, don't you want to get your two lira in as well?"

Columbus, as was his wont, hadn't been paying the least attention. He'd been exploring. Now he slowly straightened up from a bent position with something small and white in his hand. "Look, fellas, I find'a the mushroom!"

Then his triumphant grin faded as he saw Jo-Jeff running toward them—not that Jo-Jeff wanted to. But Manny was on the ground, not moving. You don't leave a brother, not even one as bat-crap crazy as Manny Ruiz, lying on the ground with a bunch of . . . statues?

Columbus pointed toward Jo-Jeff and mildly pointed out, "I t'ink tha's one angry fella coming."

Then Halleck saw him coming, too, and knew that finally, *finally* his own moment was at hand. He nodded to his fellows, then pointed to Jo-Jeff and roared:

"Strike—till the last armed foe expires.

Strike—for your altars and your fires;

Strike—for the green graves of your sires!"

Jo-Jeff stopped and dropped his box-cutter as if it were a red-hot iron.

Burns nudged Scott and murmured, "That's nae half bad, is it?" And Walter agreed, "No, no, it's not. I'd forgotten his

Marco Bozzaris." Even Shakespeare admitted, "Good words and well spoken."

And Harry Dillon said, "Uh, I, ah, I think I'm going to . . ." Then he, too, hit the pavement in a dead faint.

In that instant, Joseph Hardy Jefferson, who had paid scant attention when they'd read *Hamlet* in class, but kind of liked the Mel Gibson version he saw once on TV, dimly recalled someone saying that there were more things in heaven and earth, Horatio, than are dreamt of in your philosophy. . . . This *had* to be one of those things.

So he raised both hands in the air and asked, "Is it okay with you dudes if I just drag my boy's bony ass outta here?"

The statues nodded once, as one. And Jo-Jeff hauled both his and Manny's ass as he'd never hauled ass before. When Manny finally came to, he was lying on a bench on the uptown A train next to his friend. He blinked several times and then asked, "Jo, what the hell happened?" Jo-Jeff just patted his shoulder, smiled and said, "Oh, man, we just been *schooled.*"

BUT WHEN HARRY DILLON CAME to, he was still on the pavement of the Poets Walk and there was a face looking down at him, but it wasn't made of stone. It was flesh and blood and lovely—it was Jeri's.

"Harry, *Harry*, can you hear me? Honey, are you alright?"

"Hmm? Yeah . . . I think so."

As Jeri's face came into focus, he saw that she was surrounded by her friends from the restaurant.

"Harry, I saw you at the Boat House. Why did you run away like that?" Jeri asked.

"Uh, you looked kinda busy."

"Busy?"

"I thought you were with . . . where's the guy with the pony tail?"

"Roberto?" One of the other girls gave a half-snort, half-laugh. "That wuss made a beeline for Fifth Ave as soon as we locked up."

"Really?" Harry raised himself up on his elbows and looked around. Sure enough Roberto was nowhere to be seen—and neither were the gray guys.

"What happened, dude?" one of the waiters, a tall fellow asked. "Did you get jumped or did you trip or what?"

"Never mind that," Jeri cut in. "Just help me get him to his feet. Can you walk, honey?"

At that instant, Harry Dillon felt he could walk, run, or jump tall buildings in a single bound. But the concerned look on Jeri's face prompted him to milk the moment just a tad.

"I think so." Harry put one arm around Jeri's shoulders as he grinned down at her. "Lead on, MacDuff."

"Oh, honey, you *know* that's a misquote." Jeri gave him that little smile that made her nose crinkle up. God, how that smile slayed him! Harry was in heaven now "You've told me so often enough."

"You're right, you're right," he agreed happily. "It's 'Lay on, MacDuff.'"

From somewhere off to his left, he thought he heard a soft voice sigh, "*Thank you.*"

It seemed the others had heard something as well for they all stopped for a second. The girl who had hooted at Roberto's wussiness, looked around, then waved a hand in the general direction of the now seated statues and asked, "Who are these guys anyway?"

"*Tch*, Madison, you are such an illiterate!" This from the tall waiter, who happened to be an English lit major at NYU.

"This is the Poets Walk. With the exception of Christopher Columbus down there at the end of the walk, these are all men of letters. Shakespeare is way over there to the left. To either side of us is Robert Burns and Sir Walter Scott."

"Alright, *enough*," Jeri said. "I need to get Harry home and in bed."

This was followed by a wave of lascivious chuckles as the group moved forward. But Madison held back and pointed to the statue of a man, seated on a chair and holding pen to paper.

"Okay, but who's *that* guy?"

The English lit major gave the statue a cursory glance then pronounced, "Oh, that's, uh . . . that's James Fenimore Cooper."

Harry Dillon's head was still a bit muzzy, but he could swear he heard a stony voice hiss, "Son of a *bitch*!"

OLD HANDS
BY ERIN MITCHELL

"You have an old soul."
"I'm not sure about that, but I definitely have old hands."

LUNCH IS ALWAYS INTERESTING. I sit on the same bench in a relatively quiet corner of Central Park most days with a book and my sandwich because I have to get out of the store, away from the squawking, yipping, mewling . . . not to mention the smells. I must look approachable, because usually at least one of the homeless men wandering by will have a pithy comment or three. I've gotten good at responses that are dismissive without being rude. The Soul Man, for example, had no comeback for my *hands* retort, and shuffled off muttering about pigeons.

This isn't where I intended to be. Killing a person has a funny way of getting your life off-track.

Don't misunderstand . . . I'm not a glamorous or interesting hitwoman. I have no idea how a silencer works, wouldn't know how to buy a gun if my life depended on it, and I don't collect stamps. I'm kind of dowdy; my most attractive feature, my Dublin accent, is fading fast into a typical New York twang. I've spent my entire life taking directions from those in positions more powerful than my own.

I was a nurse. Technically, I still am; my license is good for life, and my registration has another year before it expires. But I hadn't deliberately chosen nursing so much as I'd fallen into it by default, and my illustrious career ended when Mr. Richards took his last breath. I gave him the right painkiller—but the wrong dose. I had glanced at the chart, filled the syringe, and with all the efficiency in the world, depressed the plunger into his IV. He was dead within minutes.

There was a morbidity and mortality conference, of course. The resident gave his presentation, after which it was abundantly clear that the mistake was mine. The order was correct, but I had misread it. When I met with the HR woman who was trying just a little bit too hard, she explained that I would get a reprimand. The Incident would be recorded in My File.

"But given that you've never had something like this happen before, we don't see the need to take any further action."

"Really?"

"Yes. You seem surprised."

"I am. I mean, I expected to be fired. I *should* be fired."

"We don't see it that way."

"I was negligent. A man died. It was my fault. How else is there to see it?"

"These situations are always difficult. We have a counselor we'd recommend you talk to."

Instead of making an appointment with the counselor, I used the typewriter at the nurses' station to prepare my resignation—it only took a few minutes thanks to typing skills courtesy Sister Lamb at St Mary's Holy Faith—and slipped it under HR's door before leaving that night.

I grabbed a newspaper on the way home and saw a help-wanted ad for a small pet store on West Seventy-first. I figured I could handle furry and scaled creatures. The owner of the store is eighty if he's a day, and he was impressed by my credentials so he hired me on the spot, and now I spend my lunch hour here.

"WHAT ARE YOU READING?"

"A book."

"Which one?"

"One from the library."

"Is it *The Joy Luck Club*?"

"No."

"Have you read that? Seems to be all the rage."

"No."

"*No* as in not the rage, or *no* as in you haven't read it?"

At this point, I looked up, because it seemed this particular pesterer wasn't going to meander away any time soon. Much to my surprise, it was the physician who had been the attending on Mr. Richards's case. Almost a year older and sporting longer hair than I recalled, but definitely the same guy.

"What do you want?" I believe in getting right to the point.

"It's been a while. I was wondering how you are."

"Why? And how did you find me?"

"Because you had a traumatic experience, and then you disappeared. And the phonebook. If you're hiding, you're not very good at it."

"Bullshit. The phonebook doesn't list my work address."

"No, but your neighbor was happy to tell me where the store is. And the old guy there told me you'd be here."

"Go away." Again, the point.

"Have dinner with me."

"No."

"Look, I've been worried about you. You shouldn't have quit. You're an excellent nurse."

"Excellent nurses don't kill patients."

"It was a mistake. They happen. It's horrible, but they do. Hell, I wrote the order, and I know my handwriting is not always clear."

"That's an understatement, but you're no different from any other doctor. It was my responsibility to double-check if it wasn't clear."

He looked like he was getting ready to either babble or lecture. "I miss seeing you around, talking with you, and—"

"Fuck off."

So much for witty retorts. But I'd had enough. As much as I hated to, I stood up, ready to cut short my precious lunch hour by a few minutes and head back to the shop.

"Have dinner with me."

"No." As I started down the path toward the sidewalk, I stepped in a pile of gray goo. It might have once been food or even a bird, but now it was just . . . slippery.

And slip I did, forward, right onto my knees. My book— *Lullaby*, as it happened—went flying. In that instant, I fully expected to feel his hand on my arm, being oh-so chivalrous, helping me up, but he went for the book instead.

"Ed McBain. I've heard of him." I rolled my eyes. "Look, that was karma telling you to talk to me."

"No, that was this gray . . . shite that's now all over my trousers and will probably ruin them. Just give me my book."

He handed it to me. I wasn't lying to the homeless guy; my hands are wrinkly and knobby and look like they belong on an old woman. I gripped the novel so hard that my ante-diluvian mitt slipped on the cellophane cover.

Not long after dark as I was about to close up the shop, in he walked, doing that Doctor Strut like he owned the place.

"I'm persistent." He grinned.

"You say that like it's a good thing: the perseverance of the stupid. And we're closed."

"Have dinner with me."

"You already asked, and I declined the invitation."

"This is where I'm hoping my persistence pays off. I really want to talk to you. And it's just dinner. Nothing fancy."

"You make it sound *so-o* appealing." He guffawed. "Even if I wanted to, I can't. I have to go home. I need to feed the cat."

"I think the cat can wait."

"You don't know this cat. She's gets grumpy when she's hungry. And she doesn't appreciate dinner being late."

"Luckily, cats can't tell time."

"Again, you don't know this cat. She can."

"I'll spring for an extra entrée you can bring home to her."

"You have an answer for everything."

"Not really, but I've been practicing this conversation for months now. I feel so guilty, like I participated in your giving up your calling. If I'd—"

"I also need to change my trousers. They're stained."

"You can barely see it. Nobody will notice. You look great. You—"

"Fine. I'll have dinner with you." I said it as much to shut him up as anything, but I'd wanted to say yes because I found him weirdly, if amusingly, sincere. I grabbed the slightly tatty purple LeSportsac that I carried everywhere and headed toward the door. As he fell in step next to me, I noticed that he had a slight limp.

"Can we get a bottle of the house red, Judy?"

The restaurant was typically anonymous—lime green walls, glass-topped tables, a generic Italian menu—but he must have been a regular. Judy's glance told me I should make a little more effort. Before I could think of something to say, he asked, "So where are you from?"

"You made such a fuss about dinner to ask me that?"

A grin. "Yeah, okay. I know you're Irish."

"If you have a third cousin twice removed in Ennis, I don't know her."

Still grinning. "No, no Irish relatives. I'm from Davenport. Iowa. That's—"

"I know where fecking Iowa is. How'd you get the limp?"

"Football. American football. My ACL is shot."

He traded the grin for what I assumed he figured was a meaningful stare into the depths of my soul.

"I guess I should tell you why I've called you here."

"You didn't call me. You just appeared. Twice." I should have been curious what he really wanted, but for the moment, I was enjoying our little tête-à-tête, which a shrink probably would have characterized as some kind of powerplay.

"I work with a lot of nurses. I can tell when someone is meant to be a nurse. You shouldn't have quit."

"Perhaps your perceptions aren't as astute as you think. Mr. Richards's family sure wouldn't agree with you." I emptied my wine glass in one go.

He reached out as if to take my hand, but stopped short and showed me his palm.

"Listen to me. I know not a day goes by that you don't think about that night. About Mr. Richards. You didn't do it deliberately, but I'll never forget your expression when you realized what had happened. You looked at your hands. Just like you're doing now."

He was right. I was staring at my hands.

"Your life is stuck, and unless you want it to stay stuck forever, you need to do something about it. You need to go back to nursing."

"Look, not that it's any of your business, but I'm fine. I have a great job. Wonderful friends. A cute flat. Apartment. I said my Hail Marys and moved on. Really. I guess I appreciate what you're trying to do—you've sure made an effort—but it's not necessary."

"That's great, even if it is a pack of lies. I know it is. I saw how you interacted with patients. The depth of your compassion is unmistakable. You have to forgive yourself. You made a mistake that had a terrible outcome, but that shouldn't stop you from fulfilling your potential."

I tried his stare-into-the-soul back at him. "I appreciate that you care. But I'm finished with nursing. Now, can we change the subject?"

He obliged, sort of. He regaled me with tales from the hospital, about hilarious patients and inept colleagues. As he talked, I realized his eyes were a lovely dark green flecked with gold bits. The veal was better than I expected it to be, and I wondered if that had something to do with the company.

"I'll pay the check and then let's go for a nightcap."

"No, I really do have to get home and feed the cat."

"Okay, I'll just get a chicken breast to go and I'll walk you home."

I laughed. I couldn't help myself. "Don't worry about the chicken, but I will take you up on the walk home. I've been on edge with all the Central Park Jogger crap."

WE ENDED UP RUNNING MOST of the way back to my building through a fierce drizzle. I didn't have a proper awning, so I pulled him into the foyer with me. As I checked the box for mail, I asked whether he'd like to come up for a coffee. I barely had the words out before he'd accepted and started toward the staircase.

My flat was tidy, if tiny. I couldn't remember the last time I'd had a visitor, and wasn't sure what exactly the protocol was. The cat met us at the door, making it abundantly clear that she was not pleased that her dinner was late. She was all white with blue eyes and deaf as a doornail. As I set about emptying a can of mystery-meat pate into her bowl, he reached down and petted her cautiously.

"She likes you."

"I'm glad. I would hate to be on her shit list. She's obviously important to you."

I'd offered coffee, so I grabbed the bag of Bewley's my da had sent, turned the gas on under the kettle that I always left full on the cooker, and pulled the top off the French press.

"Cream and sugar?" I figured I sounded like a flight attendant.

"Yes, please." He was looking through the cassettes on the shelf attached to the wall.

"You like traditional Irish music."

"Congratulations. You can read tape covers." I realized I sounded like a real bitch. "Sorry. Yes. My da is a musician."

"I like the Chieftains."

"Everybody likes the Chieftains."

"Do you get back to Ireland much?"

"No, not really. My sister was over for a visit a few months ago, and I ring my parents every weekend."

"Do you have a big family?"

"Enough about me." I put the mugs on the upside-down wooden crate that served as a coffee table in front of my miniature loveseat. He squeezed down next to me and took my hand.

"I—"

"I know." I kissed him. Or let him kiss me. Either way, the coffee went cold while we relocated ourselves to my twin bed. The sex was entirely passable—not workmanlike and nothing to set off fireworks. It was . . . comfortable. Nice.

Afterwards, he snored while I dug my book out of my bag and relocated back to the loveseat. The cat joined me; as much as she could be cranky, she was good company. When we were alone, I would read to her sometimes even though she couldn't hear a word.

I finished the last few pages of *Lullaby* and noted that the snoring had been replaced by the steady breathing of deep sleep. I stopped at the fridge en route back to the loveseat.

The cat kneaded my lap while I observed my prehistoric hands scratching behind her ears. After a few minutes, she decided I was softened up enough and sat down, purring and still digging her nails into the side of my leg in the rhythm that's built into feline DNA.

I kept petting her as I thought about what he'd said, about my being meant to be a nurse. I was still considering this, wondering what about me had made him so certain, as I picked up the chilly syringe I'd already filled and had retrieved from the fridge. The cat didn't feel a thing when her breathing slowed then stopped as the tranquilizer flooded her little body.

I hadn't been absolutely sure what would happen because etorphine is normally only used to subdue big wild animals. I had made some assumptions about the dosage, and had no idea whether it would cause seizures or other dramatic reactions. I had expected someone to question the order coming from a small Manhattan pet store that dealt in nothing larger than a French Bulldog, but it had simply arrived in the post.

The cat's death had been painless and peaceful, just like Mr. Richards's had been.

It had been easier in the hospital because I'd known exactly what he would be prescribed and when and precisely how much extra to administer to make sure he died before anyone realized what had happened. And I had the perfect cover story, of course—The Great Mistake—but I wasn't thinking about that as I depressed the plunger. I was overwhelmed by the simple satisfaction of finally doing what I was meant to.

My reverie was interrupted by a cough from the bed. I laid the cat's corporeal form aside gently and picked up the second syringe.

He jerked his arm and opened his eyes just as the needle pricked his vein. I suppose my expression was curious, because patients tend to reflect what they see in their caregivers, and his countenance held a thousand queries, but confidence made my grip strong and my ancient hands held. As his heart slowed and he pulled a few last labored breaths, he must have realized what I said to him right after he died:

"I told you I wasn't cut out to be a nurse."

THE SAFEST FORM OF CONVEYANCE
BY JIM FUSILLI

His mind on the office, Fleming ran toward the elevator; it arrived promptly, and he was descending before he realized what he had done. Now he was trapped and would be until it arrived in the lobby twenty-seven floors below. His only hope was that no one would stop it and step in with him. If not, he would be freed in about forty seconds. Otherwise, the journey to open space and fresh air would take forever. Panic would set in, and he might collapse or he might explode; he would lose control. It had happened before and would happen again.

Once freed, if Fleming could find a taxi he could race from the Upper East Side to the World Financial Center: across Central Park, pathways cleaving its great lawns; and along the Hudson River, high clouds, ferries crossing east, west, and free. He said he would be in by noon; now it was 11:30 a.m. Given he'd worked from home up until the moment the cable man arrived late, perhaps no one noticed he was absent. He'd sent emails, made several phone calls, printed and studied the revised Excel spreadsheet; they'd moved ahead without him, but by inches only. He could still contribute.

The elevator passed the twenty-sixth floor. Already, Fleming was sweating under his suit jacket.

His wife was in Washington, DC. Amtrak out of Penn Station at 6 a.m.; the National Gallery of Art was mounting a Klimt exhibition and her employer, the Frick Collection, was lending two paintings. She was doing well: associate curator at twenty-five. Four years her senior, Fleming worked hard to keep up.

When they started dating, it had been difficult, nearly impossible, to conceal his anxiety. At Penn, he was chided for his neatness, his desire for organization, his promptness; a dormmate called him "Clock." He admitted he lacked the gift of spontaneity. Everything had to be just so and as it had been before and must always be. It reduced his sense of "what if." He sought to control the world as best he could. Sandy thought it was a sign of maturity. Everyone she'd ever gone out with, she told him, had been a boy. He behaved like a man. He was purposeful, she'd said.

Twenty-fifth floor. "I'm supposed to marry a man like you," she told him, as they lay in an upstairs room at her parents' summer home on a New Hampshire lake, his prescription Xanax serving as a stabilizer. "I trust you'll do well," her father said as he secured a position for him at one of the Big Four professional services firms in New York.

Sandy was used to him by now, and forgiving. He'd finally convinced her that it was never her fault.

Twenty-fourth floor. The elevator descended slowly; his mind raced. He thought ahead: Usually, he rode the M20 bus south; on a good day, the trip from Lincoln Center to Liberty Street took an hour, and he could jump out at any stop if he felt enclosed or restricted. But today he didn't have an hour to spend. If a taxi couldn't be found—that was possible; it happens; it's happened to him—he would have to take the subway. He'd be caught below ground in a tube jammed tight with strangers. At times, the subway was faster than a taxi. He knew that.

He had no choice; none. He'd have to risk a panic attack. He needed to be in the office. He had to make his mark.

Twenty-three. He looked at his wristwatch.

He shuffled in place. To ward off the mounting fear, he zipped open his shoulder bag, which contained his laptop and table. He had the printouts inside. He could study the numbers. They might engage him. A copy of *Fortune* was in there, too. Last year, his father-in-law had been on the cover; a lengthy profile discussed his—

The elevator jolted to a halt on the twenty-second floor.

ON HER THIRD DAY IN the United States, Maritza Daválos took herself for a late-night walk along Riverside Park. Lights on the buildings across the Hudson glittered like diamonds on the black water; she felt a sense of peace: her aunt promised work, and soon her three young children would join her in New York. As she walked under a sheet of stars, she looked to the concrete beneath her feet and saw a five-dollar bill. She bent to retrieve it, and two men grabbed her, dragged her behind a row of bushes, tore her clothes, and took turns raping her. Surgeons wired her jaw and repaired an orbital bone. Her uncle told her she was a fool to walk alone.

Two decades ago, but it explained the knife Daválos had hidden beneath the pile of laundry she carried. Though her son Pedro, who went by the name Petey, was now with the US Army at Camp Taji in Iraq, and her twins were graduate students at Marymount College, she never felt safe in America. She shuffled with her head bowed, her dark eyes drifting to avoid contact, and she screamed in bed at night.

Only her family knew why she was this way. They knew she had been broken.

Now Maritza Daválos entered the elevator, hands firm on the plastic handles of an unwieldy laundry basket. The washers and dryers were in the basement. She attended to five apartments in the white-brick building, providing maid services. She was trusted. She received a daily flat rate of thirty dollars per family; one hundred and fifty dollars a day for five hours' work. Now and then, a tenant would ask her to babysit overnight. She agreed, but didn't sleep. She sat in the darkness, the boning knife that had belonged to her uncle in her hand. It had a six-inch blade.

Fleming stared at the timid woman, who turned her back to him as the elevator doors sealed shut. He had been thinking about dashing out and trotting down to street level twenty-one stories below. But now it was too late.

He glanced at the plump woman's sneakers: something to take his mind off his mounting anxiety. He tilted his head to count the eyelets.

Daválos felt his gaze. Then she heard him begin to shuffle. His shoes scraped on the elevator floor.

She looked at the numbers overhead.

Her friend Irene worked on the eighteenth floor. Maybe she would arrive and tell the man to stop. Stop moving, stop staring, stop frightening my friend. Stop.

Nineteen.

FLEMING HAD AN ORANGE IN his shoulder bag. He took it out. He raked his thumbnail across its skin. The activity consumed five seconds.

Daválos took notice of the scent, but didn't turn. She didn't want to acknowledge the sandy-haired man in the blue suit. If he would stop pacing, she could imagine he wasn't there.

Fleming knew the precise measurements of the elevator: 27.1 square feet; 4.5 feet by 6 feet. Standard size. Larger than a coffin.

Eighteen.

He researched elevators when his father-in-law gave them the apartment as a wedding gift. When Rafael Andros made the announcement at a table for three for brunch at Caravaggio, Fleming said nothing, though his stomach knotted. Sandy hesitated, but her father insisted, not unpleasantly. The least I can do, he said then, please. I want you nearby. Am I being selfish?

No, Daddy, of course not.

Apartment 27F. Let's go see it. Mr. Andros put his napkin on the table.

Fleming begged off. A headache. Nausea. "Robert . . . " Sandy said, with sympathy. She took his hand. Mr. Andros stared. Fleming wanted to tell him that anxiety was the result of a chemical imbalance, not a lack of character.

"Enjoy," Robby Fleming said then. He had begun to shake.

An elevator was the safest form of conveyance. On average, about twenty-five Americans were killed in elevator accidents per year. The majority were the result of falls down elevator shafts. Redundancies in safety design made it next-to-impossible for an elevator to plummet to the ground floor. The per-trip fatality rate was 0.00000015 percent.

Fleming didn't worry he would be killed. He worried that he would be trapped.

Seventeen.

He was already trapped.

THE KNIFE HAD BELONGED TO Daválos's uncle. Late one night, as the moon hovered above the fire escape, he approached.

She was asleep on the sofa; a crocheted blanket provided warmth, though not enough. She was accustomed to the temperate climate of Cuenca in her native Ecuador. New York was a frigid city; the wind whipped off the river and pushed her sideways. New York did not believe in mercy.

"Maritza," her uncle whispered. Rather than touch her, he rapped the sofa arm with the side of his fist. "Wake up."

She came to.

In Spanish, he said, "Maritza, hide this. Don't let her see it."

She knew he meant her aunt. She took the knife by the handle.

"Now you know," he continued, his breathing labored. "Nobody is going to bother you no more."

She didn't understand, but said nothing as he retreated toward his bedroom.

In the morning, she retrieved the knife from under the cushion. It was dotted with dried blood.

El Diario reported that a man had been killed in Riverside Park, his throat slashed. She followed the story. The next day, the newspaper said the victim had served time in prison for sexual assault.

The victim.

Now the man behind her sighed. To himself, he said, "Let's go, let's go . . ."

Sixteen.

Clearing his throat, he said, "Excuse me."

She pretended she hadn't heard.

"Miss," he said with more urgency than he intended.

Daválos stiffened.

The man approached.

She fumbled for the knife.

He reached around her.

She slashed at him as he extended an index finger to tap the button for the fifteenth floor.

Blood spurted onto the panel.

"WHY DID YOU DO THAT?" Fleming said in disbelief. The gash crossed the back of his hand to the base of his thumb, and it continued to bleed.

Fifteen.

Daválos held the knife as if she feared he would attack. Laundry littered the elevator floor.

Fleming said, "I was trying to—"

She jabbed at him. He retreated.

"I wanted to get out. That's all."

He looked at his hand. He needed to stop the bleeding.

Fourteen.

There was a tiny T-shirt in the laundry, baby sized. Sliding his bag off his shoulder, he knelt down to retrieve it.

Daválos stared, the knife ready.

Fleming dabbed at his wound with the T-shirt, which was not much bigger than his hand.

"Jesus," he said. He looked at her. "You could've slit my wrist."

"*Se mantenga alejado de mí,*" the frightened woman said.

"What?"

She stabbed the air. "Stay away."

"Why did you do that?"

He lifted the baby tee to examine the wound. She saw the shirt was dotted with blood.

Thirteen.

"Look at this," he said.

She kept her eyes on his face. She saw that he was hurt and confused.

He flexed his hand. A fist, then open, a fist, then open. A curtain of blood ran toward his shirt cuff.

The elevator passed the twelfth floor.

"Why did you do that?" he repeated.

She said, "Sorry." She had known this moment would come, but it had been nothing like she imagined.

He gazed past the knife toward her face. Skin sagged on her jaw, and she seemed to have melted into a permanent sadness. She saw nothing in her dark eyes.

"Put the knife down," he said. "Okay?"

Eleven.

She thought about it.

Laundry was piled between them. "Maybe there's a towel in there." He went to a knee and began to wade through the soiled clothes.

Daválos couldn't decide. Clearly, the man hadn't intended to harm her. But, injured, perhaps he would strike now.

If she wanted to, she could drive the knife through the top of his head.

Ten.

Now he was tossing laundry into the plastic basket.

Nine.

WHEN THEY HAD REACHED THE seventh floor, Fleming stood. At first, he thought he was lightheaded due to blood loss. But no, he was dizzy only for a second or so. Upright, he wrapped a dish towel around his hand.

"I'm sorry," Maritza Daválos said, her voice a squeak.

Fleming looked at her. "You shouldn't be so afraid." Then he added, "But you never know, I guess."

"Do you need a doctor?" She was frowning in concern.

"Maybe. Maybe so."

Six.

Now the woman had the knife at her side.

Fleming groped for his shoulder bag with his foot. He looked at the towel wrapped around his hand. "No, I think it'll be alright."

A mother, Daválos had tended to wounds. She dropped the knife onto the laundry, and she removed the towel.

A thin red line crossed the top of the man's hand.

"It's stopped," he said. "The blood."

Five. She saw that it hadn't, not really.

She held his fingers to study the wound. "I'm very sorry."

"Forget it. I should've said something. You never know who's getting in an elevator with you."

She dabbed at the leaking blood.

Four.

He smiled. "You know, I actually have Band-Aids in my bag."

"I can—"

"No. I'll do it."

Three.

Then he said, "I have insurance."

She hadn't thought that she might have to pay. She was thinking a cloud had lifted, and she understood: there was a time to be cautious and a time to live. She had been waiting for this moment for twenty years. Twenty years in mounting fear. It had happened and now it was done.

"I put the knife away," she said.

Fleming thought she was speaking to him. "Good idea."

Two.

He looked at the numbers on the panel. Next stop the lobby. From the moment he was cut until now, he realized, he had thought nothing about his anxiety and fear. He had been trapped, yes, and something had happened. He could have been killed. But he wasn't, and he hadn't exploded. Nothing had happened.

He didn't want to live this way anymore. It had to change. The pressure: What was it? It was nothing compared to a knife across the wrist, across the throat. There is what's real, and there is what's not. He would no longer contribute to his own injury.

The elevator drifted to a halt and the door opened effortlessly.

Daválos stepped aside.

"Well," said Fleming as he retrieved his bag, "that was . . ."

"Thank you," she said, nodding politely.

"Yes," he replied as he exited. "I guess so."

The door sealed again and Daválos proceeded to the basement.

Fleming stepped into the alcove near the mailboxes to call the office. Late, not late, trapped, not trapped. He stared at the red line across the top of his hand.

SEE/SAW SOMETHING
BY PETER CARLAFTES

STARING UP THE TUNNEL FOR the faintest hint of light, I can see the disconnection from what used to be my life. Love and all pursuit is a future of blank. Now the train shows itself—so there's direction for a moment.

I should've been at work but I covered my shift because I felt like hanging with Lateef on his truck. It's an old bookmobile he's pimped out to look like a giant street cart and parks outside clubs in the Meatpacking District and creates wild snacks to sell drunks.

I board the downtown 6 and take the first seat on my right. The car's empty at eight o'clock on Friday night—hold on! I pull myself up to make sure it's not some ghost train and, satisfied by the sight of other riders fore and aft, I sit back and embrace solitude.

Lateef concocts these crazy things, like hot dogs shaped like soft, salted pretzels and pretzels that look like hot dogs and a bun. I've helped him twice before and we really hit it off. We met about a month ago outside Zuccotti Park.

Here comes Eighty-sixth Street. And probably eight little men playing panpipes.

The train stops. The doors open. No one gets on. Okay. The doors close. I'm used to such rejection. No. That isn't really true. I'm used to being alone.

Hell. In most circles, I'd be considered nuts to take off work to have a few laughs instead. Well. These days, laughs come too far between. And while it may seem to some that my ducks were out of order, the crucial factor that enabled me to make such a foolish choice was that I haven't paid rent for over twenty-seven months.

Along comes Seventy-seventh Street comprised of flickering faces, yet once the doors slide open not a one steps in the car. Here I am all by my lonesome. Just like in my building.

See. Four years ago, my landlord had this greedy little notion he could chase out every tenant and then triple all his rents. Well. Four years later, I remain the last man standing. But after daily loud construction through my walls from all directions, I'm glad there's no place like home. The only good thing that's happened to me lately's been finding her again. Josie. Maybe it was meant to be. No way of knowing—yet.

She was on the top floor—five. I'm still on two, as then. You know. We'd run into each other in the hall and started talking. On one of those occasions, she came into my room. It went like this awhile, but she moved and we lost track after that—until last Monday afternoon, when her long red hair caught my eye on Lex pushing a baby carriage.

Thin face. Green eyes. Sexy. Slightly taller. We put four years behind us in a minute and a half. Then Josie introduced me to her six-month-old, Coquette. Another redhead. What a cutie. She asked if I could babysit tomorrow (Tuesday morning). She had to deal with "issues" concerning Coquette's father, whose status she left at—Out of Our Lives. They lived just off Park on 104th. I told Josie, "Why not."

Sixty-eighth Street/Hunter College. Reminds me of when, as a young man, I used to sit in on a lot of classes, but none held my interest long enough to really want to become someone else.

I lean out the door and watch people get on, only not on the car that I'm in! The doors slide shut. Something must be wrong. Then dropping to my seat, I caught first sight of the bag. By the far doors, catty-cornered to my right.

Okay. I'm on some inane new TV show. Where all of them pop up from inside the seats the second I touch the bag. I mean, it's been here all this time. There's no way in frozen hell I could've missed it.

A classy, light-brown men's calfskin tote. I'd say fourteen by twenty, with finely-stitched straps. I think I've seen one in the Hermes store before. You see. With constant noise surrounding my apartment, I wind up spending lots of time mind-shopping on Madison Avenue; you know—like not really buying. And I work on the avenue, too, so I'm a guy who knows fine leather. That bag costs 3500 bucks.

The train stops at Fifty-ninth. I stand up once again, keeping one eye on the bag. The cars in front and behind are at least half full. And Nobody Gets On Mine. It's time to ask myself the question that I ask in these types of situations: What Would Bobby Short Do?

You see, I worked with Bobby Short for many years and a sweeter, nicer man you'll never meet. So, whose judgment better to draw upon for moral support than his? Now the doors close, but the train's being held, so I've time to sort out my dilemma.

I'm a waiter at the Carlyle and the prestige of that itself has lent a certain peace of mind to other aspects of my life. Even after the landlord started tearing down the building with me in it. Still, I held my ground. But ever since June, when the water went off, I couldn't sleep very well, which left me fearing the unknown.

Then I met this girl who worked at Barney's in cosmetics sometime in mid-July. Her name was Cleo. Well. She came to see me once for lunch and soon we started going to her place and all I really felt was great relief. Insomuch that, after the thrill between Cleo and I came and went, I made this deal with her and her roommate to sleep on their couch twice a week for a hundred bucks, which worked out especially well for me until they changed the lock without a word in late September. And who could blame them? That's when I started thinking about Zuccotti Park.

Now as the train goes so do I and I sit directly across from the bag under one of those IF YOU SEE SOMETHING, SAY SOMETHING signs. I'm pretty sure at this point that Bobby Short would bail and catch the express, but I'm extremely stubborn; plus I like the bag. Plus I've never come to terms with that mentality. Telling doesn't cut it in the City. You open the bag. Maybe you find something good. And maybe the next day, they find you floating in the river. Doesn't matter either way. You have to take your shot. That's what drew me to Occupy Wall Street. These people were taking their shot.

I bought a cheap tent from a sporting goods shop and went down there in October and found a place to put it up. Then spent a few nights sleeping next to others under tarps. Some of them complained about having things stolen, which got me thinking: If they couldn't figure out a way to stop small scale theft, how could they ever end the reign of corporate greed? I gave the tent to three Norwegians and spent November in a hostel. Lucky me. The cops moved everybody out the same month. The best thing was hooking up with Lateef and his truck.

The train pulls into Fifty-first street. No one else gets on the car. I'm standing by the bag as the doors close. Staring at the SAY SOMETHING sign.

Worse case scenario: I open the bag, the bag blows up; I sing old tunes forever with Bobby Short and Cole Porter. It's a win/win proposition.

Best case scenario: I sell the bag on Craigslist and buy Josie and Coquette something nice. Hell. Christmas is only three weeks away. Maybe buy them a tree. I'm sure the kid could use some diapers. Hold on. As much as I'd like to pick up again with Josie, there's no need to get this far ahead of myself. I'm too worn out from the last six months.

Next case scenario: Instead of catching the L over to Eighth from Union Square, I get off at Grand Central and check out what's in the bag, then I'll meet up with Lateef a little later. Simple. I pick up the bag and it's a Ferragamo. Damn! I could've sworn it was Hermes. Well. Here comes the *moment critique.*

I cross directly to the nearest bench and set the bag down on a seat. Then delicately undo the snap. Pausing, I sweep a quick glance around and, using both hands, open the bag, which suddenly lights up, exposing this odd mechanism with a barrel pointing out. Then a sharp voice from within commands, "Don't move or you'll be tased!"

There's quite a spell of silence. I ask the bag, "What should I do?"

"Be quiet," says the voice from the bag, adding, "Nod if you understand."

What else can I do? I nod.

The voice tells me, "Just follow my instructions."

After another long spell, I ask the bag, "What instructions?"

The voice sighs, "I thought you understood."

"Huh? Oh, yeah, right." I nod again.

The voice says, "Good. Pick up the bag. Then walk to the downtown end of the platform. After the last set of stairs turn right. You will be facing an elevator. Stand by the door. Then wave at the man to your left behind the glass in the dispatcher's booth. The door will open. Get on. And just remember—the taser mechanism *will* trigger if you try to drop the bag. Understood?"

I nod. The voice says, "MOVE!"

I lift the bag and start walking. Well. They say you'll see it all if you live in this city long enough. I wonder if I'll make the *Police Blotter*.

Here's the stairs. Turn right. There's the elevator. Look left. There's the guy behind the glass. He looks like Jerry Orbach on boredom pills. I wave at him. He nods. The door opens. The guy points. The car seems like it's on last legs.

The voice says, "Down We Go!"

I read once over twenty floors exist in this place below street level. With miles of abandoned tracks. And even colonies of people. I can't be sure. I've never seen them. We're right at floor ten. Strange. Not worried in the least. One thing I do know: Been looking for a change. Eleventh floor. Might be a blessing.

Now the elevator stops at an unmarked floor between twelve and fourteen with a jolt and opens on a stale, dank square of cement painted white. There's an old steel-gray desk straight ahead, with a thin black man wearing blue and a grim look behind a screen lit more brightly than the fixture above.

I ask, "Is this really the thirteenth floor?"

He snaps, "There ain't no such thing! Come on!"

Meaning me. Meaning now.

I go in. The rickety door clangs shut.

The man points to his right, "Put the bag on the floor by the desk."

Which I do. Then ask, "Are you the voice from the bag?"

He almost breaks. But snaps, "My name's Officer Calvin Morris. You sit down and zip it up!"

There's a dark brown folding chair by the metal door farther right, which I take and watch Morris click a mouse. Seems like a nice enough guy. Mid-thirties, dreamer. Not too many coming true.

I ask him, "You want my ID?"

"Nah," Morris shrugs. "We use facial recognition." Then leans back smugly and reads from the screen. "Name: Benjamin Cartafte. Born: 1967. 5'10". Hair: Brown. Eyes: Blue." Then he shoots a quick look to make sure that they're blue and, when rest assured, he continues, "Address: 170 E. 100th Street. Damn! You work at the Carlyle?"

When I nod, Morris frowns, "Then what was your ass doing down in Zuccotti Park?"

Right then, the metal door swings open and a short Asian man wearing black round-rimmed glasses and light-brown fatigues quickly crosses behind Morris and asks, "What's his story?"

I challenge, "Why not just ask me?"

"Because we know in our position that a perp will always lie," responds the short man, then looks at me more closely and lights up, "Weren't you in my Forensics class at John Jay right after 9/11?"

Startled, I say, "Yeah—I guess. But I was only sitting in."

He smiles, shaking his head, "Wow. You look exactly the same." Then asks Morris, "What's his name?"

Morris tells him, "Ben," and then to me, "He's Sergeant Cheung. Ben here works at the Carlyle, Sarge. Probably makes more bread than us both put together. Yet the dude's been hanging out down in Zuccotti Park."

I interject, "I only slept there a few nights. I've been having grief with my apartment."

"What grief?" asks the sergeant.

I tell him, "You don't want to know."

"That's where you're wrong," the sergeant plies. "We're here to help."

"Yeah. We're your friends," chimes in Morris.

Hmm. Good Cop/Good Cop's working. I spill my tale of woe. About no water (thus no toilet) since last summer, and the last two years of banging starting six o'clock each morning and the stairs blocked with the clutter and no heat so far this winter, and the story of my landlord doing anything he wants.

"Okay—up!" the sarge tells Morris. "Let me see what I can do."

Morris stands. The sergeant takes his seat and types. Morris quips, "You think I'm bad? This dude's a monster!"

The sergeant reads off the screen, "170 E. 100th Street. Owner: C. Scaringella."

"We call him Mighty Joe Cheung," boasts Morris.

The sergeant keeps reading, "First and second court hearing postponed. Third court hearing: judgment—tenant. June of 2009."

"Damn!" Morris rides, "You ain't paid no rent since then? You must be sitting on some serious paper."

"Ben," beams the sergeant "Hold onto your seat. Here's an email sent 12/1/11—that's yesterday, at 1:06 p.m.; from S.A. Meyer, Attorney at Law to C. Scaringella. Dear Carmine, As I have stated, it's in your best financial interest to have this matter resolved by the end of the year, so I will approach your tenant first thing next week and offer to settle for $75,000, with an agreement he vacate by the end of next month. Sincerely—hah! How much more awesome could it get?"

Morris taunts, "Show me the money! Hah! You rich now, so find an apartment."

"Give him time to get used to the idea," asserts the sergeant, and keeps typing.

I hesitate. I vacillate, "I'm not sure what I'll do."

"Why not . . . move in with the girl?" prompts the sergeant.

I slight, "We only met last week."

Their eyes look up and glower. The perp will always lie.

"Okay," I confess. "We had a thing a few years back. And as much as I'd like us to pick right up again, she has some issues with her ex. Not to mention a six-month-old daughter."

The sergeant scans the screen, "The ex won't be a problem. He's doing time in Canada for smuggling marijuana. And word is he still owes the guys he got it from money."

"Look," I explain. "Doesn't matter how it seems. Love's like a taxi with the light off. But you can't afford forever."

"Dude's a poet," chuckles Morris.

The sergeant reads more from the screen. "Here's a message she sent to her sister on Facebook: You remember the man in my old building that I thought I was in love with a few years ago? Well—now I know I was, so wish me luck. I'm in love with Ben again."

Morris quips, "You in like Flynn!"

I ask, "So am I free to go?" Their eyes meet up and grin. I stand.

The sergeant says, "Ben. We're only one of seven experimental subway crime prevention programs."

"What do the other six do?" I ask.

The elevator door shakes open behind me. I take one last look at the bag. Morris says, "It's a knockoff."

The sergeant waves, "Come back and see us." As the door shuts.

Just like life, it was over much too soon. And just like life, there weren't any answers. But like that one-in-an-eight-million great New York moment, I didn't need one.

I couldn't wait to tell Lateef that there were angels on the bottom. And there, rising to the skin from the bowels of the city, I never had so much direction in my life.

THE SOLDIER, THE DANCER, AND ALL THAT GLITTERS
BY TOM CALLAHAN

THE ILLEGAL IMMIGRANT IRISH STRIPPER with the long red hair jumped back and doubled over as if punched in the gut when the thick white fist drove south into her green satin G-string. The invasion was sudden and powerful like the Allies hitting the beach at Normandy, snapping her undies in two. The dollar bills attached to her hips fluttered to the rug of the small square stage like the first flakes of winter in the Bronx. Before the first Washington hit the deck, the tall man in an army jacket had the invading fist doubled behind the man's back and his head in a chokehold.

The masher, a man in his fifties with a gray crew cut and the prominent beer belly and heavy build of a construction worker had not noticed the man in the army jacket lurking nearby. He struggled to no avail to buck off the younger man.

"Get off of me. Lemme go."

"Stop struggling or I'll break your arm off."

"Motherfucker, I'll kill you. Fight like a man."

They danced around a bit but slowly the masher stopped struggling and they were facing the floor-length dusty mirror right behind the stage. The ill-fitting mirror looked like it had come from an Irish dance studio that went broke and it did.

"That was neither polite nor smart," the man in the army jacket said into the masher's ear. "Didn't you see the sign? In big letters: No Touching Dancers. Patrons Must Keep Five Feet Away. That's the law, mac. You can read, can't ya?"

Recognition suddenly dawned on the older man's face as he looked at the reflection of the man with the shoulder-length brown hair. He was called Soldier in the neighbor-hood. Soldier, meanwhile, was looking behind him at the two guys, also middle aged, who were with the masher. He knew he was about to get jumped and then there would be real trouble. He glanced past the small back room they were in and saw Frankie moving fast behind the bar.

"Hey, I know you!" the masher croaked.

"That so?"

"Yeah, you're the neighborhood kid who went to Vietnam and came back a hippie communist peace freak. Faggot!"

Soldier tightened his grip on both arm and throat. Masher grabbed the arm around his throat with his free hand.

"Lemme tell you something, Soldier. I faced Nazi machine guns in France and won. You faced a bunch of gooks in black pajamas and got your ass beat. No wonder why the only way you can fight is to jump on a man's back. And this is your idea of honor: jumping a real American in defense of some ugly, skinny Irish hoor in a ginmill."

The snap echoed through the now silent bar like a cannon shot.

"Aaaaaiiiiiee! You busted my wrist."

Soldier shoved the man into the mirror and swung around and ducked just as the other two moved in on him. A loud *click!* echoed through the bar as Frankie the bartender elbowed Soldier aside and stood in front of the masher's friends with a sawed-off shotgun raised.

"Out now! Night's over, boys!"

They just stood there looking at the gun.

"Move! Now!"

They turned and shuffled toward the front door of the bar. The masher was leaning against the mirror, face etched in pain, holding his damaged hand.

"Frankie, your thug busted my wrist. I am going to sue, man. I am going to sue your father and this bar for hiring this brain-damaged maniac."

"Alright, let's go talk about it outside, huh? We don't want to disturb these nice people anymore," Frankie said, despite the fact there were no more than half-a-dozen people left in the joint. Frankie was as big as Soldier but fatter with dark hair that covered his ears—in style back then—and a big walrus mustache. "Here, hold this." He handed the shotgun to Soldier, put his arm around the Masher's shoulder in a friendly way and gently led him to the door.

Soldier looked around for the first time and saw Norma several feet to the left of the elevated stage, leaning against the mirror, one arm covering her glittering tea-cup-sized breasts and the other holding what was left of her undies against her full red pubic bush in a failed attempt at modesty. Soldier saw the huge, wide green eyes, surrounded by little-girl freckles on the bridge of her sharp-featured nose. He realized he was looking at a terrified little girl. He'd seen them before in the villages. All he could do was go over to the stage, bend down and pick up the dollars lying there.

He walked over, bills outstretched in his left hand, as if he was offering candy. She hesitated for a moment before taking them. As Soldier admired her body, as he did four nights a week, he saw where the terrified eyes were looking. He looked down and saw the shotgun in his right hand. He had completely forgotten it was there. Panic rose in his throat as he saw his finger on the trigger.

His hands started shaking and he wanted to drop the gun but was terrified that if he did, he would accidently pull the trigger and put a huge hole in the beautiful creature before him. He'd seen that back in the villages as well.

His whole body trembling now, he backed away from her, turned and ran to the bar.

Breathing hard, he got ahold of himself long enough to disarm the gun and was putting it in the rack Frankie's father had built for it right beneath the taps when Frankie moseyed in as if he did not have a care in the world.

"Frankie, I'm really sorry, man. I lost it."

Frankie took a seat on the customer's side of the bar across from Soldier. "Hey, no worries. You were doing your job protecting Norma. Is she okay?"

"I . . . I think so. She did not look hurt."

"Are you okay? You are as white as a ghost."

"Fine. I'm fine."

"Look, that asshole could have cost us our liquor license if there was an inspector in here tonight. We ain't running some Times Square stroke palace."

Norma appeared from the back and walked over. Fully dressed now in jeans, a dark red sweater and leather jacket, the long Irish straight red hair that spilled to the middle of her back tied in a bun at the back of her head. Over her shoulder was a large, fringed denim bag.

"Hey, I was just asking about you. You okay?"

"I am, thanks to my savior here." She looked right in Soldier's blue-gray eyes and he was speechless.

"I'm sorry about that, Norma. He won't be back in here to bother you."

"Ah, just another ejit showing the world how small his mickey is. I just wish he had a twenty instead of a one in his fist when he played drop-the-hand with me." The ring of Kerry was thick in her voice.

"Wanna drink? You deserve it."

"Thanks, Frankie, but I'm gonna run if it is all the same with ye. Night, gents. And thank you, Jimmy. My savior." Everybody called him Soldier in the Kingsbridge neighborhood where he and Frankie had grown up. Only Frankie called him by his Christian name. And now Norma.

Jimmy the Soldier silently watched her leave. Frankie watched him.

"Savior, huh? At this rate you'll want a raise. So what's bugging you?"

"This ain't good, Frankie. You heard that guy. When he tells your father and files a lawsuit, your dad will go through the roof. He can barely cover the rent now."

"Not a problem, Jimmy. There won't be a lawsuit."

"You heard him not twenty minutes ago . . ."

"And you and I asked him to leave and he left, peacefully, if a little upset. Then the damnedest thing. Doncha know he walked outside, somehow got his feet tangled up and fell hard into the gutter. Think he landed on his wrist. Drunks do the stupidest shit."

"But . . ."

"No, not his butt, his wrist. He should have been lucky enough to land on his ass. Hell, he should have stayed home and watched Carson or gone over to the Laconia Theater on White Plains Road and jerked off to the nonstop pornos, new feature every Wednesday. Last I saw, his friends were taking him over to Montefiore. Wouldn't be surprised if he didn't break both wrists. Hard fall, well deserved."

A FEW WEEKS LATER, JIMMY the Soldier was sitting in his customary seat at the GreenLeaf Pub at the far end of the dark mahogany bar. From there he could see the door and TV on the wall beside it. Behind him, also in dark wood, half a wall divider stood cheaply. On the other side of that, a few feet away, was the small stage, surrounded by the legally mandated wooden rail on three sides with chairs in front of it; the fourth side was the mirrored wall. Dancers could lean against the mirror and watch themselves as they shook their asses. There was no dancer pole; this was not a big, high-class operation. Strictly neighborhood.

Directly on the ceiling opposite the stage was a single large light that had in front of it a slowly rotating red, white, and blue disk. It was off now during the early afternoon. In the back sat the modest DJ booth, although there was no booth. Just an elevated table with a huge tape player and sound board for the bar's audio system. This was where Soldier played Bob Seeger and the Eagles and whatever else the dancers brought him on tape. Now, in the afternoon, only the radio was on low tuned to the great NYC progressive rock station, WNEW-FM.

On his stool, Soldier drank his Barry's Irish Tea—cup after cup—and read his book. If it did not look like he was working, it was because technically he did not work for the bar or anywhere else, though Frankie or his father managed to slip him some cash every week in a brown envelope.

Frankie and Jimmy were best friends their entire lives, but a bad leg from birth kept Frankie out of the draft, something that caused him no end of guilt. Jimmy went and everybody noticed the change when he came home and it was not just the wounds he would never talk about. He was, for one thing, radicalized, something unheard of in the neighborhood except among the old IRA guys.

He had joined Vietnam Veterans Against the War, went to DC and tossed his Purple Heart and medals over the White House fence and then drove a year later down to Miami to protest the GOP convention that re-nominated Nixon/Agnew, getting busted and tear gassed there. Then he and a lot of his buddies got indicted on some sort of RICO sedition rap in Gainesville. They beat it with the help of radical lawyers. He did no jail time and came back to hang around the old neighborhood all day and night.

Several years went by, disco came and Nixon/Agnew went, but Jimmy kept on the army jacket.

Most folks gave him wide berth—"There's something off with him, ya know" was the common whisper—but he didn't mind. He kept mostly to himself except for Frankie and his old man. They welcomed him into their bar and it was his second home. Tea and whatever he wanted was on the arm.

And that is where he was sitting when Frankie came in, grabbed a bottle of Jack from the shelf behind the bar, moseyed over in that friendly way of his, and poured a generous shot into Jimmy's tea.

"Whoa, dude, it is kinda early in the day for me."

"It's late somewhere, brother. Whatcha reading?"

"It's called *A People's History of the United States* by Professor Howard Zinn. It's a new book sent to me by one of my 'Nam brothers."

"Sounds like you are going to walk up the hill to Manhattan College and use your GI benefits to become a history major with that book."

"Doubt it."

"Why?"

"Well, for one thing, they are not teaching that book up there."

"Why not?"

"It tells the truth."

Frankie reached over, got a glass, and poured himself a drink.

"Listen, man, some business I gotta talk over with you. How'd you like to make five Gs?"

"Who I have to kill?"

"Nobody, nothing like that."

"Then like what?"

"In about a month, I have to go to Atlantic City on some business."

"A shithole despite the new casinos. So?"

"I was thinking of making it a holiday weekend. We will ask the girls to come and we can watch them frolic on the beach in their bikinis."

"We watch them frolic here four nights a week wearing a lot less."

"Better light at the beach."

"And that's worth five grand?"

"No, I got to see a man in room 1209 of the Claridge Hotel. I need you to stand with me."

"No fucking way, Frankie. Count me out. No."

"Relax, will ya, Jimmy? You are getting your panties in an uproar over nothing. You don't have to do nothing or say anything. Ten, twenty minutes tops and it will be back to the beach and the frolicking girls."

"No fucking way am I carrying a piece, Frankie, much less using one."

"It's not that at all, Jimmy. No rough stuff involved. I promise. It's just I feel better when I am standing next to you and others feel . . . well . . . calmer with you around."

"Does your father know about this?"

"No, and he is not going to hear it from you or anybody else."

"Frankie, have you lost your mind, continuing to deal with those Dominicans from Washington Heights? That is just insane. And it is just going to lead to disaster, man. Mark my words."

"Just think about it, okay? I need you. As a friend. Oh, added bonus . . ."

"What would that be? Another RICO indictment?"

"Norma says she is going to go and buy a new bathing suit for it. She has never seen Atlantic City or the Jersey shore. Imagine?"

"I can imagine alright."

"JIMMY, CAN I SEE YOU for a sec?"

The GreenLeaf Pub did not start out as a go-go bar. It was just one of a zillion New York Irish joints that popped up when New York was Irish. But times change and by the 1970s the demographics of New York and the Bronx had changed enough that Irish taverns were struggling.

Ironically enough, some were saved by the sexual revolution that changed mores and loosened the ban on women dancing mostly naked in bars. Bet the Church never counted on that! And as long as they kept their bottoms on and did not interact with the customers or engage in acts of prostitution, "Stopless Dancing" was within the law. And that is what the sign said outside the GreenLeaf: STOPLESS—in big bold letters.

So the dressing room, such as it was, for the three dancers the GreenLeaf employed besides Norma, was actually the liquor storage room, which Frankie's father equipped with a lighted makeup table he got from God-knows-where and two battered dressers where the girls could hang up their clothes and a battered couch where they could sleep or read between sets. There had been a phone until the first month's bill arrived.

Jimmy cautiously entered when Norma called. It was still over an hour before the show and no other girls were there yet. But Norma was already in her stage outfit: tonight a gold lame G-string and sheer gold see-through top. Her breasts were not huge, but Soldier had never in his life or travels seen nipples so long or erect or pointy, like pencil erasers for the sins of the world. They mesmerized him, although he was cursed with the knowledge that there was precious little he could do about them.

On stage, she'd cover them with glitter so the colored lights made them sparkle when she moved. She had her leather jacket over them now as he entered, probably to ward off the constant chill in the bar, or some weird sense of modesty. She took a seat at the makeup table and crossed her slender thighs. Jimmy found a box of Jameson nearby to use as a chair.

"You're here early tonight."

"Yeah, I am going to do the first three sets and leave early. Frankie said it is okay."

"What's up?"

She fixed him again with those big green eyes. And again he thought he saw the fear in them and noticed her freckles.

"Jimmy, I got to ask you a huge favor and I don't know how to do it."

"Ask away."

"Do you know where Dobbs Ferry is?"

"Sure, it's a town up along the Hudson, about six or seven miles north of here."

"Could you give me a ride there this Saturday?"

"Better yet, you can borrow my car, if you don't mind driving a beat up '72 Nova."

"No, Jimmy. I'd take the bus, but the bus only runs from 242nd to North Yonkers and there are no buses north from there."

She was starting to tear up. He could feel it coming, like a summer storm.

"What is it, Norma? You can tell me." The tears let go and she dropped her face into her hands.

"Ah, Jaysus! My life is yockers. It's just totally banjaxed. I ruined everything. Sorry for going on like this, Jimmy." She took a deep breath before continuing, as if to screw up her courage. "There is a women's medical center in Dobbs Ferry and I've got an appointment for Saturday morning."

"So take my car like I said."

"Will ya listen? They told me I should not drive back afterward. That . . . that I need a friend should drive me."

"Norma, are you sick?" He stood up.

"No, damn it . . . I'm up the flue."

"The what? You got the flu?" Despite herself, she had to laugh.

"No, silly. Flue is what you Yanks like to call a pussy. And there is something up there I got to take out sooner rather than later."

"Oh, no, Norma!" He sat back down hard enough to shake the bottles.

"Well, it was not intended, I assure you. I am on the pill. But maybe I messed up. And besides, they tell me it is not one hundred percent. And His Lordship would eat a Rubber Johnny before wearing one. Anyway, I need a ride."

"Does he know?"

"No, and he is not going to know. I am trying to end it with this caffer. That means idiot back home, not pussy. He is the type who does not take no for an answer."

"Did he?"

"What?"

"Use, you know, force."

"What possible difference would that make, Jimmy? Don't be an ejit on me. I need you right now to be strong for both of us. I've been shagging him for months. Of course, I'm up 'a duff. Also pussy to your tongue. Oh, I made a funny. But no. This was supposed to be the last of it. Looks like we went out with a real authentic bang the way God intended."

"You know who Tony Manucci is, right?"

"Yeah, his da is supposed to be some sort of big shot in a wop crime family."

"All the more reason not to tell him, but seriously, Norma, you got to get away from this guy. He is bad news, period."

She put her hand to her forehead and sighed.

"Jimmy, if you can't give me the ride, just say so. I'll just have to find the money for cabs, despite the fact I have about a hundred or so to my name right now."

"Don't be silly! Of course I'll drive you. No problem. Just tell me the time and I will be there with bells on."

"You can leave the fancy pants home. But, Jim?"

"Yeah?"

"Don't tell Frankie or any of the other girls. I am just humiliated by what I did, how stupid I am, just a glorified hoor."

"You're not stupid or a whore. You're just human like the rest of us. Mistakes happen. Shit, I went to Vietnam. That was a lot worse than being up the block with the Irish flu. And as far as the people here are concerned, my lips are sealed. I don't talk to anybody anyway."

"You talk to me."

"You're different. You're special. You and Frankie both, although you are a lot more beautiful than he is on his best day."

She laughed.

"You made me smile despite my troubles. You are my savior, James. You might have once been a soldier. But now, you are my angel from God."

"Well, I might not go that far. Let's just say I am here and happy to help, if I can."

"And Saint James?"

"Yes, but you can call me Jimmy?"

"Afterward, on the way home, can we stop for ice cream?"

"Hey, I will buy you two ice creams."

Her eyes lit up. "And another thing that is exciting, Frankie says he is taking us for an all-expense weekend in Atlantic City next month. Isn't that grand?"

"I used to go there with my parents when I was a little kid and it was okay back then. Last time I was there was after I got home and it is a real shithole now, believe me. The glamor left about 1925 and has never returned. So I might not get my hopes up if I were you."

"But the boardwalk is still there, right?"

"That it is."

"And the ocean and beach?"

"Be hard to get rid of them."

"And saltwater taffy?"

"Yeah still there, although your fillings might get pulled out while eating it."

"And you are coming, right? I am getting a brand new French-cut bikini. I never had one before. You don't have much use for beach clothes and sun bathing in Ireland. Please tell me you are coming."

"Wouldn't miss it for the world."

"Now, get out of here. I got to paint my teats like a dumb cow in heat, make them glitter."

MUCH TO JIMMY THE SOLDIER's relief, Atlantic City went fine and Norma seemed to be okay after the abortion, never mentioning Tony Manucci Jr. again. And Soldier did not ask. It was not his nature or any of his business.

But he was not exactly shocked when a guy who had to be Tony Jr. showed up during the final number of Norma's set one Saturday night a few weeks after Atlantic City.

He looked like he had been dipped in a vat of disco. Skin-tight red pants emphasizing his package. A multicolored satin print shirt worn open to the belly, revealing a bunch of no doubt real gold chains that probably cost more than Soldier ever had in his life. An expensive leather jacket over the shirt. His perfect-length hair was expensively barbered and blow-dried back and sprayed into place. Like every other young American male back then, he had a mustache, but it was also perfectly barbered, like William Powell in the old movies. And to bottom it off, he wore high-heeled platform shoes—red shoes with a heel that must have been three inches to boost him up over six feet.

He walked in like a wise guy in training, head moving right and left, slightly slouched shoulders, throwing hard looks at bar patrons, daring somebody, anybody, to start something. And there were the two huge bookends trailing behind him in black leather jackets, arm muscles like bowling balls straining against the leather.

The entourage moved to the entrance to the back room. Norma was dancing fast to Bowie's "Panic in Detroit" and its hard-rocking percussion riff. Mr. Cool turned on his heels and said something to his boys and they immediately retreated to the bar. Probably something about not looking at his girl while she danced mostly naked for a bunch of guys.

It was getting late and the bar was thinning out. Soldier had been sitting on a wooden chair by the stage, tilting it back with his foot, keeping an eye on everything: Norma, the guys sitting passively around during the show, except when they respectfully leaned over to put a bill on her offered out-thrust hip, and the front door. Nobody dared cop a feel with Soldier there. Word got around fast in Bronx neighborhoods. He saw Tony's crew as they walked in and quietly stood.

In front, Frankie was at the far end of the bar watching the TV up by the ceiling with the sound off. The Yankees, who were great again despite the owner fighting with Reggie over his eyesight, were on the West Coast, playing in LA. Frankie had also noticed the men come in and slowly began to walk toward the taps while glancing into the back room until he made eye contact with Soldier.

It happened fast. The song ended.

"Norma, let's go," Tony shouted in a too loud voice. "The car's right outside. You can get your stuff later."

"No, Tony."

"Okay, get your stuff. We can wait."

"No."

"No what?"

"No, leave me alone. It's over. I told you that a million times. No! No! No!"

He lurched forward and reached out his right arm to grab her when Soldier jumped in front of her, knocked the arm away, and slightly bumped into Tony, throwing him off balance in those high heels. He went backwards, losing his balance and pinwheeling both arms as he fell on his ass.

His boys raced in from the bar but they were too late. Just as one pulled a gun, Frankie had the shotgun pressed up against his ear. He put the gun back in his pants. The other guy helped his boss off the floor.

"Look at this," Tony shouted in the suddenly silent bar, making an elaborate show of brushing off his pants and pushing back his hair, though not a hair had fallen out of place. He glanced back at Frankie, who had put the shotgun down. "You run this place, fat boy? Because I was just assaulted by this tough mick in the army jacket looks like a hippie the size of a tree. And what's with that popgun? You think you are fighting for the IRA and we're the Brits? As for you," staring right at Soldier, "nobody puts their hands on me."

"Law says nobody can touch the dancers."

"I didn't touch her."

"You were about to."

"And you knocked me down."

"Looked to me like you lost your balance and tripped on those shoes. I am very sorry about that. It was not my intention that you fall, just to protect the dancer. Where did you get the shoes, by the way, Thom McAn's on Fordham Road?"

Tony's face turned beet red. He looked past Soldier, where Norma was huddled against the wall mirror, her hands once again over her breasts. Tony raised his voice.

"Let's go, Norma. Let's get out of this place where they pull rods on you and knock you down."

"No."

"I am taking you out of here."

"No."

"Seems like the lady has repeatedly said no," Soldier said. "Perhaps you should listen to her and leave."

"I ain't talking to you, mick." Now rage had him bouncing up and down on the balls of his feet. He tossed a pointed finger in the direction of Norma. Soldier's fists were balled at his side and he was motionless.

"Norma, I walk out that door and you are not with me, there is going to be trouble. And you . . ." He pointed the finger at Soldier. "You and me are not finished yet. This is not over."

"Probably not."

"Maybe we meet again when your boyfriend here does not have his shotgun. Let's go, guys. If that cunt wants to stay with this Irish filth . . . Irish girls are pigs anyway, not like Italian girls." He turned and marched out of the bar. Norma ran into the dressing room.

"Seems to know what he wants in women," Soldier said after they disappeared. "Might not be the best view to express in this neighborhood."

"Think they'll wait outside for her?" Frankie said, gun now pointing at the floor.

"Nah, they're done for the night. But we better keep Norma here until closing and then I'll drive her home."

"I'll feel better if I drive you both home. I just hope they don't come back later and throw a firebomb into the joint."

"Nah, can't collect on the insurance. There is no profit in it and it would attract cop attention his father doesn't need."

"He won't back down."

"No."

"You have a plan?"

"Deal with things as they develop."

"Well, one thing's for certain, things are certainly livelier with you around here."

"I try. Now put that gun away before your remove your toes and then I won't have anybody to dance with anymore. How about you take us to the Riverdale Diner later for French fries?"

THEY BOTH NOTICED IT IMMEDIATELY a few days later when Norma came to work. Soldier was sitting at his usual seat while Frankie polished the glasses nearby. Norma brushed by them with a "hi" and headed to the changing room. Normally, she would stop, sit at the bar, and maybe have a cup of tea. And she never wore heavy makeup; today her face looked like she was auditioning for the circus at Madison Square Garden. Even the paint job could not fully hide the shiner.

"See that?"

"Yep. I'll handle it," Jimmy said, getting off his stool.

"About time you did some work around here."

He pushed open the dressing room door without knocking. Norma was at the table painting on more makeup, if possible.

"Leave me alone, Jimmy. I don't want to talk about it."

"Just one question, Norma, did that animal do that to your face?"

"Not your problem. You are a great guy and all . . ." She burst into tears.

"Well, I am making it my problem. Remember, that wop bastard threatened me as well. Said it wasn't over and obviously it is not."

"There is nothing you can do. Nothing anybody can do. I just bollixed my life completely. I thought life over here in Amerikay would be an adventure, a bit of Ri-Ra and a lot of craic. But I got to get out of this place, away from here before something really bad happens, and I cause it."

"Wait, let's just deal with this and make sense of it."

"Ah, ya can't see. You said once I wasn't a hoor. But you got to admit I am in the same neighborhood, selling peeks of my hairy growler to strange men in a bar for dollar tips. And standing around almost in the nip while pervs leer at me. What sort of life is that? Good God, I can't even buy normal girl knickers." She reached her hand in her bag and pulled out a bunch of new G-strings. "And where does it lead when my jabs end up pointing at the floor in a few years? I'll be doing handjobs in the Port Authority."

"No, you won't. Besides, some people think exotic dancing is an art form."

"Yeah, men. I can't do this anymore I tell you. It is not a normal life."

Jimmy took a deep breath and looked away.

"Okay, one thing at a time. Where do you want to go? Home?"

"To Ireland, you mean? Are you dense, mate? Didcha forget why our people left that place to begin with?"

"Then where?"

"I got a cousin up in Boston, she just finished cosmetology school. Eventually, she wants to own her own place and get a green card, so she is not illegal anymore."

"You could do that."

"Fat chance. I'd never afford the tuition and he would never let me go."

"Nobody owns you, Norma. You can do what you want with your life."

"That's the problem with you, Jimmy."

"What is?"

"Saints can't see things as they really are in life."

"I learned to start really seeing life in a place a lot worse than you are in now."

He stood up and moved to the door.

"Jimmy?"

He turned and saw the river of tears plowing through the makeup.

"Thanks for being here for me all the time. But promise me something."

"Sure."

"You won't do something stupid and get yourself hurt."

He walked out and went back to his place at the bar.

"She alright?" Frankie asked.

"She's fine."

"And you?"

"Fine."

"Well, it sounds like everybody is fine and dandy then."

A FEW DAYS LATER, IN the late afternoon, Jimmy the Soldier was in his usual spot. The afternoon Irish bartender, Gary, who opened everyday had just served him his third cup of Barry's, as he was reading a chapter entitled "The Socialist Challenge" from Zinn's book. He looked up when Frankie came in, went behind the bar, ambled over, and dropped a fat brown envelope atop the book.

"What's that? And you look particularly happy today."

"Good news and even better news. The good news is that that is your fee from the AC trip. Put it away."

Soldier picked up the envelope, bounced it in his hands a few times, and put it in the breast pocket of his army jacket.

"And the better news is that I was talking to some people in the know this morning and Tony's Manucci's kid had an accident last night."

"Fall off his shoes?"

"Something like that. You know he has an auto body shop down in the burnt-out South Bronx, off 149th in a crappy garage. It's like the only place in the hood that custom details and repairs sports cars. Meanwhile, nobody white has gone down there in twenty-five years. You knew that, right?"

"If you say so."

"Late last night, Tony Jr. was in there alone and a Porsche fell on his head."

"Ouch! Probably left a bad bruise."

"Killed him dead from a broken neck is what they tell me."

"Hmmm."

"That all you can say?"

"Nice car? What do you want me to tell you? Accidents happen. If you are not careful, a car can slip off a jack in a Bronx second. Got to be careful with that shit. And you saw the guy, he did a swan dive in here and I barely touched him. Guy did not look all that careful to me. Besides, he was nothing but a bully, able to beat up women and the weak. Stuff always ends up happening to scum like that eventually. No big loss to the world."

"Accidents happen especially if they are helped."

"What exactly are you saying here, Frankie?"

"Look, man, nothing. I just hope there was nothing linking whatever happened down there to this bar. Tony Sr. and his friends play rough."

"Relax."

A female voice chimed in. "Why are we relaxing?"

"Some good news in the neighborhood," Frankie said, walking away. "Somebody finally took the garbage out."

Norma, looking puzzled, took a seat at the bar, way early as usual. Girl was nothing if not conscientious. Her face was not as bad as it had been. The bruise was fading yellow.

"Whatever, Frankie. Jimmy, I just want to say I'm sorry for the way I bit your head off. I was feeling sorry for myself and you were just trying to help."

Jimmy reached into the army jacket, took out the envelope, and handed it to her.

"What's this?"

"Your down payment on a new life."

Again, she fixed him with the big green eyes; this time in surprise, not fear.

"What?"

"Do not open it here. Put it right in your bag. You cannot trust the clientele in bars like this. Look at the big guy over there behind the bar. But there is enough in there to get you to Boston, find you a modest place to live and pay your beauty school tuition. With maybe a few bucks left over to buy normal girl knickers."

"You're giving me money?"

"Call it a loan."

"I can't take this from you. . . . Your money."

"You just did, darlin'."

"But I could never pay you back."

"You will eventually, when you get on your feet."

"Jimmy, thank you, but I can't."

"Stop saying that. Sure you can. Look at it as life giving you an opportunity to better yourself. Or if you prefer: Giving me an opportunity at no cost to help another human being. All you need is the guts to seize the moment. And, darlin', you got guts. I've seen them, along with your jabs and occasional glimpses of your growler—whatever the hell that is—four nights a week for a long time now. It took guts to do what you did on that stage. And it took guts to cross a giant ocean to find us in the Bronx. Now it will take guts to start that new, better life in Boston."

"I dunno about this."

"Well, there is a condition with it."

"And what is that?"

"You got to leave now, right this minute. No more dancing in here. No looking back. No hanging around the Bronx. Now. Leave. Go. Consider this your severance from the GreenLeaf. Go home, pack, call your cousin. Hey, Frankie?" The big man looked over.

"Yeah?"

"What train goes up to Boston?"

"Amtrak."

"Where does it leave from? Grand Central?"

"Penn Station, I think."

"That's fine. You call 'em, Norma, make a reservation. Heck, the 1 train right outside will take you to Penn Station. One bag is all you need to start. Anything else, leave it and I will make sure it gets there, if I have to drive it myself. Penn Station is the stop after Times Square."

"Now? I got to go now?"

"That's my one condition."

"Why are you doing this?"

"Easy. Because I can and I will and I did. Case closed."

"But what about . . ."

"What?"

"You."

"Me? What about me?"

"Well, I thought you liked me."

"I do. A lot. Enough to invest a small fortune in your future."

"No, I always thought that there was going to be, you know, an us." She reached over and put her hand on top of his. He felt something start to melt inside.

"I'm too old for you."

"Bollocks. No, you're not."

"Look, Norma, think about it. You just got out of a bad, abusive relationship. You need time to work on yourself, to take care of yourself and get your life started right . . . in school, in a new place. Believe me. You need this."

"Ah, but what about Tony coming after me?"

Frankie let out a snort. She looked over where he was fiddling with the glasses.

Jimmy answered. "Won't happen. I can assure you. He has decided to work on his cars, especially his Porsche."

A few silent moments passed, rock music low in the background from the radio. "Memory Motel" by the Stones.

"I can't believe I won't be seeing you anymore. What if I have a problem?"

"I'm a phone call away. This place still has a phone, right, Frankie? You father did not take it out?"

"We still got a phone."

"Can this really be happening?"

"It already did."

"Will you come up visit me?"

"You can count on it. Hell, you'll probably get so sick of me, you'll want me to go back to the Bronx. Besides . . ." He picked up the book. "Professor Zinn teaches in Boston. I want to go to one of his classes and talk to him. Maybe more than one. And there is another teacher up there by the name of Chomsky. Want to look him up as well. They know the truth."

"Stand up a minute, my savior, Saint James."

He stood up and she came forward and pressed her body hard into him and gave him the longest, deepest kiss of his short life. And he returned it with all his being. He leaned backward and one point and she stayed with him, briefly leaving her feet, kicking one foot behind her. When it ended finally and she broke away, tears were pouring down her face.

"Thank you, Jimmy. I could not have done this without you. I could never have gotten through this without you. Everybody in this place knows there is something serious going on between us. And that's the truth not in your book."

He just started mumbling something that did not make sense.

"Hush. I listened to you. Now, you'll listen to me. You need a savior as well. You can't go through life always the hard man. You are not as tough as you pretend. So I will do as you say. For now. I will get me head back on straight and maybe then we can pick up this conversation where we just left it. Maybe an us. That's my down payment to you, kiddo."

"Ah, yeah. Sure. Whatever you say."

"This is no joke: I love you. I will always love you and now you have made me mess up me face."

"Go, darlin', go."

With that, she grabbed her bag from the bar and turned away. Then she stopped, reached in, and took out a half-used silver tube and tossed it to him.

"What's this?" he said catching it with both hands.

"My glitter that sparkles. Maybe you can find use for it."

Then she fled the bar. "Bye, Frankie, thanks for everything. Love you, too."

Jimmy the Soldier sank down on his stool, the tube in his hands, and was suddenly very tired. He struggled unsuccessfully to stifle back his tears. Frankie ambled over.

"Have a good life," he muttered, looking at the door. But she was gone.

"Thanks. You too. But I have just one question," Frankie said.

"What?"

"You're going after her, right?"

"What, and leave you. Nah, I'm fine here."

"Like hell you are. You're a fool, Jimmy. Here's a girl deflates and inflates your lungs in a bar and pledges her love forever and you're gonna let her walk."

"Some things you can't make better by wishing, Frankie. Ever."

"Says you. Well, at least you are a romantic fool. I'll give you that."

The big man started to laugh.

"What's so funny?"

"You know, when she was kissing you there and you leaned back and she was in your arms, all you needed was a sailor's uniform and you would have recreated that famous photo of VJ Day in Times Square of the sailor and the nurse. Looked just like that. Wish I had a camera."

Jimmy the Soldier said nothing but rubbed his hand along his face. It came away wet. The hand with the tube in it was shaking slightly.

"Maybe the Soldier has finally come home, Jim. Maybe the war is over. Think about that."

"I will take a drink now, Frankie."

SPIT THE TRUTH
BY EVE KAGAN

THE FIFTH FLOOR WALK-UP HAD never been an issue before. When she moved in the summer after graduation she was surprised it was not included in the amenities: South facing. Hardwood floors. Electric stove. Built-in StairMaster to your front door! After four years of pizza and beer, and in spite of the occasional bout of anorexia or bump of coke, she figured her ass could use it.

They told her not to drive home, not that anyone she knew drove in New York City. They told her to take a cab, not that she could afford one. But no one told her to hire someone to help her up the stairs. She had it all planned out: *Friends* reruns on TBS, Ben & Jerry's Chunky Monkey, expired Vicodin stolen from her aunt Ginny. She sat down on the stoop feeling woozy, empty, and alone. She wondered if this would be her only abortion or merely her first. She wondered if this moment would become an anecdote she would tell at fancy dinner parties on the Upper West Side or rooftop barbecues in Fort Greene. She wondered how the fuck she was going to get up the stairs.

It wasn't like she slept with her professor or her boss or a married man or a stranger. His name was Teddy. He was a bartender. He made killer mojitos and his dreadlocks smelled like sweet almond oil. He wasn't interested in a relationship. He was an aspiring musician. She felt like everyone in the city was an aspiring something, except for her. Somehow her aspirations got left behind with the boxes of philosophy books in her parents' basement. There they sat, collecting dust with Hegel.

She was wearing black yoga pants and a threadbare Haverford sweatshirt that she had worn since junior high. She'd spent the fall of seventh grade chewing thumb holes into the wristbands while staring with longing at the back of Ari Cohen's head. That was 1993 grunge in suburbia. This was 2003 hell in Harlem. She shoved her thumbs through the holes. Still comforting ten years later.

When had it become fall? It was only 4:30 p.m., but the sun was already threatening to set too soon on what she figured should be an excruciatingly long day in her life. It wasn't exactly cold yet or crisp, but the light had changed from the golden glow of summer to something starker. A little girl in pigtails came skipping past the stoop and flashed her a shy smile. Her mom was close behind her wearing a newborn in a green raw silk sling. They probably thought she was fine, just fine, maybe a bit winded after a run or a Bikram class. Did anybody really know anything about anyone?

She reached for the railing. How did handicapped people survive in this city? It's not like everyone in a wheelchair could afford to live in a building with a doorman and an elevator. Not that she was comparing her present situation to being a paraplegic or a war hero. She had just read an article in *Time* about the first soldiers blown up by IEDs in Iraq. They said when you lose a limb you feel this tingling like the ghost of the arm or leg haunting the empty space that was once full of flesh. She wondered if her womb would tingle with the loss or if it would just return to business as usual, pretending nothing ever happened, like a broken heart that loves again in spite of the cracks.

She had never thought of herself as the kind of girl who would get an abortion. She was the last one to lose her virginity. Sure, she was felt up before she was ever French kissed but those things happen. Sure, she was pro-choice but that was just a position. The reality was that the condom broke. She told him she was on the pill (a lie). She told him not to worry (she was worried). She told him it was no big deal (another lie). Six weeks later she walked into the bar wearing her tightest dress, so he would notice her swollen belly. He didn't. The next morning she called the clinic.

Maybe she should have told him. Maybe she should have told someone. The lady at the front desk was clearly under the impression that a friend would be taking her home. She had friends, but after college they were scattered across the world. Amy was in London getting an MA in directing from LAMDA. Jeff was sleeping in a hammock on a beach in Laos. Sarah S was a legal assistant in San Francisco. Sarah K was on a pilgrimage to Kyoto to pay homage to her ancestors.

This wasn't exactly the kind of news you shared over the phone or in a group email. She hadn't made any real friends in the city. She moved into her place two months before 9/11 and even after two years, xenophobia was still rampant. She had acquaintances but they weren't the kind of people who would carry her up the stairs.

The wind blew another piece of hair loose from her ponytail. If she had to withstand one more car horn she would probably scream. Everyone in the city was in such a big fucking hurry. She stood up too quickly and braced her left hand against the brown door. There were tiny flecks of silver paint surrounding the doorknob that she had never noticed. They looked like a miniature constellation. She reached into her pocket for the key and jammed it into the lock. The sound of old metal on metal grating from years of lazy landlords and hurried tenants hurt her ears. Everything was throbbing with poor choices.

She opened the door.

A young black boy was hopping down the stairs from the first floor landing. He froze, dropped to a seat on the lowest step, and stared up at her with his mouth agape as if he had just been doing something naughty. This *who me?* look was clearly perfected from years of being caught in the act. He was probably around ten years old, but skinny, his long arms swimming in the oversized T-shirt sleeves, his slim jeans bunched up around the ankles, riding just above pristine white Nikes that must have been brand new for the first day of school. He had wide-set eyes with long thick lashes like a baby doll. His front teeth were two sizes too large for his mouth.

"My mama says I can play on the steps as long as I don't go outside."

"Okay."

She stumbled slightly at the sound of the door slamming shut behind her.

"You sick or something?"

She was always taken aback by how sharp kids could be, how they had no filter, how truth just spilled out of them. She was suddenly blinded by a memory of eating chocolate chip pancakes at a roadside diner with her mother. She was four. She was dipping a pancake wedge into a pool of syrup when a very overweight man pushed through the doors. She had never seen anything like him before and announced at full voice, "Mama, look at the fat man!" She was promptly slapped. That was perhaps her last moment of raw honesty.

"When I'm sick my mama makes me take my shoes off so my head won't get too hot. She says the fever gonna drip down through my toes and then I'll be all better. You don't look so good."

"Thanks."

Even at ten he could catch her hard edge. Was every kid in New York City born with an innate sense of sarcasm?

"You're right. I don't feel so good. Can I sit here with you for a minute?"

"Don't you gotta get upstairs and lie down?"

"I do but I'm not ready yet."

She slumped down on the lowest step next to the boy. The front hall always smelled like something had been left in the oven too long. The stairs were painted the same swampy brown as the front door.

"You can't take your shoes off now cause it's all kindsa dirty up in here."

"You're right."

She swallowed hard, feeling the vomit rise up in her throat, the chili basil sauce from last night's drunken noodles fomenting a riot in her gut.

"I got seven sistas."

"Excuse me?"

"I got seven sistas."

She realized she had seen him before amidst the parade of girls in various styles of cornrows tromping up to the third floor on Sundays at noon. She had assumed they were related but not that they were all sisters or that there were actually seven of them. They were anywhere between two and eighteen years old which must have landed him splat in the middle.

"What's that like? I mean, what's it like to be the only boy?"

"It's a-ight. They nice and all but they don't know how it is."

"What do you mean?"

"How it is to be the man."

"You're the man, huh?"

"Naw naw, not like, *you da man*, like cool. I mean the heavy."

"The heavy?"

"Life."

"Life? Right, life."

"Bein' a man ain't no Christmas party. My mama says I gotta win the bread and be stand up. But sometimes I just wanna sit down, you know?"

"I do."

"My sistas got it easy."

"You think so?"

"Yeah. If one of them do somethin' bad they can just blame the otha one and half the time my mama can't even tell them apart. But if I do somethin' bad they all know it was me and even if it wasn't me they gonna blame it on me anyway and there's just one of me so that's that."

"Sounds rough."

He proceeded to give her what her mother would surely call *the fish eye*.

"No really. It sounds like you get a lot of the blame."

"Mmmmhmmm. You got any sistas?"

"Nope. No sisters. No brothers. Just me."

"For serious?"

"For serious."

"Are you sure?"

"I'm pretty sure. Unless I was separated at birth from my twin and my parents kept it a secret all these years like in one of those Lifetime original movies." She watched her reference fly right over his head.

"Yeah. I wish I had a twin, too."

She could have sworn this moment was the closest to silence she had ever experienced in a city that was never silent. And of course she felt the need to fill it.

"So are you in school?"

"Duh. Why grownups always gotta ask about school? You all miss it or something?"

She had never been called a grownup before.

"I don't know. Maybe."

"Why?"

"I guess because school has structure. You know exactly how your day is going to go: Math. Science. Art. Recess. Once you get out of school everything gets kind of . . . blurry."

"Like when you open your eyes underwater?"

"What?"

"I did that last summa at the lake by my grandmama's house. My eyes stung like crazy and all I could see was brown."

"Exactly. What's your name anyway?"

"Jeremiah. What's yours?"

"Tal."

The fish eye.

"My real name is Talia but everyone calls me Tal."

"But you ain't tall, you short."

"And you aren't a bullfrog."

"Huh?"

"Don't you know that song?" She belted out: "Jeremiah was a bullfrog! Bah dah bah . . ."

"You crazy!"

"That may be true but it's a real song."

"Well, I'ma call you shorty cuz you ain't tall."

"Then I'm gonna call you bullfrog."

"You crazy!" He laughed.

She could feel the blood seeping around the wings of the pad. It was less of a pad and more of an adult diaper. Even with seven sisters she figured she would have to wait for Jeremiah to go home before she made her way up. She wondered whether she was the only one in the city bleeding on overpriced yoga pants. She was glad she went with black instead of gray.

"Are you married?"

"What? No."

"You got a boyfriend?"

"Nope. Why? Do you want to be my boyfriend?"

"Naw, I got a girlfriend. Fayth. With a Y not an I."

"Oh."

"I mean, you cool and all but I gotta be real to my girl."

"Definitely."

"We could be friends though."

"I've heard that one before. I mean, that would be nice."

"Nice?"

"Cool?"

"Dope."

"Dope? Dope it is then."

"You tryin' a get ridda me? Cuz I won't go out witchu?"

"No. Not at all."

"Good. So where was you?"

"Where was I when?"

"Where was you when you got all sick? You out all night partyin'? My Auntie D she like to party all night an' then she come over an' sleep on the floor all day long even when my sista put on *In Da Club* an we be dancin' all over her. You know that song? 50 Cent is da bomb!"

"He's the one who got shot like ten times, right?"

"Nine times. He a survivor."

"I thought that was Beyoncé."

"You know a lotta hip hop for a white lady."

"I think a lot of white ladies like hip hop."

"For serious?"

"I think you would be surprised."

"Like that dude to be or not to be."

"Hamlet?"

"Shak-a-speare. My Drama teacher say he was like the original white hip hop artist cuz his plays rhyme and he be talkin' 'bout how the system is all kindsa messed up. He spit the truth yo, like Tupac."

"That's very cool."

"You a writer?"

"No. Why, is that what you want to be?"

"Uh-uh. I wanna be a firefighter like my uncle Ray. He ran up all them flights a stairs an' saved a whole lotta people before he died. What you wanna be?"

"I don't know."

"How you don't know? Aren't you already supposta be somethin'?"

"Probably. Got any ideas?"

She watched his eyes crinkle as he looked her up and down searching earnestly for the right answer.

"You should be a teacher. Or a mama."

"Why?"

"Duh. Cuz you good with kids. Like you don't talk to me like I'm a baby, you talk to me like I'm a man."

"Thank you."

"You don't gotta get all polite or nothin'. I just tell it like it is."

"Spit the truth, right?"

"Right. Well, I gotta go."

"Really? I mean, sure, of course, you have things to do."

"Feel better, shorty."

"Thanks, bullfrog."

"You crazy!"

She stayed on the step as he ran up. She could hear the rubber of his sneakers squeak against the floor every time he hit the landing and turned sharp for the next set of stairs. She didn't watch but she was pretty sure he was climbing two at a time, racing himself like only kids do.

She brought her knees up toward her chest and slowly unlaced her shoes. She was afraid some other neighbor would walk in and ruin everything by brushing past her or worse yet asking if she needed a hand. There was no way she was willing to sacrifice this moment, this almost memory, for a few more breaths toward recovery. She flexed her toes and gingerly dipped them toward the filthy floor. She could feel generations of women in her family gasping at the sight. The floor was cold. She wondered whether it was a boy or a girl, or would have been. She pushed herself up, grabbed the banister, leaning into it slightly like a crutch, and started her way up. Her sweaty feet left little prints behind that disappeared almost before she could catch them.

THIS POSE IS A PROBLEM
BY BILL BERNICO

BOB AND SUE BERGMAN STEPPED off the plane at JFK International Airport, waited for their luggage on the carousel, and carried the bags to the first car rental counter they found. Bob chose a mid-size sedan and before they left the lot, Bob opened his suitcase and withdrew the GPS he'd brought with him from Wisconsin. He plugged it into the accessory outlet and punched in a search for hotels in New York. The screen had so many little red arrows on it that they nearly obliterated the rest of the map. He had to start over and refine the search criteria, confining the search to Manhattan only. He instinctively chose the red arrow that was closest to his present location and entered its address into the unit. The unit brought the couple right up to the front door of their hotel on Forty-second Street. The name on the front of the building identified it as the Hilton Manhattan East Hotel.

"I told you it would be better to rent a car than to take a cab," Bob told his wife. "Can you imagine what one of those cabbies would have charged us to get here? They'd have probably taken the long way around, like that cabbie did to Clint Eastwood in *Coogan's Bluff*, remember?"

Sue Bergman nodded and said, "Yes, and he wanted to charge Clint for luggage when all he had was a briefcase."

They checked into their hotel, unpacked their luggage, and stowed the suitcases in the closet before collapsing on the two full-size beds. Sue pulled a stack of glossy nine-by-twelve photos that they'd brought with them for this trip. The photos had all been bought at movie memorabilia shops over the past few years. They were stills from several of the couple's favorite movies. On the back of each photo, Bob had penciled in the street address of the particular location. The purpose of their trip to New York was to visit all these film locations and pose for pictures at those exact spots. The two Wisconsinites were both movie buffs, having seen several hundred movies from the forties through the eighties. They didn't really care for contemporary movies, preferring the classics from days gone by.

Bob changed into a pair of comfortable walking shoes, knowing that he and Sue would be doing quite a bit of travel on foot to get where they needed to be. Bob knew that the first place he wanted to visit was the twenty-third precinct police station that Coogan had visited on his trip to New York. He held his hand out toward Sue and asked for the *Coogan's Bluff* photo from the pile. She found it quickly and handed it to Bob. Bob turned the photo over and read the address to Sue.

"It's on West Thirtieth Street between Sixth and Seventh Avenues in Manhattan," Bob announced. "See why I brought along my GPS? Right after we get some lunch we can drive over there and take our shots. I'll bet we can get half a dozen good shots before the day is done. Hell, we've got three days here. That should be more than enough time to get everything we need."

"And won't they all look terrific in our scrapbook?" Sue said. "That first section we put together from the Los Angeles locations turned out great. The second section with the film location photos from Chicago was not as good. At least I didn't think so. But this section will be the best of the three. Do you realize how many movies were shot right here in New York?"

"I hope that's a rhetorical question," Bob said, "because there were hundreds and even I couldn't remember all of them."

"I know," Sue said, patting the pile of movie stills in her lap. "But we're only interested in the ones in this stack. Let's go eat. I'm hungry."

They found a restaurant nearby and spent as little time there as they could, wanting to spend the bulk of their time in the city finding movie locations. When they'd finished, Bob and Sue got back into their rented car and followed the GPS unit's directions. "Looks like we can keep going this way on Forty-second Street and then turn left on Park Avenue," Bob announced.

"I've always wanted to see Park Avenue," Sue said.

As Bob approached the intersection at Park Avenue, Sue looked out her window and pointed to a tall building. "Bob, look," she said. "It's the Pan Am Building where Coogan landed in that helicopter, remember?"

"It's the same building, alright," Bob agreed. "But it says MetLife on it. Looks like insurance was more lucrative than airlines. I'll bet they bought it from Pan Am." Bob turned right on Park Avenue and pulled to the curb. He got out and stood behind his rented car as he snapped several photos of the oddly shaped skyscraper before he slid behind the wheel again. He turned to Sue. "Good catch. I would have missed it."

Bob continued south on Park Avenue and caught Thirtieth Street heading east. As he passed Fifth Avenue Sue said, "I wonder where Saks is."

"I don't know," Bob said, but the police station has to be up ahead just a couple more blocks." He stopped for the light at the next corner and looked up at the street sign. "Avenue of the Americas," he said. "What happened to Sixth Avenue?"

Sue saw a man standing at the corner, waiting to cross. She rolled down her window and yelled to the man, "Excuse me." The man turned toward the sound of her voice. "Can you tell me where Sixth Avenue is?"

The man's brow furrowed. "What are you, some kind of wise guy?" he said and crossed when the light changed.

Sue rolled her window up again and turned to her husband. "That was odd. I guess people aren't very friendly around here."

Bob drove on and had gone only half a block when he looked out his window and spotted the familiar police station. He stopped in the middle of the block, amid horn honks and shouts behind him. "That's it," he told Sue. "I've got to find a place to park so we can get some pictures." He circled the block and then widened his search, eventually finding a parking place two blocks away. "See," he said, turning to Sue. "This is why I brought comfortable walking shoes along."

The two of them got out and walked at a brisk pace toward the 23rd precinct building. Bob looked all around him and commented, "For some reason I thought this place was a little more out in the open. Look at this street. I'll bet I could spit across it and hit the other side."

He and Sue walked up to the front of the building, touching the rough stone exterior with their hands, looking, Sue was sure, like a couple of out-of-town tourists. Bob handed Sue the camera and then stepped back against the building, pointing at the front door while she snapped several photos. They reversed their positions and Bob took a few photos of Sue in much the same pose.

Satisfied that he had what he came for, Bob took Sue's hand and walked her back to the rented car. Once back inside, Bob turned on the digital camera and brought up the photos they'd just taken. Sue leaned in to get a look and the two of them smiled at their accomplishment.

"What's next on the list?" Sue said.

Bob pulled a printed list from his pocket and looked over the locations before announcing, "According to this, we're only four or five blocks away from Macy's Department Store."

"*Miracle on 34th Street*," Sue said. "That's one of my favorite movies. Let's go see it."

When he got to the corner of West Thirty-fourth Street and Seventh Avenue, Bob looked up and down the streets. "We'll never be able to find a place to park around here. How about if we park this car somewhere else and take a cab back to this corner?"

"That's probably a good idea," Sue said. "You'll probably want a cab anyway when you want to get pictures of the Plaza Hotel. You know, a picture of you getting into a cab, posing like Cary Grant in *North by Northwest*."

"Good idea," Bob said, driving away from Macy's. They found a parking place nine blocks away and spent another fifteen minutes hailing a cab. They got out in front of Macy's and told the cabbie to wait around the corner while they took their photos. The cabbie smiled, imagining these two running up a pretty hefty bill before they were through.

Before they got back into the cab, Bob turned to Sue and whispered, "Let's try to act like we belong here, or this cabbie's gonna run us all over town. Let me do the talking."

When they got back into the backseat of the yellow cab, Bob told the driver to take them to the Plaza Hotel and then settled back in his seat.

The cab pulled up in front of the hotel and before Bob could open the cab door, a doorman from the Plaza Hotel pulled it open and swept an arm out, inviting them to step out of the cab. Bob looked at Sue and raised his eyebrows. "Now that's service," he said, sliding out of the cab and extending his hand out to Sue. She took it and stepped out of the cab, taking the camera from Bob and stepping ahead of the cab.

Bob leaned in to the front window and told the cabbie to wait for them. The doorman had closed the cab's back door but Bob opened it again, posing with his hand on the door, as if he was catching a cab. Sue snapped several photos and again switched places with Bob for her turn as the model. When they'd finished, Sue and Bob slid back into the cab and closed the door, leaving the doorman standing there, waiting for the tip that wasn't coming. The cab pulled away from the curb. "Where to now, mac?" the cabbie said.

Bob checked his list and announced, "Grand Central Terminal."

"You got it," the cabbie said, occasionally glancing at the ever-rising amount on his meter. When he got to Grand Central, he turned around in his seat and said, "You want me to wait here, too?"

"Yes," Bob said. "We won't be long."

The nervous cabbie looked Bob over and pointed to the meter. "You're running up quite a tab here, bud. Suppose you give me a little down payment while I'm waiting. I've been ripped off once too often to trust anyone."

"Oh, sure," Bob said, looking at the meter and peeling two twenties off the roll he had in his pocket. "Here, that should keep you happy until we get back. It'll just be a few minutes." He and Sue stood across the street, snapping several photos of the outside of the building before going inside to compare the glossy photos to the actual locations. They both posed again in the approximate place that Cary Grant had stood during the filming of the Alfred Hitchcock classic thriller. Bob checked another location off his list and took Sue by the hand, walking her back out to the waiting cab.

"Let me guess," the cabbie said. "The United Nations building, right?"

Bob and Sue looked at each other in wide-eyed amazement. "How'd you know?" Bob said.

The cabbie exhaled deeply. "You think you're the first tourists to want to see movie locations? *North by Northwest* was a big deal for New York when they filmed it here back in '59. Of course I was only nine years old at the time, but my mother told me all about being outside the Plaza when they were shooting that cab scene with Cary Grant, so I knew right away what you two were doing."

"Well, that should save us a few explanations," Bob told the cabbie.

"I take it you got shots inside Grand Central Terminal," the cabbie said, driving on to the UN Building.

"Uh huh," Bob agreed.

"I don't suppose I have to tell you that it was also used in *The Out-of-Towners*, do I?" the cabbie said.

"Jack Lemmon and Sandy Dennis," Bob offered. "That's another one of our favorites."

"Tell you what," the cabbie said. "When you're done taking your pictures of the UN Building, I can drive you over to the Waldorf Astoria Hotel where those two actors tried to get a room. After that I can drive you through Central Park and point out a couple more movie locations."

"Thank you very much," Bob said. "That'll save me a lot of time looking them up."

"All part of the full service," the cabbie said.

Bob and Sue got their UN photos, got back into the cab, and sat back as their personal guide drove them to the Waldorf. The cabbie waited at the curb as Bob and Sue snapped a few photos of the outside of the Waldorf before going inside to pose for a few more shots. When they had what they came for, Bob and Sue got back into the cab, smiling at their accomplishments.

The cabbie turned around and asked, "Get everything you need?"

Bob and Sue both nodded and smiled. "I think so," Sue said.

"I don't think so," the cabbie said. "Do you remember the scene in *The Out-of-Towners* where that couple sat on the steps of that church to rest and eventually went inside to pray?"

Bob and Sue looked at each other and then back at the cabbie. "You know where that church is?" Bob said.

"Sure," the cabbie said confidently. "When we come back out of Central Park on Sixty-fifth Street, we'll be less than a block away from it. You wanna see it?"

"You bet," Bob said, and off they went to fulfill yet another goal in their quest for movie locations.

After they'd taken exterior and interior photos of the church, they got back into the cab and sighed.

"Where to next?" the cabbie said.

"That's it for us for today," Bob said. "We're beat. We can pick this up again tomorrow. Hell, we've got three days. No sense knocking ourselves out the first day."

The cabbie slipped one of his business cards through the slot in the Plexiglas partition. "Call me tomorrow whenever you're ready. I can pick you up wherever you're staying. Is that where you want to go now?"

"Yes," Bob said.

"No," Sue interjected. "We have to go back and get the rental car that we left parked on the street."

"And where would that be?" the cabbie said.

Bob and Sue looked at each other. "Uh oh," Bob said. "I hope you remember where we parked it."

Sue shrugged. "I thought wrote it down before we left it there," she said.

"Let's not panic," Bob said. "Let's think back." He looked at the cabbie. It has to be somewhere near where you picked us up. You have that written down on your clipboard?"

The cabbie checked his drive sheet before offering, "It was near Bryant Park. I'll take you there now."

Bob let out a deep breath. "Thank goodness," he said. "I thought we'd lost the car."

"When we get back to it, let's turn it in," Sue said.

The cabbie turned around in his seat. "If you like I can follow you back to the car rental place and then drive you back to your hotel."

"That would be great," Sue said. "Thank you so much."

The cabbie dropped Bob and Sue off near Bryant Park and the memory of where Bob had parked the rental came back to him a little at a time. He paid the cabbie for the time on the meter so far and then drove the rental car back to the turn-in garage. He and Sue took the cab back to their hotel and promised to call the cabbie again the next morning.

Back in their room, Bob and Sue looked at what they'd photographed that day and were pleased with their results. The digital pictures on the camera matched the glossy stills in both location and pose. Their scrapbook would be one section richer when they returned home to Wisconsin two days from now.

The next morning after breakfast, Bob called the number on the card the cabbie had given him and told the cabbie they'd be standing out in front of their hotel at nine o'clock. The cabbie was there a couple minutes early and greeted the couple as they slid into the backseat to continue their quest for movie locations.

"Well," the cabbie said. "Where would you like to start this morning?"

"I was thinking about *The Odd Couple*," Bob said. "You remember that movie?"

"Indeed I do," the cabbie said. "Which locations interest you?"

Sue picked through the pile of glossy prints and selected three, handing them to Bob. Bob turned the first one over and read the address aloud. The Hotel Flanders at 133 West Forty-seventh Street. You know where that is?"

"I know where that was," the cabbie said.

"Was?"

"Yeah, they tore it down some years ago," the cabbie said. "Sorry. Anyplace else you wanna see from that movie?"

"How about Oscar's apartment at 131 Riverside Drive?" Bob said.

"Now that I know is still there," the cabbie said. "Riverside Drive it is."

When they got to the corner of Riverside and West Eighty-fifth Street, Bob smiled when he recognized the familiar building. He elbowed Sue and pointed out the window. "There it is," he said. When the cab pulled to the curb, Bob and Sue got out, camera in hand, ready to snap their photos. Sue held the glossy photo in one hand while she instructed Bob where to stand and how to pose for the correct replica shot. Bob did the same for Sue and then returned to the backseat of the cab. He turned the third photo over and read the address to the cabbie. "Soldiers' and Sailors' Memorial Monument," he said.

The cabbie laughed.

"Did I say something funny?" Bob asked.

The cabbie pointed out the windshield of his cab. "It's just up ahead, not far from here. I'll have you there in less than a minute."

Bob and Sue repeated their picture-taking routine, with each of them posing in the shot, before returning to the cab, satisfied with their efforts.

"Where to next?" the cabbie said.

Sue raised her index finger. "I'd like to see *The Goodbye Girl*'s apartment building," she said, turning over the glossy print and reading the address to the cabbie. It's at 170 West Seventy-eighth Street at Amsterdam Avenue. Are we far from there?"

"Not too far," the cabbie assured her. "Maybe a dozen blocks, give or take. Sit back and relax. I'll have you there in no time."

The cabbie headed east on Eighty-sixth Street and turned south onto Amsterdam. As promised, less than a dozen blocks to the south he pulled up to the curb and pointed to an old apartment building on the corner. "There she be," he said.

Sue grabbed Bob's hand excitedly as the two of them exited to the street. The cabbie watched as the two tourists walked around the doorway to the building, snapping pictures and posing as if they were the principal players in that Oscar-winning movie.

Bob looked up at the fire escape that hung from the front of the building. He turned to Sue. "I wonder if I could climb up there so you could get a picture of me leaning over the fire escape railing, you know, like Richard Dreyfuss did when he was calling down to Marsha Mason."

"I don't know, Bob," Sue said. "That sounds dangerous, not to mention that it might make that second story tenant mad. You wouldn't want to get shot for trespassing, would you?"

Bob thought about it for a moment and said, "I guess not. But let me get a shot of it from here anyway. Later I can use my graphics editing program and insert a picture of me in the shot."

"Okay," Sue agreed. "Then let's get out of here. I don't like the look of this neighborhood."

Bob took a few more photos and quickly led Sue back to the cab. "Get what you were after?" the cabbie said. Bob said that he did. "Okay, folks, where to next?"

Bob held out his hand and waited for Sue to hand him the next set of glossies. He turned the first one over and announced, "Park Avenue and East Sixty-eighth Street."

The cabbie smiled, knowing how many people he'd already taken to this now-famous corner. "*Midnight Cowboy*, right?" he said while still looking forward.

"Boy, you really know your movies, too, don't you?" Sue said.

"It's not that," the cabbie confessed. "It's just that I've taken more than my share of tourists to that same corner. If I remember correctly, that's the corner where Jon Voight followed that woman across the intersection and asked her for directions to the Statue of Liberty."

"Yeah," Bob agreed, "but she was on to him and knew that he was just trying to pick her up and offer his stud service."

"Right," the cabbie said. "And not far from there is the townhouse where Voight daydreamed about taking that woman. I can show you that location as well, if you like."

"If we like?" Bob said. "That was going to be our next stop." When the cabbie parked at the corner, Bob asked him if he'd like to take a couple of shots of him and Sue crossing that intersection. The cabbie agreed, knowing that the meter would be running the whole time. "When we get across the street," Bob told him, "take a picture of the two of us in the same location as Voight and that woman. Get it?"

"Clever," the cabbie said. "Sure, I'll be glad to take those pictures for you."

Bob waited until the cabbie was situated in the proper place for the right effect and then waved to him. Sue crossed the intersection with Bob following close behind her. The cabbie snapped several pictures of that event and then crossed the street himself to get the close-up shot of the two of them, with the same backdrop as in the movie.

When they finished, the three of them got back into the cab. Bob and Sue immediately checked the camera's three-inch screen, looking at the photos the cabbie had taken of them pretending to be Joe Buck and the classy woman. They were perfect. Bob looked up at the cabbie. "Great shots," he said. "Thanks a lot."

"All part of the full service," the cabbie said, parroting the phrase he'd used on them the day before. "I'll take you to that townhouse now." He drove two blocks to the location used in the movie and parked at the curb while Bob and Sue got the shots they wanted for their scrapbook. They returned to the cab and double-checked their pictures before they were satisfied that they could move on to the next project.

The sun would be setting within the hour and Bob knew he needed to get a few more shots before he and Sue called it a day. He looked at the cabbie. "There're just three more locations we want to photograph before we quit for the day," Bob said.

"And the address?" the cabbie said.

Bob looked at the back of one of the last three glossies that Sue had handed him. "Would you take us to 33 Riverside Drive at West Seventy-fifth Street, please?"

The cabbie scratched his head. "You got me on that one," he said. "Which movie are we talking about here?"

Bob smiled, proud that he'd finally stumped the knowledge-able cabbie. "That would be Paul Kersey's apartment building from *Death Wish* with Charles Bronson," Bob announced.

The cabbie snapped his fingers. "I would have gotten it in another minute. Yes, I saw that movie several times. Riverside Drive it is." He pulled away from the curb and headed for the address Bob had given him.

When they got to the address, Bob compared what he was seeing out the cab window with the glossy photo in his hand. This was the place where the muggers had followed Bronson's wife and daughter home from the grocery store and had beaten and robbed them both, raping Bronson's daughter before they left. Bob and Sue took several shots of the same area as in the glossy photo before they were satisfied that they had what they came for.

"That didn't take long," the cabbie said.

"There weren't that many scenes shot here," Bob explained. "There is another place we'd like to photograph before it gets dark. Can you take us to the corner of Eighth Avenue and West Forty-fourth Street?"

"Sure," the cabbie said. "What's there?"

"Remember in the movie when Bronson was trying to lure muggers down into the subway?" Bob said. "He sat in the café and opened his wallet, letting everyone see that he had a lot of money. He knew that someone would follow him when he left the café and he wanted to get them down into the subway and dispatch of them, so to speak."

"Yes," the cabbie said. "I remember that part. And you say that café is on Forty-fourth and Eighth?"

"If it's still there," Bob added. "Let's go find out."

It was indeed still there, as Bob learned when the cab pulled to the curb at the corner. He leaned toward the cabbie. "We won't be long," he said. "I'll just be getting exterior shots. The interiors were probably filmed on some sound stage anyway." He and Sue got out and crossed the street to the café. Bob got the shots he wanted with the two of them taking turns posing before they returned to the cab.

"That it for the day?" the cabbie said. "It'll be dark in a few more minutes. I expect you'll both be anxious to get back to your hotel."

"Just one more stop," Bob said.

"But will you be able to get the shots you want in the dark?" the cabbie said.

"They'd turn out more accurate in the dark, actually," Bob said. "Take us to Riverside Park and West Ninety-ninth Street, would you?"

The cabbie's face took on a look of concern. "Are you sure you want to go there?" he said. "It's not really safe out there this time of night."

"We just need two or three more shots before we can call this project finished," Bob said. "It'll just take a few minutes. You worry too much, you know that?"

"Okay," the cabbie said, reluctantly. "I hope you know what you're doing." He stopped at the address Bob had given him and glanced at the meter. There was enough on there to justify this foolhardy stop at night. He imagined what kind of tip he'd get from his passengers when he dropped them off at their hotel once all this picture taking was done.

Bob and Sue got out of the cab, assuring the cabbie that they'd be right back. The two of them walked over to the exact place that was shown on the glossy print Sue had in her hand. "This is it, alright," Bob said. "This is the exact spot where Charles Bronson stood when he shot that mugger at the top of the stairs. Remember? Then he turned around and took a shot at the other mugger at the bottom of the stairs. You go to the bottom of these steps and look up at me. I'll get a picture of you from up here and then I can bring the camera down to you so you can get a picture of me looking down from the top of the stairs. Then we can go home."

"Let's hurry," Sue said, nervously. She walked to the bottom of the cement stairs, camera in hand. When she was situated, she called up to Bob to quickly take the picture and then bring her the camera.

Bob did as he was told, got two shots of Sue looking up at him and then hurried down the steps to give her the camera before returning to the top again. When he got to the bottom, he stood beside his wife and pointed up at the top of the landing. "Wait until I get ready up there," he said. "I'll wave down at you and you can snap two or three pictures and then we can go home, okay?"

"Okay," Sue said. "Let's get this over with. I don't like it here."

"What's not to like?" a voice from behind the couple said.

Bob and Sue both turned toward the sound of the voice only to see two young men standing there, staring back at them. One of them was scraping dirt from under his fingernails with the tip of a switchblade knife. The other one was casually holding a snub-nosed revolver, as if it was an extension of his hand. The one with the gun was the voice they heard. "Come on, folks, you know the routine. Give me your watches, your wallets, and anything else you might have on you, like that camera. That looks like a good one." He held his hand out to receive their personal possessions.

"Give it to them, Bob," Sue said.

"But all our photos from this trip are on there," he protested.

"Give it to them, Bob," Sue repeated, more frantic this time.

Bob pulled the wallet out of his hip pocket and handed it over to the thug with the gun. He also gave the man his watch as well as Sue's watch. "Just take that and go, please. Let me keep the camera, alright?"

"I ain't gonna tell you again, pops," the thug said, gesturing with his head toward his knife-wielding partner. "Get the camera," he told the other kid.

Bob grabbed Sue by the hand and made a mad dash for the stairway.

The cabbie had waited several minutes past the time he thought he should have. He got out and walked over to where he'd seen Bob standing earlier and looked down the cement stairway. He saw two youths standing over the bodies of Bob and Sue. They were going through their pockets and looked up when they heard a noise at the top of the stairs.

The kid with the gun aimed it up at the cabbie and squeezed off three quick shots, two of them hitting the cabbie in the chest. He fell onto the top landing as the kid with the knife hurried up the steps and relieved the cabbie of his wallet as well. He stood back up and waved the cabbie's wallet overhead, smiling maniacally. The cabbie's eyes fluttered open and he could see the kid waving his wallet at his partner. The cabbie reached into his jacket and pulled out a gun of his own, firing it several times at the kid on the landing. He caught the kid once in the back of his calf, once in the hip, and once in the back of his skull before he dropped the gun again and died there on the sidewalk.

The kid holding the cabbie's wallet tumbled down the cement stairs, coming to rest on top of Bob and Sue's bodies. The thug with the gun yelled, "Oh shit," and took off running in the opposite direction.

The following day an early morning jogger found the carnage and called the police. When they lifted Bob's body up, they found the digital camera but no identification on either body. A further search of the area netted them one dead cabbie with a gun lying near his body. When the media got wind of the crime, they were all over the scene, taking pictures of their own. It eventually came out that this couple had come from Wisconsin to take pictures of movie locations and that fact was reinforced when the police got a look at the pictures on the digital camera.

The evening papers ran a front page story on the four deaths found on the stairway. The headlines read DEATH WISH and ran side-by-side photos of the murder scene as well as the glossy photo found on Sue's body. On the back, written in pencil it said, "Charles Bronson from *Death Wish*. Location: Riverside Park and West Ninety-ninth Street."

It would be one hell of an addition to someone's scrap book.

THE TOUR GUIDE
BY KAT GEORGES

"AND HERE IS A BOX of New York's Best Cannolis, for all of us to share," the tour guide said. She held a white cardboard box high above her head. Liz was a short brunette. Neat: tailored woven silk jacket over designer jeans, urban black leather boots, well-kept nails with a fresh French manicure, chic intelligent glasses shielding deep brown eyes that took in much more than they gave away. Now she was smiling on a warm spring afternoon on Bleecker Street in the West Village. Smiling, at the seventeen tourists in her group. Smiling, in that way people smile when they expect the people they're looking at to smile back exactly the same way.

They did, reflexively. Good, Liz thought. More smiles, more tips. She glanced down and opened the box lid and carefully showed off its treasure—seventeen mini cannolis. The tourists took a few photos with their cell phones, then she gently handed them one mini cannoli each.

Tourists are so damn easy to please, she thought, over their adoring clicks and coos. Goddamned sheep. I could give them dog shit and—as long as I told them a good story about it—they'd suck it up with a stupid grin and tell me over and over how delicious it was. As if they knew from delicious. I give them the best slice of pizza in the world, they get goo-goo-eyed and gush about how it reminds them of their first slice of Domino's. I give them the best cannoli in the world? To them it's the same as some crap they "just love" from Dunkin' Donuts. They've got no ability to distinguish quality from mediocrity. As long as they're eating and they don't get sick, they love it. Idiots.

Liz reached for the last cannoli in the box and held it out without looking up. A hand reached out, fingers brushed hers as they took the treat. She heard a familiar voice. A repeat customer. She had heard it a few times during the past few weeks. A man's voice: smooth, deep. "Thank you, Liz." She glanced up. He waxed on, "I just love your walking tours. Far better than any of the others! You are amazing!"

It was not a compliment. Compliments never scared her like this.

HE WAS THE DEFINITION OF a middle-aged man: medium height, a little overweight, slightly balding. Sunglasses in the top pocket of his striped short-sleeve light-blue shirt. Neat khaki pants; brown leather loafers—cheap and well-worn. He'd been on the tour two—no, three—times, always with a different woman—some dowdy out-of-towner or another. Some small-town woman past her prime. A Kansas, Georgia, Arizona type. Some lonelyheart on a weekend break from Facebook.

This time he was all alone. He smiled at her. She did not smile back.

WHEN WAS THE FIRST TIME he came on Liz's Exclusive West Village Bits and Bites Walking Tour? Hard to say. These days, she ran it so many times every week. With repetition like that, memories blur. It was all rote by now: life on repeat. Jackson Pollock's first art studio was here at 69 Carmine Street! Bigtime mobster Vincent "The Chin" Gigante roamed these very streets as a child before he became boss of the Genovese crime family! Jack Kerouac sipped espresso at this very table of Cafe Reggio!

How long had she been at it? Two—no, three—years? God. Too long. Should have stuck to walking dogs.

Her first tours—three years ago—gave her that same sheer joy she'd had as an actor back in her little theater days. She researched her part—went to the library on the weekdays and found out interesting tidbits about the West Village that she knew would make her tour The Best. Enthusiasm flew out of her—infectious. Tour groups were thrilled. They recommended her to friends back home. She was able to go from one tour a week to four a weekend, and—by summer—tours on weekdays as well.

That first year, in July, she led at least one tour a day for three weeks straight. She was able to buy real food instead of junk. She ate out once in a while. Got her hair cut and colored at the local salon instead of doing it herself. Bought new clothes. Even shoes.

It made a difference. The better she looked, the more business improved. By the end of October that first year, she was turning away customers. By December, she had saved enough to take a few weeks off during the cold months.

Bursting with newfound confidence, for the first time in years, she auditioned for a few Off-Off-Broadway plays. In February, she actually landed a small part in a staged reading (a long and not very interesting play by a middle-aged woman from Queens). Middle-aged—like me, she thought. Everyone else in the theater scene was so much younger. Liz lied about her age on her headshot, but even knocking off ten years didn't help. Her theater days were over—except for her tours.

BUT BY THE MIDDLE OF her second year of leading the tours, it was just another job. The kind of job you take when you live in a rent-controlled studio, don't have a lot of bills and don't want to work in an office or restaurant.

She stopped going to the library for research. History is finite—there's only so much you can learn about a six square block Historic District in New York City. She wondered how actors in long-running plays on Broadway could get pumped up for their roles after the three hundredth performance. That's what it was now: performance. No need to improvise.

She had figured out exactly how many steps a typical group of overweight mid-Westerners could waddle without getting sore feet. How many minutes they could endure without eating another nibble from one of the cafes they passed. She figured out exactly how much water they needed—or claimed they needed—to make it through a one-hour tour without fainting or whining about the heat. She even ordered bottled water with a custom label that had her website address printed under a cute caricature a friend had done for her back in the days where friends used to do that kind of thing for you.

LIZ HANDED A CANNOLI TO the man and gave him a quick "back off" glare. He looked away, bored. Typical. She remembered the way he would say sweet things to the other women he'd been with, then ignore their reply. The disconnect. Scary.

The cannolis were gone. The tourists looked up at her, wondering what was next. Insatiable. They'd already had a slice of pizza, sampled three kinds of cheese, a fresh-baked baguette, a prosciutto ball, gelato, and now a cannoli. Time to wrap things up with a bang and count the tips. Liz launched into her final spiel.

"Aren't these cannoli deee-lightful?" she purred sweetly, while the tourists chewed on their last bites. They nodded and grunted. "Told you so, didn't I? Well, un-for-tu-nate-ly, folks, that wraps up our tour for today. Thanks so much for coming along. I hope you had just as much fun as I did!" The tourists applauded. Liz beamed.

"So, as you know, a tour guide needs to eat between tours! Right now, you are invited to show your love and make your favorite tour guide a very happy lady with a dash of paper currency." The tourists reached for their wallets and pocketbooks like obedient children. The middle-aged man handed her a crisp twenty. The other tourists, figuring that was normal, did the same. The tour guide smiled sweetly, trying to cover up her shock as the twenties filled her small palm. Five twenties. Ten twenties. Fifteen, sixteen, seventeen. Three hundred-and-forty dollars! Holy shit! She'd never made this much in one tour before. She could barely speak her final lines.

"Don't forget to tell your pals back home to sign up for the Exclusive West Village Bits and Bites Walking Tour on their next visit to the greatest city on Earth." More applause. Then it was done. Liz gently tucked the tip money into her pocket, shook a few hands, and waited for the last stragglers to ask their final questions ("Where's the nearest ladies' room?" "Where can we catch a taxi?") and leave.

"WHY ARE YOU STILL HERE?" she asked the man, who lingered after the others had gone.

"Don't you know?" He looked earnest. Liz sneered.

"Don't give me that crap about how you just love my tours."

"Aww—but I do love your tours. You are the most interesting, most fascinating, most historically accurate, and most successful living tour guide in the neighborhood."

"What do you mean 'living'? Sounds like a threat."

"You really should think better of me—after I helped you score all those tips today."

"Actually, pal, I can get plenty of tips without anyone's help."

"For now," he said. "My name's Ken, by the way."

Liz rolled her eyes, then smiled sarcastically. "Goodbye, Ken," she said, and turned away. She started walking up Bleecker toward Sixth Avenue, hoping he wouldn't follow her.

He did. Of course. The creeps always follow you. It happened once before, the first year she led tours. Some out-of-towner with big expectations launched into a monologue about his "special" skills, asked her out for lunch, then a movie, then a weekend stay in his Times Square hotel room. She turned down each request, hailed a cab and never saw him again.

But this guy—this . . . Ken—ugh—stupid name . . . this guy had something else on his mind. And it felt like he would keep coming back until he got whatever it was that he wanted. And what he wanted wasn't simply a friend with benefits for a weekend fling. She better figure it out quick—without letting him know that she knew.

At the corner of Carmine and Bleecker, she waited for Ken to catch up to her, then suggested they talk in the corner park. They found a bench near the entrance and sat.

"So, Ken—," she said, trying to sound absolutely sincere. "You're right. You deserve better treatment. You've been on the tour—what?—two other times?"

"Three. Plus today."

"Ah, you're right!" Liz chuckled. "Four times in all. You know, I think that's a record."

"Thank you."

Liz purred. "I'm surprised that you're here by yourself today, Ken. You always seem to have a lady friend with you. From out of town. . . . You're from—where?—I forget . . ."

"Cat and mouse? Must we?" Ken's voice had an edge.

"Just trying to get to know you a bit better."

"You want facts? Okay. Name: Ken Prather. Age: Forty-eight. Birthplace: Mamaroneck."

"Profession?"

"Trust-fund baby."

"You don't look like a trust-fund baby."

"I lied. I'm a writer."

"A waiter?"

"You heard me."

"You writing about me, Ken—huh? Is that it?"

"You don't mind, do you?"

"True crime?"

"Memoir."

"Hope they're not the same thing."

"You're getting rude again, Liz," Ken said, with a cold smile. "You're much more agreeable when you are pleasant."

Liz figured he was lying about being a writer. Maybe trying to impress her, since she mentioned so many literary figures on her walking tours. Hell, the whole neighborhood was rife with literary history. Dylan Thomas, Allen Ginsberg, Edna St. Vincent Millay all had hung out or lived in this area. Today, writers lived in Brooklyn, according to all the newspapers. No one could afford the West Village anymore, since prices skyrocketed after 9/11. The only writing most of the folks around here did was signing credit card receipts and checks.

"Where do you live now?" she asked Ken. "Brooklyn?"

"Of course," he said flatly. "All writers live in Brooklyn these days."

"Somehow, I don't believe you," Liz replied.

"You don't trust me, do you?"

"Why should I? What difference would it make?"

Ken glanced down at his hands, examined them closely. Palms first, then the backside. He seemed to be looking for something in particular, some sign or a mark or the source of an itch. He became absorbed, seemed lost from the physical world. Liz saw small beads of perspiration form on his neck and forehead. A minute passed, without either of them saying a word. Liz knew she should just leave, but she couldn't help herself—she had to find out what just happened to him.

"Ken? Are you okay? What's wrong?" she asked.

He snapped out of his trance, and looked suddenly joyful.

"I've got it," he said, standing up. "Thank you, thank you, thank you."

And just like that, he left—walking up Sixth Avenue like a new man, like the kind of man who fits in with other men. His steps were solid, he smiled a bit. Just before he was out of sight, Liz saw him pull an iPhone from his pocket and start texting without breaking stride. Yep, just like other men.

A WEEK WENT BY, THEN two, then three. Liz led tour after tour, but Ken wasn't there. After a month, business seemed down a bit. She figured it was a temporary dip in the economy. But by the end of summer, people just weren't booking the Exclusive West Village Bits and Bites Walking Tour. Liz cut out the mid-week tours first, then started scaling back on the number of tours she led on the weekends. On Labor Day weekend, she led only one tour a day, down from three a day the year before. Something was definitely wrong.

SHE SPOTTED KEN A FEW weeks later. She was sitting in the corner park on the same bench they had shared the last time he took her tour. She hadn't booked a single tour this weekend, and was desperate to figure out what had happened. Ken was near the park's fountain, madly texting on his iPhone.

"Hey, Ken!" she yelled, without getting off the bench. He glanced up, gave her a little wave, then turned his back to her and kept texting.

Asshole. Liz stormed over to him.

"Hey, Ken! I want to talk to you!"

"Minute . . ." he mumbled. He kept his eyes on his cell phone screen, and kept texting, his thumbs moving like a violinist's fingers, pressing strings that made no sound.

"Hey, this is important."

"So's this," he murmured.

Liz grabbed the phone out of his hand and scanned the last few lines of conversation.

> —LOL – just booked final slot for B&B GV eTour
> —WTF? 2 mo takeover? You rock!
> —Ha! App rocks
> —:p not to mention the $$$
> —O, F—she's here.
> —Lz? Duz she no?

"Hey, jackoff!" Liz shouted. "What the fuck did you do to my damn walking tour, asshole?"

Ken looked sheepish for a moment, then stood tall and grabbed his phone back. "What tour? Doesn't look like you do much of anything now, unlike—all these folks here." Ken swept his arm toward the sidewalks. "Look at all of them, happy as could be."

"What the hell are you talking about?" Liz snarled.

"Tourists—see?" Ken mused. "Hundreds of tourists."

The sidewalks did seem a bit crowded with small groups of two and three, a family here and there. They lingered in front of the bakery, the cheese shop, the bar, the old apartment building. If you looked closely, you could see most of them wore headphones or small ear buds. And everyone looked happy.

Ken gleamed. "Personalized eTour app, can you imagine? I designed an algorithm that automatically gathers immense data for each individual user, then programs a unique user experience. They get the tour of their dreams for far less than what you charge—or should I say, 'charged'—and they don't tip anyone at the end. Ta-da!"

"You're bullshitting me."

"Still don't trust me, huh, Liz?" Ken said with a smirk. "Let's investigate."

He held her by the elbow and walked with her to the front of the bakery. A man was just finishing a mini cannoli, and smiling. He listened for a moment longer, then removed the sound buds in his ears.

"Sir," Ken said. "Excuse me, sir?"

The man glanced up. "Yes?"

"By any chance, were you just using the B&B West Village eTour app?"

The man's eyes grew wide. "How did you know?"

"Lucky guess. I've heard so much about it. Tell me—didja like it?"

"Loved it. Fantastic tour. My wife—she's right across the street—she found out about it and I tell you what—she picked a winner. This area has so much history—did you know that Jack Kerouac used to drink coffee just up the block? I love Kerouac—bought a few eBooks of his last year. I feel like I'm following in his footsteps, can you imagine?"

"Sounds great," Ken mused. "But I'm not sure if that makes sense for me. I mean, I don't know too much about this Kerry-ac fellow. Guess I'm just not really much of a reader. Oh, well . . ."

"Wait—that's okay, buddy," the man chirped. "My wife's like you—well, not exactly, of course." He and Ken laughed. Liz brooded between them. "See, my wife is more into food— if it's edible and sounds interesting, she is all over it. She's what you call a 'foodie,' see?"

Ken nodded, "That's me."

"I knew it. Well this app knows just what you like—it took the both of us to the same places, and we each found out just what we were interested in. She found out about food, and I found out about those beatnik things, and it was just like magic. A total win-win for both me and her."

Liz felt sick. She had to say something. "Wouldn't you prefer to have a real tour guide?"

The man stared at her with a curious look. "This is real."

"I mean—human. A human tour guide, who could talk and answer questions and point out interesting things and give you free samples and . . . stuff like that."

Ken and the man glanced at each other and laughed.

"I got free samples galore! And I ask all the questions I want. Here, let me show you." He held his cell phone out, turned it on speaker and asked, "Where's the nearest subway station?"

A female voice replied, "If you're headed back to your hotel, Mr. Felton, turn around, and walk up Bleecker to Carmine, then turn left on Carmine and walk three hundred-and-fifty feet to the West Fourth Street Station. Take the A train to West Forty-second Street. When you get there, I'll guide you to your hotel."

"Thank you," the man said to the phone.

"There's a train in four minutes," the phone replied. "If you like, I can contact your wife across the street, and let her know that it's time to go."

"That's okay," the man said. "I'll linger here a little longer."

"I thought you might," the phone said. "Enjoy yourself."

The man put the phone away.

"Cute, isn't it?" the man told Liz. "And it's never wrong. The difference is trust. A machine—you can trust. It makes all the difference in the world."

"What about the food?" Liz snapped. "Who gives you the samples?"

"Oh, that's the great part," the man grinned. "If I want a sample at any place, I just text 'Sample please.' And the cool thing is, they know what I like and they know what I'm allergic to and this cute little number pops open and hands me the perfect sample for me and my wife. She got a chocolate éclair here. Me—I'm allergic to chocolate, so I got a cannoli. And what a cannoli it was! Best in the city, so I'm told!"

Ken glanced at his iPhone. "Well, guess I'm just going to have to find out for myself. Thank you, Mr. Felton."

Liz wasn't finished. "Wait—this is just a tour, and you trust your little app more than a live tour guide, right? What's next? Dog walkers? Teachers? Political leaders? I mean—how far is this going to go?"

"Who knows?" the man said. "Babysitter? Lifetime tour guide?"

"You got it!" Ken said. "Those apps just keep getting better and better!"

Ken and the man looked at each other and burst out laughing.

"So long, Mr. Felton," Ken purred. "Pleased to meet you."

"Same," said the man, already texting his wife across the street, who waved.

LIZ DRIFTED AWAY. HER RENT was due in a few days. If she was careful she could live off her savings for at least three months, maybe four. She wondered how long it would take to learn enough to make her own app. Something that destroyed all the other apps. A killer app. That's what she needed. That's what she would become. A killer app—one that everyone would trust—for the rest of their lives.

WANG DANG DOODLE
BY ANNETTE MEYERS

ARTIE

"THE THING ABOUT MA IS, she got no patience. One mistake and—" He sticks his tongue out, slurpy inhale, index finger across his throat. Hilarious. "You know Ma."

"Yeah, we know Ma," Harry says.

Artie laughs so hard, he's a swamp. "She's not my Ma, she's nobody's Ma." He howls with laughter. "Magdalina Angelina, private snoop." His head lands on the table with a thud.

"Where you going with this?" Harry goes into his inside pocket and shoves over a handkerchief. Eyeballs Artie, mouths to Ray, "Shikker?"

Artie lifts his head from the snotty pool. Dries his face with the handkerchief. Fondles his mustache. "You don't think it's funny?"

"Jesus Christ," Harry says. Punk's a pothead, pinprick pupils. "You think Ma's got no patience. I'm no fucking prince of patience either." He rolls his eyes at Ray, who keeps mum.

"Listen, we're doing a routine investigation. That's why we invited you here." Ray takes a pack of gum from his pocket and offers it around. "Don't fuck with us, Artie," Ray says.

ANNETTE MEYERS

"I thought you wanted to hear my story," Artie says.

"We do."

"So don't rush me."

Ray says, "Tell it like you want."

Artie puts gum in his mouth and chaws. "Well, shit, she took me in when I was thirteen. You know all about it, right?"

"Harry doesn't."

"Look it up . . . Harry." Artie's smirk slips into hiccoughing giggles.

"Later." Harry slams his palm on the table.

Artie stops in mid-laugh. "Okay, okay. Name: Arthur Ponzini. Age: twenty-four. Address: formerly, care of Ma, private snoop, MacDougal Alley, currently the Brevoort." He yells at the mirror. "You got it?"

"Let's take a break," Ray says. "You wanna Coke or something, Artie?"

"Yeah." Grins "Some Oreos." He pats his pockets. "And Camels."

MA

"I WAS FBI. BET YOU didn't know that," Ma says. "Frizzy red hair, scrawny, like a Jew Commie. Alias, Margie Goldberg. Spent a couple of years undercover." She smiles, adjusts the seams of her nylons. She has decent gams under her tight skirt, good ankles. "The boys on both sides liked me, but I have to admit those lefties gave Margie a good time. If you know what I mean."

Ray's eyes make her beefcake. "Why'd you quit?"

"Too much like Catholic school, if you know what I mean. Besides, I had responsibilities."

"A private doll, not many of you," Harry says.

"Not many." She crosses her legs. Her jacket is open, her blouse unbuttoned enough to show plenty of cleavage. She's

296

been around this corner. Puts a thin, brown cigarillo in her lips. "Got a light?"

They both fumble to give her a light. Ray gets there first. "Any problem getting your license?"

Ma laughs. "What do you think?"

Ray and Harry do a "heh, heh."

Overhead, the fan harrumphs and harrumphs.

"So, boys, did you ask me over to talk shop?" Ma says. "I run an honest business, a little small-time maybe, but I make a living. And my license is clean."

ARTIE

"She's got this stupid business, punk wants to know if the wife is farting on the side and it's, 'Artie, follow her.' Insurance company thinks someone's faking disability? 'Artie'll check it out.' Thinks she's fucking Philip Marlowe. Fuck, I'm Philip Marlowe. 'Oh now, Arthur,' she says, 'Stop complaining. You have it good.' Sits in the backyard with her dago red, playing poker with that fat-assed stripper, Fanny, and Fanny's old man, Norman, who owns the Village Soir." He's lapping up a Good Humor on a stick.

"Fanny was some piece in her day," Harry says. He puts thumb and index finger together and smack-kisses. "Shoulda seen her feathered fan thing at Minsky's."

Ray brings them back. His mother's Italian and he doesn't like "dago," but Artie's talking now.

Harry says, "Ma know how you feel?"

Artie drops the licked-clean stick on the table. He swigs some Coke, leans in to take a light from Ray. "Yeah." Tilts his head back and makes a smoke ring. "I don't keep nothing to myself. Most times." Grimaces a grin. "She always says, 'Oh, Arthur.' Like what I say don't count."

"Okay, chum." Ray lights up his own. "Knock off the Freud crap. Get to the girl."

"What girl?" Artie's doing a tease. He winks at Ray. "There's always a girl."

"You know goddamn well what girl, mister." Harry's a big guy, over six and built like a brick wall. He gets in Artie's face.

"Shit," Artie says, spraying spittle as he pulls back. "It's my story."

"Then fucking tell it."

MA

"WE WANNA KNOW ARTIE'S STORY," Ray says.

"Artie? My nephew Arthur?"

"Yeah," Harry says. "Good kid. He's helping us out on a routine investigation."

"Arthur can't—he's my nephew—so I'm telling you, Arthur is like those monkeys. Don't see nothing, don't hear nothing. Makes like he's a hound." Ma waves her hands in the air. "Useless." She thinks, *What the fuck are these mutts up to?*

"He says he came to live with you when he was thirteen," Ray says.

"Eleven."

"How come?"

Ma sighs. It's ugly. Blocked it out. Never happened. Except Arthur, he looks more like Anthony every day. "Thirteen years ago, Jersey City, my brother Anthony killed Julia, his wife, little Angela, who was nine, and himself."

"Jeeze," Ray says.

"Arthur came home and called the police. They found him holding Julia, covered in her blood, talking to her like she was still there."

"Poor kid."

"He don't remember any of it," Ma says, giving them her squinty eye. "So spill. What's going on?"

ARTIE

"NORMAN," ARTIE SAYS. "IT WAS Norman. Yeah."

"Norman Organ, you're saying?" says Harry. It's really Argonne, but no secret he's called Norman Organ, and there's a lot of truth there. "Is this the beginning or the end?"

"Both," Artie says, burbling.

"Fuck this, wise guy," Harry says, heading for the door. "I'm done."

"No, no. You asked me to help you."

Harry comes back, sits.

"Where does the Organ come in?" Ray says.

"Norman sets up fun. He's good to me. He has a room at the Earle. The girls meet us there." Smirks. "For auditions."

"How long has he been so good to you?"

"I don't know, maybe since I came to live with Ma. Before Tamara."

"Tamara, she was one of the girls?"

"Not Tamara. You ever see her?" He gets dreamy-eyed, stares off in the distance. "At the Soir. Ringer for Ava Gardner. Sings blues, like sweet smoke. Just got a recording contract with Atlantic Records." Proud. "My girl."

"She dumped you, chum," Harry says.

Artie stares at Harry. "You're beginning to annoy me. Who told you that?"

"We ask the questions now," Ray says. "When did you see her last?"

Quiet, serious, Artie blows into his cupped hands. "We were celebrating. The contract."

"Celebrating, huh," Ray says, "What do you think, Harry? They were celebrating."

TAMARA

"Didn't last long at Vassar, did I? Too weird. But they were weirder, except for you, though come to think of it, you were a little weird yourself," Tamara says. They're drinking gin, straight. She refills their glasses, kicks off her Cubans.

Outside, a fire engine siren blares.

Tamara closes the window. Too hot. Opens the window. The siren is a distant wail.

"Yeah, I was weird, didn't grow a mustache, wore a bra," Dottie says, "Stayed parked and got the foolscap I can't do shit with."

"While I hung out at Birdland and the Three Deuces, and dives we won't even talk about."

"Have to admit, you were pretty shocking." They laugh.

Tamara is leggy and elegant. Her nose is too long, her eyes too far apart. She is not beautiful except when she laughs. Or when she sings.

"Oh, yes, shocking. They finally suggested I was not suited to be one of their young ladies. Crushed Mama, but Daddy, he didn't care. Just wanted me to be happy. He wrote a big check, and I moved into the Brevoort and here I am."

"The story of your life." Dottie puts her notebook down, tucks her pencil into her braid. She writes bits and pieces for *Mademoiselle*. Tamara's helping her out, helping both of them out. "And we haven't even gotten to the Soir."

"Thank Norman Organ for that."

Dottie shrieks. "Organ?"

They're laughing so hard, their drinks slosh. "Okay, Argonne. But everyone calls him Organ behind his back. He's always schtupping it around."

Dottie takes her pencil from her braid. "I have to ask you about Artie."

"What about him?" Tamara can't help being defensive. She knows Dottie doesn't like Artie, doesn't understand what Tamara sees in him.

"He's a spoiled rich kid going nowhere, you're a girl on your way up. He doesn't fit. The recording contract is only the beginning."

"I love him, Dottie. Except when I don't. He looks like Errol Flynn, don't you think?" Tamara says. "Besides, he's got plans. Coffee houses on West Fourth."

"Coffee houses? Sure, with a side business of benzies and barbies."

"He promises he's done."

Dottie thinks her friend wears rose-colored glasses.

"I have to find a new place," Tamara says. "They're going to tear down the Brevoort and build an apartment house."

ARTIE

"So you say you're at the Brevoort?" Harry says.

Artie blinks. He's back. "The Brevoort, yeah, me and Tamara. A suite. We gotta find another place."

Ray puts a new cig in his mouth and lights it with the butt of the old one. "Why's that, chum?"

"It's coming down. They tear everything down."

"So how does a kid like you get a babe like Tamara?"

"She's nuts about me."

Harry says, "Nuts enough to give you a shiner?"

Artie touches the skin around his eye. "Walked into a door."

"Sure, wise guy." Harry's like a bulldog. "And what happened to your hair? Looks a little singed. Walk into a candle?"

"Shove it," Artie says, getting up. "You don't want my help. I'm blowing."

"Knock it off, Harry," Ray says, making nice. "Don't be sore, Artie. Harry's got his problems at home, don't you, Harry?"

Harry growls. "Yeah, sorry, kiddo."

Artie sits back down. "Okay."

"What's she like, Tamara?

MA

"YOU HAD RESPONSIBILITIES, YOU SAY, Ma? What kind of responsibilities?"

"You're kidding me, right? I had the kid. What was I going to do with a kid?"

"What did you do?"

"Arthur inherited a lot of money. I bought a house in MacDougal Alley and put the kid in private school, Collegiate. When he's twenty-five next year, he gets the rest of the bundle."

"So he don't remember anything about the murders?"

"Come on, boys. What's cooking?"

"We're interested in why your brother did it."

Ma knows these two mutts with shields are playing her. She'd like to take off, but not without Arthur. What kind of trouble has Arthur gotten himself into now? "Are you telling me you're reopening my brother's case?"

"Could be," Harry says. "Wanna coffee?"

TAMARA

"HE DOESN'T MEAN IT," SHE says. She's dizzy, barefoot, the sleeve of her dress is torn. She has to hold on to the doorjamb to keep from falling over. Herb, the desk clerk, who runs errands for her when he's off duty, has ice for the bruise on her cheek. "I took into him." Grins, winces. "You should see him."

"Saw him. Blew past me like a bat outta hell." He follows her into the room, the living area of a suite, gives her the ice in a linen handkerchief once she's sitting. There's lit candles all around the room and the smell of something burned. "Something burning?"

"Threw a candle at him."

Herb's spooked. "You wanna burn us down?"

She tries to laugh but the swelling's in the way. "Told him we're finished," she says.

"Found a new place yet?" Herb says, not believing her. The two of them are off again, on again, fighting, throwing stuff. Like candles now. The only reason the Brevoort hasn't tossed them out is the building is coming down and no one cares.

"No. My mama and daddy are coming up from Natchez next week. Daddy will find me a place."

Herb nods. He's heard her father's rolling in dough. Padrone of the oleomargarine business across the South. No joke.

"Leave word at the desk. I don't want Artie let back up here."

"Okay. Hey—" The door opens behind him.

Artie doesn't look at him. Goes straight to Tamara and lifts her into his arms. "I'm sorry, babe. You're right. I promise. I love you. It's going to be different." He touches her cheek. "Does it hurt?"

"Oh, Artie." She snuggles into his chest. "I love you."

"Brought you some medicine," he says. "It'll make you feel better."

"Let's go shopping," she says.

Herb leaves.

MA

"MAYBE YOUR BROTHER DIDN'T DO IT," Harry says.

"Waddaya talking about? It was his gun."

"Someone coulda popped him, then set him up, right, Ray?"

"Yeah. Maybe he was having a little on the side with a local. People talk."

Harry smirks. "More like he was doing business on the side." Moves his thumb to his nose.

Ma doesn't like how they're playing her. "Big shots. Anthony wasn't perfect."

"Yeah, a real skirt chaser we hear."

"Arthur was a kid. He don't remember nothing about what happened."

"You'd be surprised, Ma."

"I wanna see him. Now."

"Later," Ray says. "He's looking at pictures. Let him look. He might remember something." He stands. "I gotta get back."

After Ray leaves, Harry says, like he's sympathetic, "You got a business. Why don't you blow and take care of business and we'll give you a ring when he's done."

Ma's got to get a report out to her client, putz carrying a torch for his ex-wife. Harry's right. She's gotta take care of business. "Don't try to put anything over on me, buster."

TAMARA

"*TELL AUTOMATIC SLIM, TELL RAZOR totin' Jim, tell butcher knife totin' Annie, tell fast talkin' Fanny . . .*" Buddy on guitar, Willie drums, nice and slow. Spot loves her. She flips back her hair, goes for the repeat. *"We're gonna pitch a wang dang doodle all night long . . ."* Spot out. When the lights come on, she's gone.

"They're sayin' you're the white Bessie Smith." Lou fills her glass with his mix of gin and orange juice. Mostly gin. Sea breeze, he calls it.

"White Bessie. That's a laugh." She's a little woozy. What did Artie give her? The dressing table mirror is flecked with age spots, her image blurs back at her. She finished her set to good-enough applause, gave them her encore of "Wang Dang Doodle," which she always closes with. She resents the chipped paint of the table and the dingy closet they call a dressing room.

"Drink up," Lou says. He's on top of the world. "You're knockin' 'em dead with that "Wang Dang Doodle." Where'd you get it?"

"Willie Davis. Mississippi blues music."

"Mississippi?"

"Where d'you think I'm from, Lou?"

"Well it's makin' 'em all sit up and take notice."

"Really? They talk, and eat while I'm singing." Lou's a good agent but understands nothing about being an artist; all he thinks about is the dough.

"Listen, kiddo, there was a line tonight and the eleven o'clock is sold out."

"Artie says I should be in a better club."

"Yeah, well Café Society is long gone." Lou does that one arm over the elbow thing. "Artie knows nothin'. Did he do that to you?" He points to her bruised cheek, which she's carefully covered with Max Factor and powder. "Good thing blues don't work in too bright light."

"It was an accident." She checks her makeup in the mirror, but her image swims. Aspirin he said he gave her, but it must have been one of his goofballs.

"Yeah, you walked into his fist. He's poison. You got ten years on him, you oughta know better. You're goin' places, and he's a loser."

"Lou, please." Tears spill. "I know. I can't help it. We have terrible fights. Drugs, girls Norman gets for him."

"Oh, shit, kiddo, don't cry." Lou squeezes her shoulder. "If you want, I'll get him to lay off."

She shakes her head. Lou has some tough friends who might hurt Artie. That's not what she wants. "No. I'll do it."

NORMAN

"Yeah, got a tip about her from a pal at the Onyx. She hanging out, playing goo-goo with the bass player, got him to set her up on a stool during the break."

"So she was good," Harry says.

"Good? A white blues singer, sings like Bessie. You kidding me? She's going places. And I wanted to be first in line."

"Who is Lou?" Ray says.

"Jesus, do you believe that punk Lou turns up from somewhere when I'm handing her a contract and says he's her manager?"

"She hired him?"

"And I have to put in this and that and if and when before she signs."

"But she signed. And you signed."

"Yeah. And she's hot stuff. Can make you cry, she's so good."

"What about Artie?" Harry says.

"What about him?" Norman lights a fag, inhales, exhales, content.

"He's a friend of yours?" Ray said

"More like protégé, know what I mean?"

"Oh, yeah. We heard about the Earle."

Norman winks, makes clicking noise with his teeth. "Oh, so that's what this is? Where I do my auditions? Every sis wants to be a star. They come to audition and have fun, we have fun. The kid is a college boy, tall, good looking. What can I say?"

"How do you know Artie?"

"He's Ma's kid. Known him since she took him in after his pop popped the rest of the family." He laughs at his joke. "Ma can be tough. Boy needs a father. I been like a father to him."

Harry and Ray make an obvious exchange of glances. "A real sport," Harry says.

"How did he come to Tamara?"

"Oh, I get it. She made a complaint because he gave her a pat on the cheek."

"Something like that," Ray says.

"A love pat. Artie was at the Soir her first night. They fell for each other. Kid stuff. It won't last."

"He moved in with her at the Brevoort."

"To get away from Ma."

"The Brevoort is coming down."

"Artie'll have his pop's dough by that time."

TAMARA

SHE CALLS THE FRONT DESK. "Herb, run round to Bigelow's. Get me a pint, House of Lords, put it on me."

"As soon as my shift ends. Fifteen maybe twenty, when Joseph gets here."

"What time is it now?"

"Quarter to."

"Okay. Tell Joseph if Artie comes in not to let him up. I don't wanna see him."

"How's Joseph going to stop him?" She doesn't answer right away. "Hello?"

"Never mind, tell Joseph to ring me up that Artie's on his way."

HERB

"Waddaya wanna know?"

"You and Tamara," Ray says. The kid has enough freckles to cover a phone booth.

"Me and Tamara? Lay off. Me, I'm the desk clerk at the Brevoort. I do errands for her, like pick up booze." He feels his cheeks get hot.

"You got a job for when the Brevoort comes down?"

"Yeah. I'm learning real estate."

"So you do stuff for her? Did you do anything yesterday?"

"Yeah. She calls down when I'm almost finished my shift— she knows when—and asks me to get her a bottle of House of Lords from the liquor store on Sixth."

"House of Lords?" Harry says.

Ray whistles. "Fancy gin."

"It's what she drinks. I say, 'Okay.' Then a coupla minutes later she calls down and says to tell her when Artie gets there."

"Why?"

"I didn't ask her. You want me to keep going?"

"Keep going."

"I don't see Artie and I tell Joseph, the night man, to tell her when Artie comes in, but Joseph is queer . . . so I don't know if he tells her . . . so—" He trails off, looks at them.

Ray says, "Just spit it out, for Chrissakes."

"So I knock on the door and she don't answer, but I hear yelling. I knock again and Artie opens the door, yells, 'Scram, punk,' and slams the door in my face. And Tamara yells, 'No, no,' and he's yelling, and he opens the door, and says, 'Get lost or I'll punch your lights out.'"

"Then what?" Harry says.

"I wait in the stairwell. They'll stop soon. She'll throw him out, or he'll leave, and she'll let me in. I got something to talk to her about."

TAMARA

"You put one of your barbies into my gin."

"So, didn't you feel better?"

"No. I went on woozy, drunk."

"Best you ever were."

"Get outta here. Don't come back."

"I'm not leaving."

Knocking on the door.

"It's Herb."

"You got that loser always sniffing around."

"I sent him for a pint."

Artie opens the door. "Get lost, punk." Starts to close the door.

"No, no. Stop." She goes for the door.

He pulls her away and slams it. Flings her across the room. She lies still, the carpet rough on her cheek.

He's lifting her. "I'm sorry, babe. You know I love you." He puts her on the bed. Goes to the door, grabs the paper bag with the bottle from Herb, slams the door in his face.

"Artie," she says. She doesn't recognize her own voice.

"I'll make you a gin," he says.

HERB

"So I'm waiting in the stairwell."

"They still yelling?" Ray says.

"No. It gets real quiet. Then I see Artie leaving. He gets on the elevator."

"What about Tamara?"

"I wait a little while to make sure he's not coming back. I knock on the door."

"She says, 'That you, Herb?'"

"Yeah," I say. "You decent?" Feels like he's in a movie when he says it.

"'Door's open,' she says. Like she don't care."

"'You sore?'" I ask her. She's wearing this black lacy thing and stockings. I try not to look."

"'Not sore at you.'" She moves stiff like she hurts."

"Why'd you really hang around?" Harry says.

"I got something I want to talk to her about."

"Oh, yeah? Spill it."

"There's a penthouse come up at 24 Fifth. The concierge is my chum. Two bedrooms, two terraces. A real beaut."

"'Herb, my hero,' she says. 'Tell your chum it's a sure thing.' "

"What a good fella," Harry says. "Don't you think, Ray?"

"A real good fella. Always doing the right thing without asking for a handout." Watches Herb's freckles turn bright red.

"I gotta admit there'll be some kickback dough for me in it."

DOTTIE

"You look awful, Tamara." Tamara has dried blood near her scalp. "He knock you around again?"

"Don't worry. We're done." She tries to light a cig but can't hold the match. Dottie gives her a light. "I'm taking a penthouse at 24 Fifth. I'll be outta here before he knows it."

Dottie knows better. "He'll find you."

"No, no," Tamara says. "This time we're finished." She's

half dressed, black lace corset, stockings. "Go take a look at the place. Tell them I want it."

LOU

"You wanna know how I come to Tamara?"

"Yeah," Harry says.

"Why you askin'? Somethin' happen I should know about?"

"We ask the questions."

"Listen, boys, I been bookin' vaudeville and variety for thirty years. Nobody I don't know. I know Norman from when he was a straight in burlesque. Fanny, too, when she took it all off." He laughs. "Hoo boy, she was somethin'." He makes like he's palming melons.

"Yeah," says Harry.

"Move it along," Ray says, giving Harry the eye.

"Fanny tells me Norman found a real talent for the Soir. She knows Norman. He's mister somethin' for nothin'. She's been there. So she makes me swear and then spills about Tamara."

"Go on."

"That Artie makin' trouble again?"

"You don't like Artie?" Harry says.

"Waddaya think?"

HERB

"I already told you."

"Tell us again. Every time you tell us, it's a little different."

Herb groans. "Okay. She's sitting at the piano when I get there with the gin. Artie's pacing back and forth. He hates me. He says, 'What you doing here, mutt?'"

"Tamara says, 'Leave him alone, Artie. He takes care of stuff for me.'"

"Artie gets real mad. 'What the f— do you think I do? Always collecting losers,' he says, or something like that. He looks like he's gonna kill me."

Harry stubs out his butt. "Losers."

"Tamara gets up quick and gives me a fiver. 'Thanks,' she says, 'And thanks for my penthouse.' Artie goes nuts, stamping around, yelling. 'What's this about a penthouse?' I don't wait around."

ARTIE
"We made up. I was hungry, she was drinking, wanted to take a bath."

"You waited?"

"No, I wanted to get something to eat. Said I'd be back."

"What about the Soir?"

"She don't do a show on Mondays. Lou took care of that."

"Where'd you go?"

"Corner Bistro, for a burger."

"You went back to the Brevoort?"

"No, met a punk and went to his place to do some . . ." He's not telling about the hashish. "Got higher than a kite."

"You got the punk's name?" Ray says.

"Sam or Joe, maybe."

"Maybe Kilroy?" Harry says.

HERB
Ray pops the cap on the Coke and hands it to Herb.

"Thanks." He's sweating. Takes a swig of Coke. "I can't."

"Sure you can. You're her hero."

He wipes his face with his handkerchief, which is damp and dirty from all the sweating he's doing. "I'm at the end of my shift and I'm doing a second shift right after."

"Yeah?"

"They're starting to let people go, and I can use the dough." He stops; he can't keep his hands steady. He grips the Coke bottle.

The ceiling fan wheezes.

"Come on now, you're doing great," Harry says.

"I give a guest directions uptown to the Shubert, then it gets quiet. I'm sitting at the front desk, maybe catching forty when something drips on my head. I look up and there's a patch of wet in the ceiling there."

"So there's a leak?"

"Yeah. I know right way where it's coming from."

"How?"

"Tamara's suite is right above the front desk, on three, and no one is in two."

"You went up."

"Yes. I told you already. Why you keep asking me?"

"Do we gotta shake it out of you? Be a man."

"I don't like to leave the desk but it's an emergency. It's two o'clock in the morning, and we're not full up, so maybe it's okay."

"Step by step now, chum," Ray says.

"I bang on her door. She don't answer. I hear the water. See it spilling from under the door. Use my house keys." He chokes up.

"Almost done."

"The rug is soaked, water's everywhere, pouring from the bathroom. I yell. Jesus. The tub is so deep. So deep. I see her hair first, floating like seaweed. Tamara's looking at me there on the bottom in her black lace underwear and the water's coming over the side."

"What did you do?"

"I shut off the water."

ARTIE

"GOT BACK TO THE BREVOORT as the sun was coming up."

"You saying you didn't come back all night?" Harry says.

The lights flicker, go on, off. The fan squeals to a stop. The room is dark except for the dots of the cigs.

"Christ," Ray says. He opens the door. "Hey!"

Someone yells, "Generator."

The lights come on again. The fan harrumphs, harrumphs.

"Where were we? Oh, yeah. You got back to the Brevoort for breakfast."

"Can't get near. The street's swarming with cops." He stops and stares at them. "What're you playing at?"

"Playing? Who's playing? You playing, Ray?"

"No, Harry, I'm not playing. You playing, Artie?"

"I'm tired. I wanna go home. Tamara's waiting for me."

"Heard she found an apartment, a penthouse."

"Where'd you hear that? Oh, I get it, that mealy mouth mutt on the desk. Yeah, we're taking the penthouse."

"Correction. She's taking the penthouse," Ray says. "She's dumping you."

"We made up. We always do. She don't always understand what she means to me." He gets up. "So if you got nothing more to say, I'm blowing."

"You wanna go home? He wants to go home, Harry."

"We're not finished yet, chum."

HERB

"HER EYES ARE OPEN, LIKE bulging. I take holda her under her arms and pull her up. Get water all over me."

"You shoulda left it for us, chum."

"She's got dark finger marks all over her neck."

ARTIE

"WHY WERE THE COPS AT the Brevoort? Where's Tamara?"

"Wise guy wants to see Tamara, Ray. Waddaya think?"

"Not very likely, punk." Ray takes out his handcuffs. "Unless you got a connection with the ME."

HERB

HARRY OPENS A COKE AND hands it to him. "You been a big help."

"We done?"

"Yeah. You can scram now." Harry stands. "We got your statement."

"Uh—uh, Tamara. Is she dead?"

"Is the Pope Catholic?" Ray says.

Herb exhales. "So I guess she's not taking the penthouse."

—END—

AUTHOR'S NOTE

I CHOSE 1953, AND GREENWICH Village as the time and setting for "Wang Dang Doodle" because the Village was in transition. Folk singers and coffee houses were replacing jazz joints. Café Society and its star Billie Holiday were long gone. Old landmarks like the Brevoort were to be demolished, replaced by high rise apartments.

Willie Dixon's "Wang Dang Doodle," written around 1951, is a blues classic, recorded by KoKo Taylor, and later, the Pointer Sisters, and the Grateful Dead.

I was in college across the river, but I might as well have been in another country.

Annette Meyers, 2014

WEDNESDAY IS VIKTOR'S
BY BRIAN KOPPELMAN

WEDNESDAY IS VIKTOR'S FAVORITE. WEDNESDAY, Alik is off. It's not Alik himself that Viktor does not like. Alik is Viktor's cousin, his older cousin, by six years. He likes him. Respects him, too. Of course. But when Alik is in, which he is the other five days the shop is open, Alik pulls business from Viktor. That is what Viktor does not like.

Alik doesn't think this way. After all, Alik opened the shop. Alik had the imagination to see that a shop could fit there, in what was once a news kiosk, then a locksmith, located in the cramped space between two buildings on the south side of West Eighty-sixth Street, almost exactly in the middle of West End Avenue and Broadway. There isn't even a proper roof; the first few years, whenever the inspector came, Alik felt his heart try to accelerate, felt the need to fight the appearance of nerves, not yet sure how many hundred-dollar bills it would take to stop the inspector from closing him down. And, although he doesn't tell it to Viktor over and over, as would be his right to, Alik remembers that he was the only one back then, in the shop, in New York City, in the entire United States of America.

Viktor and the rest were still in Kazakhstan, cutting and styling at the three shops Alik built in Almaty there, before that Major's daughter began coming in three, four times a week for blowouts, always in Alik's chair, always with makeup already applied to her cheeks and eyes, and lipstick to her thick young lips, and it was suggested that Alik consider either a different vocation or location. The words didn't rhyme in Russian. And even if they had, Alik wouldn't have cared. He noticed things like that here, appreciated them even, because he could allow himself to. Now. Before, back there, anything that might distract you from hearing the messages underneath the words people were using, anything taking your attention at all, could lead to the kind of mistake that's very difficult to undo. Such as not packing up and leaving first the town, then the country itself, within hours of a subtle but direct conversation with the Major's aide.

In the beginning, those hundred-dollar bills (two of them, it turned out), every three months from Alik's back pocket to the inspector's, were a week's profit. But Alik had lived on little for much of his life. In some way, he—well, if he didn't enjoy it, it did feed something in him, did stoke some deep knowledge that he could make do without whining, without even considering giving up. So he paid. You don't get to open three shops, nine chairs in each, in a competitive market like Almaty without knowing who to take care of. And Alik understood that the same applied in New York.

Which is why Alik owns the shop and Viktor works there. Viktor could no sooner do the negotiation/payoff dance with the inspector then he could sprout a third arm from his belly and spin around on it 'til he launched himself to the moon. Not here. Not at home. He isn't too stupid to do it, he's not stupid at all, just cold, with sharp-edges, visible in the set of his jaw, the far off, uncaring look in his eyes which narrowed when angered and seemed to go black. A real Kazakh. Even his father said it, in the way only one Kazakh could say it to another, and then, only to one with blood ties.

What would happen if Viktor were left to deal with an inspector or regulator or any bureaucrat? Alik knows: Viktor would pay the money, but he would make the officials feel dirty for taking it, so that without even being aware of their true motive, they'd be rooting against him, and would not offer support when a rival salon would show up and want to open around the corner. And before he could stop it, and without ever knowing why himself, Viktor would be out of business.

But Alik makes people feel good when they are doing something bad together, makes them believe they are conspirators in a great, joyful ruse, like they are the only honest ones in a game everyone else is too ashamed to admit they are playing. So everyone likes Alik. And most feel just a little uncomfortable around Viktor.

There are two barber chairs inside the shop—the first, two feet from the front door, the second two feet from the back wall. Five days a week, Alik cuts at the first chair, Viktor at the second. Each man hugs his own chair while cutting and has become so adroit at avoiding the other barber, there's never even a moment they come close to touching.

The chairs, the barbers, the heads. Those are the only things that fit, besides razors, scissors, combs, and the blue disinfectant in which these tools soak. There's no room even to put down a coffee. Or if there is, in a tiny nook next to the wall, it's a risky thing to do, and you have to keep half an eye on the head's leg, so you can spin the chair if he kicks unexpectedly, before he sends the scalding liquid flying. There is no back door. No emergency exit.

THERE ARE ALSO TWO CHAIRS outside the shop. Viktor unfolds and clunks them down on the sidewalk every morning when he arrives, after lifting the heavy iron security grate and before turning on the lights and sweeping. Heads wait in these outside folding chairs, and others stand beside them, also waiting, all year round, for one of the barber chairs to free up.

To Viktor, the way it's supposed to work, the way Alik told him it would work, is that whenever a head got out of a barber's chair, that chair would be filled by one of the heads in an outside chair. Simple. Fair.

But sometimes, too often as far as Viktor is concerned, the head will wait even after a barber's chair has opened up. Viktor's chair. These heads don't seem to care about the way Alik told Viktor it was going to work. They decide Alik is their special barber. Their friend. And that's that. They smile at him, and look sheepishly in Viktor's direction, with maybe a shrug of the shoulders, as if to say, "It's not you. It's me."

VIKTOR IS EVERY BIT THE cutter Alik is. Alik would admit this even. Viktor knows that. But Viktor also knows, because he is not stupid and puts those merciless eyes to good use, that Alik has a way of making heads think that he is their friend, cares about them, about their lives, about more than hair he is removing from their scalps.

Viktor sees that this matters, but cannot understand why it should. It's a transaction. Business. You sit in his chair. Tell what you want. He gives you exactly that, to the eighth of an inch. You get up eleven minutes later and pay, in cash, fourteen dollars. Nineteen if, by your request, he uses scissors instead of the razor. If you tip, you tip. Thank you. That's all.

Sometimes a customer will ask Viktor for his opinion—longer, shorter, part on this side or that. How should he know which your wife will like better? Which way is more handsome? He's a man. Not a woman. Who has time for that kind of conversation anyway? There are more heads to cut, five an hour, fifty bucks after Alik takes his share. So Viktor shuts them down, demands that they choose.

NOT ALIK. ALIK CAN LISTEN to your questions, answer them, guide you to your best look. And if some world events hold your interest, the football game or the latest terrorist action, Alik can offer an opinion on that, too. When the Muslims beheaded those journalists, Alik frowned—why torture? If you have to kill, if your interests demand that, fine, do it, quick, no need for the rest. No need to make a man suffer. And the heads frowned right along with him. Perhaps only one in ten would even wonder if Alik was speaking from experience. Perhaps one in one hundred would know by the expression on his face that he was.

Here's something that would surprise Viktor: Alik agrees. It is business. But on the nature of the transaction—that is where they would disagree, were they to discuss it. Which they don't. Alik does what he does, and his chair remains filled from nine in the morning until, sometimes, seven thirty at night. Viktor just cuts and, when his chair is not filled, he stews.

But not Wednesdays. Wednesdays, there is no Alik. Wednesdays are different. Wednesdays, Viktor cuts at Alik's chair, while Andrei, who is first cousin to both though brother to neither, cuts at Viktor's. Wednesdays are also different because the folding chairs outside, while still getting use, sit empty sometimes, and the heads waiting barely have time to open their newspapers or unlock their iPads before they are moving inside to let Viktor put shears to them.

This lack of traffic is mostly Andrei's loss. On Wednesday, the heads get no choice of barber chair. If Viktor's is empty, it must be filled before Andrei's. But Andrei is young, and his needs are simple, enough to buy exactly the amount of vodka it takes to slow him down a little in bed, without softening his *chlen*. So he cuts whichever heads happen to park themselves in his chair, barely thinking about anything other than the feeling he'll have when the cash is in his wallet and the alcohol about to hit his belly.

On Wednesday, Viktor arrives even earlier than usual. Chairs out. Broom moving across the floor. The shop is his today. It is his shop. And an actual smile breaks out across his face.

As he's placing the broom back into the far corner, he hears the front door open, turns, and that smile doesn't fade, it disappears, as quickly as it arrived. His cousin Andrei is not walking in. Alik is.

"But it's Wednesday, Alik."

"Andrei sent the text. Sick."

"But it's Wednesday."

"It's fine."

By this Alik means, it's fine that I have to work today, don't worry about me. I'll take next Wednesday and maybe a Friday, if Andrei can fill in. But Viktor isn't worried about Alik. And as much as Alik understands about people, as much as his instinct has served him, this time he misses it. Maybe the price of forgetting that even in America, even in New York City, when a man from back home is talking, you better listen closely.

Viktor nods. That's all. And begins organizing his station. Alik begins doing the same.

It's not that Viktor doesn't like Alik. Of course he likes him. Respects him, too. But that does not change the fact that Wednesday is ruined. Which means the week is ruined. And who ruined it? Alik.

Viktor takes his sharpest scissors out of the blue disinfectant, shakes them off, and takes half a step—the chairs are that close, remember—and he plunges them in between Alik's shoulder blades.

Or aims there, anyway. By the time the blade has reached Alik, he has sensed his cousin's approach, seen the quick movement in the mirror and begun to turn, so the scissors cut Alik's left bicep, but don't really penetrate and are knocked to the ground. Viktor shoots his knee up, toward Alik's groin, but Alik raises his leg, blocking it, while reaching back, grabbing his own scissors and jamming them into Viktor's liver.

Viktor falls, moaning, thick dark blood begins to pool around him. Alik looks at his watch. The heads are going to start showing up soon. Viktor moans louder. "*Tishe*," Alik says, and kicks Viktor in the face. Viktor shuts up, as he's told, lies there shuddering. Grabs for the scissors in his side.

"Don't. Leave them. You'll bleed out."

If he thought about it, Viktor might be surprised to know Alik's breathing hasn't changed, his heart hasn't begun to beat faster. But Viktor isn't thinking about anything besides the pain.

Alik goes outside, brings down the grate, slides under it, brings it the rest of the way down.

Inside, it feels like night.

As his pupils adjust, Alik admits it: he's never liked Viktor. Never respected him. But Viktor is family. So he took him in, gave him a living. He allows himself to picture their grand-mother, how she kept photos of the three of them, Alik, Viktor, and Andrei on her mantle, how proud of them she was, in business in New York City, with lines out front waiting. And all three together.

But she's still in Kazakhstan. He's here. The heads are out there, waiting, some sitting, some standing, all wondering when the grate will open. This is his business, his life.

And it's wrong to make a man suffer. If you have to kill, if it's in your interest . . .

Alik rolls the barely conscious Viktor onto his back, then yanks the scissors out of his cousin's side. Blood begins spilling across the floor, mixing with the hair that the broom can never quite wipe away. Without hesitation, Alik, gathering all the force he can muster, rams the point of the blades into Viktor's left eye, through it, and into the younger man's brain. A quick spasm and it's over.

Alik takes a moment. Watches close. When he's certain Viktor is dead, he exhales. The shop feels small to him, tight, but he knows this is adrenaline, panic, and he allows it to come for a few seconds before forcing it away.

He glances at the grate. He can feel them outside, waiting, wondering, reading their iPads, iPhones, and newspapers, but he can't do anything for them now. Nor they for him.

So he sits in his chair and breathes. Then his mind begins to work. You don't open three successful salons in Almaty and one barber shop in New York City without the ability to think clearly no matter the situation. This is a difficult spot. But it isn't the first difficult spot he's found himself in. And, although he doesn't yet know how, he's going to make sure it won't be the last.

WET DOG ON A RAINY DAY
BY S. J. ROZAN

A HEAVY, MOIST SMELL, A faint rancid bite at the back of her throat, but it's always like that. Worse today, perhaps, because of this rain in this heat, but when is it not worse, really? That would mean better. It's never better.

Snuffling, scrabbling, and both dogs are up on the lumpy floor-flat mattress, panting, wet noses painting her, nails scratching, tails waving. How do they know when she's awake? Neil never had. Neil would so-silently tiptoe, shut the bathroom door before the light, before the water, caring and careful so she could sleep. Anna would lie pretending, lying, loving the warmth of his concern while the bed grew cold. Once or twice she'd stretched, reached out, but he'd whispered, *No, no, Panda Bear, you should sleep,* and he'd gone out and left her because it was her time to sleep.

Anna never put it into words, how desolate this basement became, the heavy dread, how she had to fight to get out of bed, unbury herself, get going. She walked both dogs—Neil didn't want to go out, in, out again, it would wake her—and she had coffee, and then she stood before an unfinished canvas and wanted to die. Every morning, wanted to die.

Neil said that's what made the artist: fear, doubt, knowing it could all fall apart, it might turn out not worth it. But (kissing her forehead) she had to try, they had to try, because that's who they were, that's what it was for them. And it was a gift, this pain, this need to create, it made them not like everyone else. He went out each morning to write, sitting among everyone else, endless cups of coffee in the diner. *Smells like bacon and burgers, anyway,* he said. *Kind of yucky, even for me. You, you don't eat meat, you have such a sensitive vegan tummy. You'd barf.* He gave her a gentle smile. *You need to be alone, to have space. Your work needs it.* But Anna yearned to be surrounded, too, by waitresses and first dates, nurses off the night shift and commuters grabbing takeout before they grabbed the train to the ferry to a bigger life in the other New York.

Some days, not a streak or a spot of new paint on the canvas, she's glad when the day grows late, when the basement is layered in muddy gray shadows. She puts on her polyester smock and heads to Gristede's, to the dead-end job that pays the rent. There are people there, lights and movement. They each have a job like that, she and Neil. *Until we make it, Panda Bear.* She'd thought she might teach, work with kids, but Neil said anything that pulled her creative force away from painting would be a tragedy.

She pushes the sheet off, stands, scratches the ears of the dogs, Leo and Molly. They're both frantically wagging, climbing over each other to be closest to her. Molly steps back, she always does, happy to let Leo win. Happy just to be with him, and her. And Neil, but not Neil anymore. When Neil left he said he'd come for Leo soon, for Leo and some tools, things of his from the storage room. Anna brushes her teeth, sifts through a mound of shirts for one less musty than the others, clips on the leashes, leaves the basement through the creaking door.

She holds an umbrella, which means both leashes in one hand, so she's not surprised when Leo lunges, tears away. Neither is old man Shinn, watching from the window. He does that, watches for her, for Leo on the loose, for people he doesn't know, for anyone he wishes away from this bleak block in this sad town barely hanging onto the far ass-end of Staten Island.

Old man Shinn is on his porch now, cursing her, cursing Leo, cursing the world and while Anna hates him she doesn't blame him. Leo comes bounding back when she calls, eager to share the joy of rain, of freedom, of old man Shinn's trash, spread now in the street. *Just like a dog!* the old man screams, and of course he's right, because Leo's a dog. Without a word, even a look, she ties the dogs to a lamppost and gathers the garbage, redeposits it in the can Leo knocked over. She's done it before because he's done it before. If old man Shinn got a can that locked they wouldn't have to do this dance, his acid screaming and her garbage-smeared hands, but he won't. She's so tired.

Neil met Stacia at the diner. While he sweated out a story she bled out a poem; he put it that way. They recognized each other, their tribal affiliation—he put it that way, too—and started to talk, to commiserate. Natural and mutual support, at the start, that's all it was, he swore. In the afternoons he'd go off to work at the cabinet shop, his dead end, and he never thought about Stacia while he sawed and glued and hammered. Until he did.

Neil was honest with Anna. He always was. When he said, *Panda Bear, I never slept with her,* she believed him. Then he left her so he could.

He worried about the rent, her rent now, and he tucked money in the cookie jar for next month, until Anna could get more shifts at Gristede's. And the car, that would stay here, too, until he found a cheap place to park it up near Stacia's apartment. Stacia lived near the ferry, as close to the bigger New York as you could get without leaving the island. In a condo, on the water. Why had she ever come down to the diner, fluorescent lights, and scratched the formica at the sad far end? Neil said she said, *It's real*. Not like where she lived, not like the people she knew. Probably she did say that; Neil was honest, and Anna never met her.

Rain's soaked through her shoes by the time she unlocks the door. The smell's worse. The canvas, blues and grays and murky browns, hasn't changed in a week. Leo and Molly slip and slide in filthy happiness across the curling linoleum, roll in wet bliss on the blankets, to dry off. Wet dog. Old pizza. Mold. The new, strong stench. Anna goes into the bathroom and vomits.

The only thing she takes time to do after she straightens up is wash her face. She stuffs the money from the cookie jar in her jeans. Wallet and car keys, what else is there? She clips the leashes on, takes the dogs out to the car. Usually they go through the storage room in the back to reach the driveway but not today. They scramble in, Leo in the front, as always. When Neil used to drive, and Anna sat in the front, Leo sat in her lap. Molly swept her tail happily along the back seat.

From this sorry town, clinging to a soggy, slippery seacoast the bigger New York doesn't remember it owns, she has to drive north to the city's southernmost bridge. Now she knows that should have told her everything. Just before the bridge she pulls over. Leaving the car idling, she grabs Leo's leash and fast-walks through sheets of rain to the animal shelter door. *I can't handle this*, she says. She drops the leash and bolts. She's in the car and peeling away by the time the guy has raced out from behind the desk and through the doors. In the mirror she sees him with the leash, sees Leo with his cocked head, getting smaller, watching her. Molly's standing in the seat, looking through the back window. She whines.

Anna slides the car onto the on-ramp, slices through traffic, heading out of here, heading west. *Molly!* she says. With emphasis, with anger. Molly's whining stops. *Molly*, Anna repeats. *Come here.* Nothing. *Come here. In the front.* The dog stays where she is. *Molly, come.*

Tentatively, Molly worms between the front seats, clawing her way onto where Leo was. She sniffs, whines again. *Quiet*, says Anna. Molly curls morosely on the front seat, burrows into Leo's scent. Anna stares ahead, seeing the road, watching the windshield wipers. She bites her lip and blots out the sad, scared look on Leo's face as he stood with the shelter guy, so exactly like Neil's look when he turned in the storage room and there she stood, Anna, her, with the costly carving knife he'd been so excited about, the knife he'd been so eager to share the joy of owning, even though she doesn't eat meat.

WHY I TOOK THE JOB
BY PETER HOCHSTEIN

THERE WERE MICE IN THE garbage.

The lady who is the entire staff and management of Manhattan Typing Services Unlimited, the business that occupies the cubicle next to mine, pointed them out to me. Somebody had taken the previous day's garbage and stacked it in a couple of heavyweight green plastic garbage bags, sealed at the top with wire ties. The bags were leaning on the wall next to the service elevator. The janitor hadn't come yet to collect them. Inside one of the bags, several oblong shapes were wiggling, evidently feasting on a takeout lunch somebody had discarded the day before.

"Mice!" she said.

"This place is a dump," I agreed.

"Are you asking me or telling me?"

I pay $475 a month for a cubicle here. "Here" is a real estate entity that is euphemistically but officially named "Success Deluxe Workplaces." The truth is, the place is a dump of an office suite, full of people who are either not yet successful or who will always be less than successful. Some are total flops waiting to happen.

Success Deluxe Workplaces is on the ninth floor of a decaying former dress factory. The building is on a grungy-looking block in the Garment District, in the West Thirties, just off Eighth Avenue. In the building next door there's a gypsy fortune teller who each morning puts out a misspelled sign on a sidewalk sandwich board. The sign says, "Tarot cart reading $5 Speical." If she's so good at knowing the future, how come the spirits didn't tell her that people would notice she can't spell? Most of the other storefronts belong to wholesalers of women's garments, some carrying rather nice merchandise, but some cheesy looking, some frumpy looking, some a little too overtly sexy. I swear, one of them ought to stop calling itself "Mindy's Evening Wear" and rename itself "The Hooker Supply House."

My cubicle is wedged into a space too small for a grown man to fully stretch out his arms. For my $475 a month rent I get a desktop, one lockable cabinet, a two-drawer file, a Wi-Fi Internet connection, and a phone, along with occasional use of a conference room. Plus there's a tall willowy receptionist, a blonde with blue eyes and dimples who barely speaks English. Her name is Krystyna, and three months ago she was still living with her parents in Gdansk, Poland. She answers the phone, "Sooksess Delox Vorkplaces." I will admit her accent sounds sexy.

The men's room is filthy. One of the toilets frequently backs up. You don't want to know about the smell in there. The passenger elevators often don't work, so the tenants of Success Deluxe Workplaces frequently ride the service elevators with the bagged mice or climb eight flights of stairs when the service elevator is also down. My cubicle neighbors, in addition to the middle-aged, dyed-blonde typing lady, include a woman who puts out an Internet publication called *Stocking and Lingerie News*; somebody who describes herself as a "job coach"; an employment agent specializing in low-end hospital jobs like transporter and janitor; an unemployed advertising copywriter getting by on freelance assignments; and more of the other usual suspects you find in New York rent-a-work-space dumps—a collection of less-than-stellar lawyers, accountants, bookkeepers, software programmers, people peddling iffy investment schemes, and struggling insurance and printing salesmen.

Around the edges of the huge room are private offices with windows. Those rent for triple to quadruple what the cubicles go for, depending on what the landlord thinks he can get away with. Whenever you negotiate the rent with him (and you have to keep negotiating the rent because he keeps trying to raise it) he tells you, "Look, I'll settle with you this time, but don't tell any of the other people, because you are getting this cheaper than all the rest of them."

Right, and I am the Queen of England.

The private office occupants are mostly lawyers who are actually making what passes for a living, the majority of them either by bilking poor immigrants for their last five hundred dollars before they get deported, or making sure that divorcing lower-middle-class couples emerge from their split mutually dead broke while the lawyers pocket their former joint bank accounts. We once had an entrepreneur in one of the offices who said he was running a modeling agency. All kinds of pretty women walked in and out of there. No, he wasn't a pimp. Pimping would be too classy for a dump like Success Deluxe Workplaces. But one day the cops arrived with drawn guns, went into the model agent's office, pulled him out with his hands cuffed behind his back, under arrest for statutory rape. It turned out one of his models was fourteen years old and played "Casting Couch" with him. I hear that when the case came to court, his defense was that she told him she was thirty-seven. You can't make this stuff up.

Did I mention the cat? We used to have a white cat named Minna. Her job was to keep the mice at bay, but there's only so much one cat can do. Two or three times a week, if she was favoring you, she'd leave a decapitated rodent for you, either on your desk or on the seat of your chair. Usually when that happened, you could find her nearby, demurely purring.

It happened to me twice, after which I stopped bringing Minna cat toys and treats. I didn't mind the headless mouse cadavers on my desk. I picked up their remains with one paper towel, and washed the blood off my desk with another. It was the mouse entrails on my cheaply upholstered chair that got to me. What can you say to a cat who think she's honoring you by leaving you a pile of bloody mouse guts to sit on? You pick her up and coo, "Good girl, Minna! Let's take this catnip toy over to the *Stocking and Lingerie News* writer's cubicle. She's out right now checking out undies, but I'm sure she'd love to greet you when she gets in." All the same, Minna would sometimes come back to my desk and curl up next to my computer screen. I don't know why, after I stopped feeding her. But for some reason she liked me, before she got killed. More about that in a bit.

So by now you must be wondering who I am and what's my story. Fair enough.

My name is Rich Hovanec. Sound familiar? It might if you're old enough. I used to be an investigative reporter for one of this town's tabloids. I'm the guy who broke the story about the fire chief who was forcing the guys in one of his engine companies to renovate his house if they wanted to keep their jobs. That's strictly against the law, and after I broke the story he did time for it. I also dug up the dirt about a prison assistant warden who was sleeping with one of the inmates over at the women's section at Riker's Island. This was an especially juicy story because the warden was married and had two kids. And because both the warden and the prisoner were women. And especially because the prisoner didn't enjoy the relationship, but felt she had no choice if she ever wanted to see the sky again.

I loved my work. It was fun driving the snakes out of city government, and getting acclaim for it. The paper put me up for a Pulitzer Prize once, although I didn't get it. Instead it went to a group of reporters in Los Angeles that year. Even so, I was living a high profile life, generating the kind of bad publicity about high profile bad guys that zaps their careers. I liked writing the stories, but to tell you the truth, what I liked best was finding out stuff that nobody knew. And then making sure everybody knew it. The pay wasn't exactly great, but I lived comfortably enough. Wife, one kid, a modest house out on Long Island. What was not to like?

Well, eventually there was Stanford G. Bernys, the eminently horrid media mogul. He jetted into town one day from the West Coast on his private airplane, with his private mistress—the one half his age with the big fake eyelashes. You've seen her picture. She wears thigh-high boots and looks like she has a rawhide whip in her Gucci purse.

Stanford G. Bernys wrote a check for ninety million bucks to the ailing publisher of my paper for the whole she-bang as casually as you might write a check for the phone bill. Trust me, Old Lady Schreyer was glad to be rid of the thing. She operated it at a loss of roughly two million bucks a year, and she was thinking of closing it down anyway. But at least she loved news that was news. Bernys only loves news that sells papers, no matter how rancid the content. He once put a picture of a bloodstained corpse on the front page, under a headline that said, STOOL PIGEON STOPS COOING. On the inside right-hand page, under a standing headline, TODAY'S BOOTY BEAUTY, there's always a picture of a hot babe with too much flesh showing. Yeah, the head-line writers are having fun. But it's not really a newspaper anymore. A lot of the time, when they can't find stories that sink to the level of their subprime concept of journalism, they make stuff up.

I tried to put up with it for a while, but one day the booze-and-pill head that Bernys installed as editor called me up to his desk. His name, by the way, was Calvin Coalpister. Believe it or not.

"Hovanec," he sneered, without any preliminary pleasant-ries, "your work is shit."

I didn't know where he was going with this insult, and I wasn't interested in finding out. I must have raised my voice. Can you blame me?

"Hey, you can't talk like that to me," I said. "I'm a Pulitzer Prize nominee."

He stood up, stuck his face so close mine that I could smell the scotch on his breath, and stared at me with what I can only describe as an evil eye. "Fuck you and the Pulitzer you never got," he said.

So I decked him. It was spontaneous, but I freely admit I did it. It was as if my soul had left my body, floated up to the ceiling, and was watching me destroy my own career with one deliberately assaultive punch. It wasn't a graceful punch either, certainly not a boxer's punch. My arm straightened and went back, as if it held a tennis racket. Then suddenly my hand turned itself into a fist, my arm rotated forward, and my fist landed on the side of Coalpister's nose. There was a loud crack and he fell down. When I looked at him lying on the floor, there was blood all over his face and his nose looked like a beet that had been squished by a backhoe.

Goodbye newspaper career.

For a while I worked for a bunch of PR agencies and press agents, writing press releases and something they called "pitch letters," that try to sell editors on assigning stories about the PR clients. I didn't really hate it, but I didn't feel like there was a reason to bounce out of bed every morning, either. Once you get used to screwing crooks, con men, and connivers, it's hard to get off by giving the business equivalent of blow jobs to publicity seekers.

Then I realized that I never got into the journalism business to write in the first place. I got into the business for the sheer joy of finding stuff out. So I thought a bit about who else does that.

Well, university graduate students and professors, I guess, find stuff out. I'm talking about stuff like, is there a double-entendre in an Old English line of a poem about Beowulf? Or how many molecules of nucleic acid are in a cell that . . . oh, never mind. That's not for me.

G-men and cops also find stuff out. And they find out stuff about bad guys. Unfortunately, at the age of fifty-three I was a little long in the tooth to take the patrolman's exam.

There was once another possibility. In the old days I could have picked a subject to find stuff out about and then write a book about it. But the book business sucks these days. The publishers mostly aren't taking on new authors, half the planet is self-publishing, and I suspect that nobody except a handful of best-selling authors is making a plugged nickel.

So I did the one thing I could do. I became a private eye. Well, not really. If you think I'm going to take courses and take a licensing exam, you've got another think coming.

Instead, my business card says, "Sensitive Topic Information Researcher." Don't wrinkle your brow. I don't really know what it means either. But if somebody comes up to Success Deluxe Workplaces and asks me, "Can you find out whether my spouse is screwing around on the side? And can you get me pictures for my divorce lawyer?" the answer is yes, because I do sensitive topic information research, and sleazy affairs in motels are sensitive topics.

That more or less explains how I came to be sitting across the conference table from a woman named Carmelina Pezzetini, trying to make sure we got through the meeting as quickly as possible. ("You hoff conference room for only one hoff hour, until 2 p.m.," said Krystyna. "Next hour, conference room reserved for different meetink.")

"I want a divorce," Mrs. Pezzetini told me after she sat down and I closed the conference room door. She looked to be an attractive forty-something—big brown eyes, full lips that I suspected were made that way by Botox, a dress that was a trifle too tight, and huge black leather shoulder bag with brass studs on it.

"Divorce? That's not my department," I told Mrs. Pezzetini. "There are a couple of lawyers down the hall who handle that kind of stuff. Perhaps I should introduce you to Mr. Shmerz."

"I already know Marvin Shmerz," Mrs. Pezzetini said. "He's the one who gave me your name and pointed out your cubicle."

"Oh, I see. So you want proof that your husband is playing around. With gorgeous confirming color photographs, I assume."

She reached into her purse—I feared for a cigarette. Smoking isn't permitted on the premises of Success Deluxe Workplaces. When Mr. Grapler, the landlord, catches one of his tenants or their clients smoking, he usually retaliates by trying to raise the rent.

But I was wrong. Carmelina Pezzetini produced a pack of Juicy Fruit gum. She offered me a stick. I declined. She unwrapped three sticks for herself, stuffed them into her mouth, and began chewing vigorously.

I waited for her chewing to slow down. It took a while.

"I already know that shithead is cheating on me," Mrs. Pezzetini finally said, her anger rising as she spoke. "He's been cheating since three weeks before we got married. It's no secret. He was on fucking TV with one of his bimbos, coming out of a Chinese restaurant, last month. I don't want more evidence. I want him out of my life."

"Well, that's why you need a divorce lawyer, not me," I said.

"You don't understand. I've already seen three different divorce lawyers, not counting Shmerz. I pay them their retainer, cash money. They take my case. They file divorce papers against my husband. Then a week or two later they call up and tell me they just remembered they're too busy to take my case, and they send back the money."

"You mean you didn't have to chase a matrimonial lawyer to get your retainer back?"

"They find out about the life I'm from. I think my husband or some of his people visited one of the lawyers and threw the furniture around. Anyway, everybody's scared to take my case. Or to try to keep my money."

Then it hit me. Pezzetini . . . Pezzetini.

"Your husband is he, uh . . . ?"

"Connected? The Mafia? Is that what you're asking?"

"Well, now that you bring it up."

She took a couple of hard chews on her gum before she spoke.

"Yeah, that's him. Al. Al Pezzetini. In the write-ups in the press, they usually call him Icepick Al."

"So where do I come in with all this?"

"I want him dead."

"Umm, with all due respect, Mrs. Pezzetini, killing people is not my profession. I just do research. And I'm not sure I'd want to find out too much about your husband, even if that was all you wanted. It could be bad for my health."

"You look like a pretty healthy-looking guy to me," she said. "Stop acting like a divorce lawyer. Get a pair of balls!"

I've been around newspaper city editors too long to take most nasty putdowns personally.

"You don't have to get all agitated," I told her. "I can under-stand your frustration. I'm simply saying, what you seem to be asking for isn't my area of expertise."

"You like money?" she asked. She took her bag off her shoulder and plunged her arm into it up to her elbow. A second later her hand emerged holding a fat wad of hundred dollar bills, fastened together with a thick rubber band.

"Ten thousand dollars down," she said, "cash money. No record of the transaction."

"Not interested," I said.

"When he's dead, you get another twenty. Here's my card. Just call when it's done and I'll get you the money. It's all tax free. Nobody files 1099s on hit men. I don't know your tax bracket, but bare minimum, with no taxes this is worth the the same as . . ."

"You don't understand, I don't do hits. I don't even want to hear about them."

"Money," she said, "money, money, money, money!"

"I'm a researcher, not a hit man."

"Okay, then do some research for me," she said.

For a moment, that sounded like a quick and welcome change of assignment.

"What kind of research are you talking about?" I asked.

"Find out what will make my husband dead, and how to get it done. Then let me know how it went." She rose from her chair and opened the conference room door.

I started to say, "Hey, you can't . . ."

But she was gone. I usually stand waiting for the elevator for a full ten minutes. For her, one of the elevators opened its doors the second she pressed the down button. I could run after her and try to hand back her money in the crowded Garment District streets, but that would attract unwelcome attention and might invite a passerby to make a grab for it. Nah, I decided I'd simply lock the money away and do nothing. Sooner or later, she'd fire me and ask for her money back. And I'd happily return it.

That, I figured, would take four, or maybe six weeks. But I didn't have a chance to find out. Two days later, I was sitting in my cubicle, at my computer, researching offshore banking. My client was one of the heirs to his father's estate. He was convinced that while his father slowly faded into the fog of Alzheimer's disease, a sibling was raiding the old man's assets and shipping money to some money-laundering bank, either in Switzerland or the Bahamas. To my surprise, I was discovering all kinds of banks in the United States will be happy to help you cheat—cheat on taxes, cheat your siblings, cheat the company you're stealing from, or hide drug money—by placing your money offshore. They don't put it that way. Citibank talks about "investing" abroad, but in quirky places like the

Isle of Jersey, which is independent of English banking laws, and Switzerland, which strictly enforces banking privacy. You don't need a very powerful magnifying glass to read between the lines.

When my phone rang, Minna the cat twitched. She had decided to take a nap on my desk, draping herself over the phone cord. She took an annoyed swipe at my hand when I tried to pull the cord from under her, then lazily accommodated me by moving eight inches down my desk and going back to sleep atop a stack of papers.

"Man comink to see you," said Krystyna's voice over the phone.

"Who? What man? When?"

Before Krystyna could answer, a hand forcefully clapped my left shoulder. I turned. There was a nicely dressed guy, about fifty years old, standing over me. He was wearing a thoroughly conservative dark gray suit, a blue button-down shirt, and a gray-and-blue striped tie that picked up the colors in his shirt and his suit.

"I wonder if you know who I am?" he asked me pleasantly. His voice was strong, but unremarkable. He could have been any ivy league guy inquiring about the time of day.

I hung up the phone, and looked at him. He seemed familiar, but I couldn't place the face. I told him that.

"Well, let me give you a hint. I hear via the grapevine that my wife went to see you the other day. She keeps trying to hire lawyers to get a divorce from me. My name is Alvin Pezzetini. Some people call me Al."

His dress and demeanor may have been perfectly gentlemanly, but the mere mention of his name gave me the creeps.

"Look, I'm not a lawyer," I said.

"I know that. I checked up on you. You're some kind of private investigator."

"I'm actually a researcher," I said.

"Really? Is that your cat?" he asked, pointing to Minna.

"She's the office cat. Doesn't belong to anybody, really."

"Good," he said. "In that case you won't mind a little demonstration."

He snatched Minna from my desk, holding her in the air by the scruff of her neck with his left hand. She let out a protesting screech. He reached into the breast pocket of his elegant suit with his right hand and pulled out an object. And yes, it really was an ice pick, about nine inches long, a small plastic cap of some kind covering the point.

Al Pezzetini took the cap off with his teeth and then shoved the ice pick deep down through Minna's chest. The point came out of her body somewhere near her anus, followed by a stream of blood. The whole action took maybe three seconds, and mercifully it appeared to be over for Minna in three seconds after that.

Pezzetini shook the handle of the ice pick vigorously. Minna's bleeding corpse slid off, and onto my computer keyboard. Pezzetini calmly and meaningfully wiped the ice pick dry on the sleeve of my shirt, while I sat in silent horror. Then he put the cap back on the point, and returned the weapon to an inside pocket of his suit.

"Kindly cease any and all contact with my wife," he told me. Then he walked out.

I thought about it for about a minute, sitting almost paralyzed, as if I had no legs to stand on. I was breathing hard, my hands trembling a little. Then my soul left my body again and floated up toward the ceiling. I hadn't felt this way since the day I decked Calvin Coalpister and broke his nose in the newsroom of Stanford G. Bernys' tabloid newspaper. Only this time, it wasn't my fist that seemed to have a life of its own. It was my mind that was running on autopilot. I found the card that Pezzetini's wife had left me and dialed her telephone number.

"Mrs. Pezzetini?" I said, "Rich Hovanec here. Tell me about your husband's daily routine."

KELLER THE DOGKILLER
BY LAWRENCE BLOCK

KELLER, TRYING NOT TO FEEL foolish, hoisted his flight bag and stepped to the curb. Two cabs darted his way, and he got into the winner, even as the runner-up filled the air with curses. "JFK," he said, and settled back in his seat.

"Which airline?"

He had to think about it. "American."

"International or domestic?"

"Domestic."

"What time's your flight?"

Usually they just took you there. Today, when he didn't have a plane to catch, he got a full-scale inquiry.

"Not to worry," he told the driver. "We've got plenty of time."

Which was just as well, because it took longer than usual to get through the tunnel, and the traffic on the Long Island Expressway was heavier than usual for that hour. He'd picked this time—early afternoon—because the traffic tended to be light, but today for some reason it wasn't. Fortunately, he reminded himself, it didn't matter. Time, for a change, was not of the essence.

"Where you headed?" the driver asked, while Keller's mind was wandering.

"Panama," he said, without thinking.

"Then you want International, don't you?"

Why on earth had he said Panama? He'd been wondering if he should buy a straw hat, that was why. "Panama City," he corrected himself. "That's in Florida, you change planes in Miami."

"You got to fly all the way down to Miami and then back up again to Panama City? Ought to be a better way to do it."

Thousands of cab drivers in New York, and for once he had to draw one who could speak English. "Air miles," he said, in a tone that brooked no argument, and they left it at that.

At the designated terminal, Keller paid and tipped the guy, then carried his flight bag past the curbside check-in. He followed the signs down to Baggage Claim, and walked around until he found a woman holding a hand-lettered sign that read "Niebauer."

She hadn't noticed him, so he took a moment to notice her, and to determine that no one else was paying any attention to either of them. She was around forty, a trimly built woman wearing a skirt and blouse and glasses. Her brown hair was medium length, attractive if not stylish, her sharp nose contrasted with her generous mouth, and on balance he'd have to say she had a kind face. This, he knew, was no guarantee of anything. You didn't have to be kind to have a kind face.

He approached her from the side, and got within a few feet of her before she sensed his presence, turned, and stepped back, looking a little startled. "I'm Mr. Niebauer," he said.

"Oh," she said. "Oh, of course. I . . . you surprised me."

"I'm sorry."

"I had noticed you, but I didn't think . . ." She swallowed, started over. "I guess you don't look the way I expected you to look."

"Well, I'm older than I was a few hours ago."

"No, I don't mean . . . I don't know what I mean. I'm sorry. How was your flight?"

"Routine."

"I guess we have to collect your luggage."

"I just have this," he said, holding up the flight bag. "So we can go to your car."

"We can't," she said. She managed a smile. "I don't have one, and couldn't drive it if I did. I'm a city girl, Mr. Niebauer. I never learned to drive. We'll have to take a cab."

There was a moment, of course, when Keller was sure he'd get the same cab, and he could see himself trying to field the driver's questions without alarming the woman. Instead they got into a cab driven by a jittery little man who talked on his cell phone in a language Keller couldn't recognize while his radio was tuned to a talk program in what may or may not have been the same unrecognizable language.

Keller, once again trying not to feel foolish, settled in for the drive back to Manhattan.

Two DAYS EARLIER, ON THE wraparound porch of the big old house in White Plains, Keller hadn't felt foolish. What he'd felt was confused.

"It's in New York," he said, starting with the job's least objectionable aspect. "I live in New York. I don't work there."

"You have."

"A couple of times," he allowed, "and it worked out alright, all things considered, but that doesn't make it a good idea."

"I know," Dot said, "and I almost turned it down without consulting you. And not just because it's local."

"That's the least of it."

"Right."

"It's short money," he said. "It's ten thousand dollars. It's not exactly chump change, but it's a fraction of what I usually get."

"The danger of working for short money," she said, "is word gets around. But one thing we'd make sure of is nobody knows you're the one who took this job. So it's not a question of ten thousand dollars versus your usual fee, because your usual fee doesn't come into the picture. It's ten thousand dollars for two or three days work, and I know you can use the work."

"And the money."

"Right. And, of course, there's no travel. Which was a minus the first time we looked at it, but in terms of time and money and all of that—"

"Suddenly it's a plus." He took a sip of his iced tea. "Look, this is stupid. We're not talking about the most important thing."

"I know."

"The, uh, subject is generally a man. Sometimes it's a woman."

"You're an equal-opportunity kind of guy, Keller."

"One time," he said, "somebody wanted me to do a kid. You remember?"

"Vividly."

"We turned them down."

"You're damn right we did."

"Adults," he said. "Grown-ups. That's where we draw the line."

"Well," she said, "if it matters, the subject this time around is an adult."

"How old is he?"

"Five."

"A five-year-old adult," he said, heavily.

"Do the math, Keller. He's thirty-five in dog years."

"Somebody wants to pay me ten thousand dollars to kill a dog," he said. "Why me, Dot? Why can't they call the SPCA?"

"I wondered that myself," she said. "Same token, every time we get a client who wants a spouse killed, I wonder if a divorce wouldn't be a better way to go. Why call us? Has Raoul Felder got an unlisted phone number?"

"But a dog, Dot."

She took a long look at him. "You're thinking about Nelson," she said. "Am I right or am I right?"

"You're right."

Nelson, an Australian Cattle Dog, had entered Keller's life in unexpected fashion, and made an equally surprising exit. He'd acquired the animal upon the death of a client, and lost it when the woman he'd hired to walk it—Andria, her name was, and she painted her toes all the colors of the rainbow—walked out of his life, and took Nelson with her.

"Keller," she said, "I met Nelson, and I liked Nelson. Nelson was a friend of mine. Keller, this dog is no Nelson."

"If you say so."

"In fact," she said, "if Nelson saw this dog and trotted over to give him a friendly sniff, that would be the end of Nelson. This dog's a Pit Bull, Keller, and he's enough to give the breed a bad name."

"The breed already has a bad name."

"And I can see why. If this dog was a movie actor, Keller, he'd be Jack Elam."

"I always liked Jack Elam."

"You didn't let me finish. He'd be like Jack Elam, but nasty."

"What does he do, Dot? Eat children?"

She shook her head. "If he ever bit a kid," she said, "or even snarled good and hard at one, that'd be the end of him. The law's set up to protect people from dogs. What with due process and everything, he might rip the throats out of a few tykes before the law caught up with him, but once it did he'd be out of the game and on his way to Doggie Heaven."

"Would he go to heaven? I mean, if he killed a kid—"

"All dogs go to heaven, Keller, even the bad ones. Where was I?"

"He doesn't bite children."

"Never has. Loves people, wants to make nice to everyone. If he sees another dog, however, or a cat or a ferret or a hamster, it's another story. He kills it."

"Oh."

"He lives with his owner in the middle of Manhattan," she said, "and she takes him to Central Park and lets him off his leash, and whenever he gets the chance he kills something. You're going to ask why somebody doesn't do something."

"Well, why don't they?"

"Because about all you can do, it turns out, is sue the owner, and about all you can collect is the replacement value of your pet, and you've got to go through the legal system to get that much. You can't have the dog put down for killing other dogs, and you can't press criminal charges against the owner. Meanwhile, you've still got the dog out there, a menace to other dogs."

"That doesn't make sense."

"Hardly anything does, Keller. Anyway, a couple of women lost their pets and they don't want to take it anymore. One had a twelve-year-old Yorkie and the other had a frisky Weimaraner pup, and neither one had a chance against Fluffy, and—"

"Fluffy?"

"I know."

"This killer Pit Bull is named Fluffy?"

"That's his call name. He's registered as Percy Bysshe Shelley, Keller, whom you'll recall as the author of 'Ozymandias.' I suppose they could call him Percy, or Bysshe, or even Shelley, but instead they went for Fluffy."

And Fluffy went for the Yorkie and the Weimaraner, with tragic results. As Dot explained it, this did seem like a time when one had to go outside the law to get results. But did they have to turn to a high-priced hit man? Couldn't they just do it themselves?

"You'd think so," Dot said. "But this is New York, Keller, and these are a couple of respectable middle-class women. They don't own guns. They could probably get their hands on a bread knife, but I can't see them trying to stab Fluffy, and evidently neither can they."

"Even so," he said, "how did they find their way to us?"

"Somebody knew somebody who knew somebody."

"Who knew us?"

"Not exactly. Someone's ex-husband's brother-in-law is in the garment trade, and he knows a fellow in Chicago who can get things taken care of. And this fellow in Chicago picked up the phone, and next thing you know my phone was ringing."

"And he said, 'Have you got anybody who'd like to kill a dog?'"

"I'm not sure he knows it's a dog. He gave me a number to call, and I drove twenty miles and picked up a pay phone and called it."

"And somebody answered?"

"The woman who's going to meet you at the airport."

"A woman's going to meet me? At an airport?"

"She had somebody call Chicago," Dot said, "so I told her *I* was calling from Chicago, and she thinks you're flying in from Chicago. So she'll go to JFK to meet a flight from Chicago, and you'll show up, looking like you just walked off a plane, and she'll never guess that you're local."

"I don't have a Chicago accent."

"You don't have any kind of an accent, Keller. You could be a radio announcer."

"I could?"

"Well, it's probably a little late in life for a career change, but you could have. Look, here's the thing. Unless Fluffy gets his teeth in you, your risk here is minimal. If they catch you for killing a dog, about the worst that can happen to you is a fine. But they won't catch you, because they won't look for you, because catching a dog killer doesn't get top priority at the NYPD. But what we don't want is for the client to suspect that you're local."

"Because it could blow my cover sooner or later."

"I suppose it could," she said, "but that's the least of it. The last thing we want is people thinking a top New York hit man will kill dogs for chump change."

"THE PERSON I SPOKE TO said there was no need for us to meet. She told me all I had to do was supply the name and address of the dog's owner, and you could take it from there. But that just didn't seem right to me. Suppose you got the wrong dog by mistake? I'd never forgive myself."

That seemed extreme to Keller. There had been a time in St. Louis when he'd gotten the wrong man, through no fault of his own, and it hadn't taken him terribly long to forgive himself. On the other hand, forgiving himself came easy to him. His, he'd come to realize, was a forgiving nature.

"Is the coffee alright, Mr. Niebauer? It feels strange calling you Mr. Niebauer, but I don't know your first name. Though come to think of it I probably don't know your last name either, because I don't suppose it's Niebauer, is it?"

"The coffee's fine," he said. "And no, my name's not Niebauer. It's not Paul, either, but you could call me that."

"Paul," she said. "I always liked that name."

Her name was Evelyn, and he'd never had strong feelings about it one way or another, but he'd have preferred not to know it, just as he'd have preferred not to be sitting in the kitchen of her West End Avenue apartment, and not to know that her husband was an attorney named George Augenblick, that they had no children, and that their eight-month-old Weimaraner had answered to the name of Rilke.

"I suppose we could have called him Rainer," she said, "but we called him Rilke." He must have looked blank, because she explained that they'd named him for Rainer Maria Rilke. "He had the nature of a German Romantic poet," she added, "and of course the breed is German in origin. From Weimar, as in Weimar Republic. You must think I'm silly, saying a young dog had the nature of a poet."

"Not at all."

"George thinks I'm silly. He humors me, which is good, I suppose, except he's careful to make it clear to me and every-one else that that's what he's doing. Humoring me. And I in turn pretend I don't know about his girlfriends."

"Uh," Keller said.

They'd come to her apartment because they had to talk somewhere. They'd shared long silences in the cab, inter-rupted briefly by observations about the weather, and her kitchen seemed a better bet than a coffee shop, or any other public place. Still, Keller wasn't crazy about the idea. If you were dealing with pros, a certain amount of client contact was just barely acceptable. With amateurs, you really wanted to keep your distance.

"If he knew about you," Evelyn said, "he'd have a fit. It's just a dog, he said. Let it go, he said. You want another dog, I'll buy you another dog. Maybe I am being silly, I don't know, but George, George just doesn't get the point."

She'd taken her glasses off while she was talking, and now she turned her eyes on him. They were a deep blue, and luminous.

"More coffee, Paul? No? Then maybe we should go look for that woman and her dog. If we can't find her, at least I can show you where they live."

"Rilke," he told Dot. "How do you like that for a coincidence? A Weimaraner and a Pit Bull, and they're both named after poets."

"What about the Yorkie?"

"Evelyn thinks his name was Buster. Of course that could just be his call name, and he could have been registered as John Greenleaf Whittier."

"Evelyn," Dot said, thoughtfully.

"Don't start."

"Now how do you like that for a coincidence? Because that's just what I was about to say to you."

His name aside, there was nothing remotely fluffy about Percy Bysshe Shelley. Nor did his appearance suggest an evil nature. He looked capable and confident, and so did the woman who held onto the end of his leash.

Her name, Keller had learned, was Aida Cuppering, and she was at least as striking in looks as her dog, with strong features and deeply set dark eyes and an athletic stride. She wore tight black jeans and black lace-up boots and a leather motorcycle jacket with a lot of metal on it, chains and studs and zippers, and she lived alone on West Eighty-seventh Street half a block from Central Park, and, according to Evelyn Augenblick, she had no visible means of support.

Keller wasn't so sure about that. It seemed to him that she had a means of support, and that it was all too visible. If she wasn't making a living as a dominatrix, she ought to make an appointment right away for vocational counseling.

There was no way to lurk outside her brownstone without looking as though he was doing precisely that, but Keller had learned that lurking wasn't required. Whenever Cuppering took Fluffy for a walk, they headed straight for the park. Keller, stationed on a park bench, could lurk to his heart's content without attracting attention.

And when the two of them appeared, it was easy enough to get up from the bench and tag along in their wake. Cuppering, with a powerful dog for a companion, was not likely to worry that someone might be following her.

The dog seemed perfectly well behaved. Keller, walking along behind the two of them, was impressed with the way Fluffy walked perfectly at heel, never straining at his leash, never lagging behind. As Evelyn had told him, the dog was unmuzzled. A muzzle would prevent Fluffy from biting anyone, human or animal, and Aida Cuppering had been advised to muzzle her dog, but it was evidently advice she was prepared to ignore. Still, three times a day she walked the animal and three times a day Keller was there to watch them, and he didn't see Fluffy so much as glower at anyone.

Suppose the dog was innocent? Suppose there was a larger picture here? Suppose, say, Evelyn Augenblick had found out that her husband had been dilly-dallying with Aida Cuppering. Suppose the high-powered attorney liked to lick Cuppering's boots, suppose he let her lead him around on a leash, muzzled or not. And suppose Evelyn's way of getting even was to . . .

To spend ten thousand dollars having the woman's dog killed?

Keller shook his head. This was something that needed more thought.

"EXCUSE ME," THE WOMAN SAID. "Is this seat taken?"

Keller had read all he wanted to read in *The New York Times*, and now he was taking a shot at the crossword puzzle. It was a Thursday, so that made it a fairly difficult puzzle, though nowhere near as hard as the Saturday one would be. For some reason—Keller didn't know what it might be—the *Times* puzzle started out each Monday at a grade-school level, and by Saturday became damn near impossible to finish.

Keller looked up, abandoning the search for a seven-letter word for *Diana's nemesis,* to see a slender women in her late thirties, wearing faded jeans and a Leggs Mini-Marathon T-shirt. Beyond her, he noted a pair of unoccupied benches, and a glance to either side indicated similarly empty benches on either side of him.

"No," he said, carefully. "No, make yourself comfortable."

She sat down to his right, and he waited for her to say something, and when she didn't he returned to his crossword puzzle. Diana's nemesis. Which Diana, he wondered. The English princess? The Roman goddess of the hunt?

The woman cleared her throat, and Keller figured the puzzle was a lost cause. He kept his eyes on it, but his attention was on his companion, and he waited for her to say something. What she said, hesitantly, was that she didn't know where to begin.

"Anywhere," Keller suggested.

"Alright. My name is Myra Tannen. I followed you from Evelyn's."

"You followed me . . ."

"From Evelyn's. The other day. I wanted to come along to the airport, but Evelyn insisted on going alone. I'm paying half the fee, I ought to have as much right to meet you as she has, but, well, that's Evelyn for you."

Well, Dot had said there were two women, and this one, Myra, was evidently the owner of the twelve-year-old Yorkie of whom Fluffy had made short work. It wasn't bad enough that he'd met one of his employers, but now he'd met the other. And she'd followed him from Evelyn's—followed him!—and this morning she'd come to the park and found him.

"When you followed me . . ."

"I live on the same block as Evelyn," she said. "Just two doors down, actually. I saw the two of you get out of the taxi, and I was watching when you left. And I, well, followed you."

"I see."

"I got a nice long walk out of it. I don't walk that much now that I don't have a dog to walk. But you know about that."

"Yes."

"She was the sweetest thing, my little dog. Well, never mind about that. I followed you all the way through the park and down to First Avenue and wherever it was. Forty-ninth Street? You went into a building there, and I was going to wait for you, and then I told myself I was being silly. So I got in a cab and came home."

For God's sake, he thought. This amateur, this little housewife, had followed him home. She knew where he lived.

He hesitated, looking for the right words. Would it be enough to tell her that this was no way to proceed, that contact with his clients compromised his mission? Was it in fact time to abort the whole business? If they had to give back the money, well, that was one good thing about working for chump change: a refund wasn't all that expensive.

He said, "Look, what you have to understand . . ."

"Not now. There she is."

And there she was, alright. Aida Cuppering, dressed rather like a Doberman Pinscher, all black leather and metal studs and high black lace-up boots, striding along imperiously with Fluffy, leashed, stepping along at her side. As she drew abreast of Keller and his companion, the woman stopped long enough to unclip the dog's lead from his collar. She straightened up, and for a moment her gaze swept the bench where Keller and Myra Tannen sat, dismissing them even as she took note of them. Then she walked on, and Fluffy walked along at heel, both of them looking perfectly lethal.

"She's not supposed to do that," Myra said. "In the first place he's supposed to be muzzled, and every dog's supposed to be kept on a leash."

"Well," Keller said.

"She wants him to kill other dogs. I saw her face when my Millicent was killed. It was quick, you know. He picked her up in his jaws and shook her and snapped her spine."

"Oh."

"And I saw her face. That's not where I was looking, I was watching what was happening, I was trying to do something, but my eyes went to her face, and she was . . . excited."

"Oh."

"That dog's a danger. Something has to be done about it. Are you going to—"

"Yes," he said, "but, you know, I can't have an audience when it happens. I'm not used to working under supervision."

"Oh, I know," she said, "and believe me, I won't do anything like this again. I won't approach you or follow you, nothing like that."

"Good."

"But, you see, I want to . . . well, amend the agreement."

"I beg your pardon?"

"Besides the dog."

"Oh?"

"Of course I want you to take care of the dog, but there's something else I'd like to have you do, and I'm prepared to pay extra for it. I mean, considerably extra."

The owner, too, he thought. Well, that was appropriate, wasn't it? The dog couldn't help its behavior, while the owner actively encouraged it.

She was carrying a tote bag bearing the logo of a bank, and she started to draw a large brown envelope from it, then changed her mind. "Take the whole thing," she said, handing him the tote bag. "There's nothing else in it, just the money, and it'll be easier to carry this way. Here, take it."

Not at all the professional way to do things, he thought. But he took the tote bag.

"This is irregular," he said, carefully. "I'll have to talk to my people in Chicago, and—"

"Why?"

He looked at her.

"They don't have to know about this," she said, avoiding his eyes. "This is just between you and me. It's all cash, and it's a lot more than the two of us gave you for the dog, and if you don't say anything about it to your people, well, you won't have to split with them, will you?"

He wasn't sure what to say to that, so he didn't say anything.

"I want you to kill her," she said, and there was no lack of conviction in her tone. "You can make it look like an accident, or like a mugging gone wrong, or, I don't know, a sex crime? Anything you want, it doesn't matter, just as long as she dies. And if it's painful, well, that's fine with me."

Was she wearing a wire? Were there plainclothes cops stationed behind the trees? And wouldn't that be a cute way to entrap a hit man. Bring him in to kill a dog, then raise the stakes, and—

"Let me make sure I've got this straight. You're paying me this money yourself, and it's in cash, and nobody else is going to know about it."

"That's right."

"And in return you want me to take care of Aida Cuppering."

She stared at him. "Aida Cuppering? What do I care about Aida Cuppering?"

"I thought—"

"I don't care about her," Myra Tannen said. "I don't even care about her damn dog, not really. What I want you to do is kill Evelyn."

"What a mess," Dot said.

"No kidding."

"All I can say is I'm sorry I got you into this. Two women hired you to put a dog down, and you've met each of them face to face, and one of them knows where you live."

"She doesn't know that I live there," he said. "She thinks I flew in from Chicago. But she knows the address, and probably thinks I'm staying there for the time being."

"You never noticed you were being followed?"

"It never occurred to me to check. I walk home all the time, Dot. I never feel the need to look over my shoulder."

"And you'd never have to, if I'd borne in mind the old rule about not crapping where we eat. You know what it was, Keller? There were two reasons to turn the job down, because it was in New York and because it was a dog, and what I did, I let the two of them cancel each other out. My apologies."

"How much was in the bag?"

"Twenty-five."

"I hope that's twenty-five thousand."

"It is."

"Because the way things have been going, it could have been twenty-five hundred."

"Or just plain twenty-five."

"That'd be a stretch. So the whole package is thirty-five. It's still a hard way to get rich. What's she got against Evelyn, anyway? It can't be that she's pissed she didn't get to go to the airport."

"Her husband's been having an affair with Evelyn."

"Oh. I thought it was Evelyn's husband that was fooling around."

"I thought so, too. I guess the Upper West Side's a hotbed of adultery."

"And here I always figured it was all concerts. What are you going to do, Keller?"

"I've been wondering that myself."

"I bet you have. A certain amount of damage control would seem to be indicated. I mean, two of them have seen your face."

"I know."

"And one of them followed you home. Which doesn't mean you can keep her, in case you were wondering."

"I wasn't."

"I hope not. I gather both of them are reasonably attractive."

"So?"

"And they're probably attracted to you. A dangerous man, a mysterious character—how can they resist you?"

"I don't think they're interested," he said, "and I know I'm not."

"How about the dog owner? The one who looks like a dominatrix."

"I'm not interested in her, either."

"Well, I'm relieved to hear it. You think you can find a way to make all of this go away?"

"I was ready to give back the money," he said, "but we're past that point. I'll think of something, Dot."

JUST AS KELLER REACHED TO knock on the door, it opened. Evelyn Augenblick, wearing a pants suit and a white blouse and a flowing bow tie, stood there beaming at him. "It's you," she said. "Thank God. Quick, so I can shut the door."

She did so, and turned to him, and he saw something he had somehow failed to notice before. She had a gun in her hand, a short-barreled revolver.

Keller didn't know what to make of it. She'd seemed relieved to see him, so what was the gun for? To shoot him? Or was she expecting somebody else, against whom she felt the need to defend herself?

And should he take a step toward her and swat the gun out of her hand? That would probably work, but if it didn't . . .

"I guess you saw the ad," she said.

The ad? What ad?

"'*Paul Niebauer, Please Get In Touch.*' On the front page of *The New York Times*, one of those tiny ads at the very bottom of the page. I always wondered if anybody read those ads. But you didn't, I can see by the look on your face. How did you know to come here?"

How indeed? "I just had a feeling," he said.

"Well, I'm glad you did. I didn't know how else to reach you, because I didn't want to go through the usual channels. And it was important that I see you."

"The gun," he said.

She looked at him.

"You're holding a gun," he said.

"Oh," she said, and looked at her hand, as if surprised to discover a gun in it. "That's for you," she said, and before he could react she handed the thing to him. He didn't want it, but neither did he want her to have it. So he took it, noting that it was a .38, and a loaded one at that.

"What's this for?" he asked.

She didn't exactly answer. "It belongs to my husband," she said. "It's registered. He has a permit to keep it on the premises, and that's what he does. He keeps it in the drawer of his bedside table. For burglars, he says."

"I don't really think it would be useful to me," he said. "Since it's registered to your husband, it would lead right back to you, which is the last thing we'd want, and—"

"You don't understand."

"Oh."

"This isn't for Fluffy."

"It's not?"

"No," she said. "I don't really care about Fluffy. Killing Fluffy won't bring Rilke back. And it's not so bad with Rilke gone, anyway. He was a beautiful dog, but he was really pretty stupid, and it was a pain in the ass having to walk him twice a day."

"Oh."

"So the gun has nothing to do with Fluffy," she explained. "The gun's for you to use when you kill my husband."

"Damnedest thing I ever heard of," Dot said. "And that covers a lot of ground. Well, she'd said her husband was running around on her. So she wants you to kill him?"

"With his own gun."

"Suicide?"

"Murder-suicide."

"Where does the murder come in?"

"I'm supposed to stage it," he said, "so that it looks as though he shot the woman he was having an affair with, then turned the gun on himself."

"The woman he's having the affair with."

"Right."

"Don't tell me, Keller."

"Okay."

"Keller, that's an expression. It doesn't mean I don't want to know. But I have a feeling I know already. Am I right, Keller?"

"Uh-huh."

"It's her, isn't it? Myra Tannenbaum."

"Just Tannen."

"Whatever. They both fly you in from the Windy City to kill a dog, and now neither one really gives a hoot in hell about the dog, and each one wants you to kill the other. How much did this one give you?"

"Forty-two thousand dollars."

"Forty-two thousand dollars? How did she happen to arrive at that particular number, do you happen to know?"

"It's what she got for her jewelry."

"She sold her jewelry so she could get her husband killed?

I suppose it's jewelry her husband gave her in the first place, don't you think? Keller, this is beginning to have a definite Gift-of-the-Magi quality to it."

"She was going to give me the jewelry," he said, "since it was actually worth quite a bit more than she got for it, but she figured I'd rather have the cash."

"Amazing. She actually got something right. Didn't you tell me Myra Tannen's husband was having the affair with Evelyn?"

"That's what she told me, but it may have been a lie."

"Oh."

"Or maybe each of them is having an affair with the other's husband. It's hard to say for sure."

"Oh."

"I didn't know what to do, Dot."

"Keller, neither of us has known what to do from the jump. I assume you took the money."

"And the gun."

"And now you still don't know what to do."

"As far as I can see, there's only one thing I can do."

"Oh," she said. "Well, in that case, I guess you'll just have to go ahead and do it."

MYRA TANNEN LIVED IN A brownstone, which meant there was no doorman to deal with. There was a lock, but Evelyn had provided a key, and at two thirty the following afternoon, Keller tried it in the lock. It turned easily, and he walked in and climbed four flights of stairs. There were two apartments on the top floor, and he found the right door and rang the bell.

He waited, and rang a second time, and followed it up with a knock. Finally he heard footsteps, and then the sound of the cover of the peephole being drawn back. "I can't see anything," Myra Tannen said.

He wasn't surprised; he'd covered the peephole with his palm. "It's me," he said. "The man you sat next to in the park."

"Oh?"

"I'd better come in."

There was a pause. "I'm not alone," she said at length.

"I know."

"But . . ."

"We've got a real problem here," he said, "and it's going to get a lot worse if you don't open the door."

IT WAS ALMOST THREE WHEN he picked up the phone. He wasn't sure how good an idea it was to use the Tannen telephone. The police, checking the phone records, would know the precise time the call was made. Of course it would in all likelihood be just one of many calls made from the Tannen apartment to the Augenblick household across the street, and in any event all it could do was tie the two sets of people together, and what difference could that make to him?

Evelyn Augenblick answered on the first ring.

"Paul," he said. "Across the street."

"Oh, God."

"I think you should come over here."

"Are you sure?"

"It's all taken care of," he said, "but there are some things I really need your input on."

"Oh."

"You don't have to look at anything, if you don't want to."

"It's done?"

"It's done."

"And they're both . . ."

"Yes, both of them."

"Oh, good," she said. "I'll be right over. But you've got the key."

"Ring the bell," he said. "I'll buzz you in."

It didn't take her long. Time passed slowly in the Tannen apartment, but it was only ten minutes before the bell sounded. He poked the buzzer to unlock the door, and waited while she climbed the stairs, opening the door at her approach and beckoning her inside. She was already breathing hard from the four flights of stairs, and the sight of her husband and her friend did nothing to calm her down.

"Oh, this is perfect," she said. "Myra's in her nightgown, sprawled on her back, with two bulletholes in her chest. And George—he's barefoot, and wearing his pants but no shirt. The gun's still in his hand. What did you do, stick the gun in his mouth and pull the trigger? That's wonderful, it blew the whole back of his head off."

"Well, not quite, but—"

"But close enough. God, you really did it. They're both gone, I'll never have to look at either one of them again. And this is the way I get to remember them, and that's just perfect. You're a genius for thinking of this, getting me to see them like this. But . . ."

"But what?"

"Well, I'm not complaining, but why did you want me to come over here?"

"I thought it might be exciting."

"It is, but—"

"I thought maybe you could take off all your clothes."

Her jaw dropped. "My God," she said, "and here I thought *I* was kinky. Paul, I never even thought you were interested."

"Well, I am now."

"So it's exciting for you, too. And you want me to take my clothes off? Well, why not?"

She made a rather elaborate striptease of it, which was a waste of time as far as he was concerned, but it didn't take her too long. When she was naked he picked up her husband's gun, muffled it with the same throw pillow he'd used earlier, and shot her twice in the chest. Then he put the gun back in her husband's hand and got out of there.

IT WAS HARD TO BELIEVE that they charged two dollars for a Good Humor. Keller wasn't positive. But it seemed to him he could remember paying fifteen or twenty cents for one. Of course that had been many years ago, and everything had been cheaper way back when, and cost more nowadays.

But you really noticed it when it involved something you hadn't bought in years, and a Good Humor, ice cream on a stick, was not something he'd often felt a longing for. Now, though, walking in the park, he'd seen a vendor, and the urge for a chocolate-coated ice cream bar, with a firm chocolate center and assorted gook embedded in the chocolate coating, was well nigh irresistible. He'd paid the two dollars—he probably would have paid ten dollars just then, if he'd had to—and went over to sit on a bench and enjoy his Good Humor.

If only.

Because he couldn't really characterize his own humor as particularly good, or even neutral. He was, in fact, in a fairly dismal mood, and he wasn't sure what to do about it. There were things he liked about his work, but its immediate aftermath had never been one of them; whatever feeling of satisfaction came from a job well done was mitigated by the bad feeling brought about by the job's nature. He'd just killed three people, and two of them had been his clients. That wasn't the way things were supposed to go.

But what choice had he had? Both of the women had met him and seen his face, and one of them had tracked him to his apartment. He could leave them alive, but then he'd have to relocate to Chicago; it just wouldn't be safe to stay in New York, where there'd be all too great a chance of running into one or the other of them.

Even if he didn't, sooner or later one or the other would talk. They were amateurs, and if he did just what he was supposed to do originally—send Fluffy to that great dog run in the sky—either Evelyn or Myra would have an extra drink one night and delight in telling her friends how she'd managed to solve a problem in a sensible *Sopranos*-style way.

And, of course, if he executed the extra commission from one of them by killing the other, well, sooner or later the cops would talk to the survivor, who would hold out for about five minutes before spilling everything she knew. He'd have to kill Myra, because she'd followed him home and thus knew more than Evelyn, and that's what he'd done, thinking he might be able to leave it at that, but with George dead the cops would go straight to Evelyn, and . . .

He had to do it. Period, end of story.

And the way he left things, the cops wouldn't really have any reason to look much further. A domestic triangle, all three participants dead, all shot with the same gun, with nitrate particles in the shooter's hand and the last bullet fired through the roof of his mouth and into his brain. (And, as Evelyn had observed with delight, out the back of his skull.) It'd make tabloid headlines, but there was no reason for anyone to go looking for a mystery man from Chicago or anywhere else.

Usually, after he'd finished a piece of work, the next order of business was for him to go home. Whether he drove or flew or took a train, he'd thus be putting some substantial physical distance between himself and what he'd just done. That, plus the mental tricks he used to distance himself from the job, made it easier to turn the page and get on with his life.

Walking across the park wasn't quite the same thing.

He centered his attention on his Good Humor. The sweetness helped, no question about it. Took the sourness right out of his system. The sweetness, the creaminess, the tang of the chocolate center that remained after the last of the ice cream was gone—it was all just right, and he couldn't believe he'd resented paying two dollars for it. It would have been a bargain at five dollars, he decided, and an acceptable luxury at ten. It was gone now, but . . .

Well, couldn't he have another?

The only reason not to, he decided, was that it wasn't the sort of thing a person did. You didn't buy one ice cream bar and follow it with another. But why not? He wouldn't miss the two dollars, and weight had never been a problem for him, nor was there any particular reason for him to watch his intake of fat or sugar or chocolate. So?

He found the vendor, handed him a pair of singles. "Think I'll have another," he said, and the vendor, who may or may not have spoken English, took his money and gave him his ice cream bar.

He was just finishing the second Good Humor when the woman showed up. Aida Cuppering walked briskly along the path, wearing her usual outfit and flanked by her usual companion. She stopped a few yards from Keller's bench, but Fluffy strained at his leash, making a sound that was sort of an angry whimper. Keller looked in the direction the dog was pointing, and fifty yards or so up the path he saw what Fluffy saw, a Jack Russell terrier who was lifting a leg at the base of a tree.

"Oh, you good boy," Aida Cuppering said, even as she stooped to unclip the lead from Fluffy's collar.

"Go!" she said, and Fluffy went, tearing down the path at the little terrier.

Keller couldn't watch the dogs. Instead he looked at the woman, and that was bad enough, as she glowed with the thrill of the kill. After the little dog's yelping had ceased, after Cuppering's body had shuddered with whatever sort of climax the spectacle had afforded her, she looked over and realized that Keller was watching her.

"He needs his exercise," she said, smiling benignly, and turned to clap her hands to urge the dog to return.

Keller never planned what happened next. He didn't have time, didn't even think about it. He got to his feet, reached her in three quick strides, cupped her jaw with one hand and fastened the other on her shoulder, and broke her neck every bit as efficiently as her dog had broken the neck of the little terrier.

"So you saw Fluffy make a kill."

He was in White Plains, drinking a glass of iced tea and watching Dot's television. It was tuned to the Game Show Channel, and the sound was off. Game shows, he thought, were dopey enough when you could hear what the people were saying.

"No," he said. "I couldn't watch. The animal's a killing machine, Dot."

"Now that's funny," she said, "because I was just about to say the same thing about you. I don't get it, Keller. We take a job for short money because all you have to do is kill a dog. The next thing I know, four people are dead, and two of them used to be clients of ours. I don't know how we can expect them to recommend us to their friends, let alone give us some repeat business."

"I didn't have any choice, Dot."

"I realize that. They already knew too much when it was just going to be a dog that got killed, but as soon as human beings entered the equation, it became very dangerous to leave them alive."

"That's what I thought."

"And when you come right down to it, all you did was what each of them hired you to do. A says to kill B and C, you kill B and C. And then you kill A, because that's what B hired you to do. I have to say I think D came out of left field."

"D? Oh, Aida Cuppering."

"Nobody wanted her killed," she said, "and at last report nobody paid to have her killed. Was that what you call pro bono?"

"It was an impulse."

"No kidding."

"That dog of hers, killing other dogs is his nature, but there's no question she did everything she could to encourage it. Just because she liked to watch. I was supposed to kill the dog, but he was just a dog, you know?"

"So you broke her neck. If anyone had been watching . . ."

"Nobody was."

"A good thing, or you'd have had more necks to break. The police certainly seem puzzled. They seem to think the killing might have been the work of one of her clients. It seems she really was a dominatrix after all."

"She would sort of have to have been."

"And one of her clients lived in the apartment where the love triangle murder-suicide took place earlier that afternoon."

"George was her client?"

"Not George," she said. "George lived across the street with Evelyn, remember? No, her client was a man named Edmund Tannen."

"Myra's husband. I thought he was supposed to be having an affair with Evelyn."

"I don't suppose it matters who was doing what to whom," she said, "since they're all conveniently dead now. Or inconveniently, but one way or another, they've all been wiped off the board. I don't know about you, but I can't say I'm going to miss any of them."

"No."

"And from a financial standpoint, well, it's not the best payday we ever had, but it's not the worst, either. Ten for the dog and twenty-five for Evelyn and forty-two for Myra and George. You know what that means, Keller."

"I can buy some stamps."

"You sure can. You know the real irony here? Everybody else in the picture is dead, except for the Good Humor Man. You didn't do anything to him, did you?"

"No, for God's sake. Why would I?"

"Who knows why anybody would do anything. But except for him, they're all dead. Except for the one creature you were supposed to kill in the first place."

"Fluffy."

"Uh-huh. What is it, professional courtesy? One killing machine can't bear to kill another?"

"He'll get sent to the YMCA," he said, "and when nobody adopts him, which they won't because of his history, he'll be put to sleep."

"Is that what they do at the YMCA?"

"Is that what I said? I meant the SPCA."

"That's what I figured."

"The animal shelter, whatever you want to call it. She lived alone, so there's nobody else to take the dog."

"In the paper," Dot said, "it says they found him standing over her body, crying plaintively. But I don't suppose you stuck around to watch that part."

"No, I went straight home," he said. "And this time nobody followed me."

THE FOLLOWING THURSDAY AFTERNOON, THE phone was ringing when he got back to his apartment. "Stay," he said. "Good boy." And he went and picked up the phone.

"There you are," Dot said. "I tried you earlier but I guess you were out."

"I was."

"But now you're back," she said. "Keller, is everything alright? You seemed a little out of it when you left here the other day."

"No, I'm okay."

"That's really all I called to ask, because I just . . . Keller, what's that sound?"

"It's nothing."

"It's a dog."

"Well," he said.

"This whole dog business, it made you miss Nelson, so you went out and got yourself a dog. Right?"

"Not exactly."

"'Not exactly.' What's that supposed to mean? Oh, no. Keller, tell me it's not what I think it is."

"Well."

"You went out and adopted that goddamn killing machine. Didn't you? You decided putting him to sleep would be a crime against nature, and you just couldn't bear for that to happen, softhearted creature that you are, and now you've saddled yourself with a crazed bloodthirsty beast that's going to make your life a living hell. Does that pretty much sum it up, Keller?"

"No."

"No?"

"No," he said. "Dot, they sent the dog to a shelter, just the way I said they would."

"Well, there's a big surprise. I thought for sure they'd run him for the senate on the Republican ticket."

"But it wasn't the SPCA."

"Or the YMCA either, I'll bet."

"They sent him to IBARF."

"I beg your pardon?"

"The Inter-Boro Animal Rescue Foundation, IBARF for short."

"Whatever you say."

"And the thing about IBARF," he said, "is they never euthanize an animal. If it's not adoptable, they just keep it there and keep feeding it until it dies of old age."

"How old is Fluffy?"

"Not that old. And, you know, it's not like a maximum-security institution there. Sooner or later somebody would leave a cage open, and Fluffy would get a chance to kill a dog or two."

"I think I see where this is going."

"Well, what choice did I have, Dot?"

"That's the thing with you these days, Keller. You never seem to have any choice, and you wind up doing the damnedest things. I'm surprised they let you adopt him."

"They didn't want to. I explained how I needed a vicious dog to guard a used-car lot after hours."

"One that would keep other dogs from breaking in and driving off in a late-model Honda. I hope you gave them a decent donation."

"I gave them a hundred dollars."

"Well, that'll pay for fifty Good Humors, won't it? How does it feel, having a born killer in your apartment?"

"He's very sweet and gentle," he said. "Jumps up on me, licks my face."

"Oh, God."

"Don't worry, Dot. I know what I have to do."

"What you have to do," she said, "is go straight to the SPCA, or even the YMCA, as long as it's not some chickenhearted outfit like IBARF. Some organization that you can count on to put Fluffy down in a humane manner, and to do it as soon as possible. Right?"

"Well," he said, "not exactly."

"WHAT A NICE DOG," THE young woman said.

The animal, Keller had come to realize, was an absolute babe magnet. In the mile or so he'd walked from his apartment to the park, this was the third woman to make a fuss over Fluffy. This one said the same thing the others had said: that the dog certainly looked tough and capable, but that he really was just a big baby, wasn't he? Wasn't he?

Keller wanted to urge her to get down on all fours and bark. Then she'd find out just what kind of a big old softie Fluffy was.

He'd waited until twilight, hoping to avoid as many dogs and dogwalkers as possible, but there were still some to be found, and Fluffy was remarkably good at spotting them. Whenever he caught sight of one, or caught the scent, his ears perked up and he strained at the leash. But Keller kept a good tight hold on it, and kept leading the dog to the park's less-traveled paths.

It would have been easy to follow Dot's advice, to pay another hundred dollars and palm the dog off on the SPCA or some similar institution. But suppose they got their signals crossed and let someone adopt Fluffy? Suppose, one way or another, something went wrong and he got a chance to kill more dogs?

This wasn't something to delegate. This was something he had to do for himself. That was the only way to be sure it got done, and got done properly. Besides, it was something he'd been hired on to do long ago. He'd been paid, and it was time to do the work.

He thought about Nelson. It was impossible, walking in the park with a dog on a leash, not to think about Nelson. But Nelson was gone. In all the time since Nelson's departure, it had never seriously occurred to him to get another dog. And, if it ever did, this wasn't the dog he'd get.

He patted his pocket. There was a small-caliber gun in it, an automatic, unregistered, and never fired since it came into his possession several years ago. He'd kept it, because you never knew when you might need a gun, and now he had a use for it.

"This way, Fluffy," he said. "That's a good boy."

ABOUT THE CONTRIBUTORS

BILL BERNICO has written a novel and more than three hundred short stories. His Cooper, PI series began in 1989 and now numbers 156 short stories featuring five generations of private eyes named Cooper. He and his wife, Kathie, live on the shores of Lake Michigan in Cleveland, Wisconsin.

JILL D. BLOCK's first published story appeared recently in *Ellery Queen's Mystery Magazine*. She lives in Manhattan where she is an attorney by day.

LAWRENCE BLOCK's several Life Achievement awards have made it abundantly clear to him and others that his future is largely in the past. Nevertheless, he'll follow the recent film version of his Matthew Scudder novel, *A Walk Among the Tombstones*, with a new noir thriller, *The Girl With the Deep Blue Eyes*, coming in September 2015 from Hard Case Crime. (His film agent describes it as "James M. Cain on Viagra.")

TOM CALLAHAN spent three decades as an award-winning reporter and freelance writer (*The New York Times, Parade Magazine*) and writing teacher before moving into fiction and film. Born in Harlem to a family with firm roots in the Bronx, he currently lives north of the Bronx border—but visits frequently.

PETER CARLAFTES is an author, playwright, and performer. His books include *A Year on Facebook* (humor), *Drunkyard Dog* and *I Fold With the Hand I Was Dealt* (poetry), and *Triumph for Rent (Three Plays)* and *Teatrophy (Three More Plays)*. He is co-director of Three Rooms Press.

JANE DENTINGER came to Manhattan to be an actress, and enjoyed a long run Off-Broadway in Jack Heifner's *Vanities*. When it closed, she wrote *Murder on Cue*, the first of six Jocelyn O'Roarke mysteries, all newly available from Open Road Media. She managed Murder Ink, the mystery bookstore, and has held executive positions at the Mystery Guild Book Club.

JIM FUSILLI is the author of eight novels. He also serves as the rock and pop music critic of the *Wall Street Journal* and is the founder of www.ReNewMusic.net, a music website for grownups. He lives in New York City.

KAT GEORGES is a writer, playwright, performer, and designer. Her books include *Our Lady of the Hunger, Slow Dance at 120 Beats a Minute, Maiden Claiming*, and *Punk Rock Journal*. In New York since 2003, she is co-director of Three Rooms Press.

PARNELL HALL is the author of the Stanley Hastings private eye novels, the Puzzle Lady crossword puzzle mysteries, and the Steve Winslow courtroom dramas. His books have been nominated for Edgar, Shamus, and Lefty awards. Parnell is an actor, screenwriter, singer/songwriter, and former private eye. He lives in New York City.

PETER HOCHSTEIN is a former small town and big city newspaper reporter, advertising agency creative star, and closet sex novelist. He was born in Brooklyn but has lived most of his adult life in Manhattan. If for some reason you need to know more about him, you can read his memoir, *Heiress Strangled in Molten Chocolate at Nazi Sex Orgy*.

ELAINE KAGAN is a Los Angeles-based actress, journalist (*Los Angeles Magazine, Los Angeles Times*), and novelist (*No Good-Byes, Losing Mr. North*). When she visits New York she always has a tuna melt at the Viand Coffee Shop on Madison Avenue. On rye.

EVE KAGAN is a writer, critically acclaimed actress, and international theater teaching artist. Her recent teaching adventures include a devised original production based on Virginia Woolf's unpublished short stories with students at Brandeis and running the IB Drama program at the International School of Uganda. Her first trip to New York City was when she was two—she stepped out of the hotel, clamped her hands over both ears, and smiled. Hers has been a visceral love ever since.

BRIAN KOPPELMAN is the co-writer of *Ocean's Thirteen* and *Rounders*, writer/co-director of *Solitary Man*, host of the influential podcast *The Moment*, and creator of the Vine "Six Second Screenwriting Lessons" series which has generated over thirty-seven million loops. He has never been to Kazakhstan.

DAVID LEVIEN is a screenwriter, director, and novelist, best known for occasionally eating semi-gluten free and as co-writer of the films *Ocean's Thirteen* and *Rounders* and author of the Frank Behr detective novels, including *City of the Sun* and *Where the Dead Lay*. The latest in the Behr series, *Signature Kill*, was published in March 2015.

ANNETTE MEYERS, author of the Smith & Wetzon Wall Street mysteries, enjoys exploring New York's history in her fiction. As Maan Meyers, she and her husband Martin have written seven history-mysteries known as *The Dutchman Chronicles*, and numerous short stories set in New York over the past several centuries.

The first time **ERIN MITCHELL** visited New York, she went to the Rainbow Room wearing fishnet stockings. Since then, she's spent a great deal of energy pretending to live there, when not pursuing her passion for exploring crime fiction, because, as she recently noted in *Crimespree* magazine, "It is about the human condition. It is about aspects of society we might prefer to ignore. It is rife with social commentary that gives us room for thoughtful consideration."

WARREN MOORE is the author of the crime thriller *Broken Glass Waltzes* and an English professor at a small college in the South. Despite this, none of his activities have warranted mention in *Penthouse Forum*. Instead, he lives in Newberry, SC, with his wife and daughter.

JERROLD MUNDIS is a novelist and nonfiction writer whose books have been selected by major book clubs and widely translated. His short work has appeared in publications ranging from *The New York Times Magazine* to *The Magazine of Fantasy & Science Fiction*. He has lived for most his adult life in (where else?) New York City.

ED PARK is the author of the novel *Personal Days*, which was a finalist for the PEN/Hemingway Award, and the co-editor of *Read Hard, Read Harder*, and the forthcoming *Buffalo Noir*. His stories have appeared in *The New Yorker*, *Vice*, and elsewhere. He lives in Manhattan.

THOMAS PLUCK has slung hash, worked on the docks, and even cleaned the crappers of the Guggenheim. He is the author of the World War II action thriller *Blade of Dishonor*, and the editor of the anthology *Protectors: Stories to Benefit PROTECT*, and he hosts Noir at the Bar in Manhattan, at Shade in the Village.

S. J. ROZAN has won most of crime writing's awards, including the Edgar, Shamus, and Anthony, and the Japanese Maltese Falcon. Her fifteen novels include two as part of the writing team of Sam Cabot. From the Bronx, she now lives in lower Manhattan. She teaches in the summer at Art Workshop International in Assisi, Italy, and invites you all to come join her.

JONATHAN SANTLOFER's work has earned him a Nero Award and two NEA grants; he's been a Visiting Artist at the American Academy in Rome and serves on the board of Yaddo, the oldest arts community in the United States. A distinguished novelist, short story writer, anthologist, and visual artist, he is currently at work on a new crime novel and a fully illustrated novel for children.

ROBERT SILVERBERG has been a professional writer since 1955, and is known mainly for his science fiction. In 2004, the Science Fiction Writers of America awarded him its Grand Master designation, the highest honor in the science-fiction field.

RECENT AND FORTHCOMING BOOKS FROM THREE ROOMS PRESS

FICTION

Meagan Brothers
Weird Girl and What's His Name

Ron Dakron
Hello Devilfish!

Michael T. Fournier
Hidden Wheel
Swing State

Janet Hamill
Tales from the Eternal Café
(Introduction by Patti Smith)

Eamon Loingsigh
Light of the Diddicoy

Aram Saroyan
Still Night in L.A.

Richard Vetere
The Writers Afterlife
Champagne and Cocaine

MEMOIR & BIOGRAPHY

Nassrine Azimi and
Michel Wasserman
Last Boat to Yokohama:
The Life and Legacy of
Beate Sirota Gordon

Richard Katrovas
Raising Girls in Bohemia:
Meditations of an American Father;
A Memoir in Essays

Judith Malina
Moon Over Malina: Personal notes
from 50 years of the Living Theatre

Stephen Spotte
My Watery Self:
Memoirs of a Marine Scientist

PHOTOGRAPHY-MEMOIR

Mike Watt
On & Off Bass

SHORT STORY ANTHOLOGY

Dark City Lights: New York Stories
edited by Lawrence Block

Have a NYC I, II & III:
New York Short Stories;
edited by Peter Carlaftes
& Kat Georges

HUMOR

Peter Carlaftes
A Year on Facebook

MIXED MEDIA

John S. Paul
Sign Language: A Painter's
Notebook (photography, poetry
and prose)

TRANSLATIONS

Thomas Bernhard
On Earth and in Hell
(selected poems of
Thomas Bernhard with English
translations by Peter Waugh)

Patrizia Gattaceca
Isula d'Anima / Soul Island
(poems by the author
in Corsican with English
translations)

César Vallejo | Gerard Malanga
Malanga Chasing Vallejo:
Selected poems of César Vallejo
with English translations and
additional notes by Gerard Malanga)

George Wallace
EOS: Abductor of Men
(selected poems of George
Wallace with Greek translations)

DADA

Maintenant: A Journal of
Contemporary Dada Writing & Art
(Annual, since 2008)

PLAYS

Madeline Artenberg &
Karen Hildebrand
The Old In-and-Out

Peter Carlaftes
Triumph For Rent (3 Plays)
Teatrophy (3 More Plays)

POETRY COLLECTIONS

Hala Alyan
Atrium

Peter Carlaftes
DrunkYard Dog
I Fold with the Hand I Was Dealt

Thomas Fucaloro
It Starts from the Belly and Blooms
Inheriting Craziness is Like
a Soft Halo of Light

Kat Georges
Our Lady of the Hunger

Robert Gibbons
Close to the Tree

Israel Horovitz
Heaven and Other Poems

David Lawton
Sharp Blue Stream

Jane LeCroy
Signature Play

Philip Meersman
This is Belgian Chocolate

Jane Ormerod
Recreational Vehicles on Fire
Welcome to the Museum of Cattle

Lisa Panepinto
On This Borrowed Bike

George Wallace
Poppin' Johnny

Three Rooms Press | New York, NY | Current Catalog: www.threeroomspress.com
Three Rooms Press books are distributed by PGW/Perseus: www.pgw.com